# THE FALLEN

## THE BOOK OF JAKIELE

DENISE MORAN

ISBN 978-1-961227-33-0 (paperback)
ISBN 978-1-961227-34-7 (digital)



Rushmore Press LLC
1 800 460 9188
www.rushmorepress.com

Printed in the United States of America

# ACKNOWLEDGEMENTS

A special Thank You to my sister, Terri. I authored this book with your support. I could always count on you to be there for me through thick and thin. In addition, my wonderful, loving husband encouraged me to follow my dreams and my beautiful children who bring out the best in me. I love you all!

D.B Moran

# PREFACE

Jesus once noted to his disciples, the kingdom of Heaven held many dwelling places. The highest realm houses the Seraphim, the Cherubim, and the Ophanim. These entities guard the throne of God. The middle realm houses the Dominions, Virtues, and Powers. The Dominions regulate the duties of Angels. The Virtues maintain the heavenly bodies to ensure the cosmos is in working order. Finally, the Powers are the bearers of conscience and the keepers of history.

The third realm houses the Principalities, Archangels, and lower Angels. The Principalities follow orders given by the Dominions. They are the educators and guardians of the Earth and can bequeath blessings. Seven Archangels conduct orders issued by the Principalities. They are known as Michael, Gabriel, Raphael, Uriel, Chamuel, Jophiel, and Zadkiel.

The Archangels are the guardians of nations who carefully monitor politics and military matters on Earth. They command the last tier of angels who watch over humanity.

# PROLOGUE

After God created the universe, he created humans blessed with the ability to possess a soul and be reborn. God knew that he needed to develop a planet that could sustain and protect his beloved creation. God decided planet Earth would suit this purpose. God created Adam and Eve as the first humans. Adam and Eve lived in the Garden of Eden, and they bore two sons. Abel and Cain. Cain killed Abel out of jealousy to gain God's favor. However, other civilizations and cultures existed on Earth long before God created humankind in his image. One such humanoid species were known as Neanderthals. Cain eventually married one and thus intermingled the bloodlines and begat a son named Enoch. Enoch is responsible for writing down the history of the Nephilim and the war in Heaven. Enoch is the great grandfather of Noah. The angels loyal to Lucifer were known as the fallen angels. The fallen angels have also been referred to as the Anunnaki, Annodoti, Grigori, the Watchers, and Tuatha de Danaan.

God loved Adam and Eve so much he commanded the angels who served him to bow down to the humans in respect. God wanted Earth to be known as the "Planet of the children." He wanted humanity to evolve on its own without any interference. However, the demand created jealousy and anger in some angels who felt the humans were less than the dirt from which they were made. Lucifer believed humans were ignorant beings who needed to be educated and uplifted in their knowledge. Lucifer used this controversy to convince many angels that they were superior to humans in every way.

The angels who sided with Lucifer felt that teaching humans the knowledge of the universe was the only way humans could be considered worthy of God's favor. The friction created a war in Heaven between the angels on God's side and the angels on Lucifer's side. The angels who took Lucifer's side were banished and cast down to Earth by God after being defeated by an army of angels led by the Archangel Michael. Lucifer and his fallen angels kept many of their original angelic abilities, but they could never again enter the kingdom of Heaven.

Lucifer lost his holy name after being cast down to Earth, thereafter becoming known as Satan. The angels who followed Lucifer were forever known as the fallen. Their names were Samlazaz, Araklba, Rameel, Kokablel, Ramlel, Ezequiel, Tamil, Danel, and Baraqijal. The fallen angels led the Chiefs of tens to become their first lieutenants. Their names were Asael, Batarel, Armaros, Ananel, Zaqlel, Samsapeel, Satarel, Turel, Jomjael, and Sariel. The Chiefs of Tens appointed leaders who would follow orders without question, and they were named Uzza, Remiel, and Azza. These leaders were chosen to perform specific teaching tasks to humanity, and all were banished to Mount Hermon. They began interacting and teaching humans against God's wishes.

After the Golden age ended and before the pre-dynastic period began, the fallen angels spread out over Earth to teach humans their vast universal knowledge. Many cultures recognized Satan, or the serpent, as their teacher. They created monuments and buildings to commemorate his teachings, notably in South America, Egypt, and India. Humanity continued to procreate and create daughters. The fallen angels became lustful of these human daughters and decided to make them wives. The human women the fallen angels married bore them children called the Nephilim. The Nephilim were tall, powerful, full of bloodlust, and were an abomination to God. Many different "tribes" of them existed. They spread their corruption upon the face of the Earth and consumed humanity like a fast-moving virus of evil by sharing their precious blood with humans in ancient rituals and inadvertently creating vampires.

God intervened to save his precious creation by finding the only living family left whose DNA was not yet infected by this evil and saved them. Noah, his family, along with a few of the animal species God specifically selected, became the chosen ones. God forced a great flood to come and wipe out any remaining living humans, the fallen angels, and the Nephilim. The Nephilim's body died in the enormous flood, but since they were half angels, they transformed into demons as punishment.

Demons are forever cursed to walk the Earth as bodiless creatures unless they are allowed to inhabit a human soul. Since they would never gain access to Heaven, they had no choice but to align themselves with Satan. As a result, demons have managed to infiltrate every area of society since the beginning of time to corrupt and deceive humanity into giving up their souls and following Satan.

God made a promise to Noah that he would never again flood the planet Earth in retribution for sinful behavior. He generously offered a beautiful rainbow for man to behold as a reminder of such a promise. Angels in Heaven who remained loyal to God are eternal so there is no need to marry or procreate. Angels can transform their bodies to take human form and blend in easily on Earth to remain undetected. God ordered them to infiltrate our society to keep an eye on human activities. They are only here to observe, lead, influence, and follow orders given by the Archangels. They are not allowed to disobey God. Ever. Only humans have the gift of free will.

So why would an angel ever want to give up his exalted position in Heaven and ever wish to be with a human woman knowing the awful consequences which would eventually befall him? And her? For the most potent reason in the entire universe, the most powerful cause of all, love.

# CHAPTER 1

## Summer of 2010

Jakiele or Jake Smith, as the humans had come to know him, had been on Earth watching the affairs of God's creation for more centuries than he could remember. Over the long centuries, he had managed to develop his angelic abilities to acute sharpness. His keen ability to decipher lies was legendary. He became aware that human beings would use a particular frequency in their voices when they lied that he could lock on to at once. He contributed this skill to preventing many wars. He did not want to lose faith in human beings, but he felt perilously close. He had proved himself a warrior on so many battlefields, in Heaven, and on Earth that he now reported only to the Archangel Michael.

Since the assignment required that he be always in human form, Jakiele sometimes forgot how wonderful it felt to spread his massive angelic wings and fly. The freedom he felt when he flew with his mighty wings fully spread out created a release he could not seem to duplicate on Earth. He liked the feel of a sword in his hand and practiced whenever he could with other angel warriors he ran across from time to time. He knew he needed to keep his fighting skills in top form so he would be ready if called upon by Michael to fight against the forces of darkness.

Jakiele knew that if he ever forgot who he was or why he came to Earth, it could create a lapse in judgment and a failure to complete his required assignments. So Jakiele made a special request to Michael to give him tasks to keep his adrenaline going and keep his mind and body on constant alert to prevent boredom from setting in. Jakiele participated eagerly in any forms of combat training offered by the CIA and any special weapons training he could participate in. When not engaged with these activities or his regular duties, he learned everything he could about the latest security equipment for commercial and home use.

Michael often conferred with his second in command, Gabriel, before making any crucial decisions about what angels could or could not do while stationed on Earth. Together, they decided the best job for Jakiele would be to oversee monitoring and arranging the security systems for the Secret Service of the American president. While the job could be stifling at times, Jakiele became privy to all the schedules of the president's activities since he became the one to whom the Secret Service reported. In addition, Jakiele regularly monitored the security devices specifically designed for the president and the Secret Service to use.

Jakiele was assigned to train the Secret Service agents to communicate in secret code with the ear and wrist equipment Michael had made for them. The training was the one part of the job that Jakiele enjoyed immensely. The newly trained agents could quickly and effectively relay all pertinent information to each other and Jakiele in cases of emergencies. If any glitches were reported with the equipment, it became Jakiele's job to let Michael know and fix them. In addition, Michael ordered Jakiele to offer the Secret Service members specialized defense training techniques to make them more efficient and deadly to anyone trying to harm the president.

The prestigious position allowed Jakiele to do background checks on any prospective agents the government wanted to hire and train. Jakiele vetted every one of them with Michael to figure out if any of the agents had evil agendas or if they were there to guard the president with their lives. The president was constantly made aware of any agents that did not meet approval and followed his and Michael's advice accordingly. Jakiele regularly listened in on every conversation the agents had with the president. He could hear every word the president said to other political leaders through them. He used his special angelic abilities to decipher if anyone he listened to was being truthful or not. His job assignment guidelines required that he regularly report to Michael any suspicious events which were worth noting. He left it up to Michael to decide what to do with the information. The position was one Jakiele had held and excelled at ever since America began.

The nature of the job made it easy for Jakiele to blend in with the wallpaper. Humans never suspected who he was or paid much attention to him. Human memories could be easily erased if they asked too many questions. The only times he felt like he failed at his job had been when assassination attempts ended with the successful termination of a human president's life. In Jakiele's opinion, the men who made these attempts may have been possessed demons who worked for the fallen angels.

It certainly explained why the men who conducted these attempts seemed confused and disoriented after the event and were often accused of mental illness. There was no way these men were intelligent enough to perform an assignment of such an enormous magnitude on their own without help. Demons had been infiltrating governments and kingdoms for eons to get humans to destroy themselves. The only reason they had not yet succeeded was the strategic placement of God's loyal angels to detect and counteract their activities. The ongoing war on Earth would never end until Judgment Day.

All of Heaven's angels could become invisible if they needed to. Humans would not even know an angel was present for those who had psychic powers or were empaths. These unique humans could sense his presence and knew he was not what he seemed to be, although they could not pinpoint who or what he was exactly.

He had often speculated that these humans were descendants of the Nephilim.

Jakiele had not run across empaths very often. If he did, he sent a request to Michael to erase their memories so he would not run the risk of exposure. The Archangels usually cared for any human problems or issues they considered necessary. All he knew was he was to observe, report, and follow the orders given. He avoided interacting with humans as much as possible, especially women. Women had been the downfall of man since the beginning of time as far as he was concerned, and he would never be dumb enough to tangle with a human woman other than on a strictly needed basis.

After many long, lonely years, Jakiele impulsively decided to buy a turn of the century home in the Washington D.C. area. It was a lovely old home that needed a complete renovation, but it was very private and would suit his needs. The old estate sat on a bluff overlooking the city below so he could sit on the back porch of the house and enjoy the wonderful twinkling lights of the city at dusk. The property's front yard stretched back and around approximately five acres in every direction with thickly foliaged trees that supplied cooling shade from the long hot summers. The mature trees lining the driveway leading up the long road to his home were thick with green foliage and tall. The various shrubs and lovely roses in between the trees delicately scented his house in the spring, which he enjoyed immensely. Jakiele did not know why he wanted to buy the old house. He had always lived inconspicuously in small apartments throughout different cities, which provided variety to his routine. Over time, he had stowed away a substantial amount of money and suddenly felt compelled to make his stay on Earth feel more permanent, more like home.

The home was a classic two-level white plantation-style estate with a large wrap-around porch in front. Majestic tall white pillars held up a front wooden overhang with delicate swirls carved into the wood to resemble artisan lace. He had altered the house's original design to have a 360-degree view from every window. Jakiele wanted to see and detect any trouble coming his way from every direction. He painted the shutters outlining the windows a lovely dark red color to match the handcrafted front doors. The security system he installed in the house was state of the art. There was no way anyone encroaching upon the house within five hundred yards could get anywhere close without him knowing it or unless he wanted them to. It was not like he did not have enough training to access the correct information on safeguarding his home. He enjoyed looking for ways to improve his security and keep his home safe.

Jakiele intended to install more cameras on the ten-foot-tall wrought iron black fences that encircled his entire property when he got the time. The floors inside the house had grey and white marble tile in the kitchen, bathroom, and foyer area that were imported from Italy. Lush cream-colored carpeting covered the living room and bedroom floors. The brilliance of the white walls highlighted the beautifully maintained collectible art from all over the world. A gorgeous turn-of-the-century crystal chandelier hung gracefully in the front foyer. The house's first level boasted a modern gourmet kitchen with an attached formal dining room off to the left of the long hallway which led into the house.

The main floor also featured a bathroom, laundry room, living room, and an office situated to the right of the main entrance hallway. A long winding staircase next to the office led to the upper floor, where the bedroom and guest bedroom were found. The office held the security monitoring equipment for the house, but it also contained a secret compartment hidden in the paneling behind his desk, which he could access if there were a need. The hidden room held all sorts of weaponry, from guns and ammo to explosive devices.

Unfortunately, the large estate had developed a cold, sterile feel since his favored furniture was black leather and stainless steel. The living room coffee and end tables were translucent glass with silver glazed marble inlaid around the outer edges. The massive fireplace in the living room was made with imported white and gray marble that matched the flooring beautifully. Jakiele loved to watch the flames dancing in the grates while watching his big screen TV located above the mantle. He fell asleep sprawled across the couch more often than he used the massive king-size bed in his bedroom.

Jakiele had fully transformed the basement into his combat training area. The basement floor had thick mats lining the floor. He liked to be on his bare feet to practice martial arts or weapons training. All along the walls were handcrafted cabinets made of special steel with soft blue felt lining the glass shelves that housed and protected his priceless training weapons. These cabinets were locked by ancient angelic script only an angel would know how to read and open. Jakiele installed an ultramodern lock system on the heavy steel door leading to the basement, requiring a complex code to unlock. The windows to the basement were designed to repel laser or gunfire from the outside. The glass in the windows had been altered to see outside, but no one could see inside. The motion sensors installed on the windows would alert him to anyone trying to break the glass or pry them open.

Jakiele furnished his home to be functional and easy to keep clean. Being required to stay in human form meant he had to endure human needs. He had to eat, shower, shave, and have all the normal bodily functions of an average thirty-five-year-old human male. He kept his long thick black hair strictly contained in a ponytail down his long muscular back while working, but otherwise, he liked to let it flow freely. He knew women found him exceptionally attractive with his square, angular face, long legs, and finely sculpted body, which was as hard as diamonds. He had luxuriously long black lashes that framed his beautiful sapphire-colored eyes. Whenever he had to speak with a mortal woman, they often would become transfixed on his eyes as though seemingly hypnotized. His voice was intense and since being around women sometimes made his body react, he had to stay away from them as much as possible. There was no way he would take the risk of mating with a human woman unless he knew for sure they were incapable of having children.

Like any typical human male, Jakiele did not like to do house chores and positively hated cooking for himself. So Jakiele thought it might be good to hire a housekeeper, but he had to get permission from Michael first. After gaining Michael's consent, Jakiele chose to use an employment agency that ran all the background checks and references for people who worked for the government to find the right woman for the job. The first applicant who showed up was a woman named Anna Klackovich. Anna was a stocky, overweight woman in her early fifties who looked like if she were ever to smile, she would break her stiffly formed lips which were kept in an almost perpetual thin frown as though disapproval was evident in everything she observed.

Anna was an immigrant from Bosnia who had recently arrived in the States and needed a job. She dressed as people had during the fifties with long dark skirts falling well below the knees, functional dark blouses, dark pantyhose, sensible nondescript shoes, and a headscarf to cover her hair when she was not in the house. When Anna first walked into the house, she took a long look around very slowly as if she were memorizing every detail. Anna did not say one word until Jakiele graciously invited her into his home at the appointed interview time. Jakiele led the way down the hallway to his office and gestured for Anna to sit opposite his desk.

Jakiele took a seat behind his desk and initiated the conversation. He began the interview by telling her what he was looking for and what he did for a living. He did not detail his employment because he strictly adhered to security concerns. However, he did tell her he oversaw security monitoring for the United States government. Jakiele noticed he did not seem to have the same hypnotizing effect on Anna with his eyes. He found this revelation most interesting, although he noticed that when she did look directly at him, she did not stare directly into his eyes. Then, while carefully studying her voice for any detection of subterfuge, he asked Anna to tell him a bit of herself. Anna kept her head down, avoiding looking directly at him for several seconds before deciding to respond. Once she decided to look him in the eye, Anna hesitantly told him she was an immigrant who had recently emigrated to America from Bosnia.

Jakiele could tell Anna did not want to talk much about her experiences in Bosnia or why she came to America. Anna revealed nothing about herself except that she had a daughter. Her daughter lived in Boston and was employed by a forensics lab in Maynard. Anna told him her daughter, Katliana, sometimes did a forensic analysis of DNA at crime scenes for the Boston police department if the department got too backed up with cases. Anna's answers about herself and her past were cursory at best. He would have known if Anna was lying. After several more probing questions from Jakiele, Anna asked him what her duties would be if she were to accept employment as his housekeeper. Jakiele politely changed the subject about her past and explained her duties would include housekeeping and meal preparation. There were two rules, no one was allowed in his bedroom or basement. Ever. Not even her.

When the interview had concluded, Anna looked directly at Jakiele with her dark, piercing black eyes for several long seconds. Jakiele was starting to feel uncomfortable with the long silence when Anna asked him directly if he was of this world or from a different dimension. Anna sat back quietly and waited for him to answer with her arms across her chest as if defying him to dare to lie to her. Anna had told him the truth about who she was and where she came from and wondered if Jakiele would be equally honest before deciding whether she would accept the position. Jakiele was so profoundly stunned that he did not know how to answer her at first. Jakiele quickly realized Anna was an empath or a physical medium. This revelation was a complication he had not seen coming. There was no other way she could have detected something different about him. Anna was a stern older woman with a deceptively sweet gray-haired old lady countenance but with the laser stare of someone who had suffered tragedy in life and did not want to hear a bunch of nonsense.

Jakiele felt optimistic that Anna would serve him well and keep her mouth shut if he allowed her to work for him. Deep down in his belly, Jakiele felt he could trust her, but he also knew he was taking a big chance on her. Jakiele decided to trust his instincts and reveal a small amount about who he was and why he was here on Earth. Jakiele assumed Anna would be very frightened and run screaming from his presence if he told her the truth, but she did not. Anna visibly relaxed, and Jakiele could tell he made the right decision being honest with her. Jakiele had a gut feeling Anna would have gotten up and walked out if he had refused to answer or danced around the truth. Later, Jakiele would ask Michael to scan her brain to make sure they could erase her memories if necessary. Then, he politely led Anna to the front door when the interview had concluded and told her he would get back to her as soon as possible after he checked her references.

Later in the evening, Jakiele filled Michael in on the president's recent happenings and his desire to hire Anna. Michael was hesitant but gave Jakiele permission to hire her after secretly visiting Anna. Michael shared misgivings with Jakiele about Anna's ability to block information from someone trying to access her memories if she chose not to reveal them. The visions Michael had been able to glean from Anna's past were vague and ugly. Anna possessed the ability to keep the lid tightly closed on her mind about what she had endured in her life. Angels had always been able to access any memory they wished from any human they wanted information from, but not always with empaths.

This new development about Anna's ability to keep secrets gave Jakiele pause, but he decided to accept her into his home. Anna started working for him right away and ran his household like a well-oiled machine. She kept her thoughts and her past to herself, but she seemed sad and hardly ever smiled or seemed joyous about anything. Jakiele instinctively knew she was the type of person who would give her life rather than betray him or the other angels.

Anna did not try to change or rearrange his house in any way. Anna knew his schedule, likes, and dislikes but made herself scarce when Jakiele was home. Anna never asked for anything other than necessary household supplies, a grocery list, and a paycheck. She had been in his employ now for over a year. No one ever visited her, and Anna never went anywhere he could decipher except to get the goods needed to run his household. Jakiele realized it was a hardship for her to go to places in the city because she insisted on taking public transportation instead of letting him help her and take her to town. Anna always laid out the mail for him to peruse when he got home, but he noticed there never seemed to be any mail for her. He supposed she must have a post office box in the city to receive her mail. Jakiele respected her isolation and the right to have a private life. Anna was an excellent cook who loved to make a variety of meals. His dinner was always prepared, so when he got home after a long hectic day at work, all he had to do was heat the food in the oven or microwave.

Jakiele offered Anna a room in the house, but Anna preferred to stay in the small loft on the top of the renovated garage. The loft had a small kitchenette with a large living room. The only bedroom had a bathroom, so it had everything Anna needed. Jakiele assumed Anna wanted to have her own space. He did not ask, and Anna did not explain why she had refused his offer to take the spare room in his house even though it would have been more convenient for her to use.

When Jakiele remodeled the master bedroom in the main house, he installed a keypad lock on the outside of his bedroom door so no one would ever be able to come in and see the secret portal he had secretly built into his walk-in closet. The closet door would automatically shut and lock behind him so no one could see the hidden mirror. The closet was a massive extra room that held all his clothes and shoes, but a large, round silver mirror encased in glass was at the back end. The exquisitely designed mirror resembled any other mirror except for the small silver and cherubic blue faces surrounding it. It was breathtakingly beautiful in its ornamentation. It had an angelic script all around the outer edges. On the right-hand side of the closet beneath his clothes was a secret compartment that required a numeric code for the panel to pop open.

Once opened, the panel inside had a scanner device that required him to lay his hand on it. After the scanner identified his handprint, the mirror's protective glass casing would lift. The mirror would begin to shimmer and turn a bright white which shined as bright as the stars. The emanating light was blinding in its intensity. Speaking in Aramaic to the living Cherubim on the mirror would identify himself. Jakiele had to wait until the small Cherubim started singing and allowed entrance before he could go through the mirror to the angelic realm. He was looking into installing laser lights in the closet to alert him to an intruder, but he had not gotten to it yet.

Once the mirror accepted his presence, Jakiele could safely walk through the membrane which separated the Earthly plane from the Heavenly one. He had to walk through an identical mirror on the other side to reach his destination. Jakiele was not allowed entrance into all areas of the kingdom of Heaven. He could only transport to the third-tier realm above the Sirius star where the other lower angels lived until commanded otherwise. The Archangels had mansions in the Orion, Pleiades, and Cygnus constellations. The other nine realms of the universe kept to themselves.

The heavenly mansion was massive, with multiple levels full of rooms with no barriers on the open windows. It appeared like it was made entirely of marble, like an ancient Roman place of worship would have been with its broad stone stairway leading up to the mansion suspended by large white marble-looking pillars. The main floor was where the other angels were busy bustling around fulfilling whatever assignments were given by the Archangels they served. Jakiele observed angels waiting to be transported to Earth while others were supplying reports on the activities of the humans they were assigned to watch.

Jakiele had to give regular reports to Michael unless an emergency required contact with him at once. For example, if Jakiele was going to be out of town to check on the American president's security, they used other means to contact each other. Inside, an altar was made of gold and silver in the center of the mansion's room. A large angelic mirror made of red and gold rested upon it. This mirror allowed the lower angels to contact the Archangels. While lower angels such as he could not go to the second or first tier of angelic beings, the Archangels could come down to the lower heavenly realm whenever they wished.

For centuries, human leaders had all known about the existence of inter-dimensional beings. Many treaties had been signed, and wars were avoided because of this. Army bases, churches, landing pads, and designs on the Earth were used to receive visitors from other realms. If humans observed spacecraft descending from the skies in ancient times, they would try to describe what they saw by writing it down on hieroglyphs or cave etchings. With the advance of technology, humans could now visibly see and record advanced transportation methods, so angels and other inter-dimensional beings had to become more creative to avoid being noticed when they visited Earth.

In the past, all inter-dimensional beings like the Greys could use mirrors, but this unstable method of transportation had proven to be hazardous since demons could use mirrors made by humans to enter the Earthly plane. So, God commanded the Cherubim to make a mirror that would keep angels undetected by humans when they had to travel. Only Archangels could assign a mirror to a trusted lower angel. However, it was clear the Archangels would be held accountable if the mirrors ever fell into the wrong hands or were misused.

The Greys have long been considered inter-dimensional beings with secret agendas to fulfill, but they must also obey God. Some have even called them scientists of the thirteen realms. Many eons ago, when Earth was in its infancy, they came to Earth to build magnificent structures and mine gold, but their bodies were not strong enough for such arduous tasks. The fallen angels wanted to use the splendid buildings as teaching platforms and transportation devices. In exchange for using the structures, the fallen angels offered the Greys the physical strength of the Nephilim and the humans they wanted to teach to help build them. These sites had astrological importance either for mining or making special metals, transportation purposes, storing essential artifacts like historical scrolls, or storing the Ark of the Covenant. All the sites or buildings on Earth the Greys built had a purpose and needed protection.

Ancient peoples mistakenly interpreted the Greys who had visited Earth in the past as gods and tried to worship them as such. Since the Greys did not want early humanity to know what they looked like, they wore decorative masks that resembled animals such as dogs, cats, birds, or snakes. These masks made it easier for the fragile Greys to breathe the air on Earth without difficulty. Ancient peoples understood not to question but simply follow orders for secret knowledge of the universe and reincarnation. The Egyptian, Native American, Japanese, Incan, and Mayan cultures wrote down the most accurate history to commemorate these ancient beings.

When the Greys designed the ancient pyramids and other historical sites, they did so with unerring mathematical accuracy. However, it became clear that humans were becoming aware of things they did not need to know of too soon from the teachings of the fallen angels. For example, the Nephilim mated with human women and freely offered their blood in religious rituals. Ancient cultures believed blood offerings to the Gods were a sacred rite to bring about their favor. Unfortunately, old drawings or hieroglyphs are all that is left for modern-day man to explain what happened to the vast knowledge that the fallen angels were once teaching.

The frames of the mirrors all had angelic scripts engraved in the ancient Aramaic language. These mirrors were as lovely as they were functional. Since they were all individually handcrafted by the Greys, no mirror was precisely like any other. After entering the heavenly mansion, Jakiele walked up to the red and gold mirror on the altar in the middle of the room, got down on his right knee, and bowed his head in respect. He spoke his exaltations and swore his allegiance with humbleness to the God he served in the ancient tongue of the angels. Once accepted by the Cherubim, Jakiele could request to speak with Michael. The Cherubim would begin to sing to one another, and the mirror would start to vibrate and shimmer. The mirror would shine its startling bright white light until Michaels's visage would appear before him.

Michael had many responsibilities and was not always in the realm assigned to the Archangels. As the special ambassador to Israel, he also had the extra burden of weighing the value of souls, so Michael was extremely busy. Not to mention being the leader of God's formidable army. If Michael were unavailable, he would have to report to Gabriel, who was Michael's second in command. Sometimes, Michael would walk through the mirror to join Jakiele if Michael decided he wanted to get some exercise. Then, the two would take off with lightning speed toward the entrance of the heavenly mansion while spreading their massive wings to see who could get outside first and fly with astonishing speed toward the outer realms of the universe, just for fun.

Michael loved to make sure he was still the fastest at everything he tried, whether flying, wielding a sword, or dropping kicking a demon straight to the Underworld where they belonged. Jakiele loved giving him a run for his money and was not about to hand a win to Michael on a silver platter without a fight. These little contests over the centuries cemented their trust in each other and kept Jakiele from going stir crazy. He was sure some of the other angels were jealous of his closeness with Michael. However, Jakiele knew he had earned it with hard-won battles and unwavering loyalty to God, which would never diminish with time. Jakiele was determined never to be a disappointment to God or Michael if he could help it.

It had been a long, sweltering summer in Washington D.C., and things in the white house were tense as usual. Russia had been acting up, and there was unrest in the Middle East as expected. There had been upheaval in the Middle East since before Jesus was born. Such news was not particularly unusual except when Michael was gone often, keeping his eye on things. The American president was due to take his vacation at Camp David soon, so for the first time since taking his position, Jakiele decided to take a long-earned break as well.

Jakiele knew he had trained the Secret Service agents who guarded the American president relentlessly. They needed to be as alert and deadly efficient as humanly possible. The agents assigned to Camp David while the president was on vacation were lethal and expert at watching everything around them, so he knew the president would be well cared for. He had trained them personally to be superhumanly alert and trust absolutely no one. He was sure the agents gave him the utmost respect for his hard-handed authority, but they were secretly relieved Jakiele finally trusted them enough to provide them with a much-needed break too.

Jakiele thought to start learning how to try the human sport of skydiving. While it would not replicate the feeling that spreading angelic wings and flying would, he thought it might be an acceptable alternative. He made the necessary arrangements to train at a small skydiving school he had heard about near the airport. He also planned to go over the security he had around the perimeter of his property to make sure everything was in working order and up to his very exacting standards.

Jakiele also wanted to talk to Anna about taking the paid vacation she had earned as well. Jakiele had recently bought her a pale blue Chevy Malibu to use whenever she liked as a sign-on bonus. Anna had resisted at first because she thought it was an excessive gift and did not know how to drive. However, not to be deterred, Jakiele made sure she was given private driving lessons by Caleb, his chauffeur, who came to pick him up every morning for work and take him home. Caleb had been working for him for over twenty years. He was in his early fifties with the exact keep-to-himself gruff persona Anna also possessed. He had a full head of thickly graying hair but had the body of someone who still worked out every day and got plenty of fresh air and sunshine. Caleb's chauffeur outfit and hat were invariably impeccably clean and pressed. His black dress shoes were always highly polished and shiny.

Caleb had the personality of someone who did not ask questions but followed orders well. He was a former marine. His memories had been slightly tampered with to make sure he never noticed that Jakiele never seemed to age. Over the years they shared, Caleb and Jakiele slowly learned to trust each other and were friends of a sort. They had conversations about fishing, camping, and outdoor survival, which Caleb taught when he was a military survival expert before he retired. Caleb knew never to ask questions about Jakiele's job, even though he knew what Jakiele did for a living. Nor did he ever give opinions about world affairs. Caleb could have, but his nature showed he simply did not want to get involved. He had known his fair share of bloodshed in the military and preferred to live in a safe little world where ugly stuff did not exist if he did not know about it.

After losing so many friends during the war in Heaven, Jakiele understood how Caleb felt. His best friend, Remiel, had been the hardest to lose when Remiel took the wrong side in the war in Heaven and became a fallen angel. In addition, Caleb's wife of over fifteen years had died of cancer, and they had not been blessed with any children. It was haunting for Caleb to talk about his wife or his former life as a marine, so Jakiele did not press him for details.

It was beyond hilarious when Anna and Caleb had met for the first time. Caleb had driven up the driveway through the gates to pick Jakiele up for work and walked right into the house without knocking as was his custom. Jakiele had given him the code to the front door entrance, so it was not a big deal. Jakiele always had the coffee ready, so Caleb would walk into the kitchen and read the paper he had picked up on the front doorstep. Then, Caleb would have his cream-laden coffee while Jakiele finished his morning workout routine in the basement. Caleb did not have to get there early, but he did it because he wanted to. Then, Jakiele would get ready for work, and Caleb would take him to his office. On Anna's first day of work, she entered the house from the garage, so she did not notice there was a long limousine in the driveway since her view was blocked when she entered the kitchen.

Jakiele had not told Anna that anyone else would be allowed access to the house. So, when she opened the side entrance of the house with the code Jakiele had given her, she went directly into the kitchen. She shrieked and put a startled hand to her chest when she saw Caleb sitting at the counter reading his paper, and Anna at once demanded to know who he was. She began screaming and shouting for Jakiele to come upstairs before Caleb even had the chance to respond. After hearing Anna screeching his name, Jakiele rushed upstairs with supernatural speed to the kitchen to find out what had scared this stoic, unshakable woman. After carefully closing and locking the basement door, he saw Anna holding Caleb hostage with a large cast-iron skillet. She was waving it at Caleb's head menacingly and speaking vehemently in her native language. The look of horror on Caleb's face, who was a skilled military veteran, with his hands straight up in the air, made Jakiele laugh so hard his ribs ached for days.

When he could finally catch his breath, Jakiele let Anna know it was okay. Caleb was his driver. Anna was mortified that this supposed driver and Jakiele had a casual, informal relationship, but she gradually lowered the cast iron skillet, albeit grudgingly. However, after their first encounter, she always made sure Caleb had specially made treats like homemade pastries and little cakes to enjoy, which she left on the counter specifically for Caleb, but it would take medieval torture to get her to admit it. Caleb enjoyed them with so much relish and enjoyment that there was hardly a crumb ever left on the plate.

Furthermore, Caleb made sure to compliment her on them with so much enthusiasm and humbleness that there was no way Anna could not know how much her simple kindness meant to him. Although Anna never openly acknowledged Caleb's compliments, Jakiele knew how much Caleb's joyful exuberance meant to her as she never missed a beat making special goodies for Caleb. Moreover, she made sure to know what kind of treats he favored.

Caleb and Anna became cautious friends and would have limited conversations in the mornings. However, they still danced around each other as though afraid to like each other. When Caleb agreed to take Anna down to the local DMV to get her first driving license, it was the only time Jakiele could remember ever seeing Anna smile as she showed off her new driver's license to himself and Caleb. Jakiele could tell Caleb was incredibly proud of Anna for listening and following his instructions and had taken to driving like she was born to it. Caleb and Jakiele knew this was a profound new freedom for Anna, and it was an exceptionally precious moment.

Jakiele also needed to make sure Caleb was aware he could take his month-long vacation as well. Caleb had wanted to go on an extended fishing trip for quite some time and mentioned several places he would like to visit. It was not as though Jakiele could not drive himself with his own specially made Audi, which currently sat in his garage gathering dust. The simple fact was the government preferred he was driven to and from work by an approved government driver. Like many other high-ranking individuals who worked for the government, Jakiele knew it was the administration's way of tracking him.

Jakiele's car was dark black with shiny silver rims, but the inside made it special. The console had a handprint scanner and voice recognition system, allowing the ignition to start if the computer recognized the driver as being him. Jakiele had also had it altered to make it faster. Whenever he allowed himself the freedom to take it out and evaluate it, it was exhilarating to see how fast his car could take razor-sharp turns and accelerate to speeds that would make professional race car drivers envious. Nevertheless, Jakiele had to be incredibly careful about sustaining bodily injuries. If he died, that was it. His life was over. Only human beings were allowed to be reborn.

# CHAPTER 2

Anna had decided her month-long vacation would be spent visiting her daughter in Boston, and she left the following week. Caleb had been eagerly anticipating trying out his new deep sea fishing gear, so he paid for an adventure on a boat that would take him from the Boston Harbor out toward the Grand Banks. It was dangerous to go out on those choppy waters of the Atlantic alone, which was why it was so expensive to hire a boat crew. However, fishing in wild waters off the coast was what Caleb enjoyed. It was an extreme adrenaline rush to go deep-sea fishing with the local Gloucester men whose families had been fishing the waters for hundreds of years and knew the sea well.

Jakiele's house felt too quiet without Caleb and Anna. Too empty. He at first thought he would enjoy his long-awaited privacy but not anymore. He had gotten used to the exotic aromas emanating throughout his home, which signaled Anna had been baking her fabulous desserts for Caleb. He found he liked listening to the lighthearted chatter which signaled Anna and Caleb were having their usual morning debate over one thing or another and the easy laughter which had developed lately between the two of them. Now his home felt sterile once again, with the two of them being gone. And lonely. This new development made Jakiele feel uneasy. He did not want to become too accustomed to humans being in his home.

Somehow, he let his guard down, and he had become used to their sounds and smells. Human lives were so short and fragile, and he did not want to become attached to humans being in his life or feel anything for them.

Jakiele resolved in his mind that what he needed to do was go downstairs and give himself a vigorous workout that would take his mind off this strange uneasiness about being alone. However, as Jakiele began walking down the thickly carpeted stairs, he got the sense that someone was already waiting for him in his basement. So, with his senses on high alert, he crept silently down the stairs until he could peer cautiously around the corner to get a better view of who had invaded his home uninvited.

Michael stood in the middle of the room staring into the glass and silver shelves that housed Jakiele's lethal weapons and had his back turned to Jakiele. Jakiele silently observed that Michael appeared to be lost deep in thought as he watched Michael slowly begin to bow his head. Michael often laced his fingers behind his back which meant something serious was going on. A braided silver thong neatly held Michaels's long flowing black hair. A silver filigree headband was the only other adornment on his head which signaled he was of the Archangel class of angels. Michael's body length armor was made of metallic silver, which could outshine even the brightest star. It was covered in ancient angelic protective designs. His long flowing white cape disguised his massive, folded wings.

However, it was Michael's magnificent sword that could immediately capture one's attention. It was deceptively sharp and made to inspire fear in the heart of his enemy. The blade was made to resemble a long, jagged length of silver lightning with fiery blue flames around the edges, which sprang to life whenever Michael wielded it. A glowing white spherical orb adorned with specially shaped smaller white diamond orbs were welded on the sword's end above the hilt. The spheres refracted light and could blind enemies. Wrapped around the handle were silver and powder blue metallic strands which would wrap around Michael's hand if he were ever to become separated from his sword. Michael always had his left hand resting on the hilt of his sword in its custom-made silver sheath spectacularly covered in angelic protective symbols unless he was in deep thought or streaking through the heavens at supernatural speed stretching his wings.

Michael slowly turned around and opened his eyes to stare at Jakiele with his piercing light blue eyes and nailed Jakiele to the wall with his hard stare. It was as though Michael could stare right through someone with laser precision and see every thought. It was a most intimidating glare if someone did not know him and certainly more so if they did. Michael's voice was quiet, deep, and soothing to the ear. It could lure anyone into telling him anything he wished to know or lull the senses into feeling safe and secure. One did not become the leader of God's army without using every asset or ability to whatever advantage was needed. Whether they were his skills or someone else's needing to be developed, all was fair in love and war as far as Michael was concerned.

"How quiet and peaceful your home is, Jakiele. I see you have made many improvements since my last visit, and you have been updating your security systems," Michael stated in his deceptively soft tones. "What are your plans now that you have decided to take your vacation?" Michael must have used Jakiele's private portal upstairs to enter his home, which would explain why Jakiele did not hear him come in. The glass case would automatically open when accessed by Michael or Jakiele from the other side. Michael did not let him know he was coming for a visit, which concerned Jakiele. Michael did not show up randomly as he was too busy for such nonsense most of the time. Michael must have had a particular reason to come.

Jakiele hesitated to reply for a moment because he was not sure what Michael's agenda was but said, "I have plans to walk the perimeter of my estate and check my security systems to make sure they are all working properly with the new cameras and laser motion sensors I purchased a few weeks ago. I also want to investigate a more advanced monitoring system for the glass casing of the mirror.

It needs to be more protected. Since my servants are on vacation, I would like to ambush and trap the demons I know have been watching me. I do not yet know who they are, but I have detected their presence around my home. I also plan to learn how to skydive. I have heard it is quite a thrill for humans. Why do you ask?"

It was Michael's turn to hesitate before he replied, "I have been informed Israel may become seriously involved in matters which will require my attention for an extended period, and I wanted to let you know it will be difficult to reach me. As you know, the Middle East is in quite an upheaval. I wanted to tell you personally to report only to Gabriel. Gabriel will contact me if it is deemed necessary." Michael turned around again and studied the assortment of weapons at Jakiele's disposal. He was quite impressed at the ensemble Jakiele had managed to acquire over the years, with some dating back to the days of the Samurai and ancient Mayans. Michael also added, "If you plan on trapping demons while I am not around, I expect you to take all necessary precautions to protect yourself. It will be difficult to reach me except in the case of an absolute emergency."

Jakiele walked over to where Michael stood and turned to face him. Jakiele knew he did not have a choice in the matter about having to report to Gabriel, but he did not have to like it. "I will do as commanded as always, Michael, but I do not feel comfortable reporting to Gabriel. I do not feel as though he takes my reports as seriously as you would. He does not trust me as you do." Michael thought on this for a moment before slowly turning and looking directly into Jakiele's eyes. Michael raised his right hand, placed it softly on Jakiele's left shoulder, and gave a reassuring squeeze before he replied, "My most loyal friend, do you not trust my judgment in this matter? Do you believe I would ever put your life or work here on Earth in jeopardy if I did not trust Gabriel?"

Michael lifted his right eyebrow in consternation as he always did when asking a serious question to which he expected an honest answer. Jakiele was humbled at once. He trusted Michael with his life and would never try to offend him. "Of course, Michael. Always.

My most sincere apologies if I have offended you. It was not my intention." Michael quietly laughed and, with a thought, quickly shed his armaments and clothing except for a pair of tightly fitting workout pants that showed off his impressively muscled physique. He had his beautiful sword in hand.

"Your unwavering loyalty and friendship would never allow me to put someone in charge of receiving your reports if I did not trust them implicitly, Jakiele. I would not ever put you deliberately in danger. Gabriel is trustworthy and has proven himself as my friend and ally as often as you have. Do not concern yourself with these matters. Enjoy your vacation but be careful with your human body. I would not want to come back and find you had grown fat and sloppy in my absence," Michael said mockingly and raised his right eyebrow in challenge. He quickly spread his bare feet and placed his legs in a stance of an open challenge for a much-needed energy release.

Jakiele spoke a command in Aramaic to the cabinet nearest him, which housed his own individually made sword. Jakiele's sword, upon his order, immediately flew to his right hand. While not as ornamental and beautifully made as Michael's, it was still deadly in its own right. It was long, straight, and thick with a curve at the end with black and silver threads lining the hilt. It looked like a Saracen sword of old. The knob at the end was made of silver and was solid all the way through. The sword was made to fit Jakiele's hand perfectly.

Michael and Jakiele prepared themselves for the ancient dance of swordplay and soon clashed swords. Michael had been an excellent teacher, and Jakiele had been his most ardent student. It was hard for Michael to gain the upper hand and just as tricky for Jakiele to make sure Michael did not achieve it. For hours, they danced until they were each bathed in pools of sweat. Their long black hair became plastered to their heads with their thighs and arms aching from the exertion. Nevertheless, they were so exhilarated by the action that they lost all track of time.

Finally, Michael lowered his sword a fraction and mockingly taunted Jakiele with, "I do not know about you, but I could sure use some fresh air, but only if you think you still have what it takes to keep up." In an instant, Michael was at the portal waiting for Jakiele to catch up and activate the mirror standing right before him. Michael took off like a flash of lightning as soon as the mirror started to shimmer and open. Jakiele had to use everything he had to keep up with Michael's extraordinary speed as they streaked across the universe, leaving an angelic trail that looked like a heavenly comet had passed.

Laughing all the way, they stretched out their massive wings to their total capacity. This freedom was the closest an angel ever came to being one hundred percent at peace. When they had finally had enough and were standing by the entrance to the lower tier of the heavenly mansion, looking out over the clouds, they grasped each other's forearms and said their goodbyes for now. Michael was now gone, and Jakiele knew it would be a long time before he would see him again.

Jakiele went back through his closet portal and softly closed the door behind him. He leaned back against the door and closed his eyes with a sigh of resignation. A new chapter in his life was beginning, and he had to resign himself to the fact that things were constantly evolving and changing, and he would have to accept it. What he could not countenance was this overwhelming sense of loneliness he now felt. He had never felt this way before. Why now? He thought. Since he could not find an answer, he walked downstairs to try and find something to eat. He figured there had to be some leftovers Anna had made for him before leaving.

Anna always kept the house clean and the refrigerator well-stocked. But, as Jakiele perused the contents of his refrigerator, he turned around. He suddenly noticed something he had not seen before. On the counter where Anna placed her cookies and cakes for Caleb was a single five-by-seven picture of the most beautiful human woman he had ever witnessed. In the plainly framed black picture frame was a portrait of a young woman sitting in a field of wildflowers playing with a small puppy of unknown origin. She appeared to be in her mid-twenties, he would have guessed. Yet, it was the look of pure joy and innocence on the woman's face that seemed almost ethereal that captured his attention.

The beautiful woman in the picture had lovely long hair colored like soft corn silk with honey brown highlights that swayed gently away from her face in the breeze. The woman looked down at the puppy, so he could not see what color her eyes were. Her skin tone was fair, and her face was shaped in a delicate oval. Jakiele could see she was about to give the puppy a sweet kiss with her full pink lips. Her hair was gleaming, and it looked like a halo of light had surrounded it as it reflected the rays of the shining sun. His mind and body instantly reacted violently to the sight of her. His male organs became hard and erect and bordered on pain instantly. He backed away from the counter so fast it looked like he had been shot. The woman in the picture had to be Anna's daughter, Katliana.

Jakiele had never experienced this sort of reaction before by looking at a woman or being in the presence of one. What was wrong with him? Whenever he needed to care for his human needs, he had always used female escorts who would take care of his every desire. These carefully selected human women were incapable of bearing children because they were barren, and he knew his seed could not take hold even though he was always sure to wear a condom to protect himself. These escorts had all been checked out by the Archangels to make sure, though the women never knew they were being scrutinized so thoroughly. The madam who ran the establishment the angels frequented had always been well paid to keep her mouth shut. The madam did not know what his kind was, but she did not care either if she was given the money promised to her so generously.

The women Jakiele chose to have sex with always wanted to return to him, not because of the money he paid them, but because all angels had long, thick male organs human women enjoyed immensely. All angels were intrinsically beautiful to behold and were generous lovers. In addition, angels had stamina from all their constant training. As a result, the angels and those chosen to be with them could enjoy long sensual hours. Most angels took what they needed, but Jakiele enjoyed giving women multiple forms of ecstasy either from his mouth, hands, or the male organ with which he was so gifted. It was pure joy for him to see their looks of rapture as he took them over the edge so many times. The women lost count before he would eventually seek his own release.

Jakiele often spent time with an older woman named Rochelle the most. She kept her forty-plus-year-old body in shape but with the soft curves of an older woman. She loved to wear the naughtiest lingerie for him to feast his eyes on. She had long dark red curly hair with soft amber highlights, which was naturally wavy and fell well below her waist. She had lovely green eyes fringed with dark black lashes indicating an intelligence Jakiele was careful not ever to forget. She wore only minimal make-up. Rochelle was naturally lovely and liked to display her assets openly to keep his interest running at peak capacity.

Jakiele had asked her once why she was an escort when she could be so much more. Jakiele sensed she was inordinately intelligent and even cunning. She simply looked at him and smiled but never gave him a direct answer. She simply put her mouth on him and suckled him until he gave the most explosive release he could ever remember. Her response was all the answer he needed because he never thought to ask her again. While she did not have huge breasts, the ones she had were natural and full. Rochelle loved to come to the designated hotel room they always shared wearing a long black trench coat made of pure silk. She would let him discover what she had on underneath in his own time. Rochelle favored wearing stiletto thigh-high boots so that she could be as tall as he was when she went to kiss him. Like most angels, he was over six feet tall.

Rochelle taught him how to pleasure a woman, and she relished finding out what made him hard as a rock. She genuinely seemed interested in getting to know him better after their many episodes of hot steamy sex together. Rochelle would ask what he did for a living, what books he liked, his favorite meals, anything about his personal life. Nevertheless, Jakiele was extremely cautious and knew only to tell her the bare minimum. She did not need to know anything about him other than taking care of his human desires. Too much knowledge could be dangerous for her to know.

Once Jakiele recovered from the shock of seeing the picture of Anna's daughter on the counter, he forgot all about eating. Instead, he grabbed his car keys off the holder by the front door and went outside to set his house alarm code to "armed" status. After opening the garage with the fob on his key chain, he unlocked the door of his Audi and slid in. The car dialed the number to the escort service upon his voice command. He asked if Rochelle was available for the night. The answering service said they would get back to him and took down his phone number.

While he waited, he called his favorite hotel, the Ritz Carlton, to let them know he would need his standard room ready. He liked the hotel staff at the Ritz because they were well-known for their discretion. High-ranking officials stayed in this hotel from time to time, and privacy was expected and essential. When the escort service called him back to let him know Rochelle would be available, Jakiele was relieved. However, the receptionist wanted to know the details of the meeting place. All Jakiele replied to her was, "Please tell her the usual will be fine." Which, of course, Rochelle knew well.

After hanging up, Jakiele backed out of his circular driveway, closed the garage with his remote, and sped down the road leading away from his house toward his armed front gates. He let the window slide down as he entered the code to open the black wrought iron double gates leading out onto the main road. As the gates slowly opened outward, Jake hit the accelerator and sped toward the twinkling lights of the city. The gates had been programmed to close by themselves. Jakiele was lost deep in thought, thinking about the strange reactions he had been having lately to humans, like being lonely without them, and about the extraordinary response to seeing the picture of Anna's daughter. Had he looked in his rearview mirror, he would have seen the stealthily clad being who was quickly sneaking through his gates before they completely closed to have a look around his property and to take inventory of all Jakiele had been working on.

After arriving at the hotel and handing off his car to the valet, Jakiele went up the elevator to the penthouse suite. The luxurious suite was always paid for well in advance by the Archangels, so it was always available. The Archangels like to use it for meetings with important government officials, but Jakiele was allowed to use it for his own purposes on occasion. It was one of the rewards of being stationed permanently on Earth. Michael liked to keep his angels happy who had proven themselves worthy, so being asked to exist alongside the humans was not so tedious a task.

Jakiele had ordered champagne and strawberries from room service to be chilled and ready and on the coffee table when he arrived. As he walked into the suite, he started stripping off his clothes. Rochelle would arrive at her appointed time in a matter of minutes and let herself into the suite. She was never late, which is one of the qualities he admired about her. He had started to head for the shower when he heard her swipe her pre-programmed room card at the door. She walked in wearing her trademark black silk trench coat and long black shiny thigh-high boots. She did not say a word. Instead, she walked over to the coffee table and laid her purse down.

Rochelle left her hair falling gloriously all the way down to her waist. It was a magnificent mass that Jakiele loved to run his hands through or snatch in his fist when she wanted him to let go and get down to business. As she turned around and faced him, she started to reveal what she was wearing underneath. She slowly let the coat fall off her shoulders so he could only see a small amount at a time. She wore a red sheath that fell above her mid-thighs. The dress suited her body perfectly but was not clingy. Her breasts filled the top of the outfit but did not spill out. Her stockings were held up by lacy black garters he could not wait to take off with his teeth. She wore shiny red lipstick and mascara, but they were light in the application. She was breathtakingly beautiful. He watched as she sauntered seductively up to him and kissed him squarely on the lips.

Jakiele put his large hands on her waist and kissed her back. The woman was an expert with her mouth and tongue and very skilled hands. She naughtily rubbed up against his manhood while mating her tongue with his so that before long, she would have him panting for more. Rochelle instantly broke the embrace and sauntered away from him to pour them both a glass of the chilled champagne, which was of the finest quality. "What have you been up to, lover?" she queried quietly. "It has been quite a while since you last called." She pursed her lips in a pretty pout and said silkily, "I thought you had forgotten about me."

Jakiele detected a note of hurt in her voice. Jakiele thought Rochelle would think he had grown tired of her, so he said, "I have had many things to take care of with my job, and it has been kind of hectic. Of course, you were on my mind, but it is not always easy for me to be able to have a private life." Not having any privacy was undoubtedly true, he thought to himself. Jakiele replied firmly to her, "I made arrangements to have some time with you as soon as I could. I certainly enjoy our time together, but I do not need any complications or commitments I cannot keep right now. I hope you can understand and accept these necessary boundaries." He scrutinized her reaction carefully and waited for her to respond.

Rochelle smiled her siren smile at him and emptied her glass of champagne in one long swallow. Next, she took one of the large strawberries, dipped it in the whipped cream, and placed it strategically next to her lips. She took her time staring at him while she swirled her delicate pink tongue all around the strawberry, slowly licking and sucking the cream off before she sank her pearly white teeth into the flesh of the ripe fruit seductively. He thoroughly enjoyed watching her sensuous movements as she slowly ate the sumptuous fare.

Jakiele could take it no more. He strode over to where she stood and picked her straight up as though she weighed absolutely nothing to him. He forced her long legs to wrap around his waist and walked her straight into the shower, clothes on and all. After turning on the showerhead and setting it to a comfortable temperature for them both, he kneeled in front of her and slowly unzipped her long boots. He put the boots outside on the bathroom floor and focused his attention on her sexy black garters. After unfastening them with his fingers and slipping them off with his teeth, he slid his long fingers inside her pantyhose. He slowly slid them down her legs while placing soft kisses on her legs.

Next, he focused on the small fire red strip of nylon which was supposed to pass as underwear under her dress. He ran his tongue over her sensitive womanly nub and softly blew hot air on her until she started to writhe and moan. Then she ran her fingers through his thick black mass of hair and massaged his scalp. Finally, her legs began to tremble and would have given out on her, except for the fact he tantalizingly slipped two fingers inside her and started slowly moving them in and out while still ravishing her with his tongue and breath. Jakiele was driving her crazy with lust.

Before Rochelle could gain her release, Jakiele abruptly stopped and slid her thong down her long legs and off her body, exposing her secret nub for him to explore more fully. He pulled her closer to his mouth and very slowly swirled his talented tongue around her until she screamed in a powerful release. He pulled her back up and slowly stripped off the dress over her head. He took one of her breasts into his mouth while he held her hand's prisoner above her head with his so she could not move. He kissed and suckled her breasts until they were achingly sensitive. Jakiele grabbed a handful of the liquid soap and slowly washed her from head to toe.

Not to be outdone, Rochelle wanted to do the same to him. Rochelle put a small amount of soap in her hand and began stroking his engorged organ until he began to ache. Rochelle paid attention to all the other sensitive spots she knew so well on his body. She began running her hands all over the muscled planes of his body, slowly exploring and caressing every inch. Rochelle would never look him in the eyes while they pleasured each other. She did not like looking him directly in his eyes for too long because she almost became mesmerized or hypnotized by him, and she could not afford to have any tender feelings for him. There was too much at risk for her.

After rinsing each other off, Jakiele lifted her once again and wrapped her long legs around his waist. He put her up against the shower wall and entered her with his massive erection. There was no tenderness, no emotion, only a mad lust between the two of them. Over and over, he pounded into her until suddenly, the vision of Anna's daughter materialized in his mind. He came so fast and so hard it shook him to his core. Jakiele rested his head against Rochelle's breasts and tried to regain his breath as though he had finished running a long-distance race. He was stunned. Never had he lost control and gained his release so quickly. Rochelle softly chuckled and said, "Did you miss me, baby? I can always make house calls, you know."

Even though Jakiele thought she was only teasing him, Jakiele separated from her and turned away so he could wash. He was embarrassed and did not respond to her teasing jibes. Rochelle encircled her arms around his waist from behind and rested her cheek on his back. She softly whispered to him, "Do not worry. It happens to all men occasionally. Nothing to be concerned with. If you would only let me come to your house, we could do this more often." She paused for a moment before adding, "I certainly would not mind being at your beck and call."

Jakiele turned to look at her and started washing her as well, being exceptionally careful to wash away all traces of his seed. It was not like him to be careless and not wear a condom, but he knew it was only an extra precaution and not necessary where Rochelle was concerned. "I have been doing extensive renovations on my home, and now is not a suitable time for anyone to visit. I want you to understand that I feel more comfortable meeting you here at the hotel. We need to keep our relationship on a strictly professional level, and there are reasons I have not invited you to my home, Rochelle. I do not want anything emotional or personal. I sincerely hope you can accept these parameters because I would like to have our affiliation continue." Jakiele said these words sternly as he needed Rochelle to understand that their relationship could not be anything more than what it already was. Jakiele knew that once he sensed Rochelle was becoming emotionally attached in any way, he would have to sever their contact at once.

Rochelle at first had a stricken expression, but she quickly recovered and stepped out of the shower to dry off. Over her shoulder, she glanced back at him and smiled very sweetly when she said, "Of course I understand. I was merely making an offer that could be more convenient for you because of your schedule and afford us more privacy. If it is easier for you to meet me here at the hotel, so be it. I could care less as long as you pay me what we have agreed. After all, you are only another client to me as well." With her last biting remark, she left the bathroom and walked across the room to the coffee table to dig for something in her purse.

Jakiele immediately heard the lie in her voice. Jakiele watched her cautiously as he padded softly behind her and crossed silently across the room to the enormous bed. He laid down on his back and put his left hand behind his head to allow him a better view of her. Jakiele continued to watch her very closely. Something was off with her tonight, and he could sense something was wrong. He did not want to pry, and she did not offer any explanations. She had never lied to him before, or he would have detected it. Rochelle let the towel fall sensuously off her body as she walked over to the bed. She had something hidden behind her back in her hands.

As Rochelle sat down on the bed, she reached forward and revealed to him what she had hidden in her hands. It was a pair of black fur-lined handcuffs and a little key to open them. Rochelle sat up on her knees next to him and handed them to him. She put her right hand on his flaccid member and saucily asked him if he was done for the night or if the shower scene was all he had to give her. She took him into her mouth and swirled her tongue around him until he could not breathe. Jakiele quickly flipped her over to lie on her stomach and handcuffed her wrists to the bedpost. He expertly gave her the ride she wanted by grabbing her waist on either side with his large hands and began taking her hard and fast. One should not challenge an angel and expect to get away with it.

He tangled the fingers of one hand into her luxurious hair, and the other he used to stroke her wet womanhood repeatedly. Jakiele's lovemaking kept her screaming and panting her orgasmic releases until the break of dawn when he finally gave in to his pleasure and let her hands go with the key she had given him. Rochelle gave him a quick hard kiss and quickly dressed to retrieve the money he had previously set out for her on the bedside table. Then, she said goodbye to him and quietly left the room. Rochelle had courteously left the television on a low volume for him to fall asleep to, which he quickly did as soon as she left.

After Rochelle took the elevator down to the lobby and turned in the room card, she asked the concierge if he would arrange for a taxi to take her home. As she waited in the lobby for the taxi to arrive, the tiny hairs on the back of her nape stood up. Fear and dread began to creep slowly up her spine. She knew she was being watched. Rochelle did not need to guess who it was. It was the same creature who had been tormenting her for months. Zadikiele.

Rochelle could not remember much about her life before Zadikiele had come into it and caused her life to be one continuous nightmare. Whenever she allowed herself access to her memories, all visualizing it would do was drive her gut-wrenching pain. It seemed like a beautiful dream from long ago, as though she was looking at someone else's life through a distorted-looking glass instead of her own.

She remembered having a small quaint house on the outskirts of town she had once shared with an amazing and loving husband. Their union had produced a sweet five-year-old little boy named Nathaniel. She thought of Nathaniel as her miracle baby since she and her husband had tried so long to conceive as a couple. She and her husband Steve had been high school sweethearts and married after Steve graduated from college. When she had finally managed to become pregnant, she and Steve had been ecstatic. Unfortunately, Rochelle was diagnosed with severe endometriosis, and the doctors had been forced to remove her womb during an emergency cesarean section after the delivery of her son. Her husband was hired as an investigative reporter for the local paper shortly after graduating from college, and she had been a loving stay-at-home mom who doted on her husband and their little boy.

One day, Rochelle remembered answering the door after taking her son to his afternoon kindergarten class. Her husband, Steve, had left town a couple of days before following the trail of a hot news story. There had been a knock on her front door, and a strangely dressed man stood on her front porch. She had spent the afternoon baking cookies for her son to eat when he got home from school. The screen door was locked, so she talked to the stranger at her entrance through the screen after slowly opening the main door. "May I help you?" she asked cautiously while carefully peering around the door. The man's head was bowed, so she could not see what he looked like.

She could see the stranger had on a black felt hat with silver beading on the crown, but it obscured his facial features since he was looking straight down. His hair was pale, light blond, straight, silky, and fell well below his waist. His long hair beheld one long braid on either side of his head at the front of each ear. His face was clean-shaven with a strong jawline from what she could see. He wore a long black trench coat and no shirt. She could see all the rugged ridges of his well-defined abdominal muscles. He wore black riding gloves on his hands. He reminded her of a picture she had seen of a Viking warrior. The stranger had on black, tightly fitted jeans, which covered his thickly muscled thighs, and wore black motorcycle riding boots on his large feet.

The man kept his head bowed when he replied in the slightly gravelly voice of someone who smoked cigarettes or drank too much whiskey, "I do not know if you can help. It depends on whether you want your son to live or not." The stranger swiftly reached behind his back and pulled out a long hunting knife to cut the steel mesh lining the screen door. He unlatched the door lock so fast that she did not even have time to blink. Rochelle tried to slam the front door shut on him, but the man was too fast. He slammed the front door open with a mighty crash against the wall. Rochelle instinctively backed up a few steps in horror before she bellowed at him, "I do not know what you are talking about or what you think you are doing, but you had better get the hell out of here, or I will scream and call the cops!" Her cell phone was on a small table next to the door, so she lunged out to try and snatch it, but she was not quick enough. Zadikiele raced across the room, grabbed her right wrist with a bruising force, and squeezed it hard. Finally, he forced her to fall to her knees and kneel in front of him.

Rochelle could finally see the stranger's full facial features. She had a weird sense of déjà vu of suddenly as though she somehow knew this man but knew she had never seen him before. He had dark, fathomless eyes with long black spiky lashes framed by equally dark brows. His face was pale, but he was darkly handsome. He had straight white teeth and full lips. If he were not so cruel, one could imagine playing out dark, sensual fantasies with him. He bent down, put his face within one inch of hers, and began to speak to her again very softly and slowly as if he were speaking to a slow-witted child.

He began by saying to her, "My name is Zadikiele, and you will come to know me well. We are holding your husband and your son. Your husband was foolishly digging into things he did not need to know about, and he deliberately chose not to heed the warnings given to him. Now your son will be forced to pay a high price for his father's stupidity and arrogance. Your husband has a message for you." The stranger yanked her to her feet. Zadikiele jerked her next to him and led her over to the entertainment center in the living room. Once there, he forced her to insert a disc into the DVD player.

Rochelle was breathless with fear as she watched in horror as her husband appeared on screen surrounded by a large group of people only visible from the waist down. They were all wearing dark jeans, dark t-shirts, and black leather gloves. Her husband was securely bound with his hands tied behind him in a chair, while some unknown person had a grip on his hair with one hand and a knife held across her husband's throat with the other.

A video camera was trained to look at him so her husband could speak directly into the camera. "Speak," shouted the man who held the knife to her husband's throat as he yanked her husband's head back in one violent motion. Her husband visibly gulped as though trying to gain air into his tortured lungs. It seemed difficult to speak as her husband had been noticeably beaten. His lip was cut and bleeding, and his nose was broken and bleeding profusely. His eyes were red and swollen shut. Steve was shaking violently as he spoke. He was obviously terrified out of his wits.

When Steve finally gained his breath enough to speak, her husband looked straight into the camera. He said, "Listen to me very carefully, Rochelle. They have our son held hostage, and if you do not do exactly what I say, they will kill Nathaniel. He will be allowed to live if you do what they want. Do not try to go to the police. If you do, we will all die." The picture went black for a moment and came back on with the camera showing her son playing on a blanket surrounded by his favorite toys. He was laughing and smiling his innocent little boy smile at the camera. This is not possible, and this is not happening, Rochelle screamed silently to herself. She suddenly wrenched herself loose from Zadikiele's grip and ran upstairs to her son's room. The entire contents of his room had been taken. His bed, blankets, toys, everything. She stared in silent, horrified disbelief. Somehow, Nathaniel's belongings had been taken from his room after driving her son to kindergarten earlier in the afternoon.

Zadikiele came up behind her so silently that she had not even heard him come up her creaky stairs to the second floor. Zadikiele put his mouth close to her right ear and whispered in a silky sweet voice, "We are not done yet, my little vixen. We still have work to do. You want your son to live, don't you?" Then, he violently grabbed her by the back of her hair and forced her to go back down the stairs to finish watching the DVD. He pushed her in front of him and moved her finger with his hand to press the play button on the DVD player.

Her husband came back on screen, still being held by the unknown hands which held the knife across his throat. Zadikiele whispered once again in her ear, "We want you to understand you and your family mean nothing to us. You are insignificant if you do what we ask. You are insignificant to us if you do not. However, let us make sure you clearly understand we mean what we say. We do what we say we are going to do. Let us hope you are wise enough to follow orders since your husband did not." He forced Rochelle's gaze back to the screen so she could watch her husband's throat being cut right in front of her. Horrified beyond belief, Rochelle watched Steve's life force flow from his body until he died. Rochelle cried out and fainted into a crumpled heap of grief at Zadikiele's feet. He reached down and threw her over her shoulder like a bag of garbage and softly closed the front door behind them. Zadikiele went outside to the waiting van, tossed Rochelle inside, and began the long drive back to his compound located far outside the city.

Rochelle did not know where she was when she woke up. All she knew was she was lying on a bed and been stripped naked with her hands tied above her head to a black metal scrolled headboard. The bed was pushed into the far-right corner of a small room. The tiny room had concrete walls, a bare concrete floor, and no decorations on the wall. The room reminded her of a jail cell. As she slowly took note of her surroundings, she noticed there were no windows.

There was a single light bulb in the center of the ceiling with a pull cord to turn the light on or off. Rochelle had duct tape firmly fastened around her mouth. She tried to pull on the cloth strips holding her captive, but she had been unable to loosen them. From the corner of her right eye, she could see a metal sink to draw water from and a toilet in the corner. The only entrance to the room was a metal door. A surveillance camera in the upper right corner of the room was videotaping her every move. She could see soft muted light from underneath the door, and she could hear soft murmuring voices on the other side.

Suddenly, she could hear footsteps approaching, which stopped right outside the metal door. Zadikiele walked into the room and shut the door closed softly behind him, and she could hear the click of someone locking the door from the outside. She was locked in this room with the man who had ordered her husband to be killed. They were all alone together. To her horror, he started to take his clothes off deliberately and slowly while he watched her twist and writhe in fear trying to get loose from her bonds. Zadikiele kept staring coldly at her the whole time he was shedding his clothes. Rochelle could tell he enjoyed having her at his mercy. She could see his body was thickly muscled, and he had a substantial erection. Finally, he came straight toward her and climbed into the bed. He moved slowly and positioned himself to sit back on his haunches between her legs.

Zadikiele lifted her legs off the bed, threw them over his shoulders, and lithely stretched his body over hers. He bent down, so his lips were within a hair's breadth from hers, and whispered softly against her mouth, "I am now the link between life and death for you and your son. The only thing stopping you and your son from being ripped to shreds for my people's amusement is me. I will make you into an exceptional whore to fulfill a specific purpose. You will become an expert at all areas of pleasing a man to get close to someone I want to have information about. Your only function will be to see he is well pleased and kept preoccupied. You are not intelligent enough to gain any information I need which will be worthwhile to my cause. He only uses one whorehouse, and you will become the one he asks for, or I will kill you and your son. You are a means to an end only! Do you understand what I am telling you? Or would you prefer me to prove this to you by killing your child and throw you away like the human garbage you are to me?"

Rochelle was terrified beyond reason. All she could do was nod her head. She could not have spoken if she tried. Zadikiele did what he said he was going to do. He sheathed himself quickly in her and went at her for what seemed forever. The way he was going about it made her have orgasm after orgasm against her will with his fingers, his mouth, and large erect male organ until he finally spilled his seed onto her abdomen. Zadikiele got up from the bed, put his clothes back on, and banged on the door with his fist. He ordered a woman outside the room to come into the room to clean her up and untie her. His human servants came to her room every day to dress her and take care of her human needs. Zadikiele routinely showed her different videos of her son every week so she would never forget why she was there.

Zadikiele's groupies looked they had come from a Goth concert. They wore black clothing, dark makeup and smoked cigarettes, marijuana, and alcohol. They did everything and anything Zadikiele demanded without question. Strangely, some appeared to be working professionals. Most people would never suspect them of being involved in Zadikiele's nefarious deeds. They were of different ages and backgrounds.

Nevertheless, they were all disgusting as far as Rochelle was concerned. They had made it clear to her they were a cult that worshipped Satan and would do anything Zadikiele required them to do with the intent to prove they were obedient servants. They reminded her of rabid dogs.

Zadikiele had initially intended to abuse Rochelle and make her see that he was serious, but something about her made him stop. He made love to her all night instead and enjoyed giving her pleasure instead of pain. He instinctively knew he had to come to his senses. Caring about her in any way could cost him his life and rank. So Zadikiele usually left her to the care of his minions except for when he was teaching her how to be what he wanted. Zadikiele spent months teaching Rochelle how to please him in every way. He never allowed any of the other cult members to abuse her. They were not to interact with her other than to see to her daily needs. It was contradictory to Rochelle that Zadikiele seemed to take great satisfaction in pleasuring her. It was not as though she wanted to have gratification from him, but she simply could not help it as her body seemed to have a mind of its own. Zadikiele could be so kind and gentle in his touch when he wanted, but Rochelle knew he was only tender with her to get her to do what he wanted.

Rochelle had been lying on the soiled bed face down after a particularly long lovemaking session with Zadikiele when she decided to challenge him by asking him sarcastically why he even bothered to try to make her feel anything other than pain. Zadikiele gruffly walked back over to the bed after dressing himself, yanked her up by her hair, and turned her to face him. When he had her face within one inch of his, he cruelly told her she was nothing to him and threw her back on the bed so hard she hit her head on the wall while he caustically added, "One must know how to receive pleasure to give it back. I would not like to know I failed in my mission by not training you properly. You will do absolutely everything I tell you to do, or you and your son will die a slow lingering death. Each of you will watch the other suffer. You can most certainly count on me to keep my word! Would you prefer that outcome instead?"

Rochelle was not stupid, nor would she risk her son's precious life. Rochelle nodded quietly in understanding and said dejectedly, "I understand, Zadikiele." She lay back on the bed face down in quiet defeat. Zadikiele stared at her for what seemed like an eternity while he quietly studied her. He felt something for her that he did not want to and most certainly could not afford to. The situation was driving him crazy. Finally, Zadikiele stormed out of the room and locked the door behind him. Rochelle reflected on what Zadikiele had revealed. A mission? What mission? For whom did he work? These were all questions she wanted answers to but was too afraid for her son and herself to ask. All Rochelle knew was that somehow, she was going to do whatever it took to free herself of his evil if she ever got the chance.

When Zadikiele felt she was finally up to his exacting standards in bed, he taught her how to walk, dress, eat and talk like a courtesan or geisha of old. He got her the job with the escort service he knew

Jakiele frequented and made sure the madam understood Rochelle was only to serve Jakiele and no one else. Zadikiele set her up in a small apartment under his constant surveillance and sent videos to her daily so she could watch her son grow and play. Rochelle was able to visit with her son once a week in her apartment for an hour before Zadikiele would snap his fingers, and one of his many servants would snatch her boy away from her once again.

Zadikiele did not appear to enjoy tormenting her and her child after watching their anguish when they had to be forcibly parted from each other. Rochelle thought his behavior was very odd, but she never commented on it. He made sure the madam was well paid to introduce Rochelle to Jakiele, and he damn well wanted to see his efforts get him his desired results. He never let Rochelle out of his sight except when she was with Jakiele. He had fully intended to kill her and her brat when he was done using them but was beginning to have second thoughts. Zadikiele intended to kill all his followers at the compound as soon as they fulfilled their purpose. He did not like loose ends. Failure for him was not an option. To become a highly ranked demon, one had to prove themselves regularly to be worthy of such an honor.

A human body had to be expressly chosen by the fallen angels for a demon to have permission to possess it. A demon had to blend in with humans and remain unseen by the angels who would destroy them on sight and send them straight back to the Underworld if they detected their presence. Humans could force a demon out of a host body if they could detect them quickly, but if a demon stayed in a mortal body long enough, the demon got to keep it. The human spirit inside was deeply repressed until it died and went on to the next realm. Human priests knew the proper incantations to force demons out of a host body. It was a long, grueling process for the humans who had learned to do it successfully. However, angels only had to draw their swords, cut a demon's head off, and pierce the heart with their mighty swords. Like angels, demons could not be reborn once they were killed.

Once upon a time, Zadikiele had been a powerful Nephilim with a family of his own, but now he was only a lowly foot soldier. He was trying to prove he was worthy of moving up in rank. His assignment for years had been to watch and observe Jakiele. Zadikiele followed Jakiele's every move. Jakiele was so careful in everything he did and said it was difficult to get close to him. Jakiele became more interesting when he bought his grand house, but what had prompted him to buy it? Why was he fixing it up? Installing security systems? Hiring a house cleaner? Jakiele had not done anything unusual for centuries. Why now? Zadikiele intended to find out. He was going to use whatever means he had at his disposal to spy on Jakiele. Zadikiele had to be careful, in any case. If Jakiele suspected his presence in any way, he would hunt him down mercilessly like a bloodhound and destroy him. Remiel, his father, would not be pleased about losing his only son. Again.

# CHAPTER 3

Rochelle's husband, Steve, had worked for the Washington Post since he graduated from college. For years, Steve had worked diligently as a fact-checker before being promoted to an investigative reporter. He had a knack for digging deeper into stories and getting people to reveal things to him unwillingly. He was so unassuming and bland in appearance that people automatically trusted him when he approached people he wanted information from. They would give him any information needed to help him get to the truth. Steve was easy to look at with his shortly cropped blond hair and light golden-brown eyes.

Most people did not know Steve was willing to succeed in his career at any cost. He was hungry to be recognized for his accomplishments. Steve devotedly listened to police scanners every day from several different counties in the surrounding cities and his hometown for reporting opportunities. He was more than willing to exploit anyone and everyone to get what he wanted. He would walk through fire to get to the top of the heap. These traits were welcomed and rewarded most generously with promotions in the unsavory world of journalism.

Steve had been sitting at his desk in his downtown office listening to one of his scanners when a response to a 911 call was made by a couple of teenage boys. The boys had been out sightseeing and taking pictures of the animals at a local wildlife preserve. The pictures were for a biology assignment for their school. The boys walked the trails through the Assabet Animal Preserve, found a few miles outside Maynard's small town. The preserve was about twenty miles west of Boston, Massachusetts.

After doing a quick computer search, Steve learned the Assabet Wildlife Preserve was known to house a large wetland complex and offered up forested areas that were imperative for the feeding and breeding of migratory birds and other wildlife and spanned over two thousand acres. Fifteen miles of trails were open to the public regularly. The U.S. Army had initially used the preserve, but then the army transferred ownership of the preserve to the U.S. Fish and Wildlife Service in the fall of 2000. He quickly wrote down the address and directions to the preserve.

The police dispatcher relaying the information to the responding police officers in the area said the kids were reporting they had found the dead body of a young girl. Steve jumped so hard from behind his desk that he spilled his newly retrieved cup of black coffee all over the front of his recently purchased white oxford shirt and khakis. Hot coffee spilling on him did not stop him. Steve raced from behind his desk and out of his office with the address to the preserve in his hand. He went to his secretary and told her he would be checking on a story in Maynard and to tell his boss he would be back in a couple of days.

Steve raced home as quick as he could from his office to his house to let Rochelle know he was leaving town to check out a story. Rochelle packed an overnight bag for him with his necessities, and before long, Steve was on his way after he changed out of his coffee-soaked clothes. Steve often left to check out stories, and Rochelle was used to the routine and did not question it. However, the trip would take him approximately eight hours if he traveled all through the night as it was already after two in the afternoon.

After finally arriving in Maynard, Steve checked in to a local motel within a few miles of the preserve. The motel clerk politely asked him what had brought him to Maynard. Steve was quick to tell him about the story he was following about the two boys who had recently found a dead body. The young motel clerk stared at him a little strangely and asked him if Steve knew the preserve had been taped off and closed while the police searched the area. Steve smiled patiently at the clerk and let him know he was a reporter for the Washington Post, and the report of the dead girl was the reason he was there. Steve openly bragged to the clerk that not even the police would keep him out. Steve pompously showed the clerk his press pass, which displayed his credentials.

The clerk reluctantly handed Steve his room key and gave him a local map. The clerk patiently pointed out the area on the preserve where the girl's dead body had been found. Since it was so late in the evening, Steve decided he would check it out first thing in the morning. As soon as Steve left the lobby, the clerk privately made a phone call to Zadikiele to let him know there was a reporter who was going to be snooping around the preserve. The clerk had been given explicit instructions by Zadikiele earlier in the day to let him know if anyone came around the preserve or motel asking any questions about the dead girl. Zadikiele had learned about the death a few hours earlier by the detective in charge of the case. The clerk relayed to Zadikiele that the reporter was named Steve Windham and gave Zadikiele Steve's room number. The clerk was one of the devotees loyal to Zadikiele's cause. The clerk hoped Zadikiele would reward him handsomely for the information.

Since Zadikiele had already been informed about the dead body by the police detective in charge of the investigation, he felt he had the situation well in hand. The detective in charge of the case and the medical examiner had been called in from Boston. They assured Zadikiele no evidence of this dead girl's body would ever be found and would make sure this case would simply vanish from the official records. They were demons themselves and had been ordered by Zadikiele to keep this incident as quiet as possible. Both the detective and the medical examiner knew how essential it was for the media not to know how the girl died. Zadikiele began to feel that he should deal with this problem himself to ensure everyone did their jobs. He did not want to risk any angels becoming aware of the dead girl and how she died.

Zadikiele left at once for Maynard after receiving the phone call from the idiot motel clerk. He jumped on his custom-made Harley and sped off long into the night to head off the potential disaster. The detective in charge of the case and the medical examiner were already trying valiantly to keep the media out of the investigation. Zadikiele knew he could control the police, but a reporter from the Washington Post was an altogether different animal. Reporters only cared about being the first to have an exclusive story about something significant, not whether there were any consequences to their actions. Being humane would require conscience and an ability to care. Unfortunately, neither of those traits hardly ever applied to hungry journalists looking to make a name for themselves.

After arriving at the motel several hours later, the clerk pointed out to Zadikiele which room Steve was staying in. Zadikiele gave the young, skinny, pockmarked clerk his thanks and let him know he would be duly rewarded for his loyalty, which, of course, meant he would disappear mysteriously and be found floating in the nearby river with his throat slit when Zadikiele was done with him and was of no more use. The clerk handed Zadikiele a key which opened a room next to Steve's so Zadikiele could keep a close eye on where Steve went and to whom he talked. Zadikiele would not hesitate to skewer Steve on a long pointy stick and watch him burn over a fire if it were necessary to keep Zadikiele's presence a secret from any angels who might be keeping an eye on this story or who may be residing in the surrounding area.

The following day, Steve made sure he had his camera, flashlight, cell phone, and makeshift DNA collecting kit. He stuffed them quickly and securely into his well-used duffel bag. Steve kept his trusty voice recorder in his hand to record his thoughts and any conversations with the locals or the police. Upon leaving his room, he felt uneasy, as though someone was watching him. Steve scanned with his eyes all around him but could not name the source of his uneasiness. He shrugged it off and jumped into his grey BMW and headed off to town in search of breakfast. Steve planned to question the locals while he ate his breakfast at the local diner to see if he could glean any information or insights into who this dead girl was. He would also try to talk to the young kids who had found the body if he could get access to them. Zadikiele followed from a safe distance, always keeping Steve in his field of view.

After breakfast, Steve's first stop was to stop by the local police department and see if he could glean any details about this young girl's death. He learned that the dead girl was a transient since no official records could be found from her fingerprints and no family had come forward to claim the body. Unfortunately, Steve had been unable to speak with the detective in charge since the lead detective, James Wills, was still combing the crime scene at the preserve. Little information would be forthcoming while the police were awaiting the autopsy results, which would be conducted shortly by the medical examiner.

Steve wanted to question the two young teenage boys who had initially found the body, but they were being held for questioning by the police. They could not talk to anyone other than their respective attorneys and families. Steve had requested to speak to at least one of the attorneys or one of the boys' family members, but his request was denied since the families of the two young boys wanted their privacy protected. The attorneys were more interested in protecting the boys' constitutional rights than helping nosy reporters. Since this potential lead had proven to be a dead-end, Steve jumped back into his car and decided to head out to the animal preserve.

Steve put the directions into his car GPS and soon arrived at the gruesome scene, which was surrounded by police cars and the local media. Great, he thought to himself. It was no longer going to be an exclusive story for him. Since Steve was already there, he figured he would find out what he could from the other press members. So, he walked up to where some of them stood outside the taped-off area the police were combing for clues. Steve recognized one of the press members as a fact-checker for the Boston Globe. Howard Dunbar was a newshound who could sniff out even the most mundane and often overlooked facts and would be an asset if Steve could convince him to share what he had ferreted out so far. They had met a few years ago at an awards presentation for journalistic excellence and had become casual acquaintances.

Howard saw Steve get out of his car with his duffel bag in hand and quickly walked over to the car to greet Steve. Howard extended his right hand and said to Steve, "Hey man, good to see you again. It has been a long time." Steve smiled and warmly shook Harry's extended hand. Harry was fifty-plus years old with a large paunch and a growing bald spot on top of his thinning brown hair, but he was good at what he did. "This is a long way for you to come out for a story. Been listening to your scanners again?" Harry teased Steve lightheartedly. Steve took the ribbing in stride and replied, "You know how it goes, old man. Have to do what you must do to get ahead. No rest for the weary," to which Harry laughed good-naturedly. They walked side by side back to the crime scene and stood before the taped line watching as the crime scene investigators took pictures and samples of the crushed down brush where the body had been found. Steve thought it was odd that the girl had been murdered in such an accessible area, and the killer had not made any attempt at trying to cover up the crime at all.

Steve whispered to Harry quietly, "What have you been able to find out? Everyone I have asked at the police department or at the local restaurant I ate at this morning did not seem to know anything or were unwilling to reveal anything of value. Everyone is surprisingly closed-mouthed, except for the fact no one I talked to seems to know who this girl was."

Harry grabbed Steve by the left arm and pulled him back a few yards from the gruesome scene to say softly to Steve, "I do not know much, but everything I have learned so far from observing many crime scenes in the past has left me with quite a few questions about this one. Unfortunately, the police refuse to answer any questions until the autopsy reports come in from the medical examiner. When I first got here, I noticed there was no blood or bodily fluids anywhere. The only evidence that the girl had died here was the indent left in the brush. There is no evidence of a body being dragged, no footprints, no signs of a struggle, nothing. It was as though this girl materialized out of thin air and died right on the spot. It is absurd as well as strange."

Steve digested the information Harry had revealed. What he was looking at did not make any sense to him either. There had to be evidence somewhere else. Instinctively, Steve knew something was wrong with this scene. He thanked Harry, started to walk outside the taped-off area, and talked into his voice recorder about what he had learned from Harry. Several yards away from the brush where the young girl had been found was a walking path. Maybe this girl went for a nature hike through the preserve on one of the many scheduled tours.

Zadikiele had heard everything Harry and Steve said to each other with his exceptionally advanced hearing. He started to casually stroll behind Steve to listen to what Steve was speaking into his voice recorder. Steve was approximately a hundred yards away from the crime scene when he looked down at the walking trail and spotted tiny droplets of blood. The blood appeared fresh, although it had been 24 hours since the Maynard police dispatcher first reported a body was discovered. Steve put his voice recorder in his back pocket so he could reach into his duffel bag to retrieve his camera. He quickly started snapping pictures of the blood and the surrounding area concerning the crime scene. Next, he took out his makeshift DNA kit from his duffel bag and was about to do a swab of the blood.

One of the crime scene investigators taking brush samples noticed what Steve was doing and nodded to one of the police officers standing nearby. The crime scene investigator stood up and walked over to the officer and whispered something in his ear. The police officer nodded and marched over to where Steve was bending down, digging into his duffel bag. The police officer snatched Steve's camera and duffel bag from Steve's hands, grabbed Steve by the arm, and yanked him back to a standing position. Steve was so startled that he did not have the chance to try and resist. Instead, Steve yelled at the police officer, "Hey, pal, you are not allowed to take my property. Get your damn hands off me! Don't you know who I am? I am with the press. I work for the Washington Post, and I have every right to be here!" Steve shouted at the officer once he finally found his voice.

After the officer forcibly made Steve stand up, he marched Steve over to where Steve's car was parked, yanked open the door, and shoved him inside the vehicle. Once Steve was seated, the officer menacingly bent down close to Steve's face and enunciated his words with quiet steel by saying to Steve, "You are actively impeding a police investigation, and you need to leave right now." Next, the officer reached over and ripped the press badge off Steve's left shirt pocket and then stated menacingly, "I will have you thrown in jail and held until after this investigation is over! You can pick up your belongings from the police station tomorrow. Now get the hell out of here!" Finally, the police officer effectively slammed the car door shut and pointed out the way back to town. Since Steve did not have a choice, he left to go back to the motel. Steve grabbed his keys out of his trousers and grudgingly put the key in the ignition to start the car.

Steve was fuming. As he was speeding away from the crime scene, he glanced into his rearview mirror to see if the police officer was still watching him. Steve saw a man with long blond hair wearing a long black trench coat approach the officer and talk to him. As the police officer and the blonde-haired man turned their heads in unison, Steve was instantly startled when he realized they were both watching him as he sped away back toward town. Steve looked away worriedly from the rearview mirror and redirected his attention to getting back to his motel room. This whole situation he now found himself in was weird, Steve thought silently to himself. It was not unusual for police to chase off onlookers, but they were not usually hostile or aggressive to the press, especially one of his ilk. On the contrary, they often liked the help investigative reporters could bring to the table with any evidence they could uncover. It was not like Steve was going to hide any evidence from them.

The police officer's bizarre behavior and the strange man who had come and stood next to him watching Steve drive away aggravated his nerves to no end. However, on the other hand, it got his senses stirred up as he started mentally going over all the facts he had managed to put together so far. Something was strange about the crime scene by the way the police were reacting. By trying to put him off the trail of finding out what had happened, it had the opposite effect of what the police officer had intended. It made Steve want to discover what really happened to the dead girl found at the preserve more than ever.

When he got back to the motel, Steve slammed on his breaks and threw his car door shut so hard it caused the car to shake violently. He let himself into his hotel room and called his boss's cell phone from the phone in his room. His boss, Terrence Drake, was a no-nonsense, get the story whatever it takes kind of a guy. He expected results, and if you could not or would not get him good stories, he would find someone who would. Steve wanted to get ahead in his career so urgently that he was willing to do whatever it took to be Terrence's top reporter.

Terrence answered his cell phone by demanding, "Where the hell are you, Steve! What is going on? What caused you to run out of your office without discussing why you were leaving with me first? You know I like to be asked first, not informed. So, you had better have a good explanation!" Finally, Steve was able to go over the incomplete details he had obtained so far, as well as the fact that the police officer at the preserve had confiscated his badge, duffel bag, and camera. When Terrance finally calmed down, he warned Steve to tread cautiously. He told Steve to wait until he had all the available information and only report the facts. Terrence was always afraid of lawsuits and having to bail his reporters out of jail. Terrence loved results, but he did not like the grisly details on how far the reporters had to go to get them.

Steve agreed to wait until after the autopsy by the medical examiner to file his report. The autopsy was due to be performed first thing tomorrow morning. Steve decided to call Rochelle to check in on her and Nathaniel. They were both doing fine, so he left his room to check out the town and see what he could dig up. As he went to open the front door, a giant figure of a man stood right before him, looming in the doorway. Before Steve even had the chance to gulp down a breath of air, Zadikiele shoved him powerfully back into the motel room and forcibly closed the door.

Steve backed up a few steps before shouting, "Who are you? What do you think you are doing?" Steve recognized Zadikiele as the man who had watched him speed away from the crime scene. Zadikiele slowly and menacingly approached Steve until he was standing within an inch of Steve's face. Zadikiele grabbed Steve by his throat and held him up with his right hand until Steve was an entire foot off the ground, and then he began to squeeze the life out slowly and brutally of Steve.

When Steve was within an inch of his life, Zadikiele threw Steve across the room into the wall above the bed. Steve cracked his head on the wall with brutal force. The impact of Steve's head left a small dent in the wall. Steve unceremoniously landed on the bed in a tangled heap of limbs. As soon as Steve was able, he sat up and grasped his throat with his right hand and began the arduous process of trying to draw precious air back into his tortured lungs.

Zadikiele patiently waited while Steve regained his senses so that what Zadikiele had to say would be truly clear. When Steve could finally breathe evenly again, Zadikiele yanked him up by the arm and shoved Steve violently against the motel room door. Zadikiele pinned Steve on either side of his body with his large hands resting next to Steve's head. Zadikiele then wedged his right knee securely between Steve's thighs so that Steve could not move. "You are delving into things which do not concern you. I will be expecting you to leave town first thing tomorrow morning after you collect your things from the police department. If you persist in investigating the girl's death, I will do things to your family they will never recover from. I will kill you and everyone you love, and there will not be enough of you left for the animals to find. If you care about them at all, you will leave this place at once and not ever return."

Zadikiele grabbed Steve once again by the throat with his right hand and threw him forcibly across the room to crash into the opposite wall. Steve's head hit so hard on the wall he passed out. Zadikiele left the room and jumped on his Harley to leave. Zadikiele headed back to the police department to deal with the teenage boys to see if his suspicions were correct about the dead girl and how she died. This mess had to be cleaned up as quickly and quietly as possible if he was right.

After arriving at the police station, Zadikiele motioned to one of the police officers to come over and speak to him. Zadikiele placed his right hand out to shake the officer's hand. When the officer went to shake his hand, Zadikiele brought him close and looked deep into the officer's eyes. "I want a room with the two boys alone, and I do not want any cameras running. Get it done." The young police officer had been entirely hypnotized by staring into Zadikiele's eyes and rushed off to do his bidding by showing him into an empty jail cell currently not in use. The police officer quickly returned with the two young teenage boys and released them from their handcuffs. After quietly closing the cell door, he shoved the two boys into the empty cell with Zadikiele and left to return to his station. The police officer would not remember what he had done as soon as Zadikiele released him from his zombie-like trance.

Zadikiele wasted no time. He came to stand right before the two teenaged boys and put one hand on each of their heads. He filtered quickly through their memories and what they had accidentally stumbled upon at the preserve. The boys had not seen anything of value other than a dead body. Next, he filled their heads with nightmarish visions so that if they tried to recall any details about the dead girl, their minds would immediately go to the horrific visions he implanted. They would become screaming lunatics and panic every time they were asked to recall what they had found. Finally, he put the boys into a deep sleep and watched as they fell to the cell floor. Zadikiele left the cell and intended to head back to his motel room after finishing at the police station. As he walked back out front, he nodded to the police officer who had let him in the jail cell with the two boys. The officer woke the boys from their deep sleep and led them back to their respective cells.

Zadikiele knew Steve would be out of commission for the rest of the day, so he knew he had enough time to learn everything he could about Steve. His address, where he worked, who his family was, everything. Zadikiele waited until the police officer he had under his control was done with the boys and had him retrieve all the information on Steve he needed. Once the information had been printed out, Zadikiele released the young police officer from his spell and headed back to the motel to make the arrangements necessary to deal with Steve. His crew of devotees was already on their way to Maynard to take Steve forcibly back their compound in Washington DC.

Zadikiele headed back to the motel to fill the leaders of the fallen angels in on all he had learned so far. The only way to communicate with them would be for Zadikiele to shed his earthly body and travel to the Underworld. While he was in the Underworld, his body would appear to be asleep. It was a perilous communication method, but he had no other choice but to leave his body unprotected and vulnerable.

The following day, Zadikiele headed in the direction of Emerson Hospital in Boston, Massachusetts, where the autopsy was being conducted. Zadikiele walked into the foul-smelling autopsy room and looked down at the dead body of a charming young Asian woman who appeared to be in her early teens. She was exceptionally white, and it appeared as though she did not have a drop of blood left in her body. Her skin resembled the purest white porcelain. The medical examiner was about to take the sheet entirely off the lower part of her body when something caught Zadikiele's eye.

The dead girl's left breast had two small, identical puncture wounds. The two puncture wounds sat directly above her heart. Zadikiele had all the proof he needed to confirm his suspicions about how she had died. He needed to relay this information to his father. If what he suspected was true, this was not good. It meant a rogue vampire needed to be tracked down and eliminated immediately. Zadikiele was the best hunter the fallen angels had, but he could not figure out how a vampire had been created in the first place when they had all been executed centuries ago.

When Zadikiele was done thoroughly examining the body, he turned to face the medical examiner. He calmly announced, "Your autopsy will state this girl had a severe case of Ebola and was very contagious. There was no blood found on the scene. The surrounding animals drank it off the ground. The area will now have to be quarantined until the authorities are sure the animals are safe and cleared of any contagion. Her body is to be destroyed. She is a vagrant, and no one will care. Do it quickly!"

The medical examiner, Josef Kiernan, hastily went over to the phone on the wall and called the Boston morgue. The examiner arranged to have the body of the dead girl picked up and disposed of later in the day. The medical examiner was infinitely relieved Zadikiele was satisfied and had left. Since Josef was a low-level demon, he did what he was told. Zadikiele did not like to be disappointed with lack of results or disobedience. Zadikiele jumped on his Harley and sped back out toward the preserve. He did not bother going back to the hotel room to see if Steve had followed his orders to leave town.

Steve woke up in his motel room the following day with a massive headache. His body ached all over. He was furious that a stranger had been able to assault him, and the stranger knew the police detective in charge of this investigation. These facts could mean one of two things. Either the police were actively involved in this girl's death, or they were helping to cover it up. This story was getting more interesting by the minute. However, Steve was not the kind of guy who would be put off easily by a little roughing up. He gathered up his car keys and intended to head over to the local police station to retrieve his duffel bag and camera, which the police officer had confiscated at the preserve. There was no way he was going to let this story slip from his grasp.

After arriving at the local police station, Steve marched up to the front desk. He demanded that the officer at the desk take a report on the stranger who had assaulted him in his hotel room the night before. Steve still had questions in his mind about what the assault was all about. Was this stranger in competition with Steve to get an exclusive to the dead girl's story? If so, Steve would do what he could to eliminate the competition by having him arrested. The sergeant held up his right hand and signaled to Steve to wait a moment and that he would be right with him as soon as he was done talking on the phone. Steve's whole body ached from head to toe in protest, but he had been threatened many times before in his profession, and it never threw him off the trail of a hot story. Something was wrong here. He felt it in his gut. He was more determined than ever the strange circumstances of this girl's death were being covered up for a reason, and he was going to find out what it was.

Suddenly, he heard loud wailing and terrified screams from the jail cells behind the locked steel door to his left in the lobby. Two attorneys wearing identifying name tags came out of the steel door and started talking agitatedly amongst themselves. Then, they started walking toward the front entrance together and were about to leave. It was clear from their body language that they were very shaken by hearing the wails and screams from the jail cells. Steve quickly walked over to where they were and asked them if they were okay. One of the attorneys looked very white, as though he was about to pass out. Steve identified himself and told them he was there to speak with the boys about what they had found. Both attorneys turned even grayer if possible and let Steve know they were the attorneys whom the teenage boys' families had hired.

One of the attorneys shakily replied, "Yeah, I guess we can let you speak with them now. The two boys and their families fired us. Every time we tried to ask the boys what they saw when they found the dead girl on the preserve, something would send them into screaming fits of hysteria and fear. They act like they are being possessed by demons or something. Those kids scared the heck out of us. Good luck trying to talk to them. We are out of here!" The two attorneys beat a very hasty retreat out the door and did not look back. Steve slowly went back up to the front desk and asked the officer if his press things had been turned in and if he could collect them. He showed the officer his photo I.D. Steve forgot all about trying to press charges on the stranger who had beaten him up the night before. Steve asked the officer if he knew where the autopsy was being conducted for the body found at the reserve. The officer told him he thought it was held in Boston at Emerson Hospital. Steve intended to head straight over to where the medical examiner was doing his evaluation and look at the dead girl's body for himself since talking to the boys who found her would be useless.

The sergeant went to a back room and grabbed Steve's things. Steve looked through his belongings to ensure everything was there and thanked the helpful officer. He jumped back into his car and headed off in the direction of where the medical examiner was performing the autopsy. As Steve pulled up to the hospital, he got an eerie feeling he was being watched again. He looked all around him but did not see anyone. He went to the hospital administration office and asked to speak to the hospital administrator. The secretary looked at Steve's credentials and dialed a number on the phone to let the administrator know a reporter from the Washington Post wished to speak with him.

The administrator was a tall man with a thick waist. He had thinning white hair and an equally thin white mustache which curled slightly at the ends. His gray silk suit was of the most delicate cut and quality, and his shirt was impeccably starched and bright white. His expensive silk tie matched his suit perfectly. His name was William Russell, and he liked getting his name in the paper, so he was more than willing to help Steve in any way he could. After shaking Steve's hand, he ushered Steve into his office and graciously offered Steve a seat across from his desk.

After seating himself behind his desk, the administrator asked Steve if he would like a cup of coffee or a bottled Perrier the administrator liked to keep in a little refrigerator by his desk. Steve politely declined. The administrator asked him, "What can I do for you today, Mr. Windham? It is not often we get reporters from the Washington post in our little neck of the woods." The administrator casually leaned back in his office chair and started twirling the end of his mustache with his left hand while he waited for Steve to answer.

Steve folded his right leg over his left, placed his folded hands in his lap, looked the administrator right in the eye, and politely requested to see the body of the dead girl, which had been found at the animal reserve. Next, Steve filled the administrator in on what he had gleaned so far from observing the crime scene. Steve deliberately left out the minor skirmish with the stranger in his hotel room on purpose. He did not want people to think he was a wimp and could not handle himself. Finally, the administrator picked up the phone and asked to speak with the medical examiner, Josef Kiernan, who was conducting the autopsy.

The administrator asked if it would be convenient to see the dead girl's body. A reporter from out of town named Steve Windham would like to look at the body. The administrator listened for a few minutes while Josef replied back to the request and ended the call with, "Oh, how awful. Oh, my goodness. Okay. Thank you for your assistance." He hung up the phone and said to Steve, "I am sorry, Mr. Windham. The body is already on the way to the morgue and will be destroyed. Unfortunately, the woman's body was riddled with the Ebola virus, and we could not risk the town becoming contaminated. My apologies. Is there anything else I can assist you with?"

Steve asked the administrator which morgue the body was being dispatched to. The administrator relayed that contagious bodies were taken to the Boston Morgue per the city's quarantine procedures. Steve thanked him and shook the administrator's hand again before leaving the room. He went back out to his car and dialed his boss's number to fill him in on what he had found out so far. Steve's boss did not think it was anything worth pursuing and ordered him to head straight home right away as other stories were waiting to be reported on, which were far more critical.

Something was niggling in the back of Steve's brain. If the girl died from the Ebola virus, it would have been a gruesome death, to be sure, but there would have also been bodily fluids of some kind on the brush where she was found. And what about the blood droplets on the preserve trail a few yards away from the body? It did not add up. Nevertheless, Steve was not done yet. He plugged the directions to the Boston Morgue into his GPS and headed in the indicated direction.

As soon as Josef hung up with the administrator, he called Zadikiele on his cell phone to let him know a reporter had been at the hospital asking to see the body. He let Zadikiele know the reporter's name was Steve Windham. Zadikiele swore under his breath and tersely demanded the examiner get back to completing the report as quickly as possible. Finishing the autopsy results and releasing them to the press was imperative. Zadikiele was currently at the preserve talking to the detective about releasing the two teenage boys to a mental health hospital and letting the detective know the medical examiner's story had been taken care of. Zadikiele realized Steve was going to continue to be a problem. He intended to dispose of Steve as soon as he got back to the motel.

# CHAPTER 4

Steve arrived at Boston Morgue after getting lost a few times trying to maneuver around the busy streets of Boston. Once he finally found the morgue, he walked in and was amazed at how clean and beautiful the old building was. It was a two-story stone-washed structure surrounded by neatly tended gardens with a stone walkway that led up to the double-wide front doors. The front entrance was graced on the right side of the door with an engraved gold plaque that indicated Steve had arrived at the correct address. After Steve stepped inside the front door, he noticed a wide-open and spacious foyer boasting floors made of precious faux gold and taupe marble.

Lush tropical plants were placed in perfect arrangements on either side of the reception area, found to the left of the front door across the foyer. On either side of the foyer were two golden wrought iron staircases leading to upstairs offices and were joined together over a wide-open staircase underneath the two parallel staircases. The lower flight of steps led to the labs, and crematory areas were kept. The walls and floors displayed a very peaceful taupe marble with gold accents, designed to have a soothing effect on one's soul.

Steve gaped in awe at the magnificent building structure for quite a while before slowly walking across the foyer to speak with a young girl seated behind a finely made mahogany desk. Steve presumed she was the receptionist. The young woman sitting at the front desk completely ignored him for several minutes before finally looked up unwillingly from the fingernails she had been filing angrily. She snappily asked him if she could help him after he produced his press I.D and set his duffel bag down beside his right leg. Steve graciously replied, "Yes, Ma'am. I am Steve Windham, and I work for the Washington Post out of Washington, D.C. I wondered if I could view the dead body of a young girl recently brought here from Emerson Hospital a little while ago. Is there someone I could talk to about viewing her?"

The girl was a college student and was not particularly enthused about what she did for a living. She reluctantly set down her nail file, picked up the phone, and covered the phone with her hand so Steve could not hear what she was saying to the person on the other end of the phone. After hanging up the phone, the receptionist let him know Kyle Oakes, the director, would be with him in a few minutes and to have a seat on one of the expensively appointed turn of the century antique couches which had been provided along the foyer walls for visitors to sit on. The girl returned to filing her nails while chewing and snapping her gum with unladylike enthusiasm. Steve picked up his duffel back and went to sit down and check for any messages on his phone while he waited for Mr. Oakes.

After about ten minutes, a man he presumed to be Mr. Oakes came down the stairs from one of the offices upstairs and walked to where Steve was sitting. He greeted Steve with his hand outstretched for a warm handshake. Dr. Oakes was a very somber-looking older man in his early fifties with dark black, shortly cropped hair and a pasty white complexion as though he had not seen the sun in years. His black eyebrows were very thick, and with his slender face, his facial features showed he was always perpetually morose. He was slender in stature, and with his six-foot height, he looked emaciated and slightly stooped over from age or sadness. Steve did not know which, but he grasped the man's extended hand in greeting.

After the initial handshake, Mr. Oakes stood back with his hands behind his back as though in deep thought and asked Steve what he could do for him. Steve explained why he was there and why he was looking into the death of a young girl found dead at the Assabet preserve. Steve also added that he would like to view the young girl's body. Steve revealed he knew the young girl's body would be cremated at the Boston Morgue. Mr. Oakes digested the request for a few minutes. Then, he began to speak to Steve in a softly whispered voice, "As I am sure you are aware, Mr. Windham, only the families of the deceased are approved to view the recently departed unless they give you their permission, or the police have given you leave to view the body. I am not authorized to let anyone access the body without prior written approval by either of these two entities. So, unless you have the required documentation, there is nothing I can do for you at this time."

Steve was disappointed, but he was not about to give up on such a juicy story, especially one as odd as this one. Never one to be beaten down, Steve was quick to reply, "This girl has not had anyone come forward to claim her body, sir. I am sure her family would be devastated to find out she had been cremated before being properly identified. My only goal in coming here today is to examine the body for tattoos or other identifying marks that I could release to the local news media. I am sure that will help her family come forward and claim her. Surely, you would not begrudge her family the chance to be able to grieve properly and bury her body, would you?" Steve was not about to divulge he had other ulterior motives like getting an award for his perseverance if he was the one who cracked this case.

Mr. Oakes was an associate professor at Boston College as well as the director of the morgue, so he had to be careful not to cross any ethical lines, but he was also reluctant to be considered as being truculent with the media as it tended to create an illusion there was some cover-up. Kyle paced back and forth across the marbled floor for a few minutes with his hands clasped securely behind his back before he turned and studied Steve quietly for a moment before coming to a decision. Finally, he responded to Steve's request by gravely saying, "The young lady is highly contagious, and I will not allow anyone near her without the proper protective clothing, and I will not be held responsible if I allow you to see her and you become sick. Furthermore, you would have to sign a disclaimer before being shown the body."

Steve nodded his assent readily and agreed to sign the necessary paperwork. After doing so, the director led Steve across the large foyer and down the three steps underneath the two parallel staircases directly over their heads. He led them down a long hallway that held a series of rooms on either side of the hallway. The smell of disinfectant and embalming fluid was strong. It was all Steve could do to concentrate on why he had come to the Morgue instead of vomiting and running back upstairs and out the door like a green schoolboy. As they went down the long hallway, Steve noticed that medical technicians were working on various medical equipment or looking through microscopes in two of the rooms. Some of the techs in the other rooms they passed were preparing bodies for embalming, and other rooms had refrigerators where the dead bodies were being kept. The last room on the left was where the dead bodies consigned to cremation were held.

The director led Steve into one of the rooms off to the right of the hallway, which held all the protective clothing and eye masks. Kyle showed Steve what to put on and changed himself into the required clothing and mask. Once they were done, the director led Steve to the room where the dead girl was being kept. The director went over to the only desk in the room and picked up a clipboard that held the names of the deceased and their respective drawer assignments. Kyle quickly scanned down the list for the Jane Doe he was searching for and walked over to the refrigerated drawer unit holding the young girl's body. After opening the unit's door, the director slid out the stainless-steel plank, which suspended the dead girl's body. The young girl looked so beautiful and young. She looked as though she was in a deep, peaceful sleep.

The young Asian girl showed no signs of trauma on her body. There were no ligature marks on her neck, no broken nails, and no discernible bruises. Her body bore no indications of violent death in any way. Her long black hair was not full of debris. No sign of dirt was under her nails, and none were broken to show she fought for her life either. She was completely naked and looked like a regal princess in her final death state. Steve thought it was odd that the girl showed no signs of having died from the Ebola virus. When a person died of such a contagious disease, the endless suffering would have ravaged the body such disease caused. Then, something unusual caught Steve's eye. Steve bent down to take a closer look at the girl's left breast and noticed the two identical small pinprick marks right above the girl's heart and was stunned. Steve stood back up and asked the director what he thought could have caused them.

The director looked at the pinpricks on the girl's skin very closely for quite a while before he replied, "I am not sure. I have never seen anything like twin pinprick marks before of this size. Maybe she brushed up against a bush out there on the preserve, or maybe they are bug bites. It is an animal preserve, so it is hard to say. I would hate to speculate, though, and have my opinions get printed in your paper if I am incorrect, so please do not quote me on anything I say to you." The director refused to say more. Mr. Oakes started to walk away from Steve, but he turned suddenly back around to stand on the opposite side of the plank to face Steve once again.

The director paused for a long moment and waited for Steve to acknowledge what he had said. It was clear to Steve that whatever the director wanted to reveal, he did not want the information printed in the paper. When Steve gestured his understanding with his hand for the director to continue, Kyle bent close to Steve and softly whispered, "I also thought these wounds were unusual, so even though I was not required to do so, I took a swab of the wound and sent it to a friend of mine who works nearby at a forensics lab. I want to know if anything of note will be discovered. I also sent pictures I took of the wound. If she finds anything, I will let you and the police know. However, I am required by state law to dispose of the body immediately, so please do what you can to find her family." Kyle paused for a fraction of a second before adding firmly, "The only reason I have agreed to help you, Mr. Windham, is I know what it is like to lose a daughter, and I would not wish that kind of undue pain on anyone, so I will do what I can to help you get to the bottom of what happened to her, but not so this girl's death can be exploited! Do we understand each other?"

Steve nodded profusely and thanked Kyle and assured him that he was only trying to help find her family. Any of Kyle's opinions or speculations would not be quoted in the paper, which of course, was entirely untrue. Still, Kyle did not need to know the truth of that at this time. Steve took a business card out of his wallet with his cell phone number and handed it to the director. Another thing Steve noticed was how there did not seem to be any blood left in the dead girl's body. Her body was bright white, and all the veins were clearly showing through her translucent skin. Steve chose to keep this new observation to himself for now. Steve left the morgue and decided to head back to Maynard. While he was driving, he decided to record his thoughts into his voice recorder about what he had learned so far. When he was done recording his thoughts, he stopped by the local post office in Maynard. On a whim, he decided to mail back his voice recorder to his office in Washington, D.C. He did not want the police trying to confiscate it again. He did not want to send it to his house in case Rochelle accidentally turned it on and heard all the macabre details he had uncovered so far about this case.

Steve arrived back at his motel around noon and intended to check out. He would find another place to stay in Boston so that he could continue his investigation without the fear of the blonde-haired stranger showing up at his door again. Steve wanted to head back out to the preserve unmolested and see what else could be discovered. He also wanted to see if Harry had found out anything more useful. Unfortunately, when Steve turned the knob to enter his motel room, he was viciously knocked out cold by an unknown assailant. Zadikiele's followers had shown up and had been let into

Steve's room by the obedient desk clerk who would be thrilled to let Zadikiele know he had done his job as commanded. After Steve's body had been dragged into the room and the door was closed, the clerk made sure Steve's duffel bag and his wallet were left out on the bed for Zadikiele to examine at his leisure.

After thoroughly searching Steve's belongings and the room, Zadikiele's men carried Steve out of the room. They made sure the room showed no signs Steve had ever been there. The motel clerk had already contacted the motel repair person to repair the dent made by Steve's head where it had crashed into the headboard wall. They dumped Steve's limp body unceremoniously on the floor of the waiting van that was parked next to the motel room door. After Steve was dumped inside the van, they bound his hands and feet and covered his mouth tightly with duct tape. Once Steve was secured, Zadikiele's followers sped off to Washington D.C. One of the followers who stayed behind took Steve's keys and followed the van back to the city with Steve's car. He would take the vehicle to the seedier parts of the city, where it would be stripped and disposed of in less than an hour. Of course, no one would ever find the car, and if they did, all traces of Steve's ownership would be destroyed.

Zadikiele arrived back at the motel less than an hour later and made quick work of the motel clerk. The clerk's body would be found in the nearby river after ensuring the motel room where Steve stayed had been thoroughly sanitized. Zadikiele looked through the duffel bag and found Steve's cell phone. One of the benefits of being a demon was that he could mimic any voice he had heard. Zadikiele decided to make a call to Steve's boss using Steve's cell phone and let Steve's employer know he was suddenly feeling extremely ill and needed to take a little time off. After seeing such a terrible crime scene, Terrence was disappointed but let Steve know a leave of absence would be perfectly understandable.

Zadikiele was satisfied that the loose ends had been neatly tied up at this location. Uzza, a fallen angel leader, had ordered Zadikiele's father Remiel to talk with the other fallen angels and find out if any of them knew anything about any rogue vampires that were unaccounted for. As far as Remiel and the others could recollect, the children of the fallen angels and all vampires had all been destroyed in the great flood of Noah.

If their recollections were correct, though, what could explain what Zadikiele had seen on the dead girl? Vampires had to be construed as a myth, a legend of the Nephilim by the humans. The only way a vampire could have been created was if a Nephilim shared his blood with a human. It was a puzzle, to be sure, but he had more critical issues to deal with. He had to make sure Jakiele and the other angels were not made aware of this girl and how she died. His task right now was to keep an eye on Jakiele, see what he was up to, and get rid of Steve.

As Zadikiele was rifling through Steve's wallet, he saw a picture of Steve sitting next to a beautiful woman with gorgeous red hair, and she was holding a small boy in her arms. The pictures in the wallet fit in with the dossier he had on Steve from the police department. Steve was a married man with a beautiful wife, and they had a son. Steve and his family lived in the Washington D.C area, which meant Steve's little family would be easy targets for Zadikiele to gain access to. A nefarious idea formed in his mind about how he could get what he wanted. He would get rid of Steve but use his wife to keep an eye on Jakiele. He would use Steve's boy to keep Rochelle in line, perfect.

Remiel was concerned that the preserve and anyone connected with this story needed to be destroyed. Zadikiele had to stay behind to make sure the crime scene at the preserve was all taken care of, and the demons who had helped him were disposed of once they had completed their duties. Demons were not known to be trustworthy and keep important secrets if they were somehow discovered, so it became Zadikiele's task to get rid of anyone who knew what had happened to the dead girl.

Zadikiele had made sure to come to Maynard with a vial of the Ebola virus he had managed to buy at considerable cost and was able to secretly sneak it into the lead detective's coffee cup the day before when they had been at the animal preserve together. He had also managed to covertly put the virus into the medical examiner's water bottle so both demons would die from being exposed to the deadly virus. He had watched both men drink from the contaminated containers. No one would question how they died since they had both been exposed to the dead girl's body.

It was late in the day, but Zadikiele knew he had everything well in hand. Once he got back to his compound in Washington D.C., he would interrogate Steve and set his previously formed thoughts into motion. Rochelle was a beautiful woman, and he knew Jakiele favored red-headed women. She could be transformed into someone useful to his purposes. He knew human women would do everything they could to protect their offspring. If Steve's wife chose not to cooperate with his plans, he would have to get rid of her and her son quickly so news of Steve's disappearance would not make it to the police or the news media. It was a dangerous plan that could backfire easily should Rochelle become emboldened and sought Jakiele's aid in trying to free herself and her son. Zadikiele had to make sure she was frightened enough never to choose the path to her destruction.

Once back in Washington D.C., Zadikiele went straight to his secluded compound, an old, dilapidated farmhouse located two miles from the main road. The house was weather-worn with loose gray slat boards on the outside, which had not seen paint in years, and the tiles on the roof looked like they could rot and fall off at any time. The old farmhouse was chosen because it was on the outskirts of town, and very few people traveled to the remote area since it was hard to get there. The winding road leading up to the house was a long stretch of crusty dirt overgrown with ugly weeds and trees, making the old building hard to see. The one-story dilapidated structure was made to appear deserted entirely. It was surrounded by thick brush and large leafy trees and could hardly be seen unless you looked for it. Zadikiele purchased the property exclusively for these reasons and because there were no surrounding neighbors for miles.

Zadikiele had been given command of two demons named Latkia and Dariah. Latkia had inhabited a human body made of stone. His body was bulging with muscles and was rock hard. He was Samoan in appearance and stood well over six feet tall with long black hair he preferred to keep in a long braid flowing down his back. He had a perpetual frown and an intense rumbling voice. His face was as unyielding as his dark piercing eyes. He was very skilled with a sword and all manner of other weapons and exceptionally deadly at hand-to-hand combat training. Latkia oversaw security and kept Zadikiele's followers in line with any orders given. Latkia followed orders without question.

Dariah oversaw surveillance and tracked anyone Zadikiele wanted surveillance performed on. Dariah was small but stealthy. He only stood about five feet tall because he had taken the form of a small Asian man who could be easily hidden if necessary. He was also stoic in appearance and kept his body in excellent shape. He also had long flowing black hair but liked to let it flow free. He regularly practiced martial arts with weapons made from the Asian culture. Both Latkia and Dariah were extremely lethal in their specialties in warfare. They were significant assets to Zadikiele, and each played their parts very well.

It was good for Zadikiele to see that Latkia had posted sentries to watch for any unwelcome visitors as he was traveling to the farmhouse. However, the guards were well hidden to human eyes. Demons had to use humans for such tasks, and they had to be well trained to be undetected by anyone passing by. Demons could not use animals to aid in protecting them. Animals sensed a demon's presence and would either try to kill them or become so afraid they would become useless. If Latkia felt any of his human sentries did not measure up and perform their assigned tasks up to his standards, their heads would be put upon a stake in the backyard to warn others not to fail.

Dariah was exceptionally good at setting up security systems and educated himself on new technological developments. He had set up the farmhouse and surrounding area with all the latest gadgets and cameras so they would alert him to anyone trying to come or go from the building within a two-mile radius. In addition, the farmhouse had a basement that had been converted into many rooms with a trapdoor set above it, so if anyone ever came to the house and managed to enter, it would appear deserted since everyone would be underground.

The old rug above the trapdoor easily slid back into place once the trapdoor was closed. The trapdoor underneath could be locked by a large steel bar opened and closed by a panel box underneath it in the basement. Once the trapdoor was locked, it would be challenging for someone standing above it to open it. The basement was twice the size of the farmhouse structure resting unassumingly above it. The walls and floors were finished and functional, but the basement had no windows. The main living room had a large television for everyone to share and a modest kitchen area. The only bathroom had toilets with stalls and communal showers for everyone. The other rooms were for surveillance and living quarters for himself and his followers. They were connected by a long hallway at the end of the living room. At the end of the long hallway was an emergency exit. The emergency exit tunnel led two miles away back to the main road. The exit walls had all been concreted in to protect it from caving in.

A heavy-duty steel door sealed the emergency exit. Only Zadikiele had the key, which he always kept around his neck. The exit led to a deserted barn where all the different vehicles were kept if needed. The barn, house, and surrounding area were under constant surveillance by the followers Dariah and Latkia had specifically chosen and trained.

Zadikiele drove past the front of the house and around to the farmhouse's back and parked his bike. Latkia and Dariah came out of the backdoor. They greeted him in typical warrior fashion, a slight nod of the head in greeting, nothing more. Next, they each folded their arms across their chests in anticipation of Zadikiele's subsequent commands. Finally, Zadikiele tersely asked them, "Where did you take the reporter from Maynard? Did you set everything up as I commanded?" Latkia and Dariah nodded in unison and led Zadikiele back into the house and through the trapdoor to take him to the empty room Steve was being held in.

The room where Steve was held was empty except for the single chair he was restrained in. His hands were tied behind his back, and his mouth was covered in duct tape. His feet had been tied and bound to the legs of his chair. There was a single light overhead attached to a dangling chain. Zadikiele strode into the room with Latkia and Dariah close on his heels. Zadikiele yanked the harsh light on so Steve could finally see where he was and who held him prisoner. Steve started angrily, trying to break his bonds. He vainly tried to gurgle hateful words from behind his duct tape at the trio of men staring coldly down at him with their arms folded across their chests.

Zadikiele looked about the room and nodded to Dariah. Dariah went out of the room to gather up his videotape equipment. Zadikiele nodded once to Latkia. Latkia knew what to do. Latkia walked over to Steve and violently ripped the duct tape off Steve's mouth. He was not to kill Steve but hurt him badly enough to get the answers to the questions they needed to know. Latkia went to stand behind Steve with his knife at the ready across Steve's throat and violently pulled Steve's head back with his right hand so Steve would realize they were serious.

Zadikiele stood directly in front of Steve and bent his head down to within an inch of Steve's face. "Did I not warn you? Did I not tell you exactly what I would do to you and your family?" Zadikiele pulled out Steve's wallet, showed Steve the picture he had taken of Steve and his family, and put it right up to Steve's face. Steve struggled against his bonds and cursed violently at Zadikiele. Zadikiele nodded to Latkia. Then, Latkia hit Steve in the mouth hard with the hilt of his knife. Steve stopped struggling immediately. He now knew he was in considerable trouble this time. Zadikiele bent close to Steve once again and whispered very quietly in Steve's face, "You will answer every question I have. Failure to do so will result in the rape and killing of your wife and the death of your son for our amusement. Or do they mean nothing to you?"

Steve shakily nodded his head in agreement. He did not want to die, but he did not know much of anything either yet. Finally, Steve shouted back to Zadikiele, "My family is everything to me, but I was not able to get anyone to tell me anything about the girl!" Steve paused for a long moment before quietly finishing with, "There is not anything I can tell you." After an hour of relentlessly questioning and beating Steve, Zadikiele concluded this insignificant human did not know anything of importance. Steve knew the only ace in his pocket was the voice recorder he had mailed to his office. There was no way he was going to give up his life by telling Zadikiele about the only thing of value he had in his possession. It might be the only thing capable of saving his life, and he fully intended to use it as a bargaining chip if given a chance.

The rest of Zadikiele's followers had slowly crept into the room to watch what was happening to Steve. Zadikiele snapped his fingers to Latkia, signaling him to stop the brutal beatings. He let Steve gain his breath for a few minutes but let Steve know he had two choices. Either make a video reciting everything Zadikiele told him to say to his wife Rochelle and could save his wife and child or have his throat slit. Zadikiele snapped his fingers, and the rest of his followers gathered around Steve while Latkia once again put a knife to Steve's throat. Steve would do anything to save himself and his family, so he woodenly recited everything Zadikiele told him to say verbatim into the camera recording his message. They were the last words Steve would ever say to his beloved Rochelle. Latkia violently yanked Steve's head back and slit Steve's throat from ear to ear.

Zadikiele ordered Latkia to take care of the bloody mess in the room and get rid of Steve's body. He left the room and headed for his bedroom, which could only be opened by a numeric code that had to be punched in on the keypad to the right of the door. Once inside, he started to strip off his dusty clothes and pull off his biking boots. Unfortunately, he had forgotten to close the door, and in walked his favorite female follower, Larissa Rhodes. Larissa had been a runaway vagabond before she had become involved in his satanic cult. She had been a prostitute for years on the street, and she knew how to survive.

She moved to stand right next to him and began to help him finish stripping off his clothes. They never said a word to each other, and they did not have to. He knew what she wanted, and he was more than eager to satisfy her and himself. He had much to take care of the next day with Rochelle and her child, but for now, he wanted to take care of his human needs with someone who would fulfill his every desire before he laid down to take his rest for the night. She led him slowly down the hall to the communal shower and turned the showerhead on to a comfortable temperature. She soaped his body and herself from head to toe until she was satisfied and began to dry them both off seductively. When she was done drying them off, she led Zadikiele's back to his room and proceeded to show him why she always wanted to be his favorite toy.

# CHAPTER 5

When she was only six years old, Anna had sent her only daughter to live in Boston. Anna managed to smuggle her daughter out of war-torn Vukovar, a Bosnian City, quietly and quickly. Anna had sent her to live with her brother and sister-in-law, Stephen and Alaina. They had immigrated to the United States before the war had started. Katliana was Anna's only child because her father, Uri, had been killed in the battle. Anna knew that her daughter had vague memories of her father, but they were not pleasant ones.

Anna knew that her daughter remembered her father, Uri, yelling and screaming at them both. Uri would brutally hit Katliana when she would try to get between her parents to get them to quit fighting. Katliana had once told Anna that she remembered her mother covering her own fragile body with hers so that her father could not hurt her. Anna knew instinctively back then that she had to get her daughter away somehow from Uri or her child would end up dead.

Anna had no choice but to stay in Bosnia due to financial reasons, but she made sure her daughter made it safely out of the country. It cost Anna every dime she had but making sure her daughter was safe in America was worth it. Anna had labored for years as a housekeeper and had secreted money away her husband was unaware of so he would not drink or gamble it away to pay for her daughter's passage. In addition, Anna's brother, Stephan, was a kind and scholarly man who worked for Boston College in Massachusetts as a math teacher.

Katliana's uncle passionately believed in the value of an education. Since he and his wife Alaina could not have children, they were ecstatic to take little Katliana in and raise her as their own. They showered her with love and kindness and ensured Katliana lacked for nothing, including a college education. Katliana's passion was biology and DNA studies. She earned high marks in her schooling, which landed her a coveted position working as a forensics analyst in Maynard, Massachusetts, only a few miles outside Boston. Anna had made sure Uri had no idea where Stephan or Alaina lived or worked by destroying any addresses or phone numbers she had. She memorized everything and kept the information tightly locked inside her mind.

Anna would send secret coded messages to her brother whenever she could to let Katliana know she would come to the United States to join her as soon as she could get away safely. Anna would write letters during her break at work and ask her employer to mail them by deducting the cost from her paycheck. Her employer was an elderly lady who suspected Uri of beating Anna and had no problem expressing her thoughts to Anna. Uri was a useless waste of a man as far as her employer was concerned. Nevertheless, she was glad to help Anna in whatever way she could. Anna's employer would always wait until Uri came and picked up Anna. Then, after she was sure Anna was long gone, would she have her trusted driver deliver Anna's messages to the western union office.

Katliana was not told at the time that her father liked to keep her mother under constant lock and key and was torturing her mother to find out what she had done with Katliana. It was not as though Uri loved his child or wanted her back. The issue was that Anna had defied him. Uri was not going to accept any defiance out of his wife. He allowed her to work to make money for them, but only because she earned a living for them. After Anna got home from work, Uri would barricade Anna in their bedroom with barely enough food to survive. He had stopped beating her with his fists and turned to psychological and emotional torture tactics instead. He did not want anyone to know what a sadist he was by leaving too many bruises on her others could notice. The abuse went on for weeks after Katliana made it safely to America. Still, Anna did not want her family to worry, so she did not let them know anything was happening to her.

One cold wintery day, Uri did not come to pick Anna up from work. It was odd, as Uri was always punctual and liked to keep her firmly under control. Anna had no choice but to walk home alone. She did not have any money, and few people had cars or could afford them since the city was still torn up from the war. Crumbled buildings and starving children in the streets were a common occurrence to see. Her tiny apartment was a few blocks away, so she made it to her home in short order by walking briskly to ward off the bitter cold. When she slid her key into her apartment door, she was surprised to see a note attached to the door. An official notice from the war department said her husband had been found dead in the street. The message stated Anna should come down to the morgue to identify her husband's body as soon as possible.

Anna was dumbfounded. She knew she should feel something other than relief, but she did not. Uri was once a handsome young blonde soldier, and Anna quickly fell for him with his romantic lines and easy looks. Still, those traits had hidden the true darkness within him. Anna's parents had died when she was in her late teens, and her brother had already gone to America, so she was all alone. As soon as she and Uri married, his true colors came out.

Uri drank and gambled away every cent he could get his hands on and would punish Anna severely if she ever disobeyed his commands. He often made her submit to whatever things he wanted, which would satisfy his unending hunger for abuse. He repeatedly cheated on her with harlots, and Anna knew it, but she became grateful that he turned his sadistic sexual attention on someone else. Anna's only joy in her bleak existence was her daughter, Katliana.

Anna had vowed to herself after Katliana was born that she would protect her daughter with every fiber of her being, even if it would cost her the ultimate sacrifice of her own life.

After reading the notice on her door, Anna left her apartment door and headed back to town to go to the broken-down hotel in the city's center. The city used the hotel as a temporary place for the dead to be taken since the hospital and morgue had been bombed to the ground. She had to force herself to go up the jagged, crumbled steps to the barely hanging wooden door and go in. Soldiers were standing everywhere, and Anna began to feel uncomfortable as if she were out of place. Many soldiers were covered in bloody bandages, and some were looking upward toward the ceiling in a shell-shocked state. There were bodily fluids everywhere, and the acrid smell of smoke filled the air. Anna sensed the spirits of the dead were trying valiantly to communicate their pain to her, and she felt it with every nerve in her body. Typically, she would have helped them ascend, but now was not the time. She needed desperately to know if Uri was genuinely dead.

A young woman in a nurse's uniform came up to greet her with a warm smile, and all Anna could do was hold out the paper with the information on it the war department had left for her. Anna could not seem to force any words out of her frozen throat for some reason. The young nurse looked down at the clipboard she was holding and looked up Uri's name and where Uri's body had been placed. The nurse put down the clipboard on a nearby table, grabbed Anna's cold hands with her own, and gave Anna's hands a reassuring squeeze. Then, the nurse began leading Anna by the shoulders gently down the long hall to the cold room where all the dead soldiers from the day's skirmish were brought. The young nurse led Anna over to the hospital gurney, where her husband now lay dead. He looked so peaceful and young as though in death, he finally found the serenity he could not find in life. His chest had been blown wide open by an explosion of some kind, and half of his face had been torn open by flying shrapnel. She watched him for quite a bit of time to make sure he was dead. Anna eventually realized he was truly gone. Finally.

Anna could feel his spirit trying desperately to communicate to her, but she refused to open the closed doors of her mind and let him in. Uri had done enough damage in his short life to leave permanent scars on her soul already, and she was not going to let him do more. Anna did not kiss him goodbye, hold his hand, or shed a tear. Instead, Anna simply nodded at the nurse that she was positively identifying him as her husband and that the staff at the hotel could take possession of his body now. Anna woodenly turned around and walked home after filling out the necessary paperwork. She had never told Uri or anyone else about her gift of communicating with spirits. Her husband would have found one way or another to exploit her gift for monetary gain for himself, and she would have become a laughingstock in their community or shunned. She certainly had no intention of helping her husband transcend straight to the Underworld where he belonged and would most surely be welcomed.

After arriving home, Anna turned the key again and walked into her tiny apartment, closed the door behind her, and locked it. She slowly slumped to the floor and went to sleep. She was in a very deep slumber when she heard a soft voice coming to her as if from a lofty distance. The voice sweetly whispered to her, "All will be well now, my child. Have no fear as I will be watching over you always. I have seen to it you will be taken care of. Believe in what I say, and I will reward you. It would be best if you stayed here in Bosnia until your child reaches the proper age for you to rejoin her. I will see to your every need. Have faith." Anna awoke to a feeling of such peace, love, and warmth that she intrinsically knew a celestial being had visited her. She did not know why, but she felt compelled to obey what the voice told her.

Anna awoke the following day after having the best night's sleep she could ever remember having. It was as if a dark, suffocating cloud had been lifted from her life. Anna was finally free to hear the birds singing, see the sunshine coming in through her windows, and smell the fresh snow swirling around and gently scenting the air. Anna went over to the refrigerator to retrieve some bacon and eggs to fix herself breakfast since it was Saturday, and she did not have to work. There was a sudden sharp knock on the door.

Anna was so startled that she almost dropped the bacon on the floor. Anna walked cautiously over to her front door to not alert any unwanted visitors that she was home if she did not want to open the door. When Anna looked through the peephole, she saw a young man in his early thirties standing on the threshold wearing a very fine-looking dark silk suit. She undid the deadbolt but kept the security latch on the door so she could peer a few inches around the door without opening it all the way.

"May I help you?" Anna asked cautiously, to which the man replied, "Are you Anna Klackovich?" The young man took his black fedora hat off his head and placed it in his hands, and patiently waited for her to respond. "Who wants to know?" Anna asked more boldly and with obvious suspicion. The young man hesitated for a moment before bowing his head and saying in a remorsefully kind tone, "My apologies, Ma'am. I know this must be a challenging time for you. I am the Klackovich family solicitor. As your recently deceased husband was the last living relative of the Klackovich legacy, the inheritance he was due now falls to you as his wife. Your husband was to have come into his inheritance next year, but you are now the beneficiary of the Klackovich estate since he is deceased. Are you indeed Anna Klackovich?"

Anna nodded very slowly in complete shock. Anna's left hand flew to her chest in agitated surprise. She gulped in a huge breath and let it back out in an agitated whoosh. She asked the young man if he had identification to prove who he was. The card the solicitor produced showed the business logo of a legal firm named Aragen, Lativina, and Keruger. The card was made of thick, rich vellum with gold leaf engraving. Anna instinctively knew that the fancy card had to be awfully expensive. Anna's life had taught her to be cautious about whom she let into her home or her life, so she asked the young solicitor if he would agree to meet her at the location listed on the card on Monday after she got off work to go over the details. She did not want to let him inside the apartment, where she felt uncomfortable sitting down with someone she did not know. The man graciously agreed to meet her at 5 PM on Monday and turned around and walked away. Anna slowly relocked the door in stunned silence.

Uri had never mentioned in seven years of marriage anything about coming into an inheritance or his family leaving him anything of value. She wondered if he even knew he had one coming since his family had all been killed in the repeated bombings of the city when an entire apartment complex caved in. The falling debris killed his parents and his older sister in one devastating crush. At seventeen, Uri joined the military and vowed to avenge his family's death by killing as many enemies as possible. Uri did not talk about having any other relatives, so Anna was getting more suspicious and curious by the minute. Then, after a moment of reflection, she remembered the soft voice in her dream telling her to have faith and believe. Anna took a deep cleansing lungful of air and felt at once at peace again in the comfort that everything would be okay. Anna continued to make herself the delicious breakfast she had started to prepare earlier.

Anna tried to keep herself busy by cleansing her apartment from end to end, opening all the windows to let in the fresh air. It was refreshing and exhilarating to exorcise Uri's smell and presence from what was now her space alone. She washed all her bedding and cleaned every surface, nook, and cranny on which she could lay her hands. As a couple, they did not have much, to begin with, which was not broken or second rate, but at least everything felt clean, new, and only belonged to her. She did not want to have time to think or feel. She tried to keep thoughts of Uri locked up tight within a little box in her mind, which could not be opened unless she wanted to. Until she was ready, the memory of him would never again enter her mind.

Monday morning rolled around, and Anna went to work as usual. Word gets around fast about war casualties, and her employer already knew Anna's husband had died. Her employer was not too surprised to see Anna come to work anyway. She knew Anna was unhappy in her troubled marriage, although Anna had never really confided in her. Anna never said a word about it or showed any emotion, so she let Anna do her duties without saying anything about her husband's death. The old lady figured Anna would talk about Uri when she was ready and let Anna be. Anna left for the day when she had completed her duties and walked to the address listed on the card. It was located on the outskirts of town, so it took Anna over a half hour to get there. It was a small, quaint office that appeared as though it had been renovated out of someone's old family home. After opening the front door, a small bell tinkled over the entrance to herald her arrival.

A very elegantly dressed older woman was seated behind a desk that had been made of the finest oak Anna had ever laid eyes on and had been meticulously polished to a high sheen. The receptionist had a pair of glasses perched perilously at the end of her nose while she was reading a document to an unknown person on the other end of the phone. She saw Anna come in and motioned for Anna to go and sit down on one of the stylishly lined chaise lounges on either side of the foyer. Anna took off her shabby, worn coat and gloves and slowly looked around at the wood-paneled walls of the lobby, which had also been polished to a high luster and looked to be without a trace of dust. Anna assumed the expensively framed pictures on the walls had to be portraits of the law firm owners. Underneath the photographs were little gold plaques with identifying names engraved on them. She did not see any pictures of the young man who visited her on Saturday.

The receptionist finished her phone call with the firm's client and very professionally asked Anna, "Do you have an appointment, Ma'am?" Anna suddenly felt foolish. She wondered if she were being misled somehow or was the victim of a joke and decided she would leave before making a laughingstock of herself. Before turning around to go, Anna heard a door open at the end of the hall. Anna could see the young man who had visited her at her apartment start walking down the lushly carpeted aisle towards the receptionist. Before reaching the desk, he turned and saw Anna putting on her gloves and hat. He walked up to Anna, grabbed her hands in his, profusely apologized if he kept her waiting, and started leading Anna back towards his very expensively appointed office.

"How is it your portrait is not in the lobby? I thought you said you represented this firm?" Anna demanded after the young man politely seated her in the comfortable leather chair across from his desk. The solicitor went around his desk and sat back in his office chair, laced his fingers in front of his chest, and looked Anna directly in the eye before replying politely, "I am not yet a partner in this firm. My father is one of the owners, and when my father and the other partners feel I am ready, I will be made a partner. For right now, I am overseeing estate cases. If you wish, I can set up a time to meet my father and the other partners if it would make you feel more comfortable. My name is Kurt Aragen. My father is American, and my mother is Bosnian. Would you like to see any other credentials which could potentially ease your mind?"

Anna was immediately contrite, "I apologize if I appear rude, Mr. Aragen, but I find all of this hard to believe. My husband never mentioned any of this, and I have a tough time believing this is not some joke. However, I do not have time to waste on any silliness or games, so please get to the heart of what it is you want to discuss with me so I can be on my way." Kurt paused and pulled out a folder with Anna's name on it for a moment.

"As soon as I have your signature, Ms. Klackovich, I can release the assets left to you. You will be inheriting the sum of one hundred thousand dollars held for you in a retirement savings account per the orders of the will. Also, you will be given a yearly stipend of twenty thousand dollars to live on as long as you still are in this town. There is an additional ten thousand per year to maintain the house and grounds of the family estate left to you in the will. However, the terms of the will say that you must remain a resident of Bosnia to continue to receive the yearly stipends. If you leave the city, you give up your inheritance. This stipulation does not, however, apply to the savings account. You may have access to the money any time after the age of sixty-five. Do you understand the terms and stipulations of the will?"

Anna nodded very slowly. If she agreed to the terms of the will, she would not go to America. Her brother would have to bring her daughter to this war-torn country to see her mother. If she decided not to accept, she would not have the funds to get to America and apply for citizenship for a considerably long time, if ever. "Why did the family insist on the beneficiaries remaining in Bosnia?" Anna asked after a long pause. Kurt replied in a matter-of-fact tone, "The Klackovichs were devout patriots of this country, Anna, and they believed in fighting for it. They felt any inheritance should go to the family members who were willing to stay and try to rebuild what was lost. They did not want any money going to anyone unwilling to do what was necessary to protect what they had left. Do you need time to think this over, or do you wish to go over to the bank and get your accounts set up and sign the necessary documents?"

Anna felt like she was in a daze, but she nodded numbly, followed Kurt out of the office, and let him escort her to a sleek black limousine already parked out front waiting for them. Kurt had anticipated Anna agreeing to the terms of the will. Why wouldn't he? Anna was dirt poor and did not have many options if she ever wanted to see her daughter again, so she did not have a lot of choices. Stubbornness and pride would not get her what she wanted. Uri may have been a horrible husband, but at least he was finally contributing to his wife and daughter's future happiness, even if it was not a willing acknowledgment on his part. He was rolling over in his grave in anger, thinking about Anna having any enjoyment without him. The thought alone made Anna smile.

Anna spent the next twenty years running a soup kitchen for the homeless orphans who needed a warm meal and a safe place to sleep. She used the estate funds to convert the Klackovich family estate into a cooperative housing project. Nothing was ever official on the books, but the street kids knew Anna's large house was the place to go to get a much-needed helping hand. Anna did not believe in doing this service for free, so any child who stayed with her had to attend school and better their situation. They all had to do house chores, watch their mouths and manners, and help look after the smaller children. Anna had a big heart for kids and wanted to help, but she would not be bullied by anyone and had no problem kicking out ungrateful children who were thankless for the help she lovingly gave.

Anna had managed to save a little nest egg for her new life in America from her yearly stipends until she could access her retirement funds. Her visa was finally approved because of her generous contributions to her country. In addition, her brother had arranged and paid for yearly visits between Anna and Katliana. As a result, they had all forged a remarkably close bond with one another. Anna and Katliana also regularly wrote to each other to keep their connection as close as possible until Anna could come to America.

Her daughter had understood the devastating sacrifices Anna made on her behalf when her mother finally revealed why she had to stay behind in Bosnia and was grateful she had such a strong, loving mother who had given so much. On the other hand, Katliana was sad that her father had been such a monster to her mother and had caused Anna to suffer so much pain and loneliness. Katliana was also immensely proud of her mother for taking in starving homeless orphans and offering them the warmth of a loving home. She could not wait until her mother moved to America and they could start a new life together.

While living in her uncle's house, Katliana had known nothing but love and tenderness, but she had also felt an overwhelming sense of isolation. She missed her mother terribly throughout the long years. Since she had no brothers, sisters, or cousins to play with, Katliana had turned her attention to her studies and had excelled. However, she always felt like she was outside looking in on everyone else's life and liked to keep to herself.

She did not have many friends when she had attended school. She was such a petite girl when she was in high school. The popular girls shunned her and taunted her whenever she walked by in the hall. Boys had wanted to date her, but since none of them interested her on an intellectual or physical level, she saw no point in wasting her time on them. She got the title "Ice Queen" because she came across as so frozen and emotionless. However, she was not cold at all. She was just shy, and she had no intention of letting a man get close to her after she had witnessed all the abuse her mother had suffered.

After graduating from Boston College, Anna called her at her uncle's house to congratulate her and let her know it would not be too much longer until she moved to America. Katliana was excited to let her mother know she had been offered an excellent job at a lab in Maynard and would soon be moving out of her uncle's house to get an apartment in Boston. It was a two-bedroom apartment with a lovely balcony overlooking the city at night. It boasted a large living area and two bathrooms. Katliana hoped her mother would consider staying with her at her new apartment until she got settled. Katliana had tried extremely hard to make her apartment warm and inviting with soft suede sofas and armchairs with gently muted tones on the walls so her mother could relax and watch a lovely fire dancing in the grates and be able to enjoy a comfortable life.

Her mother had worked so hard her whole life without any entertainment or fun, so Katliana wanted her mother to finally have time to herself to enjoy the sights and wonders of Boston. She did not want her mother to want for anything. When Anna had learned of Katliana's plans, she became overwhelmed with emotion and love. Anna was proud that her daughter had turned into such a kind and generous person.

Anna also felt a profound sense of relief that her daughter had finally been told the whole truth about why Anna was forced to stay behind. Anna's painful sacrifice had everything to do with how much she loved her child and would do whatever it took to be with her again. Katliana had not held her mother's sacrifice against her. On the contrary, Katliana loved her more for it. Katliana's forgiveness and acceptance were more than Anna had ever hoped for, and she was comforted by it even though she knew it would be hard to find forgiveness for herself.

What Anna had wanted for so long was finally coming to fruition. In her dreams, the strange voice which had whispered to her the night her husband died had often come back to offer her consolation and encouragement. The voice told her that if she had faith and belief, everything would work out the way she hoped for. After going through the endless red tape, Anna had finally arrived in Boston to live with her daughter. She had been in America living with Katliana for only three months when an advertisement in the newspaper caught her eye. It was for an employment agency specializing in housekeeping assignments, but applicants had to pass an extensive background check to work for government officials.

Katliana had come home from work one Friday afternoon and noticed the open newspaper on the kitchen table. She noted several ads circled in red ink. Katliana set her purse slowly down onto the kitchen table, quietly padded down the hall to her mother's room, and knocked softly on her mother's bedroom door, but the door was not all the way shut. Katliana cautiously opened the door to find her mother lying peacefully on her bed, taking a much-needed rest. Katliana slowly closed the door and went silently back into their shared kitchen to make dinner for herself and her mother.

Anna awakened a few minutes later and came into the kitchen to see if Katliana was home yet. Katliana had her back to her mother as she was preparing dinner, so Anna opened the conversation with, "I applied to an employment agency, and they are currently doing a background check on me. As a result, I may have to leave here to work in another town. I love you dearly and have enjoyed being here with you immensely, but I need a place of my own. I hope you can support me and understand that I desperately need my own sense of identity and independence.

Nevertheless, I want you to know I am here now, and we can see each other as much as we want. I have loved every single minute I have spent here with you, but you need to meet someone nice and start your own family. I want you to have children someday, and I do not think anything romantic is going to happen with me being in the room next door." Anna told this to Katliana in a lighthearted, funny tone, but she could tell Katliana was devastated by the news that Anna would be leaving. Anna went over to her daughter, turned her around to face her, gently folded her daughter in her arms, and whispered encouraging words. Anna knew Katliana was crying and trying not to let Anna see how distressed she was at the news of her mother leaving her. Katliana raised her head and looked into her mother's tear-stained face, which had been ravaged through the long years by pain. She kissed her mother gently on the cheek and sobbed even harder after seeing she had upset her poor mother by her endless need never to be alone. She felt it was her turn to do what was right by her mother and knew it meant letting her mother go to finally live the life she wanted, fought for, and deserved. It was Katliana's turn to sacrifice for her mother to be happy. She hugged her mother tightly and asked if she could do anything to help. Anna happily replied, "How about getting married and having a couple of kids?" They giggled over the subject for a while and spent the rest of the evening talking and enjoying the precious moments they had left to enjoy.

# CHAPTER 6

Katliana was so excited when she learned her mother wanted to spend some of her hard-earned vacation time in Boston with her. One long year had passed since Anna had left to start her new job. It had been difficult for Katliana to let Anna leave and go to work in Washington D.C., even though the distance was not as far as when Anna had lived in Bosnia. Instead, they had stayed in touch with each other often through phone calls and letters to keep their newfound connection strong so that they could forge a new adult relationship with one another. Their scarred past was hard to leave behind, but they were working diligently to leave it where it ought to be, in the past.

After Anna had left Boston to work in Washington D.C, Katliana had often found herself once again overwhelmed with pain and loneliness. She knew it was selfish, but she felt bereft, as though she was an orphan all over again. Katliana knew it did not make any sense, but it was how she felt. Katliana was happy for her mother that she had found steady employment quickly and reported that her employer, Jake Smith, was an industrious young man who treated her very well. The money he paid her was more than enough to supplement what Anna had managed to stow away for her retirement years. Anna was happy at her new home and felt she finally fit in somewhere.

After a while, Katliana did what she did best, buried her emotions, and immersed herself in her job. It was the only way she knew how to keep her emotional demons at bay. Once she got back into the routine of not having her mother's comforting presence in her home, she tried to go on dates with a select few men she thought might have at least the potential to keep her intellectually interested, if not physically attracted enough to see them again. However, most often, they simply bored her to tears, so she opted to spend time alone in the haven of her apartment. The only outlet she gave herself was occasionally reading an enjoyable book. Katliana liked to read nestled on her sofa with the soft flickering lights of her fireplace dancing in the background.

She had often thought about the suggestion her mother had made about producing children, but she would have to get married to one of the mealy-mouthed suitors who had been brave enough to ask her for a date. Being able to stomach their presence long enough to enable her to get pregnant made her nauseous. The very idea of pregnancy was so repugnant to her that the mere thought conjured up visions of how her father had treated her mother. There was no way any man would get close enough to her or make her want to place herself in the care of any man and give up her independence. She was comfortable making her own money and therefore making her own decisions without giving any thought to the deference of some man.

It was an average summer Monday morning when Katliana arrived to work at 8 AM sharp. At the Maynard lab where Katliana was employed, she was considered an expert in DNA analysis. She wrote a software program that could delineate any kind of DNA on the planet. After coming into her office and seating herself at her desk with her regular morning coffee, she noticed a special overnight package from her former Boston University professor, Kyle Oakes, sitting atop her desk. Katliana became cautiously curious and opened the envelope to find pictures of the dead girl that had been found at the Assabet Animal Preserve, along with tissue samples and a case file

Kyle had rushed to put together. The dead girl's story had been all over the news recently, so Katliana was vaguely aware of the strange story.

Kyle Oakes was considered highly educated himself, so Katliana wondered why he would send her tissue samples and a case file with pictures of the dead girl when he could run DNA profile tests himself. The contents of the envelope did not make any sense. The only conclusion she could come to was that Kyle must want a second opinion. She had worked for him at the morgue while going to college for extra credit to learn more about post and premortem DNA and retrieve blood samples from the deceased. She respected his knowledge and professionalism as much as he admired her drive to be acknowledged and respected in her field of DNA study.

Katliana wanted to get a good idea of what she was dealing with before her mother arrived the following Sunday to spend time with her on her vacation. Katliana knew that once she became involved in a project, all time and space melted away until she finished what she was working on. She wanted to spend quality time with her mother. She had envisioned shopping sprees and long lunches spent on the beach sipping wine and watching time going slowly by while revisiting thoughts of how they wanted to spend their lives in the future. However, there must be something she was missing about the importance of the package Kyle sent her, so she pulled a magnifying glass out of her top desk drawer and examined the picture Kyle sent her of the dead Asian girl more closely. The note Kyle sent along with the DNA sample and the picture read simply, "Look very closely at this young girl who was found dead at the Assabet Animal Preserve and let me know if the reported cause of death is consistent with what you find."

The case file Kyle sent reported that the girl died of the Ebola virus. It was odd for Kyle to go to such great lengths to question results a medical examiner found. Katliana was becoming more curious by the second. She put the photograph under her small desk lamp so her view of the young girl's body could become more illuminated.

Katliana held the magnifying glass over the image of the body, carefully going over every single inch. The body was ghostly white and showed no visible signs of trauma except for the barely noticeable twin pinpricks over the top of the girl's left breast. Bug bites, maybe? Katliana thought. But identical ones right next to each other? Such a conclusion did not seem right to her. The only way Katliana would get any answers was to take the tissue samples Kyle sent her and start running tests on them to see if she could find anything that would answer her and Kyle's questions.

Katliana prepared several slides of the tissue material to avoid any questions of accuracy and verification and processed them through her specially made software and hardware equipment, then waited for the results. It could sometimes take hours, so she decided to go out and get some sunshine by stretching her legs and going for a walk. She had not realized so many hours had gone by since she had arrived at work in the morning, and it was now lunchtime.

A small cafe nearby specialized in handmade sandwiches and soups, so she decided to eat lunch. While she was enjoying her meal, the television above the diner's heads came on with the local news broadcast. The detective and the medical examiner who had overseen the dead girl's case had died from being exposed to the Ebola virus. The media reported that the public should avoid visiting the Animal Preserve until the area could be quarantined appropriately and sanitized.

Katliana was stunned. She had come into contact with the lead detective and medical examiner from Boston on several cases. She knew from experience that both men knew how to take precautions when dealing with contagious diseases and corpses. If the girl found at the preserve was already dead, and the proper protection was used, how could they both have become infected? The dead girl would not transmit the disease unless they both directly contacted her blood or bodily fluids. It was mandatory always to wear gloves at crime scenes when performing any medical examinations.

It seemed highly unlikely two veterans of their respective professions would be so careless, especially when dealing with any contagion whether they knew someone was infected or not. Moreover, the case profile Kyle sent her was making less sense by the minute. Katliana hurried up with her meal and paid to exit the cafe as quickly as possible. She was anxious to see if her computer had produced any results.

Katliana rushed back to her office to see if the results had come in, and they most certainly had. The first sample she had run confirmed the DNA of the young girl came back as a female human with the exact DNA sequencing code she had expected to find. One of the tissue samples was taken from the girl's skin above the right breast since no blood sample had been sent to her by Kyle. The Ebola virus caused a victim to bleed from every orifice in the body and internal organs, so this theory could explain why no blood sample was sent. The second sample Katliana ran of the young girl's body showed no disease, virus, or other contagions in the girl's body. Her white blood cell count fell into the normal range, which meant she did not have a bacterial infection either. Every test she ran confirmed that the dead girl had been completely healthy at the time of her death.

The swabs taken of the twin pinpricks above the young girl's left breast had entirely unexpected and surprising results. The computer flashed the results, "NO MATCH FOUND." Her software program was designed to tell her the exact DNA sequence of any species, human or otherwise. She ran all five samples she created and kept producing the same results. The left breast sample should have saliva traces of the bug or the plant that may have punctured her skin. However, the computer kept producing the same results on the sample. So, if her computer could not find what bit the victim, and there was no disease in her body, and no plant had damaged her skin, how did this young girl die?

Since the Maynard lab employed advanced level computer technicians to keep their hardware up to date and virus free, Katliana decided to ask their resident computer analyst, Jim Thorne, to run tests on her computer and software and make sure they were all running correctly and were not corrupted in any way. After running every comprehensive test he could think of, Jim confirmed her equipment was in working order. The results Katliana had discovered had to be correct. Too tired to run any more tests for the day, Katliana wanted to stop for the day and go home. She would rerun the tests the next day and see if she generated the same results. Before leaving, Katliana decided to call Kyle to discuss her findings. Unfortunately, all she got was his answering machine, so she decided to call him from work tomorrow.

Katliana was utterly exhausted and decided she would go home and forget about work after getting dinner and a beer at the local bar. She was used to being hit on by the drunks and those looking to make an easy score, so she had learned how to defend herself through many long hours of Tae kwon do and karate classes. She had also gotten her concealed weapons permit last year since violent crimes against women always seemed to be on the rise. She always carried her small semi-automatic handgun in her purse or the back of her waistband if she went for walks to clear her head after long days of staring through microscopes. No one bothered her enough to have to produce a weapon. Still, Katliana felt better if she carried her handgun to protect herself if she needed to use it.

After letting herself into her apartment after work, Katliana decided to watch a little of the local news before going to bed. After sitting down in her reclining armchair and putting up her feet, Katliana picked up her remote control from the side table and turned the television on to her favorite news channel. Not much was going on, except the local news was still focusing on following the story of the dead girl at the Assabet Animal Preserve and showing pictures of where the young girl was found. Unfortunately, interviews with the preserve's tour guides had yielded extraordinarily little information as they had so many tourists at this time of year, and no one remembered this poor little girl as being a part of their entourage. So instead, the news once again focused on how three people were dead from encountering the Ebola virus and how people should contact the center for disease control if they start coming down with any symptoms.

This case intrigued Katliana. How could the two pinprick tissue samples not yield any DNA? She knew how meticulous Kyle was in taking accurate swabs as he was the one who had taught her how to take them from corpses. Could the sample have become contaminated somehow? None of it made any scientific sense to her. The more she thought about it, the more she was convinced that the samples needed to be re-evaluated to see if she had made any errors somehow. She would get up early the next day and go in to work to repeat the DNA scans.

Katliana was convinced that she was missing something somehow, and the more she focused on it, the more the mystery was starting to ensnare her in a web of curiosity. Katliana loved to solve puzzles, and she became more determined than ever to find the underlying cause of whatever was going on.

The only way Katliana knew how to relax was to take a long hot bath and put on soft music with the lights turned down low. Her mind tended to spin long into the night on any projects she was working on until she figured out a way to solve whatever enigma she was trying to solve. She filled her tub up with rose and lavender-scented water, slowly immersed herself into the luxurious bubbles, and began to wash from head to toe. She put a nice cool cloth over her eyes and eased back into the tub to give her mind and muscles time to slowly unwind themselves from the tension she put them through daily.

Katliana was not vain and could care less when men ogled her impressively sculpted body, resulting from her workouts at the local martial arts school she attended. Her only purpose in keeping her body in top form was so she would be able to defend herself from predators. She had no intention of being so weak that any man would have the ability to ever beat on her again as her father had.

She often woke up in the middle of the night, covered in sweat from nightmares. Her heart would be racing and ready to pound out of her chest from recalling memories of her early childhood in Bosnia and the feeling of being too small and helpless to defend herself from her father's brutal and endless abuse.

She had learned that long relaxing baths would sometimes ease her mind and body long enough to be able to fall into a deep, restful sleep. Of course, it did not always work, but she did it to give herself the best chance she could to get the rejuvenating rest her body so desperately needed for her to be the best at her job, which required an immense amount of concentration and dedication to the tasks she needed to complete. After drying herself off with a fluffy towel, Katliana put on her pajamas and crawled into bed. She had learned to count backward from two hundred and concentrate on relaxing her muscles one at a time so her mind would be occupied with other things instead of her work.

Katliana was intrigued and could not wait to get back to the office to work on the samples Kyle had sent her. After arriving at her office, she noticed a memo on her desk asking her to please come and speak to the director of the lab, Markus Lambert, at his office immediately. Katliana frowned in concern. Had she done something wrong? Markus loved the spotlight and took credit for solving crime scene analysis issues in murder cases, but he did not ever deign to praise those under him who did the work. His employees were usually only asked to come to his office if they were in trouble. Feeling uneasy, Katliana went down the hall from her office to his and knocked quietly on the door. Hearing the muffled words from Markus to enter, Katliana cautiously opened the door and walked in.

Markus was seated behind his desk, dressed impeccably in a black silk suit with a matching silk tie and crisp white shirt underneath. He was an expert in charm and liked to be unassuming and kind underneath his wealth of slicked-back black hair and perfectly groomed facial features. Markus was quite handsome and certainly knew how to use his assets to his advantage with the ladies who worked at the lab. He had never made a pass at her, though, for which Katliana was eternally grateful. She wanted to be respected for her abilities and not her body. However, she had caught Markus on several occasions admiring her bottom when he thought she was not looking.

Markus signaled for her to come and sit down across from his desk as he was still speaking on the other end of the phone to someone else. After ending his phone conversation, he placed the receiver back in its cradle. Then, he put his long fingers together in a steeple on the desk before addressing Katliana. Markus took a long pause and a deep breath before he began to speak softly to her. Then, he looked her straight in the eye and said, "Did you receive a package yesterday from a Mr. Kyle Oakes in Boston?" Stunned, Katliana stammered, "Why yes, I did. He asked me to look at a couple of tissue samples. I assumed he wanted a second opinion. Why? Is there something wrong?"

"Why would a mortician send tissue samples to you?" Markus demanded to know while looking at her with a puzzled frown on his face. Katliana was confused but answered him, "I have no idea, and Kyle did not explain why he wanted me to examine the tissues in the note he sent." Katliana explained she had once been a student of Kyle's during her college years. She revealed that Kyle and her uncle were friends and associate professors at Boston University. "I assumed he wanted a second opinion from me, but when I tried to call him last night, he did not answer his phone," Katliana added.

Markus covered his face for a moment with his hands before he lowered them again and continued, "The phone conversation I was having was with a detective from the Boston Police Department. Kyle Oakes was found dead at his desk from a heart attack last night. His receptionist found him this morning and called the police. After the police arrived and called for an ambulance, they questioned the receptionist about why he would have been working so late. Although the receptionist was not any help, she remembered the last thing he asked her to do for the day was send out a package to you."

Markus paused for a long moment before continuing with, "Apparently, a family has come forward identifying the body of the dead girl found at the Assabet Animal Preserve. Her name was Sue Kwon, and she was an exchange student from China, and now China is demanding to know precisely how Miss Kwon died, and they want answers right now! This case could potentially cause an international incident, and we need to do everything we can to cooperate with the authorities and turn over any evidence we have." Kyle's voice had risen in agitated crescendo with every sentence until his face and throat had turned a dark shade of red.

Katliana was mortified and shocked. She did not know how to respond to this devastating news. Kyle Oakes had taken her under his wing in college and taught her everything he learned in the field of forensic DNA. He had always treated her like the daughter he had lost years before. He had always been a genuinely kind and patient teacher as well as a friend of the family. Markus waited for her to absorb this horrifying news and handed her a tissue from his desk in case she needed it. Katliana was too mortified to cry.

Markus interrupted her thoughts by saying, "We need to turn over to the Boston Police everything that was in the overnight package Mr. Oakes sent you. Trust me when I tell you we do not want to be involved in this case if China decides we are tied to this murder in any way. So, I need you to please go to your office and retrieve whatever Kyle sent you. I will manage this situation by using as much diplomacy and transparency as possible to keep us out of the media spotlight. Believe me when I say I am so sorry for your loss. I can see your friend Kyle must have meant a lot to you and if there is anything I can do, please let me know."

Markus was uncommonly kind and tender with her, and she appreciated it, but she knew Kyle would have never sent her the overnight package without a good reason. Katliana stood up and walked out of the office in a daze. She had to think quickly. As she walked back to her own office, she came up with a plan. She had already made files she could copy to her personal computer on her office computer of all the information Kyle had sent. All she had to do was transfer the file and send it to her home computer, which she did as soon as she walked into her office. Markus did not need to know she had made a copy, so she removed the incriminating files from her office computer to make sure no one would ever know what she had done. Katliana gathered up the hard evidence except for the picture of the dead Asian girl, which she discreetly slipped into the back pocket of her jeans.

Katliana walked slowly back down the hall to Markus' office and handed him the file and the tissue samples, as well as the results from her analysis. Markus looked everything over very carefully before sliding the evidence into a new manila envelope. After sealing up the envelope, Markus very gently said, "I know you have vacation time saved up, so I am going to advise you to take some time off and grieve for your friend. The funeral is tomorrow in Boston, and I am sure you and your family would like to attend the service." Katliana bowed her head and finally slowly let the tears fall down her cheeks. Markus stood up and came around the desk to stand before her and grasped both of her shoulders in his hands, "I know you view me as only being your employer, Katliana, but you are invaluable to me here at the lab, and we need you. I know this is hard on you, but your job will be here for you in a month when you return. So again, if I can do anything, please do not hesitate to call me."

Katliana gratefully thanked him and returned to her office to gather everything she needed to work from home. It was only Tuesday, and her mother was not due to show up until Sunday morning. At least their vacations would coincide together, and they could spend more time with one another. Katliana planned to go home and speak with her uncle about going to the funeral together. She knew her uncle was going to be utterly devastated. Her uncle and Kyle had been friends for over twenty years. Kyle was the first to befriend her uncle at the university, and the two had been inseparable ever since. Unfortunately, Katliana had never met Kyle's daughter because she had been murdered before Katliana had arrived in the states. Kyle's wife had died shortly after his daughter's death from a stroke, and Kyle had never remarried or had other children.

Katliana arrived back at her apartment and put her office things away to access them easily from her laptop computer she kept in a tiny nook in her living room. She could not always stay at the office to do her work, or she would be there night and day. She spent a considerable amount of money duplicating the same equipment and software in her home to continue to work on her projects, especially on the nights when she could not sleep. Katliana went over to her laptop and accessed her email to see if the file she had sent from her office had made it safely and had not become corrupted from the transfer. She was infinitely relieved to see that the files and test results were indeed safe. She put the zip file into her laptop and downloaded the encrypted files she had sent so she could safely delete the dangerous information. Katliana hoped there would be no traces of the file transfer that anyone could trace back to her. Now she could readily look at the data from her zip file without having a hard copy on her computer.

Katliana knew the tricks of the trade when it came to protecting information and making sure no one could access her files. If anyone tried to hack her computer or software she created, a virus would corrupt the complete system unless they had her password. Since the password was only in Katliana's mind, there was no way anyone would be able to find out she had transferred or saved the files she created from the information Kyle had sent her.

Finally able to relax, Katliana sat down in her living room recliner to absorb what had happened to Kyle and allow herself time to grieve over the death of her beloved friend. Katliana had few friends and losing someone as close to her as Kyle was beyond overwhelming. Grief, unlike anything she had ever experienced before, suddenly reared its ugly head. Sobs were wrenched from the bottom of her very soul, and giant rivulets of tears began cascading from her eyes. The weight of the pain was so crushing that it felt like her ribs were going to break from the exertion.

Before she was even aware of it, hours had passed, and Katliana found herself curled up on the floor of her living room, watching the sun slowly setting across the dancing shadows of her carpet. Finally, she pulled herself up off the floor and forced herself to make the dreaded phone call to her uncle. She was not surprised to find out her uncle had already been informed about the awful news from his college contacts and had planned to call her in the morning to see if she wanted to attend the services for Kyle. She could tell by her uncle's shaky demeanor on the phone that he was as devastated as she was. They made plans to meet up at the cemetery in Boston, where the services were being held the next day.

Dressing the next morning somberly in a long black calf-length dress with matching heels, Katliana woodenly made her way to the cemetery where the funeral was going to be held. There was a large turnout for the event. Kyle was well known and respected by many of his colleagues even though the university had arranged the funeral on such short notice. Her aunt and uncle were standing close to the casket, so Katliana made her way over to stand next to them.

Once the church's parish priest started the funerary commencement speech, Katliana's uncle drew her close under his protective shoulder. Together, they cried as they watched Kyle being lowered into the ground for his final rest. After everyone had started to walk away, Katliana was the only one left still standing looking into the ground at the casket. She silently prayed for his soul to find everlasting peace as he was finally rejoined with his wife and daughter. Finally, Katliana vowed to Kyle and herself she would find a way to get to the bottom of the mystery about the dead Asian girl, Sue Kwon.

Katliana did not know that she was being carefully watched by the receptionist who had worked for Kyle. Andrea Lambert had been a college student dabbling in the occult for weekend entertainment and had been quickly recruited by other members of Zadikiele's cult when they found out she also worked at the morgue. Andrea had access to various chemicals and poisons which could be used if she needed them. Dariah had ordered Andrea to reveal anything of interest about the dead girl due to be cremated at the morgue where she worked.

When Kyle asked her to mail the overnight envelope to Katliana at the Maynard lab, the receptionist had secretly opened the envelope and peered at the contents inside. She had written down what was in the envelope and the address of the person to whom Kyle had wanted it sent. Andrea did as she was instructed and mailed the envelope to Katliana. Then, Andrea made the mandatory phone call to Dariah to tell him what the envelope contents held and sent them.

Dariah took down the information and ordered Andrea to make sure Kyle was taken care of quickly and told her which poison to put into Kyle's coffee so the evidence would point to a heart attack and be untraceable. Kyle was an elderly man, so no one would suspect his death was anything other than what it seemed. Andrea did as directed and made sure to bring the poisoned coffee to Kyle. It was Kyle's custom to have a cup of coffee in hand if he was working late into the evening. Andrea was instructed to leave right after giving the cup of coffee to Kyle and go home since it was the end of the workday to avoid suspicion. Dariah wanted Katliana under surveillance, so Andrea spent the rest of the night taking surveillance pictures of Katliana. He wanted to know where she worked, lived, and where she ate dinner at night. Andrea took her roll of film to the local convenience store and had the pictures developed so she could overnight them in the mail to Dariah. Finally, she called Dariah to let him know her mission was complete.

Dariah instructed Andrea to come to the morgue the following day, make sure Kyle was dead, and call the police. He told her to dispose of the poisoned coffee cup by putting it in the outdoor trash in the building next door to the morgue so it would not be found. After disposing of the coffee cup, she went upstairs to Kyle's office, wiped down the professor's mouth with a sanitary wipe, and disposed of the contaminated wipe by flushing it down the toilet in the downstairs public bathrooms.

Dariah warned Andrea to be careful not to disturb the body, and if there were any mistakes, it would be Andrea who would pay the price. Andrea was to make sure to inform the police about the envelope Kyle had sent so they would be hot on the trail of Katliana, and any evidence she had been sent would be turned over to them. Dariah felt confident in Andrea's ability to follow orders, so he did not send a backup to ensure it was done correctly.

Andrea had been very vigilant in ensuring everything appeared exactly how Dariah had demanded. Then, after the police were gone and the ambulance carrying Kyle's body had left, Andrea made another call to Dariah to let him know she had done everything she had been instructed to do. Dariah had another task for her, however. He wanted her to continue to keep Katliana under surveillance until otherwise noted.

Andrea sighed heavily in resignation, but she did as she was told. No one would question why she would come to her boss's funeral to pay her last respects. However, Andrea still made sure to stay in the background to not draw any attention to herself. At the same time, she secretly took surveillance photos of Katliana and her family. The only way to get rewarded and move up in Zadikiele's organization was not to screw up and to make sure you followed orders without question. Andrea intended to be an excellent soldier and do as she was told.

After the funeral, Katliana declined the invitation from her aunt and uncle to come and stay with them for a while or to go to dinner. Instead, she told them her mother was due to come for a visit and how she needed to clean her apartment and stock up on groceries. She knew they were apprehensive about her being alone since she looked sleep-deprived and had dark circles under her eyes from grief. Still, Katliana needed to be alone to grieve. Like any wounded animal, she did not want to share her pain. She wanted to get away from everyone and everything and heal in private. Her aunt and uncle looked as grief-stricken as she was, but they respected her wishes and went back home to manage their own grief. At least they had each other to lean on and give comfort to one another.

After leaving the cemetery and getting into her car to complete her errands, Katliana felt like her body and mind were on autopilot. She was functioning, but only barely above the surface. She did not want to think or feel anything. She simply wanted to complete her errands, finish grocery shopping, and be left alone. When she finished putting the groceries away, she wanted to cuddle on her couch with a warm snuggly blanket, block out the world and its many injustices and blank out the agony for a while. Her life had taught her how to block out any pain and focus on basic survival.

The days leading up to her mother's arrival went by in a blur. Katliana could barely manage to get out of bed and brush her teeth, let alone make a meal for herself. She had not predicted how much Kyle's sudden death would affect her. Her tiny little world consisted of so few people she loved and trusted, and losing one of them had completely turned her life and emotions upside down. She could not seem to force herself to care about anything anymore. Nothing excited or motivated her to get up and out of bed and keep living, not even her work. She had vowed on Kyle's grave that she would find the underlying cause of what happened to the poor dead girl, Sue Kwon, but she could not get past the pain that would be generated by going over to her living room office and examining the files. She hoped that if she did not open the files and dig any deeper, the unbearable pain in her chest would begin to subside.

On Sunday morning, Anna silently let herself into Katliana's apartment with the key she kept for emergencies. Anna's brother called her early that morning to tell her he had not heard from Katliana since Tuesday. He was genuinely concerned about her mental health after the death of their friend Kyle Oakes. Anna had been informed about how much Katliana had loved and admired Kyle and how Kyle had acted like a surrogate father to Katliana. Katliana's Uncle knew the only person who would have any potential of bringing Katliana back around was her mother. Anna was at once troubled and concerned for her daughter. Anna knew Katliana had not wanted to be away from her, and the decision Anna had made to go to Washington D.C. to live and work had been tough on Katliana to accept.

Anna crept silently down the hallway to her daughter's room and slowly opened the bedroom door. It was still reasonably early, so she figured Katliana would be asleep, but she was wide awake. Katliana was sitting on the edge of her bed in an almost catatonic state, staring off deep into space. Her hair was a mess, and she looked like she had not slept all week and indeed had lost weight since the last time Anna saw her. Anna was crushed from the inside out to see her daughter in a state of shock. Katliana turned to see who had entered the room. There did not seem to be any recognition in her eyes when she looked directly at her mother.

Anna carefully went over to the bed and sat down next to her daughter. She grabbed Katliana tightly around the shoulders with her left arm and placed Katliana's head next to her chest and gently rocked her back and forth, and murmured comforting words into Katliana's ears. Katliana did not shed any tears, but she slowly came back around and acknowledged her mother sitting there soothing back the tangled hair from Katliana's face. "Mom, when did you get here?" Katliana asked softly as though puzzled her mother was even there. Anna kept rocking her and gently replied, "I arrived this morning and came in here to check on you. Your uncle called me and told me about what happened to your friend Kyle. I am so sorry, baby. I know he meant a great deal to you. No words I can say will take away your pain, but I refuse to let you slowly waste away like this. When was the last time you ate anything?"

Katliana honestly could not remember. She was confused and dazed and could not think properly. Finally, Anna stood up and simply picked Katliana up under her arms and forced Katliana into the bathroom to take a much-needed shower. Katliana did not have enough energy to get undressed, so Anna took over. It was not like

Anna had not seen hundreds of children through various states of shock after surviving the war in Bosnia.

Anna was a tough old bird and knew how to bring shell-shocked children back to life whether they wanted to or not. She was not going to lose her only daughter. So, after Anna bathed and dressed Katliana, she forced Katliana into the recliner in the living room and turned on the television to try and engage Katliana back to life. Next, Anna went into the kitchen to prepare a nourishing meal for them both. Anna was glad to see Katliana had the apartment well stocked with groceries, so it took little effort for Anna to make a good breakfast for her daughter.

Anna could easily see her daughter was in denial and in a deep state of grief over Kyle's death. While it took an immense emotional toll to see her daughter in such a state, Anna watched over like a hawk for the next few days, forcing Katliana to eat, bathe, and rest. She did not leave Katliana alone for one minute. Finally, slowly on the fourth day, Katliana seemed to come out of her daze.

Anna was preparing lunch when she observed Katliana sitting on the couch staring off into space. Anna's heart wrenched in her chest as, suddenly, mountains of tears started, falling down Katliana's cheeks. It was a good sign, Anna thought to herself. As painful as it was to see her daughter so devastated, it meant Katliana was feeling again, even if the pain was overwhelming.

Anna rushed over to sit next to her daughter and pulled her daughter close to her chest. The tears and gut-wrenching sobs seemed like they would never end. Finally, when the tears subsided, Katliana lifted her head, stared into her mother's eyes, and said, "Mom, I am so sorry you came here and had to see me like this. This is unfair to you. I am so sorry." Katliana had managed to say between broken sobs.

Anna knew she had finally broken through the pain and shock of what Katliana had been enduring. The tears from Anna's eyes combined with her daughters in an endless pool of grief for what they had lost and the joy that they had found each other again. "II am not going anywhere, baby girl. I promise never to be far from you. I will always be here for you whenever you need me. Always." Anna hugged her daughter tightly to her and let her daughter finally let go of the deep pain she had kept too tightly bound to her soul.

Anna had investigated the various tour sites Boston had to offer. Every day, Anna would hire a taxi to take them around the city to see the different historical attractions. She kept Katliana busy from sunup to sundown with constant activities. Before long, Katliana returned to a normal state and began to eagerly anticipate the days spent with her mother, actively planning what they would do the next day.

Almost two weeks had passed since Anna had arrived in Boston before Katliana felt like she was back to her old self again. Katliana was so grateful to her mother for being there for her and helping her heal. She did feel a little guilty, though, that her mother had spent half of their joint vacation time trying to help Katliana deal with the unexpected consequences of Kyle's sudden death. Nevertheless, Katliana called her uncle several times to see how he was doing and found some level of comfort in knowing Kyle had finally found peace in being rejoined with his beloved wife and daughter.

It was now headline news that China and the United States were having diplomatic tension over the death of Sue Kwon. China did not believe the story they were being told about how the girl died. China had sent over their emissaries to investigate the young girl's death. However, the Chinese emissaries were becoming increasingly frustrated with the lack of intelligible evidence being revealed and the fact that one of their citizens had already been cremated before they could learn for themselves precisely what had happened.

The dead girl's family was demanding answers, and so was the Chinese government. The Maynard forensics lab where Katliana worked had already been investigated, and Markus had been interviewed extensively. So far, Markus had protected Katliana's involvement and had made sure Katliana's name was left out of the press. In addition, the morgue where Kyle had worked, Emerson hospital, and the Boston police had all been found to have followed correct procedures, so they were not being held liable for any wrongdoing.

# CHAPTER 7

Although it was late in the evening the following Monday, Katliana felt like she was finally up to the task of opening the zip file she had created about Sue Kwon. She had been actively following the news about the unfortunate girl. She felt like she had an obligation to solve the mystery. Katliana was unaware her mother had silently crept up behind her and looked at Katliana's computer screen over Katliana's right shoulder. Katliana had secretly scanned the picture she had taken from the lab, and it was in full view on her computer screen. Katliana was holding up a magnifying glass close to the screen so she could get a better close-up view of the two pinpricks above Sue's left breast.

Upon hearing Anna's horrified gulp of air over her right shoulder, a startled Katliana swung around in her chair and dropped the magnifying glass. "Are you looking at a picture of the dead girl that has been all over the news?" Anna shrieked. Katliana silently nodded and told her mother Kyle had sent over the case file for her to review right before he died and how her boss had ordered her to turn over all the material Kyle had sent her to the Boston Police.

Katliana revealed that she felt compelled to make a duplicate file and find out why Kyle had sent her the case file and tissue samples. "Kyle must have had a serious reason for sending me this case file, Mom. It was essential for him to find out what happened to this girl, and I owe it to him to find the answers. Everything I have uncovered so far leads me to believe the cause of death being reported is wrong, but I still have not figured out exactly how she died. However, what bothers me is that everyone connected to this case is now dead. Both the lead detective and the medical examiner were somehow exposed to the same virus which killed this young girl. Kyle was connected to this by sending me this file, and now he, too, is dead. This whole thing does not make any sense, and I need to find out why my computer cannot find any DNA left from whatever caused the two pinprick marks above this girl's left breast." Katliana calmly pointed with her finger at the enhanced computer screen so her mother could more closely view the marks on the girl's body.

Anna became very agitated and started pacing back and forth across the living room carpet. She stopped suddenly and turned around to face Katliana once again. Anna quietly and adamantly said, "Listen to me very carefully, Katliana. You said everyone who has been involved in investigating this girl's death is now dead. I am sure the detective and medical examiner knew how to protect themselves from encountering bodily fluids. Don't you find how they both died strangely? This information concerns me, Katliana. I agree with you that something is wrong here.

If this girl's death is causing tension between the U.S. and China, you are in way over your head. Although Kyle may have wanted you to look at this case file, he most certainly would not have wanted you to risk your life to find the answers. My employer collaborates very closely with the American president, and he will know how to help us. It is only a matter of time before your name gets mentioned somehow, and you end up entangled or imprisoned in this mess. We are leaving right now! Pack your things, Katliana. We are going to Washington D.C., and we are going to try and find out what happened to this girl, but I will not allow you to endanger your life!"

Anna snatched the zip file from Katliana's laptop computer so quickly Katliana was momentarily stunned into silence before she retorted, "Mom, no one knows I made a copy of the file. I removed every single trace leading back to me. Trust me, no one knows I have this information, so please do not worry. Everything will be fine. Markus will not reveal that the package was sent to me. He has kept the information to himself, and he will protect me." Anna was quick to reply, "Didn't you say your boss ordered you to turn everything over to him? How did he even know Kyle had sent a package to you?" Anna demanded to know. Katliana had forgotten that Kyle's receptionist had let the police know she had mailed out the packet for Kyle. The receptionist gave the police Katliana's work information and how to find her.

Katliana paled. Her mother was right. It was only a matter of time before the Chinese government or American government agencies could track her down. Their agents would be relentless in garnering any information she could potentially reveal. If they somehow found out she had made a duplicate case file, they would think she was somehow involved. They would believe she was trying to cover up either the cause of the girl's death or she was somehow involved in causing it. These terrifying thoughts propelled Katliana into action quickly. She and her mother packed full suitcases and locked the apartment, but not before Katliana grabbed her laptop and retrieved the photographs as well as the zip file she created from her mother and secured them secretly inside her suitcase.

The women put their suitcases into Anna's car and sped off quickly to reach Washington D.C. as fast as possible without drawing attention to themselves. Andrea was not far behind them and always kept Anna's car in full view since she was still under orders to keep Katliana under surveillance. She had no idea where Anna and Katliana were headed, but she knew they would not have loaded the car with full suitcases if they were not planning to stay somewhere for a while.

Andrea called Dariah from her cell phone and told him she was following Katliana. There was another passenger in the car who was driving. Andrea gave Dariah the license plate number and told him the vehicle was licensed for Washington D.C. Dariah quickly learned that the woman traveling with Katliana lived at the same address as Jakiele. Although Jakiele had not been at his home, Dariah had managed to sneak into Jakiele's estate multiple times. Dariah had given the secret bypass codes to the master bedroom and main gates to Zadikiele. Dariah had not been able to break the codes to the basement or garage yet, but he was diligently working on it.

Unbeknownst to Dariah, every time during the last two weeks when Jakiele had left to go to the airport to take skydiving lessons, Zadikiele would sneak into Jakiele's house and snoop around. Zadikiele knew Jakiele's staff had been put on their respective vacations from Dariah's surveillance reports, so he was not worried about anyone coming home unexpectedly and finding him. In Jakiele's office, he noticed that new home security equipment was lying around waiting to be installed. He realized Jakiele must be planning to install them sometime in the future, so he knew he needed to act quickly to set up his reconnaissance equipment in the house before Jakiele changed codes or updated anything else.

Zadikiele had managed to bypass the code to Jakiele's bedroom once Dariah had successfully broken the code. He placed a secret video camera capable of panning around the room at any sign of movement. It was well hidden behind the left corner of the sizeable six-drawer dresser, which sat directly across the room from the closet. Still, it could give a full view of the closet and the bedroom area. Zadikiele had also put two other cameras in the house. One was found behind a large living room picture, and the other was in the kitchen area behind one of the glass cabinets. He did not want to put too many recording devices in the house for fear that one of the devices might be detected, so he only placed them in critical areas.

It was not as though Jakiele was doing anything unusual except for buying the house and hiring servants, but Zadikiele believed in being thorough. He wanted to keep close tabs on Jakiele and what he did for his daily routines. Dariah gave daily reports on what Jakiele was up to since Zadikiele planned on hunting down the creature that had taken the dead girl's life. His father would want to question it and use the vampire for other nefarious tasks. Zadikiele thought he had tied up as many loose ends in Maynard and Boston as possible, but he failed. His father was not too happy about this girl's death becoming headline news across the country. If any angels in the area had the same suspicions as he did, they would know a vampire had somehow survived and killed a human. They would track it down and kill it without remorse.

Dariah brought Zadikiele entirely up to speed about what had happened in Boston once Zadikiele had returned to Washington D.C. Andrea had sent pictures of Katliana and Anna to Dariah from her phone so that Dariah would know what they both looked like. After Dariah and Zadikiele reviewed the photos, Zadikiele recognized the older woman as Jakiele's housekeeper, but he did not know the young woman traveling with her. Zadikiele swore softly under his breath. Somehow, these women knew of the dead girl and were connected to Jakiele. This was not good. If Jakiele were somehow informed of anything important these women might know about the dead girl, it would mean Michael and Gabriel would become informed as well. It was a good thing he had installed the cameras. At least he would be notified if either of the women revealed anything about the dead girl to Jakiele.

Zadikiele ordered a meeting between himself, Latkia, and Dariah. The three of them started forming plans to figure out how best to go ahead. Zadikiele informed them he had installed the new monitoring equipment in Jakiele's house earlier. They should be able to monitor activity in the house for now. Latkia and Dariah were tied to Zadikiele, so if he failed in his mission, the fallen angels would believe Latkia and Dariah failed as well, and all three would be punished as one. Latkia and Dariah had as much at stake as Zadikiele did in solving this problem.

Latkia was the first to speak, "I do not understand what the big deal is about this dead girl. When we were Nephilim, we all knew that we would create vampires if we shared our blood with a human and transmitted our virus. If it is truly a vampire who killed her, why did the creature not simply take the blood needed for sustenance and use his skills to block out the memories of the event? Not to mention that God made sure to wipe out the entire population on Earth of vampires and Nephilim. Only Noah and his family were chosen to live because they had not been infected with the virus. We are chasing shadows, and we do not have enough facts to know what is happening here. Isn't it possible this girl simply was bitten by an animal and had a bad reaction and died?"

Dariah did not add his thoughts to the conversation. Instead, Dariah stayed quiet with arms across his chest, looked directly at Zadikiele, and awaited orders. Latkia imitated Dariah by folding his arms across his chest after speaking and waited for Zadikiele to form his thoughts. "I do not have any idea what we are dealing with here." Zadikiele growled at both of them, "But I know we are under orders from Remiel to find out. Latkia, I expect you to make sure Rochelle keeps Jakiele as distracted as possible and make sure she is doing what she is told. She is not to be touched by anyone or harassed while I am gone. Make sure she does not know I have left town. If she fails, kill her and her brat. Dariah, I expect you to keep a constant eye on Jakiele and watch the cameras I installed this morning. Both of you are to report to me if anything happens that I need to know about. Are we clear?"

Zadikiele's tone was clipped and angry because he was anxious to begin the hunt for the creature, causing them so much trouble. Latkia and Dariah exchanged a silent look, and both nodded their assent to Zadikiele. Then, Zadikiele stormed out of the room and went to his bedroom to pack a change of clothes and travel essentials. Zadikiele's lover, Larissa, walked silently into the room, and a frown quickly traveled across her features when she realized Zadikiele was planning on leaving again so soon after he had so recently returned.

Larissa had been the one charged with the responsibility of taking care of Rochelle's son and making sure the little boy's needs were met. She hated the task and only did what she was told to keep

Zadikiele happy with her. Larissa detested kids and their neediness. She kept the boy at arm's length and did not give him any attention or affection unless she had to. The boy was held in an apartment with a nanny in the city, close to Rochelle's for convenience.

Larissa deeply resented Rochelle for having any of Zadikiele's attention for the long months it had taken to get Rochelle up to Zadikiele's very exacting sexual standards. Zadikiele had completely ignored Larissa until he was ready to resume their relationship. Although when he finally came back around, Larissa was more than eager to prove to him she would freely please him in whatever way he wanted, while Rochelle had to be forced.

Larissa walked up behind Zadikiele, wrapped her arms around Zadikiele's waist, and laid her left cheek gently against his back. Larissa softly purred, "Where are you going, gorgeous? You only got back this morning, and I have missed your touch amongst other things." Zadikiele shrugged her off him roughly and turned around to face Larissa. Zadikiele angrily shouted at her, "It is none of your business where I am going. You are here to see to my needs and follow orders. So, if this is a problem for you, get the hell out and do not come back."

Larissa was hurt and stunned and instantly became violently angry. "Do I suddenly mean so little to you? Or is the real reason you are such an ass is you are missing your little bitch Rochelle, and you would rather have her?" She hissed at Zadikiele. Zadikiele had mixed feelings about Rochelle and had no intention of revealing anything about how he felt about her to Larissa. He was not supposed to feel anything for Rochelle, yet he did.

He could not explain it to himself and felt no remorse in not explaining himself to a woman like Larissa. Zadikiele shouted back at her, "I have to leave town to take care of something, Larissa! We all have jobs to do, and if I somehow favored Rochelle over you, deal with it! You are not forced to be here. If you do not like how things are, leave! It is not like I cannot replace whores like you in a minute. There is always someone willing to take your place, and I suggest you never forget it! Now, get the hell out of my room and do what you were told, or I will find someone who will."

Larissa was blindingly furious as she stormed out of Zadikiele's room. She would wait until Zadikiele left. Larissa was patient and would wait until the right time and conduct the plans she had been working on for some time. She was convinced Rochelle was to blame for taking Zadikiele's attention from her. It was Rochelle who needed to be disposed of. She had to make it look like an accident so Zadikiele would never suspect she was behind it.

Latkia had often looked after Larissa whenever Zadikiele was not around. While Latkia was strong and fierce-looking, he was not always as aware as he should be of his surroundings. He depended too much on those he trained to do the dirty work while he got lazy and enjoyed the women's attention in the compound. He could be swayed most easily to leave his post if a naked woman and a bottle of Vodka were being offered, and he could be counted on to enjoy both for hours at a time.

Zadikiele rushed out of the compound a few minutes later without saying goodbye to Larissa. Larissa watched Zadikiele go up the stairs and out the hatch door without looking back at her once to see how she was feeling. This angered Larissa even more. She flounced herself off the living room couch and began walking furiously down the hallway to her room to gather her things.

Larissa had no intention of being somewhere where she was not wanted or valued. She was due to be at Rochelle's son's apartment in an hour to check in on the boy anyway. Latkia was supposed to escort Rochelle to the hotel room for her weekly liaison with Jakiele, which had already been predetermined on Rochelle's last visit to Jakiele. So, no one would question why Larissa was leaving the compound since everyone knew what the plan for the night was.

Latkia had already brought the van around to the compound's front and had left the keys in the ignition. After gathering her things in a small knapsack, Larissa walked out to the front porch to talk directly with Latkia, who was busy instructing one of the new guards stationed outside where the best places were to hide to watch out for trespassers and remain unseen. She was standing there alone until her friend Noella came out of the house to stand beside her. A plan was beginning to form in Larissa's mind on distracting Latkia and keeping him entertained for the evening.

Latkia watched Larissa glide seductively toward him across the yard until she stood within one inch of him and placed her lips within a hair's breadth of his left ear and whispered to him, "You do not need to escort me tonight to Rochelle's place. I will make sure Rochelle gets to the hotel on time and her visit with her son goes well. I will come right back as soon as I drop Rochelle off at her apartment, and you, my friend, can enjoy the lovely Noella for the evening."

Larissa motioned for her new friend Noella to come outside and come over to where Larissa and Latkia were. Noella was new to their little group, wanted to shore up her position, and felt Latkia was an excellent steppingstone toward her goals. Noella had all the attributes Latkia liked. Shapely legs, no brains, long blond silky hair, big breasts, and she carried a tall bottle of Vodka in her hands.

Latkia could not keep his eyes off Noella, and it was clear he was excited at the prospect of breaking in a recruit he had not slept with yet. He motioned for his lead yard captain to come over and finish the training of the newest guard. Latkia led Noella back into the courtyard and through the house without a backward glance at Larissa.

Larissa smirked in satisfaction. Demon or man, they were all the same. Give them what they wanted, and they were satisfied. A woman simply had to figure out what made them tick and fulfill their desires. So, Larissa was not surprised Zadikiele had cast her aside. Men had been throwing her away from her whole life. What made her angry was how Zadikiele thought he could do what he wanted to her and get away with it without consequence. She was determined to prove to Zadikiele that a woman scorned was something to fear, and he would think twice before disregarding another woman and treating them like trash.

Larissa arrived at the apartment complex at the appointed hour. She retrieved Rochelle's son to take him to the prearranged visit with Rochelle. However, not before she slit the throat of the nanny who had been in charge of watching the little boy. Larissa was careful not to let the little boy see what she had done to the nanny so he would not make a fuss. Larissa did not want to leave behind any witnesses to her plans. Rochelle brought the little boy to Rochelle's apartment and stood by soundlessly next to the front door to watch them.

Rochelle and her son spent the next hour playing on the floor with Lego blocks and watching cartoons in front of the TV. Rochelle did not pay any attention to what Larissa took out of her knapsack as she stood next to the apartment's front door. Larissa had stealthily grabbed a can of pepper spray out of her bag and walked over to where Rochelle and her son were seated on the floor in the living room and lightly sprayed Rochelle right in the eyes with the pepper spray. It would hurt like hell, but it would not cause any permanent damage. While Rochelle lay huddled on the floor screaming in pain, Larissa gathered up Rochelle's son. She tied him to the bed in the apartment's only bedroom. She mercilessly duct-taped his little mouth shut and made sure his arms and feet were tightly bound. The boy stared at her in wide-eyed horror and never made a sound. He was too terrified and did not understand what was going on.

Larissa came back into the living room, slapped Rochelle hard across the face, and told Rochelle that if she did not stop screaming, she would slit her throat and kill her son. Rochelle knew Zadikiele's followers would do what they threatened to do. Even though the pain in her eyes hurt unbearably, she stopped screaming immediately. Rochelle knew Larissa was not making idle threats, and even though her eyes were screaming in pain and her throat felt choked, Rochelle sat back up off the floor and tried to remain calm. Larissa wanted answers to where Zadikiele had fled, and she felt that Rochelle would know. If Rochelle did not provide information about Zadikiele, Larissa would continue with her previously formed plan and kill her and her son. It did not matter to Larissa anymore one way or the other. She planned on torturing Rochelle for pure enjoyment.

It had been over a week since Jakiele had last seen Rochelle, and he was looking forward to their weekly liaison. Anna and Jacob had now been gone for two weeks, and Jakiele was feeling more restless than ever, even though he had tried taking up skydiving. He enjoyed the sport for what it was, but it was different from spreading his wings and flying across the universe. While his servants were away, Jakiele planned to make his house extremely easy for the demons to access. Jakiele suspected the demons in the area were watching him. So, he wanted to make it simple for them to get into the house to identify them and find out where they were in the city.

Angels could easily detect their scent, follow them back to their lairs, dispatch them quickly, and send them straight to the Underworld. Since his housekeeper and driver were on vacation, now was the time to get rid of any snooping around without anyone getting hurt who might get in the way. He knew at least two demons had been in his house recently and had been successful in bypassing at least two of his codes. He suspected at least one of them was his longtime nemesis Zadikiele, Remiel's son.

However, he was becoming preoccupied with worrying about what kept Rochelle from arriving at the hotel. It was now 6 PM, and Rochelle was due to be at the hotel at 5:30 PM. Rochelle was always very punctual. Something was very wrong. He could sense it. He called the escort service, and the answering service on the other end of the phone had no idea what could be keeping Rochelle.

They agreed to call and speak to the madam and see if she knew what could be keeping her, and they would get back to Jakiele as soon as they heard anything. Jakiele knew the agency office was near the hotel, so he grabbed his hotel key card off the end table where he had thrown it earlier and quickly walked the few blocks from the hotel to the small building the madam owned. The madam had labeled the signage on the business as a "Temp" service to avoid detection by the police. He knew the business was closed and used an answering service, but he needed to find the address of where Rochelle lived and find out if she was okay.

Jakiele studied the building from the outside for several minutes before finding they did not use a security system. He went around to the back of the building, broke the glass on the back door, and let himself in. The building was tiny and had only two offices. He assumed the head office belonged to the madam herself, so he went into that office first. There was a large desk, a telephone, and nothing except a locked file cabinet. It did not take much work for him to be able to shimmy open the locked cabinet with the pocketknife he had in his back pocket. He found Rochelle's file and quickly scanned the contents for her address. Her address listed an apartment complex located a few miles from the hotel. Jakiele ran back to the hotel and asked the front desk clerk to bring his car. The parking valet brought Jakiele's car around to the front of the hotel, and he quickly sped off in the direction of the apartment complex.

The apartment complex was a dilapidated structure with three stories and was in a rundown section of the city. Small children ran around everywhere while the adults casually watched them from their small balconies outside their apartments. Rochelle lived in apartment 301 on the third floor. The apartment complex was divided into three sections by long metal stairways, which led to the various levels.

Jake went up the first long metal stairway and stood in front of the battered front door, signaling he had found Rochelle's apartment. He listened quietly for a few seconds before noticing muffled screams within the apartment with his advanced hearing. Jakiele stood back from the door and kicked the door in with one loud crash of his foot. What he saw when he entered the apartment made his blood freeze. He at once took an offensive stance, ready to fight.

As soon as the door burst open and Larissa could see Jakiele standing there, she moved even closer to Rochelle. Larissa looked away from Jakiele and resumed staring viciously down at Rochelle. Larissa knew Jakiele had kicked the door in, but she was too intent on her lust for revenge to care. Jakiele took in the scene in an instant.

Rochelle was tied up in a seated position on the living room floor. At the same time, Larissa leaned over her, brandishing a knife in front of Rochelle's left pupil as though she was about ready to plunge the knife right through Rochelle's eye. The blade's tip was centimeters away from seriously injuring Rochelle when Jakiele leaped into action so quickly that Larissa did not have time to respond. Jakiele grabbed the front of Larissa's blouse and sent Larissa flying across the room with one hand to land unconscious on the kitchen floor. Jakiele angrily strode across the living room into the kitchen and took the knife from Larissa's right hand that she was still holding onto tightly in a death grip.

Larissa's deadly intention to kill Rochelle had been made clear. Jakiele placed his left hand on Larissa's forehead and began to read Larissa's memories. He found out what he needed to know about Zadikiele and his compound of Satan worshippers and what Larissa's intentions had been toward Rochelle and her son. Larissa had become consumed with jealousy and hate for Rochelle and her little boy.

He erased Larissa's memories and planted her memory of partying too hard the night before. She would find herself with one heck of a hangover the next day when the police found her dumped outside of their headquarters. Larissa would have no memory of Rochelle, Zadikiele, or anyone else involved in this mess. Jakiele now knew for sure Zadikiele was in the area and was the puppet master in this rag-tag group of fools. Jakiele also saw in Larissa's memories who Zadikiele's second lieutenants were. Latkia and Dariah. These two were not meant to be trifled with any more than Zadikiele was. They were all direct descendants of the fallen angels. Jakiele had to be careful to manage this situation quickly and quietly.

Rochelle did not know Jakiele had broken in her door because she could not see anything. Jakiele walked back into Rochelle's living room and started to untie her tightly woven bonds on her wrists gently. Rochelle started to panic because she did not know who was touching her. Jakiele used his softest voice when he spoke gently into her ear, "It is me. Jakiele. The woman who attacked has been taken care of. When you did not show up at the hotel, I became worried, and I tracked you down to make sure you were okay." Rochelle calmed down, threw her arms around Jakiele, and sobbed against his chest while he untied the thick ropes holding her feet prisoner.

As soon as Rochelle was free, she jumped up and blindly stumbled around before she found the bedroom door where Larissa had taken her son and opened it in a sudden panic to get to her boy quickly. Rochelle ran as fast as she could into the room where her son had been held prisoner and rushed around blindly, trying to feel where she was going. She needed to release him quickly from his bonds as she knew her boy was terrified tremendously. Her eyes were in terrible shape from the pepper spray, but it did not stop the tears from falling helplessly down her bruised cheeks. Jakiele helped her quickly to untie the boy and placed him gently in Rochelle's arms as she slid down to the floor next to the bed in abject relief once she realized her boy was unharmed but scared.

Rochelle held her little boy close to her and refused to relinquish him from her arms while Jakiele tried to assess Rochelle's wounds. Finally, he told her to stay where he was so he could get rid of Larissa. Jakiele gathered up Larissa's limp body and threw her in the trunk of his car after he had gone down to the parking lot and repositioned the car to be as close to the apartment as possible to avoid anyone seeing what he was doing. After the ugly deed was done of depositing Larissa in front of the police station, Jakiele raced back to the apartment and found Rochelle had stayed exactly where he told her. He picked both her and her little boy up into his massive arms and carried them both out to his car. Jakiele took them both to the nearest hospital. When he told the hospital staff his friend had been attacked in her apartment by an unknown assailant, they quickly went into action to make sure both mother and son were taken care of.

Jakiele showed the hospital admission staff his government identification and informed them he would pay any hospital bills resulting from Rochelle's injuries. If possible, they responded even quicker by ensuring Rochelle was put into a private room with an extra bed for her son. When Jakiele was finally allowed into the room to see them for himself, he was saddened to see the thick bandages covering Rochelle's eyes and the many bandages now covering the minor inflicted knife wounds on her arms and chest. Rochelle sensed his presence as he entered the room and started to panic by saying hysterically, "Jake, is my son okay? I cannot see anything! Please tell me he is okay!"

Jakiele walked over to her, grasped her left hand in both of his, and murmured very softly to her, "He is fine, Rochelle. Your child is in bed next to you, sleeping very soundly. The hospital gave him a mild sedative to keep him calm until they could take the bandages off your eyes. I will stay here with you and keep you both safe. I know who you are, Rochelle, and what you had to go through with Zadikiele and Larissa. I understand why you did what you did. Unfortunately, I cannot tell you how I found this information due to my government clearance. I am so sorry one of my enemies made you and your family suffer. I will make sure you are never at their mercy ever again. You are courageous to go through what you did to keep your son safe."

Rochelle cried out her anger and frustration in huge gulping sobs of pain, but she gratefully thanked him and finally fell into a deep sleep. Once he knew she was deeply asleep, he placed his left hand over her forehead and closed his eyes to read her memories. Visions of the abuse Zadikiele put her through, as well as images of himself being pleasured by her flashed before his eyes in rapid succession.

Reaching further back into her memories, Jakiele saw her husband Steve and watched how he had been brutally killed. Visions of where they had lived in her quaint little rental house on the outskirts of Washington D.C. and the happy life she once had filled him with anger because he had not asked enough questions when he sensed she was more than a prostitute working for an escort service. His instincts had told him more was to the story. Still, he was too interested in using her like everyone else had to satisfy his manly desires. Jakiele felt nothing but absolute disgust for himself and how he and everyone else had treated her.

At least he could do something about it now. He made calls to his contacts, and within minutes, Rochelle had her room surrounded by the best security guards the government had to offer. Jakiele had trained Secret Service agents and former Military personnel for years. They had all looked up to him with the utmost respect and had offered their services multiple times should a need ever arise. Rochelle was in dire need, and Jakiele was relieved so many had shown up on such short notice.

There were three men stationed in her room and three outside her door. Two on each end of the wing leading into her hospital wing and two stationed outside the elevator. The hospital staff was growing a little alarmed at the number of armed guards, but they were very accommodating. All the men who answered Jakiele's summons were armed to the teeth. A former marine Jakiele trusted implicitly, named John Howard, came forward to shake Jakiele's hand after he had made sure all the men who came had been placed in their proper positions.

"I need you to take Rochelle and her son to a safe house at this address and stay with her until I know for sure she is safe." Jakiele handed John a piece of paper with the safe house address, which John quickly memorized. John took a lighter out of his pocket and set the piece of paper on fire to destroy it. Jakiele continued with, "She is sleeping for now, and so is her boy. As soon as they wake, give her my business card so she knows she can trust you. Do not underestimate my enemies. They will kill her, her son, and any of you on sight without hesitation. Once you are at the safe house and your men are in place, I will tell you where the money is hidden in the house. Then, I will get the necessary passports to get her safely out of the country into a safe house I keep in England. Make sure no one follows or traces your movements in any way. Do you understand what I am asking of you and how dangerous this mission is?" Jakiele waited apprehensively for John to respond. He knew this favor would be hazardous to all who agreed to undertake it.

John had been on covert missions for the government unsanctioned by the government. This mission would be simple in comparison, but he would never take what Jakiele had told him lightly. He shook Jakiele's hand again and simply nodded his head. Jakiele knew Rochelle was safe for the moment. Jakiele took off in the direction of the Washington Post where Steve Windham had once worked. He had gleaned all he could about Steve from Rochelle's memories. Jakiele very stealthily crept from floor to floor of the Washington Post headquarters, trying to blend in and not be noticed. Everyone was so busy bustling around following up on news stories or leaving work for the day that no one paid attention to him. He found Steve's office quickly by reading the elevator listings of all the different departments and on what floor their offices were located. Steve's office was on the fifth floor.

After stepping off the elevator on the fifth floor, finding Steve's office was not hard to find. Likewise, the employees for this section of the newspaper had already gone home for the day. Jakiele walked over to the glass door bearing Steve's name and title on it and slowly opened the door. He was surprised to find it unlocked. On Steve's desk was a plain brown package. The package had Steve's work address, but the return address had Steve's home address on it.

Curious, Jakiele picked up the package and found it was weighty. He grabbed a letter opener from Steve's desk and opened the box. Inside was Steve's voice recorder. Hearing the elevator running, which signaled someone was coming up, Jakiele quickly snatched up the recorder. Jakiele exited Steve's office door quietly and ran across the vast area of small cubicles. He quickly hid behind a large potted plant located to the left of the elevator door. Jakiele could have turned invisible if he chose, but to do so cost him considerable energy that he did not have to spend at the moment.

A young woman walked out of the elevator. She quickly walked over to a small cubicle to retrieve the purse she had inadvertently left behind. Jakiele watched her closely as she stepped back into the elevator and left. Jakiele let out a massive sigh of relief. He wanted to get out of there quickly and get back to his house to see what information the voice recorder held. He did not need the complications of being caught stealing this recorder from Steve's office.

Jakiele managed to get back to his car without anyone noticing him and sped off into the night to get back to his house. Once he pulled up to his wrought iron front gates and punched in the code, he started to relax. He had not realized how keyed up he had gotten from this whole ordeal. John Howard knew Jakiele's number and would call if there were any problems, and the hospital staff had been directed to do the same. He knew Rochelle would be asleep for a couple of hours before John moved her and her son to the safe house.

After pulling up to the garage, Jakiele noticed Anna's car in the driveway. He knew she had taken it to see her daughter in Boston, so why was Anna back? Was something wrong? Jakiele quickly parked his car and gathered up the voice recorder on the passenger seat. Next, Jakiele exited the garage and went through the outer door to set the alarm on the garage before walking across the small clearing between the garage and the outside kitchen entrance to enter the code to open the kitchen door. The smell of cookies and pot roast assailed his senses, but not before he locked eyes with the most beautiful woman he had ever seen. Katliana was seated on a small stool next to the kitchen island, watching her mother chop up vegetables. Katliana looked up when Jakiele opened the kitchen door. However, Jakiele seemed solely focused on Katliana when he strode purposefully into the room to stand next to her while looking down into her eyes. They simply stared at each other for several long moments before Anna loudly cleared her throat in embarrassment and gruffly said, "Master Jake, I would like to introduce my daughter Katliana. Katliana, this is my employer, Jake Smith.

# CHAPTER 8

Neither Katliana nor Jakiele could seem to stop staring at each other. It was as though they had become completely mesmerized by each other simultaneously. Jakiele snapped out of it first and shook his head slightly as though trying to shake out the cobwebs from his suddenly-addled brain. Katliana felt herself blushing an alarming shade of red up from the tips of her toes to the roots of her hair.

Katliana was embarrassed at being caught staring intently at her mother's employer. Katliana shyly dropped her eyes quickly and stared at her shoes instead. After a moment of awkward silence, she somehow managed to muster the courage to raise her emerald-colored eyes and stare into Jakiele's sapphire-inspired blue ones. This was not going to be easy since she suddenly found her mouth so dry, she could not speak or form a coherent thought. Finally, with wobbly knees shaking, she stood up to introduce herself and shake Jakiele's hand in a proper greeting.

Upon standing, Katliana realized how tall Jakiele was. He had to be well over six feet tall since the top of her head barely reached his shoulder. However, Katliana considered herself very tall at 5 feet, 8 inches. She had to bend her head back to be able to look directly into his impressive eyes framed by long dark silky lashes. His eyebrows were the same ebony color as his thick black hair.

She suddenly had the wildest urge to run her fingers through the luxurious strands to see if the strands were as soft as they looked. He also had the most beautiful scent surrounding him. It was soothing and sexy at the same time. If she had to guess what he smelled like, she would have said soft meadows after a good morning rain with a subtle hint of roses.

Mortified by her errant thoughts, Katliana cleared her throat to introduce herself, "It is so nice to meet you, Mr. Smith. My mother has nothing but wonderful things to say about you. I hope our untimely arrival at your home will not be an inconvenience. I can always stay at a hotel nearby if it is any trouble." Katliana extended her right hand for a handshake. Jakiele once again found himself drowning in Katliana's eyes as she spoke. She had acquired a slight Boston accent. She blended it with the Bosnian accent she had grown up with, which Jakiele found utterly charming.

Jakiele suddenly found himself at a loss for words as he studied her. Katliana was prettier than she had seemed in the picture he had seen on the counter. Her eyes reminded him of the forest after a light mist. Dark eyelashes framed her gorgeous green eyes. She had a fragile, heart-shaped face. Jakiele suddenly had an overwhelming urge to cup her face in his large hands and pull her close to him so he could inhale her scent and taste her forbidden treasures.

It took Jakiele a moment to regain his senses and manners as well. Jakiele set the voice recorder down on the kitchen counter and completely forgot about it as he silently studied Katliana. He went to clasp Katliana's right hand with his, and the moment they touched, it was like an electrical current went through them both. It shocked both to the core, and they withdrew quickly from each other. They both felt the current and were alarmed by the shock of the electrical jolt.

An awful sulfuric scent began slowly permeating Jakiele's dazed senses. It was the unmistakable putrid scent of a demon. Jakiele turned his head slightly to the right and left to see which way the scent was more pungent. This was not good. Letting the women stay in the house put them in mortal danger because if one of them came upon a demon, they would not know what it was or be able to defend themselves.

"My apologies, ladies. The house has been broken into a couple of times since Anna and Caleb left to go on their vacations. I do not feel it would be safe for you until I update my security systems. Perhaps staying at a hotel would be better. Please excuse me, I must take care of urgent business which involves a close friend of mine, and I would prefer to remain undisturbed for the next few hours." Jakiele said it in a tone that indicated he would brook no argument from the women. Jakiele started to retreat from the kitchen to his office when Anna suddenly came around the kitchen corner and grasped Jakiele by the left forearm to halt his progress. Anna motioned for Jakiele to follow her down the hall out of earshot of Katliana, who was still standing in the kitchen in utter mortification of being dismissed so summarily by Jakiele.

"Master Jake. My most sincere apologies for bringing my daughter to your home without first having your permission. I would not have done so without an excellent reason. Please listen to what I have to say, and if you still want us to stay in a hotel until your security is up to date, we will leave tonight. My daughter is in grave danger, and we need your help. Are you aware of what is going on with the United States and China? About the dead Chinese girl found at the Assabet Animal Preserve?" Anna waited pensively for Jakiele to respond. Anna worriedly rubbed her hands together on her apron in agitation.

"Yes, of course, I am aware, Anna," Jakiele replied tersely. "The president of the United States has invited the Chinese Ambassador to come to America to work together collectively. However, the President wishes to remain at Camp David to keep the joint summit as secretive as possible and keep the media out of the investigation. The summit was negotiated to ease the tension between the two countries. The Chinese Ambassador will be here in one week. What does any of this have to do with your daughter?" Anna's interruption perturbed Jakiele, but he was also starting to become alarmed by Anna's evident agitation over the matter.

Anna took a deep breath to calm herself the best she could and went on to explain how Katliana was sent a DNA case file from Kyle Oakes at her office in Boston. Anna went into extensive detail about what she had learned about the suspicious deaths of everyone who had come into contact with this case. Anna also included in her explanation the details about what she had seen for herself on Katliana's computer screen and why they were both so afraid they had somehow stumbled onto something which could potentially bring them both harm. Unfortunately, Anna's statements had come out in a rush of terror for her daughter. Jakiele was having trouble disseminating what Anna was revealing about Katliana's involvement.

"I understand most of what you have told me, Anna, although I am a little vague on some of the details you provided. However, I cannot say you and your daughter would be safe here in good conscience. I have many enemies you do not know about, and they would not hesitate to hurt you or your daughter to get to me. I can try and find someone who can help your daughter try to resolve this case better than I can, but for now, I have very pressing matters I need to address." Jakiele again tried to walk away, but Anna again put a restraining hand on his arm.

"Master Jake, please do not forget I know who and what you are! There is not anyone on this planet I would trust my daughter's safety with more. Do you believe we would be safer out there?" Anna waved her arm, indicating the outside world. "I know we are better off taking our chances here with you.

Furthermore, I know exactly who your enemies are! So, trust me when I say we will do everything you tell us to do, and we will not take any unnecessary risks. We will do anything you ask. So please let us stay." Anna added the last request with a catch in her voice as though trying not to cry as she begged him to look after her and her daughter with a sorrowful, worried look on her face. She was terrified and this alarmed Jakiele more than anything else could have come from this stoic woman who rarely, if ever, showed any emotion.

Jakiele knew it took everything Anna had to make such a request of him, and he was moved by how much she loved her daughter and wanted to protect her. He was incredibly touched that Anna was putting so much faith in his ability to protect them. He also knew why he hesitated to consent to such a request. Katliana could profoundly affect his senses, and she could easily distract him from appropriately protecting her and her mother. He was not sure he would be able to hide his powerful attraction to her. It was extremely risky for her daughter to be in his presence. He wanted to devour her with lust on sight. He had barely managed to control himself while they had all been in the kitchen. His survival instincts and not falling prey to Katliana's charms would put his considerable resistance to the test to not succumb to her many temptations.

Jakiele could not say no to Anna. How could he? She was a survivor of some of the worst atrocities known to man. Michael had been able to glean only vague details of her past, but it was enough to make Jakiele's stomach turn. Very softly, Jakiele answered her, "Okay, Anna. I will see what I can do to help.

Nevertheless, you must agree to follow my instructions implicitly and without question. You and your daughter are not to go outside of the house at all. I must get new security set up, and I will do so in the morning.

In the meantime, Katliana is to stay in the guest bedroom so I can keep a close eye on her. You should also remain in the house. You can use my room if you like. I will sleep on the couch. I will call Caleb to see if he can return early from his vacation. Can you please see that your daughter gets settled in while I finish the work I need to take care of?" Jakiele looked directly into Anna's eyes to make sure she understood what he had dictated.

Anna rushed toward him in a rush of relief, and it was the first time she had ever hugged him. She gave him such a bear hug of affection it almost toppled him over, and he had a tough time taking a breath of air. Jakiele chuckled softly and hugged her back. When Anna stood back from him a moment later, he could see there were genuine tears in her eyes. "Thank you! I do not know how I can thank you!" Anna gratefully sobbed.

"You have given me thanks enough just by being who you are, Anna. I could, however, be talked into enjoying the delicious meal I had smelled earlier. Would you please let me know when dinner is ready and bring it into the office for me?" Anna's smile quickly spread across her face as she dashed out of the hallway to head back into the kitchen to finish preparing the evening meal and to tell her daughter the good news. Anna quickly reassured Katliana that Jakiele had initially refused to let them stay for a good reason. Anna explained to Katliana that it had to do with keeping them safe until Jakiele could care for the security system. Katliana suspected Jakiele was not telling them the whole truth, but she did not reveal her thoughts on the matter to her mother.

While dinner was cooking, Anna showed Katliana to the guest bedroom where she would be staying and helped her unpack. After being shown around the house, Katliana thought the place could use a woman's touch. Everything seemed so sterile, white, and clean, as though it had not ever been lived in. Katliana was told not ever to try to enter the basement or Jakiele's bedroom as they were off-limits and were protected by security codes. Katliana thought this bit of information was bizarre but did not comment on it. Her bedroom, however, was decorated in lovely tones of gold, rose, and emerald green. A large four-poster bed dominated the room with a beautiful bedspread of the same colors. The bathroom adjoining the room was stocked entirely with large white fluffy towels, various exotic soaps, and lotions. It boasted an exquisite, deeply sunken tub.

It was as though the room had been decorated just for her. It was soothing, comforting, and styled to suit her tastes perfectly. How odd, she thought, the one room in the house with any personality at all was going to be hers for the next two weeks. She loved the deep luxurious cream-colored carpet. The carpet was so soft that it allowed her to sink her toes into it whenever she walked across it. It was divine. Once she arranged her items on the dressing room bureau to her satisfaction, she decided she needed a bath to try and unwind her tense muscles from the last couple of weeks. So, she filled the tub with her customary lavender and rose-scented bubble bath and looked forward to reclining her body in the hot steamy water and letting all the stress she had endured melt away.

Jakiele spent the time away from the women in his office making sure the arrangements for Rochelle's transfer from the hospital to his safe house in London were all taken care of. He asked John to call him when the private plane he had booked landed in London the following day. John reassured Jakiele that he had the situation well in hand and would call first thing in the morning. Rochelle had awoken earlier than expected at the hospital, so John and his team had already moved her and her son to Jakiele's safe house in Washington D.C.

It took several phone calls to get the passports taken care of, but within a couple of hours, everything was completed to Jakiele's satisfaction. There was a large duffel bag Jakiele kept at the safe house, which had money and credit cards in it should they ever be needed to make a hasty escape. Jakiele told John to take the money and make sure Rochelle would have everything she needed to start a new life in London. Jakiele informed John he had placed the duffel bag under three loose floorboards in the kitchen. Jakiele had always been especially careful to make sure no one had ever followed him to his safe house in case he needed it for an emergency. Jakiele was extremely glad now he had been so secretive in not letting anyone know about it, not even Michael.

Jakiele looked up from his desk at his office door, which he had left partially ajar so Anna could carry in his dinner when it was ready. He was startled to see Katliana standing there instead, holding the voice recorder he had left on the kitchen counter earlier. When Katliana realized Jakiele had become aware of her standing there, she politely knocked on the door and asked if she could come in. Jakiele motioned for her to come in and silently watched her cross the room.

She had changed into a sundress with small lacy straps holding up the gown's bodice on either side of her shoulders. The skirt and bodice were white and had gold stripes lining the pleated skirt. It was form-fitting and showed her sculpted body to perfection. She did not have large breasts, but the ones she had were full and filled out the bodice of her dress in lovely proportion. Her skin was creamy and flawlessly white. Jakiele noticed she did not wear a wedding ring or any other jewelry except for a pair of small pearl earrings.

Katliana laid the voice recorder on Jakiele's desk and was about to exit the room when Jakiele stopped her. "Katliana, please stay for a moment. I hope your mother expressed to you my concerns about your safety. Your mother already revealed the reason you both came here to seek my help. I will try to do everything I can to try to help with the case, but you must promise me you will follow whatever directions I deem necessary to protect you." Jakiele waited patiently for Katliana to respond while he studied the myriad of facial expressions crossing her lovely face.

"Mr. Smith, first, I did not want to impose on your hospitality uninvited. My mother insisted it was not safe for me to stay in Boston. Second, I am not particularly good at following orders without explanation. I apologize for my intrusion into your life and, most certainly, your home. I will do my best to stay out of your way while I try to solve the mystery of what happened to Sue Kwon, which, as you say, you have been made aware of by my mother. However, I made a vow to my friend that I would follow this investigation through to the end, and I fully intend to do so with or without your permission. I have been fully trained on how to take care of myself, so you may rest easy in that regard! I, for one, do not need any man to ever watch over me and protect me!" Katliana responded vehemently.

Jakiele was secretly impressed with Katliana's loyalty to her friend, and he admired her spirit. This tiny wisp of a girl in front of him liked to speak her mind and was not shy about letting him know exactly what her feelings were about him giving her orders. However, any meager skills she may have learned would amount to nothing should she come up against a demon hell-bent on killing her. Jakiele stood up and rounded his desk so he could stand in front of her and lean back against his desk. He folded his arms across his massive chest. With her tall gold pumps on her dainty feet, they were now eye to eye facing each other.

"Katliana," Jake spoke softly, "you are young and vulnerable. According to your mother, the people who have already investigated Sue Kwon's death and tried to solve this case are now dead. You need to turn over the evidence in this case to me so I can hand it over to proper professionals who are experts at uncovering evidence and investigating crimes. There is no need for you to be further involved in this matter." Jakiele impulsively reached up his right hand to cup her face tenderly.

Katliana shoved his hand away. "I am a professional in my field of study, Mr. Smith, and I may be young, but I am also fully capable of solving this mystery without your interference. If I need your help, I will let you know!" Jakiele's condescending offer of aid as though she was fresh out of school irritated her to no end. He thought she did not have the brains or skill to manage this on her own. Katliana spun on her heel, prepared to exit the room in a furor of righteous indignation when Jakiele grabbed her by the waist and turned her back around to face him once again.

He brought her close to him and held her hands behind her back with his own so she would be unequivocal on what he was about to say to her next. Her body was now trapped between his legs. "I do not doubt that any daughter of Anna's is competent at anything she chooses to pursue. However, there are forces at work here that you are not aware of and would not understand. I promised your mother I would keep you safe, and I will fulfill my promise to her whether you like it or not. You will do what I tell you to do for your safety as well as your mother's. Are we clear?"

Jakiele was not angry with her, but he quickly became irritated with her being so stubborn about her safety. Katliana was just as agitated with Jakiele's authoritative tone and refused to back down. "So, exactly how do you propose to get me to do anything l do not want to against my will?" Katliana answered sweetly. There was no way she was going to be bullied by Jakiele. He, unfortunately, did not know how stubborn she could be if she sunk her heels in.

"Perhaps I should show you instead." Jakiele seductively quipped. He moved off his desk and stood over her. He pulled her body close to his and positioned his mouth right above her own. Very slowly, Jakiele lowered his head until his lips brushed feather kisses across her tightly pursed ones. Without her even realizing it, her lips started to open on their own. His tongue invaded her mouth so sensually it felt like her nerves were on fire, and her head began to swim. When he let go of her hands, she unconsciously entwined them around his neck and began kissing him back in the same way he was kissing her. Her blood felt like molten lava was going through her veins, and her feminine core began to thrum a vibrating beat quickly matching the enticing movements of his tongue. She was utterly lost in a hazy storm of sensations she had never felt before.

Jakiele had never experienced sensations like this before either. Kissing Katliana quickly became like an intoxicating drug he could not get enough of. She tasted like honey and sunshine, which shook him to the core. Jakiele suddenly jerked back away from her and forcibly pushed her away from him. "Lesson is over, Katliana. Think hard on what I said. If you will, please excuse me now. I have important work I have to deal with." Jakiele turned forcibly away from her and sat back down at his desk. He made sure the lower part of his body was hidden beneath the desk. There was no sense in scaring Katliana with the evidence that kissing her aroused him. To avoid looking directly at her, he focused his vision on the myriad of documents awaiting his attention on the desk.

Katliana's hand flew to her mouth in utter mortification. What happened? Her brain could not seem to fathom the new sensations she was experiencing with a vengeance. She knew she must be beet red from head to toe in embarrassment and flew from Jakiele's office back to her room. She passed Anna in the hall who was carrying Jakiele's dinner, but she did not stop to talk about it with her mother. She needed to be alone to process the stunning revelations invading her mind in rapid succession. She realized the only man who had ever awakened her sensual nature had pushed her away because he was trying to teach her a lesson. This revelation was utterly devastating to her virginal sensibilities, and she was not equipped to deal with someone as masculine and virile as Jakiele, who could take her breath away with one single kiss.

Anna carried Jakiele's tray into his office, set it down on his desk, and asked him what happened to upset Katliana so much that she had run out of his office up to her room. Jakiele was sitting behind his desk, trying desperately not to let Anna see the raging erection he was valiantly trying to hide beneath the desk. His brain was still trying to process what had happened between himself and Anna's daughter. However, it was not a proper conversation to have with Anna about the kiss he and Katliana shared. So instead, Jakiele told Anna that he was trying to convince Katliana to turn over the evidence about the dead Asian girl to the proper authorities, which upset her.

Anna sat down in the seat across from his desk and replied, "I know you are only trying to keep her safe, and I will talk to her about it. Kyle Oakes was a dear family friend of Katliana's, and she feels she owes it to him to solve this case. She was completely devastated by his death. I fear this whole thing could get her killed if she dabbles in areas she should not. I do not have all the facts, but my instincts tell me there is trouble ahead we do not even know about yet. I want Katliana as far removed from this as quickly as possible. She will not give this up easily. Perhaps you could offer to help her solve it instead of trying to remove her from the case?" Anna offered hesitantly.

Jakiele thought about what Anna said for a few precious minutes while he was trying to get his erection under control before he replied, "I will think on it, Anna. Thank you for dinner, and believe me when I say that I agree with you. There is more to this case than meets the eye. My instincts are telling me the same things as yours, and I need to do some added research and investigate on my own before I can help Katliana. Can you please make sure the house is locked down tight? I have a few more hours of work to do, and I would like to remain undisturbed for the rest of the evening."

Anna was instantly relieved and answered, "Of course, Master Jake. Did you happen to notice a faint trace of sulfur in the house? I may be smelling things, but I could swear I noticed it in the kitchen and upstairs when I was helping Katliana unpack? Anna queried. Her empathic abilities told her a demon had been in the house because of the putrid smell. Still, she was desperately hoping for a more rational explanation. She was questioning whether there was a gas leak somewhere or some other practical explanation for what she had smelled. Anna had never smelled anything so disgusting, even though it was only a tiny trace amount.

"I did notice it, Anna, and I am sure you are aware of what the odor means. You are an empath and possibly a physical medium. You are most undoubtedly aware of other inter-dimensional beings like demons. It is one of the reasons you two are not safe here. I was deliberately baiting a trap for rogue demons while you and Caleb were on vacation. Unfortunately, I did not realize one of the most vicious demons named Zadikiele may have been in my house as well. Therefore, you and your daughter must follow my commands to the letter until he is caught."

Anna took in a sharp intake of breath and reconsidered staying here was not any safer than a hotel room for herself and her daughter. "Maybe us staying here is not such a good idea, after all, Master Jake. If you have another recommendation, I would be happy to hear it." Panic-stricken, Anna started to back out of the room, clearly uneasy with what Jakiele had revealed to her. Jakiele quietly reassured her, "Anna, I know you are scared, but after what you have revealed to me, I think you might be able to help me catch Zadikiele.

Most humans cannot smell his scent, but you can. I called Caleb earlier, and he will be back tomorrow morning to help us. I think you may be right. Staying here with Caleb and me is the safest thing for you and your daughter to do. You would be able to assist me greatly in capturing and destroying this bastard who thrives on hurting and humiliating women." Jakiele waited for the information he had imparted to Anna to sink in. He knew he trusted her way more than he should, but he believed strongly in Anna's abilities and her strong protective instincts.

After several moments, Anna looked down at the carpet, clearly ashamed of something. Her voice caught in her throat for a moment before she replied, "I am afraid. I know you may not understand this, but my husband lived to torture me in every way he could while he was still alive. I refused to let my daughter see the abuse or let her be harmed, so I sent my daughter to live in the States to live with my brother. It was the hardest decision I have ever had to make in my life. My poor daughter has been through so much, and she does not deserve to have to suffer any more pain because of any of my weaknesses."

Anna rose from the chair and straightened her spine into a rigid stance before she replied defiantly, "I will do whatever is necessary to keep my little girl safe. Please tell me what to do, and I will do it without hesitation. If you need my help or my own life, I will gladly give it. In return, I humbly ask you to give me the same vow to protect my daughter I have given you. In doing so, I will help you in whatever way I can to track this demon down so he will never harm another human being again." Anna was dead serious and awaited Jakiele's response.

Jakiele had not known Anna or Katliana had gone through such horror in their lives. However, his resolve to protect them was unwavering when he said, "I doubt you have ever been allowed to be weak a day in your life, Anna, and I admire you for your strength and your loyalty. I vow to you that I will do everything I can to keep everyone in my household safe, including your daughter. First, however, I want you to be aware of how dangerous dealing with demons can be. They are very clever and cunning and know a million ways to kill a human without ever being detected.

You must constantly be on your guard. You must be willing to follow my directions without the slightest hesitation, even if you disagree with what you are being told. In my hundreds of years here on Earth, I have dispatched more demons than I can count. Few are as vicious as Zadikiele. I want you to be very aware of what you are getting yourself into here without having any misconceptions of the genuine danger you are in." Jakiele enunciated every word carefully so Anna would completely understand the seriousness of the situation.

Anna nodded her understanding of the situation and left the room. Jakiele was utterly exhausted, but he finished Anna's delicious home-cooked meal in record time. Finally able to relax, he pressed "PLAY" on the voice recorder once belonging to Steve Windham and listened to the various speculations Steve had about what he had seen and heard while investigating Sue Kwon's death. Steve was incredibly good at tracking down stories from what he had seen in Rochelle's memories.

Too good. It had undoubtedly gotten him killed, and his poor wife had been made to suffer the consequences for Steve's blind ambition and stupidity. The last person Steve spoke with had been Kyle Oakes. Jakiele now knew why Kyle had been found dead in his office. Kyle suspected something was wrong with the cause of death listed on Sue Kwon's paperwork and had followed up on those suspicions by sending Katliana the DNA samples and pictures. To Jakiele, this news meant someone in Kyle's office or someone close to him worked for Zadikiele.

It was only going to be a matter of time until Zadikiele tracked Anna and Katliana back to Jakiele's house. This situation was getting more dangerous by the minute. He needed to get to the heavenly mansion and fill Gabriel in on these events at once. In addition, Michael needed to be made aware of the tension between the United States and China. After letting himself into his room, Jakiele smelled sulfur. A demon had been in his bedroom very recently, and judging by the acridness of the smell and how pungent it was, they had been in the room for quite some time.

Jakiele scoured the room but could not find anything out of place or missing. He checked everywhere he could think of. Zadikiele must have left something behind, but Jakiele could not find it. Jakiele went into his closet and placed his palm on the device that activated the mirror. After being accepted by the Cherubim, Jakiele was transported to the lower angelic tier. He needed to report everything to Gabriel so Michael would be made aware of all the current events.

Jakiele went directly to the mirror on the main floor of the heavenly mansion, got down on his right knee, and bowed his head in allegiance. He spoke his exaltations and swore his allegiance with humbleness to the God he served in the ancient tongue of the angels to the Cherubim outlining the mirror and requested to speak with Gabriel. The Cherubim began to sing to one another, and the mirror started to vibrate and shimmer. The mirror started to shine its startling bright white light until Gabriel's bored visage appeared before him before he realized it was Jakiele who had summoned him.

Gabriel had made no effort to conceal his disgust in the way Michael favored Jakiele and gave him too much credit for his ability to be able to oversee delicate political matters. Gabriel felt the angels under his direct command, like his first lieutenant, Mulakai, were far better equipped to handle sensitive issues of international espionage on Earth. "Why have you summoned me, Jakiele? This had better be important!" Gabriel demanded imperiously.

Jakiele took a deep breath and related the events between the United States and China. He calmly filled Gabriel in on what was happening in his home with Anna and Katliana and how the two problems were linked. Gabriel was less than impressed. Finally, Gabriel let out a loud sigh of exasperation, "So let me get this straight. A dead Asian girl was found at a preserve, and she was an exchange student from China. China is upset about not being notified first before her body was cremated. She had been infected with a virus and died. People exposed to her body also died from contact with her compromised body. The United States is trying to soothe China's ruffled feathers, and they are having a summit to discuss it." Gabriel sarcastically added, "Do my conclusions about sum it up, Jakiele? It does not particularly seem like these events are so critical I need to involve Michael in this situation, now does it?"

Jakiele took another deep breath before patiently adding, "Gabriel, please listen to me. The circumstances surrounding the girl's death are unusual, and so are the deaths of the people who were investigating Sue Kwon's death. My housekeeper's daughter is staying in my home under my protection because she is trying to figure out what happened to this dead girl. Nevertheless, Remiel's son, Zadikiele, will be hot on her trail, and she will need our help. Zadikiele and his followers have been snooping around my house. They have figured out my security codes to gain access to my home. I deliberately made the codes simple to set up a trap for them while my servants were gone on vacation. However, now that I know for certain that Zadikiele is the leader of this group, I feel the humans residing in my home are in serious mortal danger."

Gabriel hissed between his teeth and barked at Jakiele, "This is what happens when you involve yourself in the lives of humans! Especially females! You should know better. Your job is to observe and report. Not get involved. Why Michael ever agreed to let you have humans in your home in the first place is beyond me. Unfortunately, you have failed to understand your duties properly, so now I am forced to send help for you to look after the humans in your home correctly.

I will allow Mulakai to provide you with some assistance since you are utterly inept at providing essential protection services for those you seem to care about. But, nevertheless, be warned, should Mulakai report to me you are stepping even one toe out of line, I will have you brought up on charges of gross misconduct! Do you understand me clearly, Jakiele?" Gabriel fairly thundered the last remark at the mirror so loud it nearly shook itself off the mantle it rested on.

Jakiele bowed his head in acceptance of what Gabriel had decreed and awaited the arrival of Mulakai through the mirror. It was hard for Jakiele to hide the smile stealing across his face. Mulakai soon appeared, and the two greeted each other in the customary warrior fashion. Neither Gabriel nor Michael knew of their close friendship, and the two of them had kept it that way on purpose. It would have caused endless friction between Gabriel and Michael, who had the best warrior at their disposal. Neither Jakiele nor Mulakai wanted to be responsible for causing any grief between the two highly competitive Archangels.

Jakiele showed Mulakai the mirror he used to travel back and forth to his home. After identifying himself in the mirror and being accepted, Jakiele and Mulakai quickly transported him back to Jakiele's closet. Mulakai was dressed in full angel uniform, so Jakiele insisted Mulakai change into acceptable human attire from the many available clothing choices in the closet. Mulakai balked at giving up his sword and insisted on keeping the sheath and sword attached to his belt. He put on one of Jakiele's long overcoats to conceal the weapon. Upon closing the portal and securing the mirror, Jakiele walked over to the closet door and indicated Mulakai should precede him into the bedroom. Jakiele followed closely behind Mulakai and closed the closet door.

Mulakai's nostrils picked up the acrid scent of sulfur. He did not wait for Jakiele to allow him to investigate the source of the smell. Instead, Mulakai started methodically checking the room for anything one of the demons may have left behind. "I have already searched the room, my friend. I was not able to find anything." Jakiele informed Mulakai. Mulakai ignored Jakiele and kept searching for himself. Jakiele crossed his arms over his chest and watched Mulakai work. Finally, a tiny pinpoint beam of light caught Mulakai's eye to the left of Jakiele's dresser. It was barely visible, and he had only detected it because of how the shadows of the evening moon were falling in the room.

Mulakai raced across the room and yanked Jakiele's dresser away from the wall with one mighty shove. The fiber optic device was so small it was a wonder he had been able to find it. Next, Mulakai unsheathed the sword he had brought with him and gouged a huge hole in the wall to unveil the video camera. Mulakai yanked it out with his left hand and threw the device on the floor. He smashed it to bits by swinging his sword high above his head and bringing it down many times with forcible crashes on the device. Jakiele had watched this happen in a matter of seconds and was still staring at Mulakai in stunned silence.

Jakiele replied, "I had forgotten your incredible speed, Mulakai. I am impressed you found the device so quickly, but I am disappointed I did not find it when I searched the room before." Mulakai accepted the praise with grace but could not help taunting Jakiele a little bit, "Well, you are getting sloppy, old man. However, I doubt the device has been able to record much since you told me you detected the smell today. So, what could they have seen or heard? You were not doing something naughty in here, were you?" Mulakai waggled his eyebrows at Jakiele in jest.

Jakiele felt all the blood freeze in his body. The demons who had installed the camera could have seen the mirror and the two of them emerging from the closet. He had gone into the closet alone and came out with Mulakai. Gabriel was going to be pissed. He had failed to protect the secrets of the mirror. However, at the look of horror flashing across Jakiele's face, Mulakai caught on immediately. He said all he needed to say. "Oh, dear God, they may have seen the mirror."

The revelation propelled both into action. Although Mulakai did not know the layout of Jakiele's house, he raced from the bedroom into the hallway. He followed the scent of demons throughout to see if he could find any more devices. But not before throwing a sarcastic challenge over his left shoulder to Jakiele, "If I find more devices before you do, you are going to owe me one of your antique Samurai swords I know you keep in your private collection. Let us see if you can still keep up, old man." Jakiele was hot on his heels, racing down the hallway after him. There was no chance his friend would outsmart him and find anything first. "Never going to happen, Mulakai. Those swords are over a thousand years old. You will owe me a dueling match downstairs if I find them first. We shall see who the best still is!"

Together, they quickly found the other two devices hidden in the living room and kitchen. Luckily, Anna and Katliana were in Katliana's room together and had no idea what was happening downstairs between Mulakai and Jakiele. The two angels knew how to be stealthily quiet when they needed to be. Jakiele and Mulakai made plans to update Jakiele's security first thing in the morning. Protecting the mirror at all costs would be their number one priority, except for guarding the women in the house. The two angels managed to cover up the damage that removing the devices from their hiding places caused. Since they had both found the devices simultaneously, they called it a draw on their fun challenge to each other. They were having an enjoyable time in the living room, sitting together and reminiscing about old times when Mulakai smelled something in the air and jumped up to investigate.

Mulakai's nose led him to the kitchen and over to the crockpot where Anna had made her famous pot roast dinner. He opened the oven and smelled the wonderful aroma of home-baked bread. Jakiele had followed Mulakai into the kitchen and was amused watching his friend inhale these new scents for the first time. The look of blissful joy on Mulakai's face reminded Jakiele of all he had and what he had started to take for granted on Earth. This humbled Jakiele at once. He silently motioned for his friend to sit down while Jakiele fixed Mulakai up a plate of the delicious dinner Anna had prepared. Mulakai was in a state of euphoria as he devoured the meal with a voracious appetite.

"I can certainly see why you like these humans, Jakiele. I have not enjoyed something so exquisite for many millennia. Please thank your human servant for me. The meal was extraordinary." Jakiele chuckled softly, "I will, Mulakai. But my guess is you may be too full from what you inhaled at such a rapid pace to accommodate having any dessert, so I will have to take care of your portion myself." Jakiele reached behind him and pulled out the cookie jar Anna had recently filled with warm chocolate chip cookies.

The look of stunned pleasure on Mulakai's face was priceless. He snatched the cookie jar from Jakiele's hand at warp speed and pulled the jar close to his chest before Jakiele even had time to react. Jakiele went over to the refrigerator, pulled out the milk, and reached up to grab two glasses from the neighboring cupboard. He deliberately placed them out of reach of Mulakai on a nearby counter. "If you want to have the ultimate human experience with chocolate chip cookies, my friend, we will each have to share. I would not want to see you miss an important human tradition. Do you surrender?"

"This one time, Jakiele, I will surrender. However, only because I want to be able to report to Gabriel that I have been able to properly assist you by having an adequate understanding of human customs." Mulakai had been able to say the last comment with a small degree of seriousness and a straight face. Jakiele walked over to where Mulakai was sitting and poured them each a glass of milk to dip their cookies in. "If such is the case, Mulakai, I accept the terms of your surrender." Both angels erupted into laughter as they enjoyed the simplest of human pastimes. They each reveled in being able to enjoy one another's company again after being kept so long apart.

Anna had crept silently back down the stairs after making sure Katliana had eaten her dinner in her room. Katliana had not wanted to come downstairs and eat dinner in the kitchen for some reason. Anna had pressed Katliana hard to let Jakiele help with the investigation. Katliana finally relented and said she would try. They visited together while Katliana ate her meal and dessert for a while longer. Finally, Katliana let Anna know she was tired and wanted to rest. Anna reassured her everything would be okay and brought Katliana's plates back downstairs with her to finish tidying up the kitchen and get ready for bed herself.

Anna was apprehensive about entering the kitchen when she overheard another male's voice she did not recognize. Jakiele and Mulakai had such advanced hearing that they both knew when Anna had stopped outside the kitchen entrance. "It is okay, Anna," Jakiele said reassuringly. "A friend of mine is going to be staying with us for a time. His name is Mulakai. Please come in and introduce yourself to our guest. He is here to help us." Anna let out the pent-up breath she had been holding and crossed the threshold to enter the kitchen with her left arm full of dirty dishes.

# CHAPTER 9

A fter Anna entered the kitchen, she gingerly placed the dirty dishes in the sink to be rinsed later. As she turned away from the sink, she slowly strode to the kitchen table where Jakiele and Mulakai sat. Mulakai and Jakiele both stood up from the table in unison upon her approach. Mulakai gave a gentlemanly old-world bow and stretched out his right hand to greet Anna. Anna went to shake Mulakai's hand, but instead, Mulakai grasped her hand up to lips with both of his hands to place a gentle kiss on the top of Anna's hand. Anna could sense that Mulakai was the same inter-dimensional being Jakiele was and relaxed.

Mulakai was as tall as Jakiele and every bit as muscular, but he was more lithely built. His hair was a deep golden brown and was as long as Jakiele's. His eyes were a deep chestnut color shining with keen intelligence. The laugh lines etched around his eyes suggested he liked to laugh often and had a good sense of humor. Anna liked him instantly and felt comfortable in his presence.

"My name is Mulakai, Miss Anna. It is such a pleasure to meet a woman who can prepare such delicious fare. I have to say the chocolate chip cookies were a delight to my long-starved palette. I have never before tasted such sumptuous delights!" Anna pulled her hands back quickly from Mulakai. Anna's face suffused a dark red color from the gracious compliments and the charming demeanor of Jakiele's friend. "It is very nice to make your acquaintance also, Mulakai." Anna paused for a moment before she realized what Mulakai had said. "Did you both eat all of the chocolate chip cookies I made for Caleb?" Anna reached out and grabbed the empty cookie jar off the table with a horrified gasp. "You naughty boys! Shame on you! Now I will have to make Caleb something else to enjoy with his morning coffee! Shoo, both of you! Out of the kitchen at once!"

Anna began hastening both men out of the kitchen with her hands. Mulakai once again thanked her for the delicious meal he had devoured earlier before he allowed himself to be banished from the kitchen. Jakiele and Anna had been smiling throughout the entire exchange, and it was easy to see they enjoyed an easy camaraderie with each other instead of a business-only relationship. Mulakai was fascinated by watching them together and acting more like mother and son rather than employer and housekeeper. He anticipated meeting the chauffeur in the morning and watching how other humans and Jakiele interacted.

Even though it was getting late in the evening, Anna cleaned up the kitchen and made some miniature cakes for Caleb to consume with his morning coffee. The smell of lemon cakes and buttery frosting soon drifted into the living room, where Jakiele and Mulakai sat discussing how they were going to update the estate's security in the morning. In addition, they discussed the best ways to keep the women safe by having rotating shifts. As a result, Caleb, Jakiele, and Mulakai would have to plan their shifts diligently throughout the coming days so everyone could stay rested and alert.

Mulakai could not resist coming back into the kitchen to see what Anna was making. The smell was so enticing that he could not help himself. The newly created mini cakes were on a cooling rack on the counter while Anna stood next to them and added the final additions to her homemade frosting. Anna looked up to see Mulakai staring at the tiny little cakes with a look of forlorn wonder on his face. It instantly reminded Anna of the sweet little street urchins she had taken in who had been starving and homeless back in Bosnia.

Jakiele had come back into the kitchen as well to see what Anna had created for Caleb on such short notice. He would have thought Anna would have been utterly exhausted from the last two weeks' events.

Jakiele did not want to see Anna work so hard, especially after she had recently endured. He very gently said, "Anna, you have to be so tired. You should go up to my room and rest when you are done here. You must be tremendously exhausted. I know how much Caleb enjoys your cooking, but you do not have to do this for him. When you are ready, let me know, and I will escort you to the garage to collect the things you need to get ready for bed." Anna paused for a moment before she replied, "Master Jake, I appreciate the offer of staying in your room next to my daughter, but I will not sleep well if I am not in my bed. I would much rather stay in the garage loft. You should be the one to stay close to Katliana. You can protect her better than I can. Perhaps Mulakai would be willing to sleep on my couch instead of the living room here in the house?"

Anna began frosting the little cakes and continued with, "My daughter and I would be under constant watch by both of you without dividing your attention. Mulakai can watch over me until Caleb gets here, and you can watch over Katliana." Jakiele thought on this plan for a moment and stole a glance at Mulakai, and waited for Mulakai to mull it over. Instead, Mulakai looked deep in thought and responded with, "I do not know, Anna. Jakiele has a big screen TV and a fireplace to fall asleep next to. Why would I want to give up these valuable luxuries when I can sleep right here in the house and enjoy the delicious aromas emanating from the kitchen?" Mulakai was teasing Anna, and she was quick to catch on after living with Jakiele for over a year.

"For one thing, Mulakai, I have an amazingly comfortable couch which can be made into a bed with warm snuggly blankets. On the other hand, the couch in Jakiele's living room is cold, narrow, and hard. Moreover, the only way you will get to have any of these little cakes is to do what I ask. Otherwise, you will not get even a whiff!" Anna quickly whisked the little cakes into a storage container with a lid and held the container close to her body out of the men's reach. Not to be outwitted, Mulakai retorted back, "Okay, Anna, you win. I will go with you to your loft and sleep on your couch, but I want another batch of cookies for my efforts. It takes energy to be on constant guard duty." Mulakai gave Anna a wide smile of triumph. He knew he had won this round of negotiations with her.

However, Anna was no fool. If making enticing entrees and desserts was what she had to do to keep everyone alive, such a small gift to give back was perfectly okay with her. Anna mentally noted the differences between the two men. Jakiele was quiet, serious, and devoted to his job, but he was also polite and not obnoxious in any way. Mulakai was sweet and gentlemanly but not afraid to negotiate whatever he wanted. Anna opened the container of cakes and offered one each to Jakiele and Mulakai. "No more for tonight. The rest of these are for Caleb. I want your words of honor that you will both stay out of these cakes." Anna stated emphatically to them both. Both men were lost in a state of ecstasy for a moment while they quickly devoured their rewards, but they nodded their heads in agreement to her request.

"I am tired and going to bed. Do I have your word as gentlemen?" Anna demanded. Both men put their hands over their hearts and promised to be good. Anna harrumphed as though she was not sure whether to believe them. Anna set the cake container back onto the counter and started to leave the kitchen to go to the garage. Mulakai was close on her heels. Mulakai turned around and winked at Jakiele before closing the kitchen door behind him and escorting Anna to the garage. Jakiele watched from the kitchen window to make sure both safely made it to the garage. When the loft lights turned on, Jakiele turned away from the window and switched the house security alarms on. Jakiele made a thorough search of the house first before climbing the stairs wearily to get ready to go to bed.

Katliana had not come downstairs since their earlier encounter in the office. Jakiele had been thoroughly shaken to the core by kissing her. He felt like he owed her an explanation for his behavior. It was not like him to act like an overbearing troglodyte with a woman. He thought he should knock on her door and make sure she was okay and see if she would be willing to accept an apology. Jakiele softly knocked twice on her door, but she did not answer. He expected to turn the handle of her door and find it locked, but the door had been left partially ajar, so he walked into the bedroom as quietly as he could so he would not disturb her if she were asleep.

Katliana looked like she was deep in the throes of a terrible nightmare she could not awaken from. She was wearing a dark blue silk chemise for a nightgown, and he could see her chest and forehead had the telltale beads of sweat forming from fear. The blankets had been pushed down by her ankles, and her body kept turning from side to side as though she was trying to get away from something. Or someone. Her soft moans of fear propelled Jakiele across the room to stand at her bedside in an instant.

Jakiele placed his left hand on her forehead to try and read her memories and to see what was scaring her so badly. Jakiele closed his eyes so he could see through her mind's eye what she was reliving. Katliana was having a very vivid and graphic memory of her mother shielding her body with her own while a man stood whipping Anna with a belt across the back and head. He was hitting Anna so hard the ends of the belt would sting Katliana in the face as well, even though Anna was doing the best she could to protect her daughter from the forceful blows. Katliana looked like she was about five years old in this memory. The man standing over her mother kept trying to pull Katliana away from her mother so he could beat her too. Anna had been the only thing standing between Katliana and this monster of a man beating them.

Katliana was terrified in the dream and did not know why her father was so angry with her or her mother. She kept repeatedly saying in the memory, "Daddy, please stop! Daddy don't. You're hurting us." However, the man would not stop regardless of his daughter's plaintive pleas. In the memory, the abuse lingered on and on for an extended length of time. The back of Anna's dress was torn to shreds, and her back was a bloody mess. The only intervals in between the beatings were when Uri, Katliana's father, wanted to take another swig of the alcohol he was imbibing at an alarming rate. Finally, the man stopped but only because he had taken one drink too many and passed out with a thud on the floor.

Katliana's whole body was quivering with fear as she relived the horrible nightmare. Jakiele became physically sick at what he had seen in her memories. It made him want to go back in time and beat the man to within an inch of his life for treating his wife and child this way. No wonder Anna worked so hard to keep her memories of the man locked behind an iron wall in her mind. Jakiele would not erase these memories from Katliana's mind unless she wanted him to. It would be an invasion of who she was as an individual. He felt the experiences one had as a human, shaped a person's personality, whether good or bad.

Those experiences also influenced the choices one had to make in all matters by being given God's gift of free will. It was not up to him to interfere. He could, however, offer her some sense of tranquility. Jakiele came around to the other side of the bed and positioned himself to lay down next to her. He pulled her body close to his, gently laid her head into the crook of his shoulder, and wrapped his left arm around her shoulders.

Katliana turned on her side, laid her cheek against his chest, and wrapped her arm around his waist as though seeking the comforting consolation of his embrace. The wracking tremors shaking her body so violently had slowly stopped. She now seemed to be sleeping peacefully. Jakiele was going to try and carefully disentangle himself not to awaken her when Katliana's eyes flew open. She realized with a startled gasp that there was someone in her bed. "Oh my God, what are you doing here?" she shrieked.

Katliana edged away from him in a panic and reached down to the end of the bed to gather the blankets of the bed to cover her scantily clad body and pull them up to her chest. Jakiele positioned himself into a sitting position directly across from her so he could look directly into her eyes. "My apologies, Katliana. I wanted to come to your room to atone for my earlier behavior with you in the office. I knocked, but when you did not answer, I noticed the door was partially open, and I wanted to make sure you were okay. I walked into the room, and I could see you were having a horrible nightmare. I promised your mother I would do everything in my power to keep you safe," Jakiele replied cautiously.

Katliana could see he was being genuine in his concern for her welfare and relented enough to softly say, "I do not need your assistance, Jake. I hope you do not mind me calling you Jake instead of Mr. Smith. I am perfectly capable of looking after myself, but I appreciate your concern." Upon seeing Jakiele tightening his lips in consternation, Katliana added, "I know you were only trying to help, but I have been having these nightmares since I was a young child. Nothing I do seems to make them ever go away. When I got older, I tried to go the counseling route, but sharing the memories only seemed to make them worse. I have mostly learned to live with them. There is nothing you can do to help me."

Katliana bowed her head in sadness but having Jakiele in the room offering his quiet reassurance made her want to confide in him about her darkest secrets. Instead, Jakiele studied her for a few moments before saying gently, "I would rather you called me Jake instead of Mr. Smith. You are a welcome guest in my home, but I must tell you something you may not understand and could terrify you. I am not what you think I am. I am not a man.

It would be best to hear what I am telling you and take what I am saying very seriously. You may as well hear this from me before you learn about me from someone else. I am not from this world. Your mother knows who I am and why I am here. I am an angel sent here from Heaven on a mission for the Archangel Michael. I realize you may find this hard to believe, but it is the truth." Jakiele knew he had to tell her about who he was before she would have enough faith in him to trust him. He also knew most humans would be terrified out of their wits if they knew who he was. So, he was apprehensive to hear what she would do once she found out the truth.

Katliana was quick to reply, "The culture I grew up in has always known about the paranormal, and my family taught me early on in life that we are not alone in the universe. Even though I grew up with Christian beliefs, I am a scientist at heart, and I know who you are. My mother already told me what you were when she came to my room earlier to try and convince me to let you help me with the investigation. I kept refusing to believe you could be of any assistance. I know I can find out what happened to Sue Kwon by myself. My mother got frustrated when I would not listen to her, so she finally wore me down by telling me about your kind and about the genuine danger we are all in. I have always known my mother could see and feel things other people cannot, and I know she would never lie to me."

Jakiele was momentarily stunned into silence. He did not know whether to be relieved or worried she knew the truth about him. Learning about him and revealing his identity to the wrong people could get them all killed. Katliana reached up and touched his cheek with her right hand to gently cup his cheek before she said, "I would never tell anyone about you or your kind. I know it would put us all in great jeopardy. My mother also revealed that the enemies we are facing are not merely mortal men but demons. I would be lying if I said what she told me did not scare the daylights out of me, but I feel safer being here with you. I know you will do all you can to protect us." Then, in jest, she laughingly added, "It is not like anyone would believe me anyway, so who would I possibly tell?"

The faith Katliana had in him to protect her made him feel even more possessive of her. Jakiele reached up and touched her hand that was softly cradling his cheek and instinctively turned his face so he could place a feather-light kiss into the palm of her hand. They both felt a familiar jolt of electricity sear through their bodies at the intimate contact. Katliana looked up and stared into his eyes in awe, but she did not pull away. Jakiele took his left hand and put it around the back of her neck to slowly bring her mouth closer to his inch by inch. He advanced slowly to give her time to stop his kiss if she did not want it.

Katliana did not want to pull away. She desperately needed to know if the sensuous bone-melting kiss she had received from him earlier in the office was an anomaly or a heightened sense of awareness because of the dangerous situation. She might still be a virgin, but she had been kissed before. As if time stood still and no longer had meaning, their lips finally met each other. As soon as their lips touched, it was as though a fire began burning at its hottest intensity and was consuming both their bodies and their minds.

Jakiele was an excellent teacher. His tongue expertly explored the hidden recesses in her mouth with slow expertise, inciting her tongue to do the same. They both sat up in bed on their knees as their bodies instinctively strived to get closer to each other. They were soon so lost in a haze of lust and sensation neither were aware that Katliana's nightgown had started to slip off her shoulders. Jakiele was the first to realize it and slipped his fingers under the lacy straps to pull the gown down to reveal Katliana's breasts to his hot gaze.

"You are exquisite, Katliana," Jakiele murmured before continuing his exploration with his tongue and mouth down her throat to her breasts. He took one exposed nipple into his mouth and nibbled and suckled until he had her moaning in excitement. Finally, he had managed to lay her down gently onto her back so he could continue his unencumbered discovery of the wonder of her body. Her body had become as feverish and flushed for him as he was for her. He lavished both of her breasts with his undivided attention until her thighs began to writhe in wanting something that she had no knowledge of yet.

Jakiele took his left hand and began to pull down her silky panties. Katliana stopped him by pulling his hand away with her own. "Wait, Jake. I cannot do this. I do not know what to do. I have never been with a man before," Katliana said in a rush of embarrassment. Katliana was ashamed of herself. What must he think of her? She was sure he had been with countless women over the eons, and he would find her lack of experience in the bedroom very dull. It took Jakiele a moment to realize what she was saying. Was she a virgin? She could become pregnant. What had he been thinking? There was no way he could become involved with her. It was impossible. Why did she have such a devastating effect on his senses? He lost all common sense around her, which was extremely dangerous for them both.

Jakiele pulled the straps of her gown back up to their rightful place and guided her body back to a prone position on the bed before he gently pulled the covers over her body. Never once taking his eyes from her, he remorsefully said, "I am sorry. I do not know what I was thinking. I should never have come to your room, Katliana. It will not happen again." Jakiele quietly left the room to go to his own and seek his rest. He had never been so shaken in his life.

What if he had taken her without proper precautions to ensure she did not get pregnant? Was he no better than the fallen angels who fell from disgrace for lusting after women? Jakiele chastised himself a thousand different ways before reaching his bedroom. Finally, he opened the door with the secret code and lay down on his bed, fully clothed. He had finally concluded it was best to stay as far away from Katliana as possible and avoid being alone with her at all costs. Jakiele fell into a restless sleep full of erotic dreams about Katliana despite his resolve not to give her another thought.

Katliana had never felt more rejected in all her life. Jakiele could not seem to get away from her fast enough once he realized she was a virgin. Was being untouched such a dreadful thing? She had never wanted a man more in her life than she did Jakiele. He was an expert at seduction and making her body thrum like a well-tuned instrument. Jakiele made it clear he did not want her and that being with her would be a mistake.

However, on the other hand, his body wanted her. She had seen and felt the evidence of his arousal. So why wouldn't he take what she had been about to offer willingly? It did not make any sense to her. Katliana resolved to find out. She also fell into an exhausted slumber after reliving Jakiele's amazing kisses with the same relentless intensity as she had when he had been kissing her.

Jakiele was up early to update his external security systems the following day. Caleb would be arriving in a few hours, and Jakiele wanted to make sure everything was up to his rigid standards before Caleb arrived. Unfortunately, Mulakai was still asleep, as was the rest of the household. It would take a few days before Mulakai's body adjusted to being in human form. He would feel fatigued and slow for several days, and it would be hard for his body to do things at the supernatural speed he was used to. Jakiele spent hours installing the outside cameras on the walls and gates leading up to his home. Finally, he changed and updated the intricate codes to the estate and the garage entrances.

Mulakai had awakened when Anna had come fully dressed out of her room to begin her morning duties. His body and mind felt sluggish, and he had difficulty getting up and about to follow her outside to go into the kitchen. Jakiele met them at the kitchen entrance and opened the door to come inside. He gave them both the new security codes and explained that he had managed to update the outside security. Mulakai was astonished that Jakiele had completed it all without his help and said, "Why didn't you wake me? I thought we were going to do the updating together?" Anna had already moved past them and was moving about the kitchen, getting breakfast ready.

Jakiele waited for Anna to be out of earshot and whispered to Mulakai, "It will take a while for your body to adjust to being human, Mulakai. However, your speed will pick back up soon, and your mind will begin to function normally again. Unfortunately, I did not sleep very well last night, so I decided to let you rest. At the same time, I finished what I had started with outside security. Do not worry. I will still need your help with the minor issue upstairs in my room. Do you think you can manage it?" Jakiele enjoyed teasing Mulakai to see if he could get a rise out of him.

"Do not be ridiculous, Jakiele," Mulakai replied stiffly. "Of course, I can manage it. I might need to eat first, however. It smells as though Anna is making something amazing again!" Mulakai's nose had picked up the scent of bacon and pancakes, and his mouth began to water. He immediately took a seat at the kitchen counter to watch Anna bustle about the kitchen with the efficiency and ease of someone exceptionally experienced at what they did for a living. Mulakai became mesmerized watching Anna produce them such a delicious meal in record time.

Before long, Anna asked Jakiele if he would please go upstairs and wake Katliana for breakfast. Jakiele hesitated for several seconds, causing both Anna's and Mulakai's heads to turn in his direction. They both had puzzled looks on their faces as if they wondered why he hesitated so long to answer Anna's request. Jakiele, for the first time in his life, felt like he was blushing like a young schoolboy and quickly nodded his agreement to wake Katliana before he embarrassed himself any further. Mulakai and Anna stared at each other in wonder at Jakiele's strange reaction before Mulakai shrugged his shoulders as if it was of no consequence and went back to watching Anna whip up some fluffy eggs to go with their meal. Anna thought Jakiele's reaction was strange but returned to preparing breakfast for everyone.

Jakiele went up the stairs to the second floor grudgingly and knocked hesitantly on Katliana's door. Katliana came to the door dressed in a pair of cutoff jeans and a halter top, which showed her body to perfection. Her hair was tied in a loose ponytail, and she was not wearing any makeup. She smelled like roses and lavender, and his body felt a sudden jolt to his nether regions. She looked stunning but innocently beautiful. Jakiele's body instantly reacted to her presence, so he gruffly said, "It is time for breakfast, Katliana. Your mother would like you to please come downstairs and join us. She sent me up here to get you." He started to turn away from her, but she grabbed his arm, pulled him into the room instead, and closed the door behind him. She went to stand directly in front of him so she could look him squarely in the eye.

Katliana was a bit surprised after last night's events to see him once again at her door. Still, she wanted to clear the air between the two of them first before they went downstairs together. "Jake, I want to thank you for coming into my room trying to give me comfort from my awful dreams. That was a very thoughtful thing to do. I do not know what to think about what is happening between us. I feel like an electrical charge is going through me every time we touch. You now know I have never been with a man before, and obviously, the fact I revealed to you I am still a virgin is what made you leave my room last night. I know it is unusual for someone my age to be untouched, but I have never been interested enough in a man to have a relationship with one. I am sure you have been with many women throughout the centuries if you have been stationed here on Earth for hundreds of years."

Katliana's cheeks had blushed a fiery red as she tried her best to have a civil conversation about what she considered to be a private subject. She bowed her head in mortification for a moment before she added hopefully, "I would like you to know I do not hold what happened last night against you. I understand if you do not feel the same way about me that I feel about you. I want to try and still be friends if we can."

Jakiele was continually fascinated by this young woman. Most women would not have ever dreamed about being this candidly honest with a man about their true feelings. Too many women danced around and played games with the men in their lives and expected those men to be clairvoyant enough to figure out what the woman wanted or needed. He appreciated the fact that Katliana was brave enough to cut right to the heart of what she was feeling, even if it made her seem vulnerable or if what she was saying mortified her. He would have known anyway if she was lying to him, and it was refreshing to be in the presence of someone who did not prevaricate.

Jakiele raised both of his hands and placed them gently on her shoulders before responding to her by saying honestly, "You misunderstood the reason I left, Katliana. Angels are not allowed to have sexual relationships with women who can become pregnant. The mating of our two species can create a hybrid species known as the Nephilim. They are the very monsters God destroyed in the great flood of Noah. I would become a fallen angel, and God would banish me from Heaven, and he would kill any offspring created by us." Jakiele bowed his head in disgust at her look of horror before being as equally candid with her as she was with him. "I have also felt the chemistry between us, Katliana, and it is overwhelmingly hard for me not to take you in my arms and have my way with you right here and now. I feel this way every time I am around you. I cannot seem to help myself, so, please, stay as far away from me as you can for both of our sakes!"

Katliana felt suddenly foolish and selfish. She had no idea she had put him in such a precarious predicament by being attracted to him and revealing her innermost thoughts to him. "I did not know, Jake, and I am so sorry I revealed how I feel about you. I will do my best to keep my thoughts to myself. However, I want you to know how much I appreciate what you have done for my mother and me. I will stay out of your way from now on, I promise." Katliana started to move away from him toward the door, but not before he grabbed her by the wrist and pulled her back in front of him. He reached up and placed both of his hands on either side of her face and kissed her lips with a crushing force. His mouth quickly devoured her lips and mouth in such a devastatingly masculine way that she felt like her whole body had turned to molten lava.

Jakiele suddenly pulled away from her and put distance between them with his arms outstretched. "This is why we have to avoid each other, Katliana. I cannot even seem to be in the same room with you without wanting you so badly my body aches. Now, do you understand?" Katliana was shaken by the violence of his need which was still very visible in the tightly molded jeans he had chosen to wear. She understood what he was saying because she was having as much trouble as he was keeping her hands to herself. She mutely nodded her understanding of what he had revealed to her and followed him down the stairs to join the others for breakfast. Caleb had arrived earlier than expected and was already busy regaling Mulakai and Anna with his latest fishing adventures.

As soon as Jakiele and Katliana entered the kitchen, all eyes turned toward them. Anna was the first to frown at Katliana when she observed Katliana's pale countenance and kiss swollen lips. Jakiele refused to look at anyone directly and walked over to the sideboard where the meal was being kept warm for them all. Katliana would not look at anyone either and followed Jakiele's lead and fixed herself a plate from the sideboard as well. Conversation halted for several moments before Anna cleared her throat and introduced Caleb and Mulakai to Katliana. Katliana greeted them politely but decided to take her plate back to her room and eat alone. She felt like everyone already knew she and Jakiele had been kissing, and she felt like the room's atmosphere had suddenly become charged, and everyone was judging her and Jakiele.

Jakiele sat down at the kitchen table to eat his breakfast but not before he watched Katliana take her plate of food back to her room. He looked across the table and noticed Mulakai scrutinizing him very carefully with a mirthful smirk on his mouth. Mulakai knew he had been kissing Katliana. So did Anna since she kept giving him mildly disapproving looks throughout the meal. Finally, Caleb was the one to break the tension as he too sat down at the table with one of the little cakes Anna had made especially for him. As soon as the lemony flavor of the cake hit his tongue, Caleb rolled his eyes to the back of his head in total pleasure.

Anna was exceptionally talented in the kitchen and prepared everything from scratch. As soon as he finished with the cake, Caleb lavished Anna with compliment after compliment on her culinary skills. Anna's attention quickly diverted from Jakiele as she glowed from the abundant praise Caleb heaped on her. Mulakai soon jumped in with his commendations of the meal and cookies Anna had made the night before. Anna always got very flustered when bombarded with such flattery and admiration.

Before long, Anna was up from the table and getting the kitchen clean. The three men retired to the living room to discuss the strategies Mulakai and Jakiele had deliberated over the night before. If they worked together, there would always be someone on guard to watch over the women while the other two either patrolled the property or were asleep. Caleb did not blink an eye when it was revealed that intruders had been sneaking into the estate's grounds and had managed to bypass Jakiele's security. "No one is going to get by me and hurt Anna or her girl. You can count on me, boss. Tell me what you need me to do, and I will see it done." Caleb was visibly upset that the women were in danger, and he would do whatever it took to protect them.

"Mulakai and I are going to have to be upstairs working on a security lapse I have in my bedroom. We must remain undisturbed for several hours. I need you to make sure the house is completely armed with the new codes and the grounds are safe. I have installed new video and audio monitoring equipment in my office, enabling you to see the entire estate from every conceivable view. We will all be using small ear devices so we can communicate easily to each other and report in every hour."

Jakiele strapped the new devices around Caleb and Mulakai's left wrists and attached one on his own. He gave them each an earpiece and proceeded to evaluate them out to make sure they could hear each other without interference. Next, Jakiele escorted Caleb and Mulakai into his office and showed them both how the equipment worked and how the various video cameras and lights would automatically turn on with even the slightest movement by anyone outside who was trying to get in. The gadgetry was all top of the line, but Jakiele knew better than to trust electronics alone. He knew they were all in a dire situation. If Zadikiele suddenly decided to show up with his legion of zealots, it would take every ounce of his legendary abilities to ward them off. Even with Mulakai by his side, it would be a terrible battle that they might not win.

When Jakiele felt Caleb had a rudimentary understanding of how the equipment functioned, Jakiele and Mulakai sauntered over to the other side of the office and retrieved the laser devices they were going to install into the closet to protect the mirror. Jakiele felt confident the new devices would at least provide some level of deterrent against any of the demons trying to steal the mirror. As the two of them trudged up the stairs to Jakiele's bedroom with the heavy boxes, Mulakai could not help but ask, "So, how is it you were sent up here to retrieve Katliana for breakfast, and yet you took your sweet time bringing her back downstairs?"

Jakiele was momentarily taken aback by the blunt question and replied curtly, "We had some things to discuss privately." Mulakai laughed good-naturedly and quipped, "So nothing else happened? So why did Katliana look like she had been kissed quite thoroughly by you, and why were you both avoiding looking directly at any of us during breakfast? Anna looked like she wanted to strangle you. It looked to me like the two of you were doing more than talking." Jakiele abruptly stopped and turned to look directly at Mulakai before he ground the words out of his mouth tersely, "Whatever is between Katliana and me is for her and me to know. I have made a vow to Anna to protect her, and I will do what I promised to do! Any more questions?" Mulakai had never seen Jakiele get so possessive or angry over a woman before, so he at once backed off. Mulakai put up his right hand in a gesture of peace.

"Whoa, there, old friend. No need to get so defensive. I am sure you know you cannot be with her intimately. The consequences would be disastrous, as I am sure you are aware. I did not mean to intrude. My apologies." Jakiele immediately felt like an ass. Mulakai was right. He did know the consequences. He could not seem to think straight whenever he was in the same room with Katliana. His senses went on mental overload, and the rest of the universe ceased to exist when they were alone together.

Jakiele contritely apologized for snapping at Mulakai and said, "I am sorry. I did not mean to take out my frustration on you. I know

I cannot be with her, Mulakai. Believe me when I say I have only the best intentions toward her, but something about her drives me to do things I would not normally do. It is like an electrical current that runs down our bodies every time we touch. It is the strangest sensation and the most sensual thing I have ever felt in my life. I am trying hard to remember my vows to God and leave her alone. Yet all I want to do when I am near her is take her to the nearest bedroom and devour her. I have never felt this way toward a human woman, and it terrifies me for us both."

Jakiele admitted the last statement with such abject misery that Mulakai felt sorry for him. Mulakai placed his right hand on Jakiele's left shoulder in a gesture of friendly support before he quietly whispered to Jakiele, "Listen to me, old friend. No matter how much you may want to be with this human, she is a woman capable of bearing children. If you were to produce a Nephilim, God would kill you all. Michael and Gabriel would both see to it, and they would force me to be a part of it as well! So, you must stay away from her at all costs! There is too much at stake here. If you need to take care of your needs, see one of the whores in the city. Taking care of us is what they get paid for." The note of desperation and fear in Mulakai's voice reached Jakiele's ears the most loudly.

Jakiele had no intention of putting his friend or his mentors in any predicament, even if it cost him his happiness. However, Mulakai could see he had finally succeeded in making Jakiele see the reasoning behind his statements. Jakiele nodded curtly and headed back toward his bedroom. The two angels worked steadily side by side until they were sure the lasers all worked adequately in the closet. The glass shield which surrounded the mirror was now as protected as they could make it. It was late afternoon before they finished installing the lasers and updating any of the remaining codes in the house.

It was Jakiele's turn to relieve Caleb from monitoring the video cameras in the office. Caleb and Mulakai retired to the kitchen to see what Anna was going to make for lunch. They would bring something into the office for Jakiele to eat when Anna was done preparing it for him. He could swear he could smell Anna making cinnamon rolls with caramel icing. She had not made them in quite some time, and the whole house smelled terrific from her efforts. Jakiele smiled silently and envisioned Mulakai's face when he tried the cinnamon rolls Anna made, which could melt right in your mouth. A slight movement on one of the video monitors caught Jakiele's attention out of the corner of his eye.

Near the front gates was a hooded figure trying to enter the old security code to access the main entrance leading into the driveway. The individual would not look up into the camera, so Jakiele could not see what the hooded figure looked like. Furthermore, Jakiele could not tell whether the figure was male or female by the baggy clothes. He raced out of the office at preternatural speed and put his fingers to his lips in a warning to be quiet as he passed by Mulakai and Caleb in the kitchen. Alarmed, both Mulakai and Caleb jumped up from the kitchen table to follow Jakiele outside. Jakiele motioned for them to stay in the kitchen as he pointed to the front gates. Jakiele indicated he was going to go and check something out and for them to stay put.

Mulakai refused to be left behind. He motioned for Jakiele to take a left, and he would take a right. Both men descended on the front gate and stood behind the tall stone pillars on either side of the wrought iron gates. They could hear a woman talking into her cell phone. "Right. They changed the code on the gates. I cannot get in. Yes, both the women are here. No, I did not see anyone else coming or going. I only saw the two women enter the compound last night, and they have not left to go anywhere. Okay. No problem, I will keep watching and let you know if anything changes."

Andrea hung up the phone in disgusted resignation. She was tired of watching Katliana and her mother. This was not the kind of excitement she envisioned for herself when she agreed to join Zadikiele's cult of Satan worshippers. Instead, Mulakai and Jakiele jumped silently over the ten feet high gates. Before Andrea even had time to blink, Mulakai knocked her out cold with one hard hit from his hand to the back of her head. No damage to her body would be done except for a mild headache when she woke. Jakiele quickly scanned her memories while Mulakai looked through the numbers in her phone to see those to whom she had been talking.

The redial feature on her phone brought up the last person she had been talking to. She had been speaking to Dariah. He was the same demon Larissa had in her memories as well. This was the tangible evidence Jakiele needed to prove Zadikiele was the hound from hell they were looking for. Both angels looked up simultaneously when they heard loud screaming coming from inside the house. Jakiele and Mulakai leaped simultaneously back over the gates to run as fast as they could back towards the house to see what had happened.

Anna was incoherent with fear when they entered the kitchen and spoke so fast her accent became very thick. She kept pointing at the stairs in horror. Mulakai and Jakiele ran up the stairs in a blur of speed. They burst through the room Katliana had been using to see Caleb lying on the floor, unconscious in a pool of blood that was steadily streaming out of the back of his head. Katliana was nowhere to be found. Jakiele shouted at Mulakai, "Have Anna call an ambulance at once! I have to find Katliana!" Jakiele's heart felt like it was going to burst from fear right out of his chest. Mulakai raced back down the stairs to tell Anna to call for help while Jakiele did what he could to stem the blood loss from Caleb's gaping head wound. He grabbed the towels from Katliana's bathroom. He gingerly lifted Caleb's body to place the thick towels under the back of Caleb's head. He prayed the ambulance would get there quickly. He did what he could to keep Caleb comfortable and left the room to try and find out what happened to Katliana.

The demons must have been watching them all morning and had used Andrea as bait to get Jakiele and Mulakai to come outside to investigate. Jakiele had left the kitchen door open in his haste to get outside and had not bothered to reset the alarm. He had failed to keep them all safe because he had grossly underestimated his enemy.

They were as lethal and cunning as he was, and he should have never forgotten it even for an instant. As he rushed from room to room, he caught sight out of the living room window of a dark-colored van speeding down the road outside of his front gates and away from his property. Jakiele raced out of his front door and fairly flew across the grounds of his estate with extraordinary speed. But he was too late. He jumped over his front gates as fast as he could, but all he could see was the fading taillights of the van as it sped away. A wave of deep-down anger began to boil over in Jakiele. He wanted to chase after the van, but he had to make sure Anna and Caleb were okay before he tracked these demons and their minions down and killed them.

There was no way he was going to fail Katliana. He would find her if it were the last thing he ever did, even if it would cost him his life. He did not know why she had suddenly become so precious to him. Jakiele knew he could not live without her being alive in this world, even if it was not with him. He raced back to the house and went upstairs to see Caleb. Anna was standing worriedly over his limp body. Caleb's face was growing greyer by the minute. He was still alive, however. The wound was severe but not life-threatening, from what little Jakiele could see.

The ambulance crew arrived in less than ten minutes, and they raced Caleb to the hospital in the city as fast as possible with Anna in the back. Jakiele and Mulakai followed closely behind in Jakiele's Audi. The hospital staff rushed Caleb into emergency surgery to quickly repair the hole in the back of Caleb's head that a blunt instrument had created. Anna was hysterical with fear and was babbling in her native language as she kept hold of Caleb's hand until the trauma unit had to gently extricate her hand from his before he could be taken into surgery.

Jakiele went to stand next to Anna and put his arm around her shoulder to comfort her. He murmured reassuring words to her telling her everything would be okay. Anna was visibly shaken and was crying so hard it broke Jakiele's heart as well as Mulakai's. When Anna had finally calmed down and had regained her self-control, she broke away gently from Jakiele's embrace to tell him, "They came in the house so fast after you and Mulakai raced out. It was like they knew exactly where Katliana was. Caleb tried to stop them from taking her, but there were two of them. One was a small Asian man, and the other man was a very tall black-haired giant. He looked Samoan. The little Asian man came up behind Caleb as he fought with the big man in Katliana's room and struck him with a weapon in the back of the head. I ran back downstairs to start screaming for you to come back."

Jakiele calmly replied, "It will be all right, Anna. We will do everything in our power to get her back safely. I have a fairly good idea where they may have taken her. Please stay here with Caleb while we track them down. This may take some time, so I will assign guards to ensure you and Caleb will not be harmed. I can arrange for you to stay in a hotel room since going back to the house is not safe if you prefer." Jakiele patiently waited for Anna to respond. "No, Master Jake. I want to stay here with Caleb to make sure they will take care of him properly. Do not worry about me. They want my daughter, not me." Anna paused for a moment before continuing tearfully, "Please do everything you can to find my daughter and help her." Anna sobbed out the last request from the very depths of her soul.

The angels left the hospital together after taking care of the necessary paperwork and reassuring Anna they would be on the hunt for Katliana. They would not stop until they found her. Caleb had made it successfully through the surgery and was resting peacefully. However, Jakiele made a critical phone call to his military friends. Before long, armed guards surrounded Anna. The guards would take excellent care of her and Caleb and take proper action to see Anna and Caleb's protection. Jakiele gave the address of his safe house in Washington D.C. to Kevin Dylan. He was the leader of the specially trained group of men Jakiele had helped years ago. Jakiele asked Kevin to take Caleb and Anna to the safe house as soon as Caleb could be moved. Jakiele warned Kevin that it was critical for him to be on his guard and to speak to no one except him.

Mulakai and Jakiele raced back to Jakiele's house and started combing the house for clues. They noticed that the young girl at the front gate who had been trying to lure them outside was now gone. Both angels were incredibly furious with themselves. Somehow, they had allowed Katliana to be taken, and Caleb had been grievously harmed. They had beaten so many demons in eons past that they had taken for granted the demons who had broken into Jakiele's house would be simple to detect and therefore dispatch.

Every second counted as they looked everywhere they could think of for how the demons had managed to get Katliana out of the house so quickly. Lastly, both men walked into Katliana's room to search for clues. Katliana's drapes were open in her room, so when Mulakai went to look out of one of them, he quickly discovered their escape route. The demons who seized Katliana had managed to tie an exceedingly long zip line cable around the chimney when they had been in the house before and attached it to a large light pole the city had installed years ago for electricity. The light pole was found at the very edge of the backyard behind his fence. So, they had simply grabbed Katliana and glided down the cable to the main road in a matter of seconds. It was an ingenious plan.

Mulakai pointed out to Jakiele how they had made their escape without the motion detectors going off. Jakiele should have expected this from his extensive training, but he had not seen this one coming. If it was possible, now he was even more disgusted with himself. Jakiele swore several times before leaving Katliana's room to check on the mirror and ensure it was not tampered with. Mulakai was close on his heels, and they both let a huge sigh of relief when they realized the mirror had yet remained undiscovered.

Jakiele walked Mulakai back to the mirror and put in the code so Mulakai could go back through the mirror and let Gabriel know all that had happened. He asked Mulakai to try and convince Gabriel to contact Michael. Angels could communicate their memories to each other without speaking if they chose. Jakiele rested his forehead on Mulakai's and showed him all he knew about Zadikiele and his minions. The look on Mulakai's face was one of stoic determination as he grasped Jakiele's forearms in support. He gave Jakiele a deep bow of respect. Mulakai did as Jakiele requested and was transported back to the angelic realm to fill Gabriel in on the recent disastrous events.

Jakiele decided to go back into Katliana's room to thoroughly search it to ensure he and Mulakai had not missed any clues. The suitcase Katliana had brought with her to his house was laid wide open on the bed. A laptop computer was sitting on top of her clothes with open files displayed on the screen. It looked as though she was trying to analyze the tissue samples Kyle had sent her when she had been taken hostage. There was a photograph lying next to the suitcase, which showed the autopsy picture of Sue Kwon.

Jakiele instantly noticed the pinprick marks above the girl's left breast and knew instantly why all the individuals involved in trying to solve this case had been eliminated. The pinprick marks were the indelible prints a vampire would leave behind on their victim. This situation now made sense as to why Zadikiele would want to track down someone he thought could be a vampire.

Zadikiele did not want angels being made aware of a vampire on the loose. Jakiele wondered if Zadikiele intended to use such a creature for a nefarious purpose. No wonder Zadikiele had gone to such great lengths to keep this information from reaching his notice. If Jakiele or the other angels were to be made aware of a vampire's or demon's presence, they would hunt them down with brutal force. Jakiele perused the case file Kyle had sent her on the zip file she created on the laptop and read it thoroughly. Jakiele mentally took notes of everything Kyle had questioned about the girl's alleged cause of death.

If Zadikiele were aware that Katliana knew more than she should about this case, he would destroy her. Jakiele did not know whether there was indeed a rogue vampire running around somehow, but he would do everything in his power to find out. Jakiele was filled with an anxious but determined fury to find Katliana and make those who took her pay with their lives. He went downstairs into the basement, dressed in full angel armor, and called to his sword.

His armor was form-fitting and molded to his muscular body perfectly. It was made to blend into any environment he was in so he could remain unseen. His helmet would hide his face, and the unique sheath he wore disguised his sword until he was ready to use it. He bent down on one knee, closed his eyes, and prayed to the God he loved for the forgiveness of his failure in protecting those who were in his care. He prayed his beloved God would be with him and help him find Katliana quickly. He still hoped God was with him when he began slaying his enemies one by one without mercy.

# CHAPTER 10

Dariah had spent the previous day after Zadikiele had left making sure to watch all the video feed recordings in Jakiele's house. Latkia and Larissa were supposed to be out taking care of the sordid business with Rochelle and her son, so he felt confident that he would be left alone to perform his duties without worrying about whether the two of them were doing what Zadikiele had ordered them to do.

The monitor Dariah was watching showed that the women in Jakiele's house were making the evening meal when Dariah observed Jakiele coming into the house carrying a black box that looked like a voice recorder. The fiber optic camera Zadikiele had installed in the kitchen gave Dariah the ability to move the camera any way he wanted to provide him with a panoramic view of the entire kitchen area and the occupants within it. He watched with fascinated amusement the way Jakiele and the young girl named Katliana interacted with each other. He could also hear the muted conversations they were having with one another. He now knew the connection between Katliana and Anna and that they were mother and daughter.

Dariah was seated at his desk for many hours before checking on Latkia and getting a progress report on Rochelle. Nothing of note was going on in Jakiele's house, and the feed was boring him to distraction. Dariah was due to give Zadikiele a report within an hour on any progress he had made with the surveillance of Jakiele and his servants. Dariah could not locate Latkia anywhere in the compound, so he went outside to ask the guards posted near the entrance if they had seen him lately. Rochelle was due to be at Jakiele's at 5:30 pm, and it was now past 8:00 pm. Larissa should have returned half an hour ago.

One of the guards he questioned told him he had seen Larissa leaving by herself to take care of Rochelle. He thought Latkia was entertaining himself with someone named Noella. Dariah was not amused with this turn of events. Zadikiele had been clear in his instructions to Latkia to take care of Rochelle and Larissa personally. Dariah had been the one left in charge to make sure everything went smoothly in Zadikiele's absence. As Dariah crossed the yard to go back inside the compound, he grew angrier with every step he took.

Dariah knew which room Noella stayed in, so he marched up to the door and kicked it in. He found Latkia and Noella passed out together on the bed in a tangled web of sheets. An empty Vodka bottle was visible on the side table next to Latkia. Dariah was beyond furious as he marched up next to the bed and grabbed Latkia by the throat. Dariah squeezed tightly with his right hand and forced Latkia's body into a sitting position. Latkia was dazed, confused, and reeked of alcohol as he opened his bloodshot eyes. Latkia realized it was Dariah who held him in a vise-like grip around the throat. Latkia struggled violently and forcefully shoved Daria's hand away so he could breathe in some much-needed air to his oxygen-starved lungs. Latkia gave Dariah a venomous glare for waking him from his drunken stupor in such a brutal way.

"Where the hell is Larissa?" Dariah demanded. "She should have been back by now, you idiot! Why did you let her go alone? You know damn good and well what Zadikiele ordered you to do! Your incompetence could get us all killed. I must report to Zadikiele in one hour. Get your lazy ass up and dressed so we can figure out why Larissa is not back yet. Move now!" Daria's voice had raised to a deafening pitch, and it was not wise to cross him when he was this angry. Noella had woken up to Dariah shouting at Latkia and had looked at the two of them arguing in horror. She pulled the sheet up to her chin to hide her nude body from Dariah's condemning gaze. The lethal look Dariah leveled in her direction was enough to make her keep her mouth firmly shut.

Latkia groaned from the pain in his head, which his overindulgence had created from drinking too much Vodka, but he was quick to do what Dariah wanted and got dressed quickly. He knew he had messed up, and Dariah would not hesitate to report his laziness to Zadikiele the first chance he got so he could get in good with the boss. As Dariah impatiently waited for Latkia to get ready, he went outside to get the van ready for them to leave. Latkia stumbled out of the front door in a half-awake stupor a few minutes later, and together, they raced toward the apartment building where Rochelle and her son had been kept captive in the city.

The first apartment on the second floor they checked on was where the nanny had been placed to watch the little boy. The door was locked, and no one answered Daria's knock at the door. He signaled to Latkia to kick the door in. As they walked into the apartment, they both smelled the scent of fresh blood. They walked over to the kitchen and found the nanny's body lying face down on the floor with her throat slit. Dariah silently signaled for Latkia to check the rest of the apartment. Latkia came back into the kitchen a few minutes later and reported no sign of Rochelle's little boy or anyone else in the apartment.

Dariah and Latkia lifted the body of the dead nanny and took her outside to throw her corpse inside the back of the van. They would send a crew later to clean up the mess. Right now, they had to track down Larissa and Rochelle. They ran up the stairs to the third floor and noticed Rochelle's apartment door had already been knocked loose and was barely attached to the hinges. They entered the apartment with caution. Something terrible had happened to the nanny downstairs, and they were not sure what they were going to find in Rochelle's house.

The apartment was empty. But it had not been for long. There were cut ropes and duct tape left on the living room floor and in the bedroom. Tiny dots of blood were on the living room carpet next to the couch. They checked every room thoroughly and concluded that no one was there. Rochelle and her son had been taken by someone. Where was Larissa? Had she helped Rochelle escape? Had she killed Rochelle and her son and escaped herself? They had no answers, but they knew they were going to be in deep trouble with Zadikiele.

Dariah pulled out his cell phone and called Zadikiele, who was at the Assabet Animal Preserve, following up on the clues he had uncovered about the dead Asian girl. Zadikiele answered the phone with a curt, "What do you have to report, Dariah? I am a little busy now. I have been tracking a scent that may lead me back to whoever killed the girl. This had better be important!" Dariah hesitated a moment before revealing what he and Latkia had been doing for the last hour. Dariah did not throw Latkia under the bus for not doing what he was supposed to because to do so would have made it look like Dariah should not have been left in charge. Leaving Latkia out of the equation did not fool Zadikiele for one minute. He knew Latkia had failed to do what he had been commanded to do. Zadikiele would deal with Latkia later. For now, he still had use for him.

Zadikiele was so enraged it took him a few minutes to get his seething fury under control before he could get his voice restrained enough to demand Dariah hand the phone over to Latkia. Latkia was hesitant to take the phone from Dariah, but when he placed the phone next to his ear, Dariah could easily hear Zadikiele tear into Latkia for disobeying his commands. Finally, Zadikiele let Latkia know any future failures would result in death so macabre it would be impossible to put it into words, and he would make sure it was a torture that would last for millennia. Latkia was visibly shaken and pale when he handed the phone back to Dariah.

Zadikiele was convinced Rochelle had somehow enlisted Jakiele's help to rescue herself and her son. He commanded Dariah and Latkia to head back to the compound at once but not before disposing of the nanny's body in an inconspicuous way to avoid any further complications. Zadikiele was not worried about Larissa in any way. If she had managed to get herself killed or had left of her own volition, so be it. He knew she was not the one who freed Rochelle. Not only was she not intelligent enough to carry a plan of that sort of magnitude, Larissa would have rather seen Rochelle dead first before she ever lifted a finger to help anyone but herself.

What made Zadikiele the most infuriated was that Rochelle was free from his grasp and was no longer under his control. For an unfathomable reason, he was worried about her safety. When Zadikiele first met her, he could have sworn that he knew her from somewhere else, but he could not figure out how. Zadikiele fully believed he had trained her thoroughly enough to be deathly afraid of him. However, such was not the case, and he looked forward to finding her and teaching her what happened to those who thought they could get away from him. He intended to punish her severely for disobeying him, but for the moment, he had to focus on the tasks at hand.

Zadikiele made it clear to Dariah he was holding him personally responsible for monitoring the video feeds from Jakiele's house and to report to him directly if any new information came to light. He was very explicit in his instructions to Latkia to keep the security very tight around the compound. Zadikiele explained to both in detail his theory that Jakiele had been the one to rescue Rochelle. If he had somehow interacted with Larissa, Jakiele might know how to find the compound. Failure was not an option if they wanted to live.

Latkia and Dariah took Zadikiele's warnings to fulfill their duties and to do so with diligence very seriously. Zadikiele would not take any future fiascos lightly, and he would not hesitate to kill them both without a second thought. Zadikiele let them know he would personally see that the apartments would be cleaned and sanitized by a cleanup crew he had recently hired. The staff was eager to get new clients and not ask many questions if they were paid well. Money was not a problem for Zadikiele as he had acquired a substantial amount of it over the years by buying and selling real estate and investing in profitable diversions.

After leaving the apartment complex, Dariah drove the van to the city dump. The dump was closed for the day, and no one was around who could witness what they were about to do. They went around to the back of the van, stuffed the nanny's corpse into a large plastic garbage bag, and tied it securely closed with ropes. They lifted the heavy bag, and together, they pitched the bag onto a large debris pile. Next, they grabbed their shovels out of the back of the van to heap as much debris as they could over the nanny. Her body was soon buried under mounds of trash and was no longer visible.

When they were satisfied the body was buried enough, they got back in the van to head back to the compound. It was getting late in the evening now, so Dariah assumed there would not be much to see on the video feed, but it was his job to review every single second of the recorded material. He was not going to be the one to suffer from Zadikiele's vengeful wrath whenever Zadikiele chose to return. Dariah had ordered Latkia to stay outside with the other cult members and watch for intruders. Latkia was not happy about it, but he knew he did not have any choice or say in the matter after his major screw-up with Larissa and Rochelle. Besides, it was not as if he could not take a bottle of Vodka outside with him and let the others do the dirty work. Dariah would never know the difference. He was going to be too consumed with his electronic toys to pay any attention to what Latkia was doing.

Latkia had ordered the outside guards to be on high alert and let him know if they saw or heard anything unusual. Next, he grabbed himself a lounge chair from inside the compound and brought it out to the front porch to lay himself down and take a much-needed nap. He had his earpiece in place, and so did his guards. They had all been trained to detect even the slightest sounds or movement, so Latkia felt entirely at ease to fall into a deep slumber.

Meanwhile, Dariah had been catching up on all the new footage he had missed while he had been helping to clean up Latkia's earlier debacle. So far, nothing of note had taken place at Jakiele's house until he saw Jakiele go into his bedroom and open his closet door. He thought he saw a strange ornamental mirror covered encased in a glass cover for a split second. What an odd thing to see in someone's closet, Dariah thought to himself. Was it an antique or something Jakiele wanted to protect? Unfortunately, the closet door had closed so quickly behind Jakiele, Dariah had not been able to get a clear view of the object.

Dariah kept watching the closet door with keen interest. Several minutes had passed when a brilliant white light suddenly began undulating and shimmering under the closet door. The bedroom light was off, but Dariah could see the light coming from under the closet door was much brighter than what any ordinary light bulb could generate. Jakiele had been the only one who went into the closet, yet when he came back out, he was joined by someone else. Dariah caught another glimpse of an ornamental mirror as the glass case closed back around it. Unfortunately, the closet door closed again automatically, and he could not see anything else.

Dariah watched closely as Jakiele and what seemed like another angel emerged out of the closet with Jakiele. They both started to search the room methodically. Jakiele had called this other individual by the name Mulakai. Mulakai was very efficient in exploring space and supernaturally fast. Therefore, he had to be another angel, Dariah concluded. Before long, Mulakai had found the secret video camera, and Dariah lost his video feed. He watched in dismay as the two angels found the rest of the cameras placed in the house, which destroyed his ability to see and hear what they were saying to each other.

Dariah called Andrea on her phone and told her to keep an eye on Jakiele's house, take notes on who was coming and going, and await further instructions. He could tell from her tone that she did not want to do it, but he had given her a direct command, and she had no other choice if she wanted to be a part of the organization.

Dariah sat back in his chair and watched the video feed from Jakiele's bedroom repeatedly to see if he had missed anything important. He knew for sure that only one angel went into the closet, and two came back out. It had to be an inter-dimensional transportation device for the angels. The fallen would want to know about this right away. This information could be his ticket into gaining the same rank as Zadikiele if he could somehow find a way to use this knowledge to his advantage. He was tired of cleaning up after Latkia and taking orders from Zadikiele.

Dariah got up from the desk in his office and went down the hall to his bedroom. He lay down on the bed and shed his Earthly body so he could transport to the Underworld. He was greeted by Uzza, who was one of the original leaders of the fallen angels. Dariah got down on his right knee and bowed his head in allegiance and respect. He waited until Uzza acknowledged him before he dared to speak. Uzza held out his right hand and gave Dariah the gesture to rise before him and reveal why he had descended to the Underworld.

As above, so it is below. There were several dimensions to the Underworld. The place where the fallen angels were kept prisoner was very dark, and it boasted many caverns and caves. Jagged black rocks jutted forth from every direction. Molten red-hot lava spewed from deep craters, and dark smoke swirled through every crevice. Giant crystalline stalagmites seemed to hang suspended in the air by themselves below the ceiling of the largest cave where the fallen angels could convene if called upon. An enormous fire pit sat in the center of the large cavern, with a single large crystal hanging above it. Large razor-sharp chains with spikes were attached alongside the pit. All around him were the cries of agony and pain of the damned who were begging incessantly for mercy. Fallen angels liked to torture wayward demons and lost souls by lowering them into the deep abyss of the inferno and leaving them there until they were done entertaining themselves with the damned. Then, when they got bored, they would devise other ways of making demons who failed in their responsibilities suffer.

Uzza was joined simultaneously by Remiel and Azza, who had materialized out of thin air in unison. They did not want to consult with Lucifer unless it was warranted. Otherwise, they would suffer the severity of his wrath by disturbing him if he deemed their information unworthy. They positioned themselves to stand on either side of Uzza as they waited for Dariah to speak. Dariah had to tread carefully and diplomatically. He did not want the fallen angels to think he was trying to usurp Zadikiele's authority by not informing him of what he had seen first before seeking their council.

As Zadikiele has already informed you, he is following up on some clues which could lead him to the creature he believes may have killed a young girl. He thinks he may be trailing a newly created vampire. He does not want to be disturbed unless I have something of vital importance to reveal to him. Zadikiele has ordered me to view video footage of an angel named Jakiele that he has been assigned to watch. Jakiele and the servants in his house have somehow become privy to information about this young girl's death. Zadikiele is concerned angels may become aware of this creature's existence and that tracking it down will somehow lead the angels back to us." Dariah paused for a moment when he realized he had become surrounded by the other fallen angels who had become interested in what he had to say.

Becoming surrounded by the fallen angels unnerved Dariah to no end. If they did not like what he was about to reveal, they would dangle him in a pit of fire for all eternity if they wished. Dariah hesitantly continued, "While I was watching one of the video feeds Zadikiele had previously installed in Jakiele's house, I witnessed Jakiele going into the closet in his bedroom. There seemed to be a large ornate mirror encased in a glass kept deep inside the closet. Unfortunately, I could not get a clear view of the mirror. When Jakiele came back out of the closet, he brought back another angel with him named Mulakai. Mulakai was the first to discover the hidden video camera in the bedroom wall because he had somehow caught Zadikiele's scent. Unfortunately, Mulakai and Jakiele destroyed all the ones we had put in the house before I could glean any more information."

Excited whispers and murmurs rippled like a wave through the fallen angels as they discussed the various possibilities of what the mirror could mean. Uzza held up his hand for silence. The room fell eerily quiet as Dariah waited anxiously to hear what Uzza had to say. "I need to see for myself what you have seen, Dariah. Will you allow me to read your memories?" Dariah nodded his head in agreement. It was not a request. If Dariah refused, it would look like he was trying to hide something from them.

Uzza put his left hand on Dariah's forehead and closed his eyes in deep concentration. Dariah closed his eyes to relax while Uzza invaded his mind. Uzza quickly and efficiently flitted through the images in Dariah's brain until he found the memory he was looking for. Through Dariah's eyes, he could see the beautifully designed mirror. Uzza had never seen another mirror created like this one. Uzza speculated the Greys were behind the mirror's elaborate design. Uzza could magnify the image in Dariah's mind to see as many details about the mirror as possible. For example, he could make out the small Cherubim surrounding the outside of the mirror. Uzza inhaled a sharp intake of air and gasped.

Uzza concluded that Cherubim must have ordered the Grays to make this mirror for the angels to transport back and forth throughout the universe and remain undetected by the humans on Earth. This was exciting news. If the fallen could somehow get their hands on this mirror, they could figure out how it worked and use it for their own purposes. Azza had prophesied the fallen would once again inhabit and rule the Earth. This mirror had the potential to make the prophecy happen.

Uzza motioned for Remiel and Azza to come over and join him. Together they moved away as a group from the others so they could confer privately about what Uzza had seen. They were all motioning to each other with wild gestures with their hands and were having a very animated conversation. It was a conversation Dariah and the others were not allowed to hear. Dariah could see Remiel was not happy with the result of the conversation. He was glaring at Dariah as though he wanted to string him up by his entrails.

Uzza stood alone once again before Dariah and held up his right hand to signal he wanted complete silence. Then, he shouted a command to Dariah so loudly that the cavern walls shook. Uzza's tone commanded instant obedience. "Get on your knees and bow your head before the great council servant!" Dariah fell to his knees at once. His body fairly shook with fear knowing he had overstepped his boundaries by not reporting this information to Zadikiele first. He bowed his head so the fallen would not see the terror emanating unwillingly from his eyes.

Uzza raised both of his hands into the air to address the rest of the fallen, "My brothers. It is not right that God banished us here because we wanted to teach our secrets to humans. Is it our fault he created such beautiful women that it made us want to mate with them? Did he not also impregnate a human woman and produce a child? How is he any better than any of us? We have been banished to the Underworld for all eternity until Judgment Day. Why should we wait any longer to take what we want? Waiting down here while we plot and scheme when it may be possible for us to fulfill the prophecy Azza has foretold and regain our rightful place on Earth? I say we take back what is ours! What say you? Are you with me?" Uzza's voice had risen in crescendo with each word he uttered until the fallen had been worked up into a frenzy of voices screaming to be heard.

Uzza raised his right hand once again to effectively silence the large gathering before he addressed Dariah once again. "Bring us the mirror, and you will be rewarded with a rise in rank to a demon of first-class, and you will be given a coven to lead. Being a coven leader is the highest honor we can bestow upon you. You are to go back and inform Zadikiele of the mirror's existence and that we want the mirror brought to us. You are still to follow his commands until you carry out this objective. Keep this warning in mind, Dariah. If you are not successful in delivering the mirror to us, we will have no problem holding you personally responsible for your failure. Do you accept these terms?"

Dariah could not speak. His throat was constricted into a tight knot of apprehension. He raised his head to look at Uzza but could only nod his head in agreement. Uzza raised his hands to signal Dariah to get up off his knees. "Rise, servant, and see it done!" Dariah lowered his head and gave a graceful bow in subservience to Uzza and the others before closing his eyes and transporting himself back to his room in the compound.

He lay on his bed with his body still shaking violently all over, and it felt like his teeth were going to rattle right out of his mouth. He had never been so frightened in all his life. The fallen angels were a dark and malevolent group who had nothing better to do than think up ways to torture demons who failed in their missions and torment humanity. Unfortunately, they were exceptionally good at it too. The humans were lucky they had God and the heavenly angels on their side to help them. The fallen angels would take great enjoyment in sending demons to Earth regularly to cause endless anguish and suffering if they could.

Dariah got up out of bed as soon as his body returned to normal and reached for his cell phone so he could contact Zadikiele. Zadikiele answered the phone in his usual abrupt manner, saying, "What is it now, Dariah? Did you find out anything useful, or did you and Latkia manage to botch something else up?" To which Dariah placidly replied, "I did find something exciting, Zadikiele. It seems Jakiele has acquired a specially made mirror he has been secretly using to transport himself and the other angels to and from Earth. I contacted the fallen to let them know what I found and to see what they thought I should do with the information before I contacted you."

Zadikiele let out a long stream of curses before he yelled back into the phone, "You contacted the fallen without conferring with me first? You know you are supposed to follow the proper chain of command. So why would you do something so stupid?" Dariah waited patiently for Zadikiele to finish berating him before he replied smoothly, "You told me not to bother you unless I had something valuable to relay to you, remember?"

Dariah waited for Zadikiele to respond. Zadikiele calmed down and sighed heavily into the phone before he said with resignation, "Yes, I remember, Dariah. What did the fallen angels have to say about the mirror?" Dariah relayed the pertinent information he felt Zadikiele needed to know. He deliberately omitted that the fallen offered to elevate his rank if the mirror could be successfully retrieved from Jakiele.

Zadikiele digested everything Dariah had relayed to him before he responded after several seconds with, "Get the mirror, Dariah. Do whatever it takes. I am headed into Boston. The scent I have been following is getting extraordinarily strong. I feel as though I am close on the trail of the creature I have been tracking. Call me as soon as you have retrieved the mirror. Do not contact the fallen under any circumstances without conferring with me first. Do you understand me clearly?"

A smile of smug satisfaction grew on Dariah's face. His scheming was going to pay off if everything he planned to do to gain possession of the mirror came to fruition. "Of course, Zadikiele. Your wish is my command, as always. I will contact you as soon as I have it." Dariah hung up the phone and went outside to find Latkia. Dariah had seen how Jakiele had interacted with Katliana, and he was sure Jakiele would surrender the mirror if Zadikiele held Katliana prisoner for ransom in exchange for it.

Dariah was disgusted when he came out of the front door to find Latkia passed out in a lounge chair on the front porch. Was this moron utterly incapable of following even the simplest of orders? If it were not for the fact that he was Uzza's son, Dariah would have dispatched Latkia long ago himself. However, it was not his place to do so. It was for Zadikiele to take care of problem demons within his coven. But such a command did not mean Dariah could not teach Latkia a much-needed lesson. Dariah noticed another empty bottle of Vodka lying next to the chair. It would not be hard for a vengeful angel to dispatch Latkia if he remained consistently inebriated. Dariah would keep this bit of information in the back of his brain if he needed to reference it in the future.

With the rigid toe of his black army boot, Dariah kicked the chair so hard it made Latkia stop snoring and come abruptly awake. Latkia jumped out of the chair, prepared to do battle with whoever had so abruptly awakened him. But, instead, he saw it was Dariah who had kicked the chair. This was the second time this little Asian wimp had woken him up rudely today. It was starting to make him seriously angry. But he was slow and sluggish from imbibing too much alcohol, and his vision was still slightly blurred. So, he did not see the hard punch coming to his gut until he felt the pain as the air whooshed out of his lungs in one gasping breath. Dariah quickly followed with a brutal side swipe kick of his legs which upended Latkia and made him land in a punishing crash onto the hard ground.

Dariah was quick to wrap his left arm around Latkia's neck to hold him in a vise so tight it was difficult for Latkia to breathe. Dariah whispered into Latkia's right ear, "Now do you see how easy it would be for an angel to take you down? I could dispose of you right here and now with the greatest of ease, and no one would be any the wiser. So, you had better lay off the alcohol and women and start paying attention to your surroundings, or you are going to get us all killed!" Dariah squeezed Latkia's neck even harder to make sure Latkia got the point. Latkia could hardly breathe, but he held up his hands in a gesture of defeat, so Dariah would release his deadly grip on him.

Dariah made sure to stand back from Latkia after releasing his neck to give enough time for Latkia to recover his composure. After taking deep cleansing breaths of air, Latkia stood back up and glowered at Dariah. He knew better than to pursue an all-out brawl with Dariah in the sad shape he was in but being drunk did not mean he would let the incident go. "Do not ever put your hands on me again, Dariah! You forget I am the son of Uzza, and you are only here because Zadikiele specifically requested your ability with electronics. Your father was no one special, and neither are you! You can be easily replaced."

Dariah snapped back, "And I suggest you do exactly as you have been instructed by Zadikiele and myself from now on! Zadikiele is the one in charge, not you! Do you think Uzza would be proud of the fact that you are an abject failure at following even the simplest of orders? Cross Zadikiele or me again, and I will make sure Uzza will be made very aware that his precious little boy is a lazy bitch!" Dariah waited for his threat to sink into Latkia's addled brain before he finished by saying, "We have a lot of work to do tomorrow. The fallen angels have ordered us to seize an extraordinary object from Jakiele that they want to steal from him. To achieve our objective, I need something valuable I can use to force him to give us what we want. So, we are going to kidnap a woman staying there named Katliana. Are you following me so far?"

Latkia's face took on a look of surprise, and he was shocked into saying, "Are you serious? Do you want us to invade an angel's house? Are you crazy? He has top-of-the-line security installed all over his property! There is no way we will bypass his alarms and get anywhere near anything of value, even if it is a woman. You have lost your mind! You are going to be the one who gets us all killed, Dariah!" Latkia's voice had risen to near panic as he envisioned the plan Dariah had in mind.

Not to be dissuaded, Dariah outlined the rapidly forming plan to Latkia. If they arrived at Jakiele's compound early enough tomorrow morning, they might be able to use the codes Dariah had bypassed and enter the estate undetected. All they needed to do was climb up onto the roof and attach a zip line cable from the chimney to the light pole Dariah had noticed was close to the main road during his earlier surveillance of the house. Then, when everything was in place, they would wait until the perfect opportunity arose, and they would snatch up Katliana and leave before Jakiele, or Mulakai even knew what hit them.

The plan was simple in design, yet it would take perfect timing and precision to pull it off. Latkia sighed heavily before agreeing to the outrageous plan and said, "We had both better get some rest before tomorrow. It sounds to me like we are both going to need it." Latkia stalked back into the compound and went down the hatch to seek his bedroom. Dariah had no time to rest. He had to go over the plan many times in his mind to see all the conceivable angles on what could go wrong and make sure to develop contingency plans to counteract them. He was up well into the night gathering supplies for the dangerous mission and making sure their van was stocked with everything they were going to need.

Dariah spent more time watching the video feed he had recorded earlier to memorize the layout of the house's interior. He had only seen the outside of the house when he had been at Jakiele's estate earlier. His job had been to break the passwords Jakiele used, and he had done so with minimal difficulty. Zadikiele was the one who used Dariah's detailed information to gain entrance to the inside of the house to put in the video cameras. Zadikiele had used sticky tape to get the fingerprints off the interior alarm pads and had given them to Dariah to figure out what button combinations Jakiele had pushed.

It was not hard to figure out which room Katliana was staying in. Dariah knew the housekeeper used the loft in the garage for her main living quarters from Andrea's constant surveillance. The chauffeur did not live there as he had his own house in town. Therefore, the rooms in the house with locking keypads outside of them would not be her assigned room. The other bedroom on the second floor was more than likely the guest bedroom. Dariah surmised this room was probably going to be the one Katliana was using.

Feeling as though he had made as many preparations as he could, Dariah got up from his desk and left his office to seek the comfort of his bed. He did not believe in having sexual relationships with Zadikiele's followers. He felt such an interlude would compromise his authority and ability to lead. It was not as though he did not have the same predatory instincts as the rest of the demons. It was just that Dariah believed he had better self-control than indulging his animal instincts whenever the urge hit. Instead, he preferred to see to his humanly needs more discreetly by visiting a local brothel in the city where no one cared who or what he was if he came loaded with cash.

The following day, everything went according to plan. Dariah and Latkia had been able to sneak into Jakiele's estate without setting off any alarms. They had parked their van right next to the light pole found directly outside of Jakiele's backyard. Latkia attached one end of the zip line to the light pole, so when they landed, they would land right on top of the parked van. Everyone in Jakiele's house was still fast asleep, and they did not hear anything.

Dariah grabbed the other end of the zip line, raced across the backyard, and scaled up the side of the house using the house shutters on the outside of the windows until he reached the roof. Silent as a mouse, he crept across the roof and attached the other end of the zip line to the chimney. Dariah brought the tools he needed to make the cable line as taut as possible from the light pole to the chimney. He put two special attachment pulleys on the line. The pulleys would hold their weight while they zipped across the vast expanse of Jakiele's backyard.

Dariah gave the signal for Latkia to join him on the roof so they could see the entire property but remain unseen behind the large chimney. Before long, they spotted Jakiele out on his property, changing the codes on his front gates and installing cameras into the trees. It was vital that Jakiele did not detect their scent, and they were relieved to find a slight breeze in the air briskly carrying their scent away from Jakiele.

Jakiele finished installing his cameras mid-morning and went back into the house through the kitchen entrance. Before long, Anna and Mulakai came out of the garage and let themselves into the house using the kitchen doorway. Dariah and Latkia observed Jakiele's driver come to the front gates and punch in the new code he had been given before his arrival. Next, the driver drove up to the right side of the house and let himself in the kitchen entrance. The kitchen entrance was going to be the easiest way in, Dariah thought silently to himself. The kitchen is where the occupants of the house seemed to congregate. Dariah theorized that Jakiele would use this same door to exit the house in an emergency.

When Dariah and Latkia passed the house earlier in their van, they saw Andrea parked down the street asleep in her car. When it was the right time, they would call her and make her presence known outside of the main gates to distract Jakiele and get him to go and check out what she was doing. With any luck, Mulakai would join him. It was approaching noon when they decided to put their plan into action.

Dariah called Andrea on her cell phone and instructed her what to do and say. In the meantime, the two demons crept silently down the side of the house the same way they had come up and silently made their way around the back to the kitchen entrance. As soon as Jakiele and Mulakai left the house and started stealthily creeping up on Andrea at the front gate, Dariah and Latkia ran into the house and up the stairs before Anna or Caleb could react.

Caleb sprinted up the stairs after them and tried to engage Latkia on the second-floor landing in a fistfight. Dariah sneaked up behind him and clubbed him on the back of the head with the police-issued baton he had managed to acquire. Katliana opened the door to her room after hearing the commotion in the hallway and was about to start screaming when Latkia backhanded her hard enough across the mouth to knock her out.

Latkia and Dariah dragged Caleb's limp body into Katliana's room and let him bleed into the carpet while they bound and gagged Katliana. Latkia threw Katliana over his shoulder while Dariah opened the bedroom window. Dariah climbed out first and climbed back onto the roof. He lowered the first pulley with a cable attachment down to Latkia. Latkia zipped quickly across the line and landed on top of the van. He threw Katliana's limp body into the back of the van, quickly closed the door, and started the van while Dariah made his descent. They did not have any time to lose before they were discovered.

Dariah jumped into the passenger side of the van, and they took off at breakneck speed back down the road the same way they had come. They saw Andrea lying outside the main gates, unconscious. Dariah quickly jumped out of the van and threw her body into the back. Dariah grabbed the keys to her car out of her jeans and followed Latkia back to the compound in Andrea's car. They had barely made their escape when they saw Jakiele racing after them in their side-view mirrors. Neither demon felt like they could take a breath of relief until they had safely reached Zadikiele's farmhouse outside of the city.

Latkia hauled Katliana's limp body out of the van, took her downstairs into the basement, put her in Rochelle's old room, and locked the door behind him. She was still bound and gagged and had no way to escape. Dariah brought Andrea in from the van and placed her on the bed in her room. He checked her vitals to ensure she was okay before leaving her room to seek his own. He was the one who had ordered her to distract the angels, and he felt a little guilty Andrea had been the one to be harmed by the avenging angels. He would see to it she was well rewarded for her efforts. He might offer her a position in his new coven.

However, for right now, his main concern was making the necessary phone call to Jakiele to try and negotiate the release of the mirror in exchange for Katliana's life. Dariah had to find a way to kill Katliana because she knew too much about what had happened to Sue Kwon. He did not want her digging any deeper into the case. Dariah had to get the mirror away from Jakiele first. He hoped he had not overestimated Jakiele's feelings for the girl. If he were wrong in his estimation of Jakiele's affection for the girl, his plans would prove to be disastrous. Dariah's life was now on the line. He could not afford to screw this up, or the fallen would never forgive him.

They would take immense pleasure in letting him know he did not measure up for all eternity in their pit of hell.

Dariah jerked his head around by the sound of the trap door closing and hearing something landing heavily with a thud on the basement floor. Dariah left his room and went down the hallway toward the main living room and noticed a young man's limp body lying face down on the floor. The man was unconscious. Zadikiele's body soon came into view as he climbed down the steps and glared menacingly down at Dariah. Unfortunately, Zadikiele was so focused on Dariah that he did not secure the trap door.

Zadikiele sarcastically said, "You did not think Remiel was going to let your lapse in judgment slide, did you? You came to the leaders of the fallen angels without consulting with me first, which was stupid!" Zadikiele laughed mockingly at him before continuing with, "I will be taking over the assignment of retrieving the mirror from Jakiele. This is way out of your league. Your job is to follow orders. So, if you want a coven of your own, you had better start following orders, or you and I can finish our dispute right here and now!" Zadikiele was calm and enunciated his words slowly, but Dariah could tell that he was serious by the look in his eyes. Zadikiele pulled out his long knife from his right boot and prepared for battle by spreading his legs into a fighting stance.

Dariah's throat was working furiously while trying to decide what the best course of action would be. Ultimately, he decided that following Zadikiele was the wisest thing to do for now and bowed his body in acceptance. He felt betrayed by the fallen angels, but he could do nothing about it other than do what he was told to save his own skin. Nevertheless, being forced to humble himself for the moment did not mean he would not take the first opportunity he could to get out from under Zadikiele's thumb.

# CHAPTER 11

Dariah cleared his throat and responded smoothly back to Zadikiele, "It was never my intention to deceive you in any way. Before contacting you, I was simply trying to decide if what I observed in Jakiele's closet had any value. The fallen angels were the ones who told me to retrieve the mirror. The best way to recover it was to take something of worth from Jakiele we could use as leverage to get what we wanted. You asked me to investigate the link between the two women who showed up at Jakiele's house. I found out through Andrea's surveillance how the two women are connected to him. As you already know, the older woman is Jakiele's housekeeper, and Katliana is the housekeeper's daughter. Katliana is a forensic DNA analyst who works at a lab in Maynard.

Katliana had been sent a case file and tissue samples from the morgue director Andrea previously worked for. Andrea found out the director wanted the case file sent to Katliana for a second opinion. Andrea wrote down the name and address of where Katliana lives in Boston, and she filled me in on what she knew. The file contains specific details and questions about Sue Kwon's cause of death. I figured you would want to question Katliana and find out what she knows before we use her to get the mirror."

Zadikiele looked Dariah over suspiciously as if trying to decide what to believe before he reached down and put his knife back in his boot. However, he never took his eyes off Dariah for one second. He did not believe Dariah's story and knew Dariah had ulterior motives. However, since Dariah could still be of use to him, Zadikiele decided not to pursue the subject of Dariah's insubordination for now.

He snapped back at Dariah by saying, "If you think for one minute that Jakiele would trade an angelic transportation device in exchange for the life of some woman, you are sadly mistaken. More than likely, he is on his way to track us down like animals and kill us. Did the thought ever cross your mind, Jakiele would want vengeance before you two idiots produced this plan without talking it over with me first? If you were going to break into his house, you should have taken the mirror instead, you incompetent fool!" Zadikiele was frustrated unbelievably but demanded to know, "Where did you put the girl?"

Dariah gritted his teeth at Zadikiele's condescending tone. He ground out his following words with great care to not lose his temper, "We did not have enough time to study the layout of the house before Jakiele and another angel he had brought back with him through the mirror discovered all of the cameras you installed! They caught your scent and knew you had been in the house! Unfortunately, I could not decipher much about what the cameras could reveal before the two of them ripped them all out of the walls in the house! Nevertheless, as you said, Jakiele is now fully aware of our existence, so it does not matter!"

Dariah paused to catch his breath so he could calmly finish the sordid detail of the day's events with, "The only choice Latkia and I had was to take the girl as quickly as we could and get the hell out of there before we got caught! I carefully observed how Jakiele reacted to Katliana's presence in his house. I believe she could be of immense value to us! Besides, she knows about the dead girl and has already told Jakiele everything she knows! Watch the video feed for yourself if you do not believe me." Dariah added placidly, "The girl is being kept in the same room where you held Rochelle. Latkia knocked her unconscious and tied her up to the bed. I have not been able to question her yet to find out how much she knows." Dariah paused for a moment and looked down at Zadikiele's feet, where the young man Zadikiele dumped was still lying motionless. "Who is the young man you brought back with you?" Dariah queried.

Zadikiele kicked the body with the toe of his boot before caustically stating, "This thing is what caused the death of Sue Kwon. I tracked its vile scent back to a motel room in Boston. His identification says his name is Andy Lautner. He was a student at a college there. I do not have all the facts about how he became a vampire because I had to race back here and make sure you and Latkia did not do something stupid, which you two did per usual. Tie him up and put him in the same room as Katliana while I watch the video feed.

Afterward, make sure you and Latkia have the compound secure. I am sure Jakiele will be on his way soon since he most likely read Larissa's memories and knows where we are. Finally, round up all the cult members and tell them to get ready to leave. We do not have much time. Do you two think you can manage at least one small task without screwing it up, or do I need to take care of everything myself?"

Zadikiele was wearing away Dariah's resolve to be calm and subservient by the second. He was sure it was Zadikiele's goal to make him lose his temper and challenge him to a fight to get rid of Dariah without having to justify it to the fallen. No demon was allowed to be dispatched without their consent as it was too difficult to find suitable human bodies to inhabit, and it took an extended time to accomplish.

Dariah was trying hard not to react to how Zadikiele talked to him as though he was nothing but an insignificant servant. Instead, Dariah nodded his acquiescence to Zadikiele's commands. Then, Dariah reached down and grabbed the young man's body, who was still lying unconscious on the floor at Zadikiele's feet, and viciously dragged the young man's limp body across the living room floor to the first door on the right of the hallway where Katliana was being held.

Dariah made quick work of tying the young man to a chair by binding his arms and legs tightly to the chair. He did not want to take the chance of Katliana being inadvertently attacked by the creature should either of them come awake. Next, Dariah went from room to room to let all their followers know they needed to leave now. There were only about thirty members currently staying at the farmhouse. The cult member's rooms had multiple bunk beds to accommodate five members at a time. Dariah went to his bedroom next to pack what he needed. Then, he went next to Andrea's room to wake her and command her to quickly get all the other members to the tunnel exit.

Dariah went back up the trap door to track down Latkia and make sure the compound's security was as tight as it could be. Once the two had the guards positioned correctly, they ensured the compound could be blown up completely without leaving any traces of anyone who had ever lived there. Now all they had to do was wait for Jakiele to show up. The guards had to check in every 15 minutes, and if they did not, it would be a warning signal that Jakiele had arrived.

Katliana woke up with a startled gasp when she finally opened her eyes. The left side of her cheek was sore, and she could taste blood on her dry lips when she ran her tongue gingerly over them. She was in a dimly lit room on a bed with her arms tied above her head to a bed railing. Her feet were tightly bound with a rope, but she was able to struggle into a sitting position and survey her surroundings. From what she could see, she was being held in a basement with no windows and no way out except for a steel door found to her right across the room. There was a toilet and a sink off to the right of the door and what looked like video equipment in the upper right-hand corner of the wall.

While scanning her eyes around the room, she noted that she was not alone. A young man was tied to a chair near the end of the bed. His head was down, and he did not appear to be awake. He was wearing jeans and a Boston University T-shirt, but his clothes were torn and bloody. Katliana began pounding her feet against the mattress to try and wake him up and whispered desperately to him, "Please wake up! We must find a way out of here! I need your help! Please, wake up."

The young man began to shake his head back and forth as though he was coming out of some fog and could not think clearly. Finally, he raised his head slowly and turned to look directly at her. His face was pale, and his eyes were as red as blood. He did not say anything, but when he turned to look at her, his mouth opened into a lascivious smile, and she could see a pair of fangs on either side of his mouth dripping with saliva. He began to violently writhe his body to escape his bonds. Katliana began to scream repeatedly while trying to loosen the tight ropes around her wrists currently holding her captive.

She could hear someone outside the metal door inserting a key and unlocking the door. A short shaft of light from outside the corridor illuminated the figure of a tall man with blonde hair. Unfortunately, the room was so dimly lit that she could not see what he looked like. The blonde man strode quickly into the room and crossed the floor to stand directly in front of the boy. He struck the boy with his right fist. The vicious blow knocked the boy unconscious again. The blonde man turned to level a glare directly at Katliana and looked her over coldly from head to toe. The man turned around to walk back out of the room silently without a word. She could hear him locking the door from the outside and hear his footsteps as he walked down the hall away from them.

Katliana was paralyzed with fear as she watched the creature tied up at the end of the bed in the chair. What was he? He looked like one of the vampires of legend she had watched in old scary movies when she was a kid. Katliana wondered if she had been drugged and might be having a hallucination. Or she was having a nightmare she could not seem to wake herself from. Vampires did not exist, did they? No matter how much her scientific brain tried to rationalize what she was looking at, she could not deny what was right in front of her eyes. She did not dare make a sound. Even though it appeared the monster was restrained, she did not want to take the chance of waking him again. Katliana had never been so petrified in her life. She could only hope somehow Jakiele would be able to find her in time to save her.

Zadikiele watched the video feed from Jakiele's house in Dariah's office when he came upon the footage showing Jakiele and Katliana meeting for the first time. He watched with bored disinterest until he noticed the couple seemed to stare at each other for an extended length of time before Anna made introductions. It was clear Jakiele was as mesmerized by Katliana as she was with him. Inevitably, the traitor Dariah had been right about his observations. Zadikiele replayed the video feed repeatedly to make sure he was right in his assumptions before fast-forwarding some of the images on the monitor and reviewing the footage of the mirror in Jakiele's closet. Remiel had explained to him earlier how vital it was to try and get the mirror so they could find out how it worked and somehow replicate the technology to transport the fallen angels back to Earth.

Zadikiele could care less about fallen angels coming back to Earth to try and take over humanity once again. When he had been a Nephilim in eons past, Zadikiele tried to follow what he believed God wanted of him. He had not asked to be born, but he accepted his existence with shame at how the humans were being treated. Zadikiele had tried to convince the fallen angels that what they were doing was wrong but to no avail. He took a wife and had two little girls with her, and they were happy together. He did not want to be involved or take part in the evil deeds of the fallen angels or other Nephilim. He kept to himself and tried to do what was right by the Lord's standards. It did not matter, in any case. When the great flood came, the Nephilim were all wiped out, and his family had been destroyed in one fell swoop of destruction. There were no exceptions. He had been forced to watch his wife and children die. His family suffered before they died and went to Heaven. At the same time, he was condemned forever because he had been born a Nephilim. He and his family would never be together again in this realm or the next.

He vowed his hateful vengeance toward God, the angels, and the humans at once. He would spend eternity making them suffer if he could. If the fallen angels wanted the mirror, he would get it for them. If the mirror could somehow bring fallen angels back to Earth and destroy humanity once again, so be it. It was not as though he had anything to gain or lose. He had loved his wife with all his heart, and his family had been the only thing of worth to him. Since he could never be rejoined with them, he would do whatever he could to help the fallen angels achieve their goals purely out of his own need to have God feel the burn of his eternal grief and wrath.

Dariah came running down the hall and came into the office to report to Zadikiele, "Latkia and I did everything you asked, but now I cannot find him anywhere! I was busy inside setting up the plastic explosives, and Latkia was supposed to be positioning the guards around the compound. So, after I finished, I went outside to ensure everyone was stationed where they were supposed to be as you ordered. However, Latkia has not checked in with me, and I cannot seem to find him or any other guards! It is like everyone has vanished! They are all dead!" Dariah was in a clear panic.

Zadikiele jumped up from the desk, ran down the hall to the escape tunnel, took the key from around his neck, and unlocked the exit door. He left it wide open to quickly make a hasty exit with their prisoners. He shouted to Dariah, "Get all of our members to the tunnels first and then get the girl. You must take her to the barn and wait for me! Next, I must get the boy and read his mind to discover how he was created. We have extraordinarily little time! Do not even think of betraying me again, Dariah, or I will make sure you never take another breath! Move now!"

Dariah did as he was bid and ushered the cult members quickly into the tunnel. When they had all gone through, Dariah quickly entered the locked room where Katliana and Andy were being held and untied Katliana. Katliana started screaming and struggling valiantly against him by kicking and hitting him as hard as she could when he untied her bonds. Dariah did not want to hurt her, but he could not very well carry her over his shoulder with her flailing her body all over the place. He finally managed to roughly pull her arms behind her back and bind her wrists with rope to keep her immobile and retied her feet. Dariah found a roll of duct tape left behind on the sink, so he crossed the room to retrieve it and quickly fastened a strip of it across her mouth to keep her quiet.

Zadikiele had come into the room only minutes before Dariah arrived. He had placed his left hand over the vampire's forehead. He was trying to access any memories he could find about how the creature had been created. However, the visions Zadikiele was getting were cloudy and fuzzy as though it was not the boys' memories. He had to be reading someone else's.

The memories seemed to belong to the one who had bitten him. The hazy pictures flitting rapidly through the man's mind showed a majestic mountain located in a thickly treed forest of some kind. Zadikiele thought he recognized the mountain range. If it was a place he remembered seeing when he had lived in Europe centuries ago, it was in the Ukrainian part of the Carpathian Mountains. Unfortunately, the vampire's memories were so obscure that it was difficult for Zadikiele to yield any further information that he could filter through quickly.

Luckily, Zadikiele had hit the creature hard enough that he was still unconscious, and the boy had not awakened during the commotion Katliana had caused by screaming and cussing at Dariah in her native language. Dariah threw Katliana over his shoulder and exited the room in a hurry. Zadikiele was close behind him with the boy in tow over his shoulder when a large crash upstairs signaled trouble was not far behind.

Jakiele had managed to locate the compound with minimal difficulty after he had followed the map from Larissa's memories.

He was careful to park his car several yards down the road from the farmhouse. He surveyed the main building from a distance to get a better layout of the land. The guards stationed outside the main entrances were hidden in the brush and trees. He quickly detected their locations and where they were assigned to hide. He had to use stealth and cunning to swiftly dispatch the guards so they would not raise any alarms before he was ready to confront the demons.

It took Jakiele quite a bit of time to go from guard to guard since there were over twenty of them to sneak up on and kill as silently as possible. He found it quicker and made less noise to creep slowly up behind them and break their necks instead of unsheathing his sword, even though no one could see him in his camouflaged armor. His disguise did not fool Latkia, who had stayed hidden while Jakiele was busy dispatching the guards. Latkia had waited until Jakiele was about ready to enter the main floor of the farmhouse and had come up behind him with his own specially made sword.

Jakiele had almost crossed the threshold to enter the house when a slight movement out of the corner of his eye made him whirl around with supernatural speed and jump several feet behind where he had been standing. He had his sword unsheathed and had planted his feet in a fighting stance before his feet ever touched the ground. He shed his camouflaged armor with a single thought so he could be lighter on his feet and less encumbered. Latkia was advancing upon Jakiele with slow deliberation, with his weapon being held by both of his hands over his right shoulder in preparation for a mighty swing at Jakiele. Latkia's eyes betrayed his murderous intent, which would have intimidated lesser angels.

Jakiele did not flinch. He kept his eyes firmly locked on Latkia. He waited patiently for Latkia to attack and made sure to keep his eye on his surroundings so no one could come up behind him. The two adversaries started to dance around each other, waiting for the other to advance. Latkia launched his attack quickly with a violent crash against Jakiele's sword. The thunderous impact forced Jakiele to back up a few steps. This demon was powerful and skilled with a sword.

Jakiele knew not to underestimate his enemy. As the two parried blow after blow with their sharp, heavy swords, Jakiele realized his enemy was starting to get frustrated that his blows did not have the desired effect he wanted on Jakiele. Jakiele was able to anticipate Latkia's every move with a counterattack. Latkia's body was starting to shine from the sweat of exerting so much brutish energy, while Jakiele appeared to be completely calm and confident.

It was only a matter of time until Latkia would make a mistake from anger or arrogance and leave an opening for Jakiele to exploit to end the demon's life. Even though Latkia was beginning to tire, and his blows became less forceful, Jakiele did not let down his guard for an instant. Thinking you had beaten your enemy before you had could mean the end of your own life was a lesson Michael had drilled into his angels repeatedly.

Jakiele finally got the opening he wanted when Latkia reared up and was about to try and swing his sword down with one mighty blow on Jakiele's head. Unfortunately, the move left Latkia's chest wide open and vulnerable. Jakiele quickly took advantage of it by stabbing Latkia straight through the heart. Then, Jakiele jerked the sword back out of Latkia's body and spun himself around with his sword to cut off Latkia's head. Latkia's body and heavy sword made a loud crashing noise as they hit the floor.

Jakiele touched his bloody sword to his forehead and closed his eyes to give thanks to God for watching out for him. Then, he rolled over the heavy, lifeless body of Latkia. Jakiele inserted his sword next to Latkia's heart to incinerate the body from the inside, and in doing so, no traces of the demon would ever be found. Next, he walked over to where Latkia's head had rolled away from the body and placed it on top of Latkia's chest to be burned up as well.

Jakiele started searching the farmhouse, trying to find a secret entrance he was sure was hidden from the naked eye. He checked all the walls before noticing a worn carpet in the middle of the floor, which appeared to be out of place. He lifted the rug to see what was underneath and found what looked like a trap door. He lifted the trapdoor lid carefully and cautiously peered through the opening. There was a ladder leading down into some other room. He had to go down and check it out, even if it was a trap.

He climbed down the short ladder into the basement. The acrid smell of sulfur was so strong that it made Jakiele want to vomit. He had his sword at the ready as he slowly advanced across the expanse of the living room and started to come closer to what looked like a long hallway. Suddenly, he came face to face with Zadikiele, who was holding an unconscious man in front of him to protect himself. Zadikiele had a knife next to the young man's throat and intently watched Jakiele. Jakiele could barely see Dariah over Zadikiele's right shoulder, and it looked like he had Katliana held hostage in front of him as well. He could see Katliana's eyes were wide with fear as she stared back at Jakiele in terror.

Jakiele planted his feet once again in a fighting stance while Zadikiele laughed coldly at him and said, "If you ever want to see Katliana again, you will do exactly as I say. You will hand over the special mirror you have in your possession, Jakiele. You know which one I am talking about, so do not toy with me. I will let you know where and when I want you to bring it to me." Zadikiele reached into his coat pocket, pulled out a cell phone, and threw it next to Jakiele's feet. Zadikiele started backing up slowly toward the entrance of the steel door with his victim still held hostage close to his chest. Jakiele advanced slowly after him with his sword over his right shoulder, ready to attack at a moment's notice. "But if it makes you feel any better, you can have this one!"

Zadikiele took the knife away from the throat of his hostage and dangled the body of the unconscious boy in front of him with his right hand. Zadikiele threw the boy so hard he landed in the middle of Jakiele's chest and almost knocked him over. Jakiele shoved the boy off him in one quick move and started running towards the steel door at full speed, but Zadikiele managed to get the door closed and sealed before Jakiele could get to him. Jakiele yanked on the door as hard as he could, but he could not budge it an inch. It had to be several inches thick. Finally, Jakiele turned back around and scooped the cell phone off the floor Zadikiele had tossed to the ground and put it into his pocket. Then, Jakiele gathered up the unconscious boy in his arms to carry him out of the farmhouse to safety.

Jakiele was barely up the steps leading to the opening of the trapdoor before he heard the telltale beeping of a timer. The slow beeping could mean a bomb was about to detonate. It would not be a surprise if the demons rigged the building to explode to cover their tracks. Jakiele fairly flew out of the trap door and out the front entrance of the farmhouse. He had managed to cross the distance of the large yard before the crumbling building blasted into a million pieces. The force of the explosive blast knocked Jakiele to his knees, and he dropped the young man he had been carrying onto the ground in front of him.

The air left his lungs in a loud whoosh, and it was hard for him to take a breath. However, he never took his eyes off the boy in front of him. The young man he had been carrying sat up and started looking in the opposite direction of where Jakiele was located. The man was looking around as if he was dazed and confused. Jakiele noticed the bloody torn clothing the boy was wearing and wondered if Zadikiele had been torturing him for information. The boy finally turned his head in and looked in Jakiele's direction. Jakiele jumped back at least ten feet when he got a good look at the boy's features. His face was deathly white, and his eyes were a dark ruby red like the color of blood.

The boy seemed to be trying to figure out his next move. The vampire was fast. He managed to get up and started running as fast as possible to get away from Jakiele toward the main road. Jakiele was faster. He ran the boy down, tackled him from behind, and landed on top of him. He guessed the vampire had been no more than twenty years old or so before the virus changed him. It was a tragedy that this boy had lost out on living everyday life, but sympathy was not something Jakiele could afford to give him. He was a monster and had to be destroyed before hurting anyone else. But first, Jakiele needed questions answered.

Jakiele lifted the young man by the back of his shirt and forced him into a standing position. The vampire tried valiantly to struggle to get away from him, but Jakiele was quick to subdue him by clubbing the boy on the back of the head with the hilt of his sword. The vampire crumpled once again to the ground, unconscious. Jakiele carried him back down the road to his car and threw the vampire's body into his trunk. Then, Jakiele jumped into the driver's seat of his car and sped back to town at breakneck speed to his house. It was only a half an hour drive if he avoided traffic as much as possible. As soon as he arrived home, he would contact Mulakai and Gabriel at once and let them know what he had uncovered.

Once Jakiele arrived at his estate, he parked the car next to the kitchen entrance. Then, he raced into the garage to gather the supplies he would need to keep the vampire suitably subdued for questioning. He left the garage with car chains, thick ropes, and duct tape in his hands and went to the kitchen entrance. Jakiele hastily entered the code and ran into the kitchen to grab one of the chairs and place it in the living room. He moved the furniture hurriedly out of the way and set the chair into the center of the room. He put his supplies down next to the chair before racing back outside to open the trunk of the car.

Luckily, the vampire appeared to be still passed out. Jakiele lifted him out of the car and quickly ran back into the house to chain the vampire all around his upper body to the chair. He secured his wrists behind the back of the chair with the heavy-duty industrial ropes. Jakiele made sure to bind the boy's feet and the front legs of the chair. Next, he took the duct tape and firmly applied it across the vampire's mouth. He evaluated the ropes and chains for weaknesses until he was satisfied they were as tight as they could be without cutting off the fluids circulating through the vampire's body.

Jakiele ran as fast as he could to his bedroom, entered the codes necessary to open his bedroom door, and then raced quickly to the closet to access the angelic mirror. All the security precautions he had taken to keep the mirror safe took more time than he would have liked to spend deactivating them. Once he made it through the portal into the angelic mansion, he ran to the Archangel mirror to summon Gabriel as fast as possible. He went through the necessary steps once he was on his knees to call Gabriel forth to speak to him.

Gabriel's visage appeared quickly before him, but before Jakiele could utter a single word, Gabriel bellowed loudly, "I have been informed by Mulakai you did not obey my last commands to stay out of trouble! You have now gotten your servants entangled in your bungled mess, and one of them has been kidnapped by demons! Do your stupidity and ineptness know no bounds?" Gabriel was so exasperated with Jakiele the table holding the mirror shook with every word Gabriel shouted at him.

Jakiele was still on his knees with his head bowed when he heard Mulakai's voice come through the mirror. He could hear Mulakai come to his defense when he growled to Gabriel, "I did not say anything of the sort, and you know it, Gabriel! Jakiele and his human friends need our help, and your stubbornness is not helping the situation. If I must go over your head and find Michael myself, I will!"

Jakiele had stood back up during the heated exchange and stared stonily at Gabriel before saying in a clipped voice, "The demons took Katliana so I would be forced to exchange the mirror for her life. Whether you want to acknowledge it or not, Gabriel, we are all in serious trouble here. The demons know about the mirror, and for some reason, they want to take it by any means necessary. So, blame me all you like, but I will find Katliana and do whatever it takes to save her life. In the meantime, I have a rogue vampire in my living room I intend to question to try and locate her."

Before Jakiele could say another word, Gabriel again raised his voice into a thunderous rage, "You could not have a vampire in your possession, Jakiele! They were all destroyed along with the fallen angels and their misbegotten offspring! Have you forgotten the great flood? It is a human playing a sick game with you! There is no way I can sanction giving you permission to take the mirror and use it to gain back a human woman's life. Whatever mess you got her in, it is your responsibility to get her back out of it, but you are going to do it alone!"

Jakiele had never been so repulsed by another angel in his life. Gabriel's ambitions to supersede Michael's place in God's eyes were blinding him to the facts clearly outlined before him by two very trusted angels. If he had to rescue Katliana by himself, he would do so without hesitation. He had no intention of taking the mirror to Zadikiele. Jakiele did not feel the need to explain his motivations to Gabriel. The Archangel could believe whatever he wanted.

Jakiele responded with equal venom right back to Gabriel, "I know what kind of creature awaits me in my house, Gabriel. I will use him to gain the information I need to find the demons and get Katliana back without your help. But believe me when I tell you Michael will not be pleased when he finds out you could have helped, and you chose not to. I will also be more than happy to inform him you refused to fill him in on all of this when you could have. You are more than welcome to come back through the portal and see the evidence for yourself, or you can stay here and face Michael and God's wrath for not interceding when you should have! What say, you Gabriel?"

Gabriel had never been talked to a lower angel in such a brazen manner before. His face twisted into a malevolent rage when he had first addressed Jakiele through the mirror. However, his demeanor changed when he looked over his left shoulder at Mulakai and saw the look of utter disgust forming in Mulakai's eyes at Gabriel's disrespectful treatment of Jakiele. Mulakai stared back at Gabriel with mutinous intensity and crossed his arms over his chest. Gabriel took a few minutes to regain his composure, resumed his authoritative tone, and again addressed Jakiele, "Fine. Have it your way, Jakiele. Mulakai will join me, and if we conclude it is necessary to contact Michael, I will do so right away. Do you agree to these terms?" The silky sweet tone of Gabriel's voice made Jakiele suspicious, but he nodded his head in agreement.

Jakiele took a couple of steps back, and Mulakai emerged from the mirror. Gabriel came through a couple of minutes later. Gabriel was an impressive-looking Archangel, to be sure. However, Jakiele understood why God would send this Archangel to be the destroyer of his enemies. Gabriel was well over six feet tall, but his thickly muscled thighs and arms made him appear much more aggressive.

His hair was pure white and hung down well past his waist. His eyes were a dark chocolate brown. Many angels reported his eyes often appeared to turn black when he was angry. The lines around his eyes and mouth suggested he had seen his fair share of blood and warfare. The long beard he favored was as long as his hair. Gabriel liked to wear long flowing white robes allowing him freedom of movement. The sword he had been gifted with was long and sharp, but it was uniquely made so that it could separate into two equally deadly swords upon Gabriel's command.

The two angels went back through the angelic portal into Jakiele's closet. They were quickly joined by Gabriel, who detested this form of travel. He only used the mirrors if he had to. The trio of angels entered Jakiele's bedroom and went as a group back down the main stairs into the living room. Gabriel followed closely behind Jakiele and Mulakai and was the last to enter the living room to see the young man restrained in the chair by several chains. "Is he still alive?" Mulakai asked the question softly to no one in particular. "The last time I checked, he was still breathing, Mulakai, but do not get too close to him unless you want to get bitten," Jakiele warned.

Since Gabriel had come into the living room last, he had to move Jakiele and Mulakai gently out of the way so he could cross the expanse of the living room and bend down close to the boy to get a good look at him. Gabriel bent down on his knees and grabbed the back of the boy's short brown hair gently with his hand so he could look at the young man's face. Gabriel's face was only a scant inch away from the vampire when the boys' eyes flew open. Gabriel let go hastily and jumped back from the boy.

The vampire began to hiss through his teeth at the angels and glared at them through his evil red eyes. Then, his body began to writhe and contort to free himself of his bonds. Although the vampire was unnaturally strong, Jakiele had tied him to the chair very tightly, and he soon stopped struggling. Once he settled down, he stared at the angels with suspicion and hatred in his eyes. Gabriel lifted his hand and ripped the duct tape off the boy's mouth in one quick motion.

Gabriel was the first to speak in a tone dripping with ice, "Who are you? How is it you became a vampire! Speak now!" The vampire focused his deadly gaze on Gabriel alone, and surprisingly, the boy's eyes and visage changed to that of an ordinary man. His eyes changed to a hazel color, and his fangs receded into his mouth. "My name is Andy Lautner. I do not know what has happened to me. The last thing I remember was I was at a frat party about a month ago. One of the guys in my fraternity invited exchange students from different countries to come over and drink with us. I drank too much and went to my room to pass out. The next thing I knew, I woke up with an uncontrollable urge to drink blood."

The boy paused and lowered his head in shame. The vampire looked back at Gabriel and continued, "At first, I started noticing my speed and strength seemed different. My vision and hearing got more acute. I started having horrible nightmares about attacking people and drinking their blood. I was terrified, and the more I tried to ignore my thirst, the worse it got. I wanted to stay as far away from people as much as possible to not hurt them. I decided to go for a nature hike at the Assabet Nature Preserve, and I noticed there was a beautiful girl who was out there alone taking pictures of the wildlife near one of the trails."

The young man once again lowered his head to continue in a tearful voice, "I did not mean to hurt her! I could not help myself. Before I even realized what I was doing, I had pounced on her like some animal and began sucking the blood out of her until I drained every drop. I know I killed her." The boy began sobbing uncontrollably. The angels all looked at each other in stunned amazement and once again focused their attention back on the boy. Gabriel walked back over and bent down in front of him to softly say, "Is there anything else you can tell us about how this happened to you?"

The boy tried hard to regain his composure and added, "After I left the girl, I went back to Boston to a motel room. I did not know what to do. I was so repulsed by what I had done. I had to be alone. I had to figure out why I had dreams of places I have never been and of people I have never met. It was as though I was seeing things through someone else's eyes. I was so scared. I had only been at the motel for a couple of days when a dude busted down my door and knocked me out. He took me to a basement room where they were keeping a woman prisoner as well. She started screaming when she saw me, so the man came back into the room and knocked me out again. The next thing I know, I have this guy chasing me down trying to kill me." Andy nodded his head in Jakiele's direction.

Jakiele gave a short, harsh laugh before he responded with, "If I wanted to kill you, rest assured you would be dead. However, the young woman you were being held hostage with is important to me. You may be the only lead I have in trying to find her. I believe your dreams are the memories of the creature who made you. Those memories could help us find where my enemy took her. If you agree to help us, I will spare your life until Michael, my superior, decides what to do with you. Otherwise, we can kill you right here and now!" Jakiele quickly placed his sword next to Andy's throat to let the boy know the threat was real.

Andy's eyes grew wide with terror. He did not want to be a vampire, but he did not want to die either. His throat was convulsing with fear as he nodded his head quickly in agreement. Gabriel stood up in front of the boy and signaled for Jakiele to lower his sword with his hand. Jakiele did so reluctantly and slowly took a few steps back from Andy and sheathed his weapon. The angels left the living room and went to converse privately in the kitchen. Gabriel appeared to be visibly shaken the most by what they had just seen.

Gabriel turned to look at Jakiele and whispered vehemently, "I will do my best to find Michael and inform him about what has transpired here. However, be warned, Jakiele, we cannot let the demons get that mirror under any circumstances! Use the creature in whatever way you can to find your friend, but I want you to be aware that no matter what, I will be bringing you up on charges of misconduct before the high council! I will give you 72 hours, and if you have not found her by the designated time, it will be too late. I will leave Mulakai here to assist you if you wish."

After returning to the living room, Gabriel turned toward Mulakai and addressed him, "I would rather you not become involved in this debacle, but if you choose to do so, I will respect your wishes." Mulakai nodded his head and said to Gabriel, "I meant what I said, Gabriel. If you do not contact Michael, I will. This is not Jakiele's fault, and I will do everything in my power to bring these demons to justice."

Gabriel's mouth tightened in disapproval, but he turned and strode quickly back up the stairs with Jakiele and Mulakai hot on his heels. Jakiele opened the portal, and Gabriel went back to the heavenly mansion. Jakiele secured the mirror once again, turned to look at Mulakai, and told him, "I have to make a few phone calls to make sure Anna and a friend of mine named Rochelle are going to be safe while we are gone. Can you see if you can read the vampire's memories and find out where we should start?"

Mulakai agreed, and the two of them parted ways. Jakiele went back into his office to make the necessary calls, while Mulakai went back into the living room and stared at Andy for a few minutes in utter disgust before he finally addressed him, "I have to put my hand on your forehead to try and see if I will be able to access the visions you have seen in your mind. But, nevertheless, know this, if you try to bite me, I will end your life. Do you understand me?"

Andy nodded his head. Mulakai slowly approached the young man and gingerly placed his left hand on the boy's forehead. Cloudy, hazy images began flitting in rapid succession in the boy's mind. Mulakai was having a tough time distinguishing the details. He had a quick flash of a tall mountain hidden in a grove of thick trees. A beautiful lake was featured prominently in the forefront of the forest. Mulakai studied the Earth and its geographies for years. He had long-awaited being given an assignment to Earth by Gabriel. He was sure the mountain range in Andy's memories was located in the Carpathian Mountains.

The boy's party he had talked about attending also flitted through the boy's memories, and Mulakai could see the group of exchange students Andy had been talking about. However, there was one boy who stood out in the group. He had long black hair and black eyes. Mulakai saw the stranger's eyes turn red in the memory for a single moment. Mulakai now knew what the vampire looked like who had created this boy. The boy appeared to be about the same age as Andy. However, appearances could be deceiving since vampires could live for hundreds of years. Therefore, it depended on what age they had been turned into one.

Mulakai was about to open his eyes and release his hand from the vampire's forehead when the boy tried to attack him. Somehow, Andy had loosened his chains and was able to get his hands free. He reached up and grabbed Mulakai's left wrist in a vise-like grip and was trying to lower Mulakai's wrist to his fangs. The fangs had elongated in anticipation of taking Mulakai's blood. Jakiele came back to the living room and could see what Andy was trying to do. Before he could intervene, Mulakai had unsheathed his sword with his right hand and rammed his sword to the hilt through the vampire's heart.

Mulakai pulled the sword back out of Andy's convulsing body and cut off his head. He did not know if the method for killing vampires was the same as demons, but he figured it could not hurt. Mulakai went around to the back of the chair and retrieved the head. He placed the head on the lap of Andy's dead body and reinserted his sword into Andy's heart to burn the body from the inside out. The white-hot burn was so intense that it only took seconds for the body to turn to ash and any blood spilled in the immediate vicinity. There would be no evidence left behind this vampire had even existed.

# CHAPTER 12

Mulakai walked over to where Jakiele was standing at the entrance to the living room. Jakiele turned away from him and strolled back to his office. Mulakai followed close behind, took the seat on the opposite side of Jakiele's desk, and exhaled a heavy breath. Mulakai was the first to speak, "The details I was able to muddle through in the boy's brain were not clear, but I think I may know where the original vampire hailed from. I remember seeing this mountain range before when I studied the geography of the Earth, but I am not completely positive. Is there any way you have access to any maps or pictures of the Carpathian Mountain Ranges?"

Jakiele chuckled softly and replied, "Welcome to the twentieth century, my friend. A computer search should be able to help us." Jakiele turned on his computer and typed in what they were searching for. Mulakai went to stand behind Jakiele so he would be able to view the images flashing on the screen. A photograph caught Mulakai's eye of the Gorgany Mountains with Lake Synevir located in the forefront of some densely forested trees. Mulakai knew instinctively that this was the location he had seen in Andy's hazy visions.

Mulakai pointed to the photograph and shouted, "Stop! This location is where we should look. Can you find out any more information about the location?" Jakiele clicked on the photograph so they could glean more details about where the vampire could have originated from. The Gorgany mountain ranges they read about were considered the least accessible and least populated part of the Ukrainian Mountains.

The peaks were separated from each other by deep ravines, and their slopes were extremely steep. The thickly forested ranges were filled with many rivers, rapids, and falls surrounded by lush foliage. The minorities who had once inhabited the area in the early part of the twentieth century no longer lived there. Large lumber mills and health resorts were the primary source of income for the territory, facilitated by the only railroad in the Gorgany. The railroad connected the Prut River valley with Transcarpathia through the Tatarski pass.

Jakiele and Mulakai reviewed the information before them on the computer monitor with trepidation. Jakiele was the first to speak, "This remote location makes sense. There is no one around for miles, and it would be easy to conceal who or what you were from the mortals or us. There are a million places to hide. It is not surprising that the humans who once lived there are now gone, which certainly speaks volumes. If the vampires are involved with the commercial enterprises in the area, they could live quite comfortably in seclusion, and no one would be any the wiser."

Mulakai nodded his head in solemn agreement before he replied, "If we go there, there will be no way Michael and Gabriel will be able to find us, let alone help us. If Zadikiele takes Katliana there, the vampires who may live there will more than likely help him versus us. We are way outnumbered here, Jakiele, and we have only been given 72 hours to find her. Since Zadikiele took Katliana, we have not heard one word from him, and he has more than a few hours' heads start on us. We are going to need reinforcements."

Jakiele knew Mulakai was right. However, he thought he might have a solution. He went over to the table where the same equipment being successfully used by the secret service still lay unused. A small homing beacon would give Mulakai the ability to find Jakiele if he were within a 1000-yard range. Jakiele attached the sensor to his lower back. Together, they assessed the handheld beacon to ensure it was in working order. Jakiele grasped Mulakai's forearms with his and looked Mulakai in the eyes before he quietly stated, "This is my fight Mulakai, not yours. You have been a good friend to me and if this is the last time I see you, know I am grateful for all you have done."

Mulakai grasped Jakiele's forearms in return before he answered, "I will do all I can to help you retrieve the woman, Jakiele. Have faith, brother, and God speed your way. Take me to the portal, and I will get us the assistance we need if I must summon every angel in Heaven! We must move quickly, but protect the mirror, or your life will be forfeit. Promise me you will not do anything to put the mirror in jeopardy, even if it means the girl dies. I must have your word of honor, Jakiele!"

Words felt like they were stuck in Jakiele's throat. His tongue refused to cooperate and utter the placating words Mulakai needed to hear. Jakiele knew he had to make the necessary vow to Mulakai. His heart felt like a tight vise was closing in, and he was losing the ability to draw air into his tortured lungs. Finally, he nodded his head in agreement. The two warriors once again grasped each other's forearms in farewell before Jakiele pressed the beacon into Mulakai's hand and escorted him to the portal so he could send Mulakai back to the angelic realm safely.

Jakiele went back to his office to make the necessary flight arrangements to travel to Europe as inconspicuously as possible. He did not want to rely on commercial flights if Zadikiele's followers watched his movements. Since he could not use his angelic wings and fly while stationed on Earth, he would have to rely on human means of travel. He could get a ride on one of the military jets to Romania after calling in a favor. The flight would take him to Cluj Napoca. His military friends could arrange for a helicopter to drop him off near Lake Synevir. The flight alone would take thirteen hours to get to Romania and at least another couple of hours to get to Lake

Synevir. Time was going to run out to find Katliana quickly. He had to figure out how to get her away from Zadikiele as fast as possible, but he had to do it safely. He made sure to take his trusted sword and armor with him so he could remain hidden while he searched for her.

The military conveyance taking him to Romania was uncomfortable. Jakiele knew he needed to get as much sleep as possible on the long flight. I was early in the morning when a taxi dropped him off in front of the City Plaza Hotel in the heart of Cluj Napoca. He went into the opulent hotel and arranged for a suite to be reserved for at least two days. After that, he was due to meet with the helicopter pilots at St. Michael's church. They would covertly drop him off a couple of miles outside Lake Synevir at 11 AM. Katliana had now been in the demon's clutches for close to twenty-four hours, and Jakiele was genuinely concerned for her safety. It was becoming increasingly difficult for him to concentrate on the tasks at hand.

He knew Katliana was only safe if Zadikiele perceived she could be of value as a bargaining tool. In turn, he also knew Zadikiele would kill her without a thought if he knew Jakiele had not brought the mirror with him to trade for her life. Therefore, to successfully retrieve Katliana, Jakiele would have to use stealth and cunning to find her without being detected by the demons or the vampires. He did not know how he was supposed to accomplish it yet. Nevertheless, Jakiele knew he had to do everything he could to save her.

Once he checked into his hotel room, he decided to shower to clear his head after calling room service and eating a hearty breakfast. He was going to need all his strength. After he was done, he dressed in warm clothes since the mountains would be chilly even in the summertime. He laid out his special armor and sword on the bed and slid down to his knees. He closed his eyes tightly and said his prayers to God, and asked the Lord to please keep Katliana tightly in his care until Jakiele could reach her. He only hoped God was still on his side and would give him the strength he needed to safely rescue Katliana.

Jakiele paused in his prayers when Zadikiele's phone began to ring. Jakiele got up off his knees, went over to the bedside table, and retrieved the phone to answer it. Zadikiele's raspy voice irritated Jakiele's sensitive ears when he said, "You know what I want, angel. Bring the mirror to me, and the woman will not be harmed. You know very well what I will do to her if you do not." Jakiele could hear Katliana's muffled sobs in the background. Jakiele's heart lurched in response, and he could feel a wave of deep anger start to burn in the depths of his belly. Finally, Jakiele replied tersely, "Put her on the phone and let me hear her voice for myself so I know she is well. Know this, though, demon, if you harm one hair on her head in any way, there is no place you will ever be able to hide from me, on Earth or in the Underworld. So do as I say, or you will get nothing!"

Zadikiele's demonic laugh in response grated on Jakiele's nerves, but Katliana's shaky voice came on the line as she tentatively queried, "Hello? Jake?" Jakiele breathed a heavy sigh of relief before he steeled himself to answer her, "Are you all right, Katliana? Are you injured?" Katliana answered back vehemently, "No! I am furious, but I am not hurt. Do not come for me! Do not give him what he wants, or he will kill us both!" The last part of her sentence had trailed off as if the phone had been jerked away suddenly from her hand. Muffled sounds of distress indicated her mouth was being forced shut with tape or cloth. Then, Jakiele heard a loud slap as though someone had struck her resounded loudly across the phone. Jakiele's hands curled into tight fists at his sides in frustrated impotence at not being able to strike out at those who were assaulting her and holding her prisoner against her will.

Zadikiele's earlier amusement had faded from his voice when he once again spoke into the receiver, "So now you know your little bitch is still alive. For now. However, be warned, Jakiele, if you try to find her or do not produce the mirror, she will not be for long, I promise you, but not before I thoroughly enjoy myself with her first. You know what I mean!" The phone line went dead as Zadikiele ended the call with his final threat. What Zadikiele did not know was that Jakiele was waiting for the phone call so he could put a trace on Zadikiele's location through the GPS tracking device he had downloaded into the phone. He had been given access to the NSA's satellite many years ago if an emergency had ever arisen. He needed to track down the president's location. Jakiele looked at the laptop he had synchronized to the phone he had left lying open on the bed. Zadikiele was calling from another hotel a couple of blocks down the street.

Jakiele dressed in his specially made armor quickly and headed to the hotel where Zadikiele had called from. His camouflaged armor made him appear invisible, and he was quick to take advantage of it as he walked out of the hotel and crossed the street. He waited patiently for Zadikiele to make an appearance. A taxi appeared in front of the hotel, and Zadikiele, Katliana, and Dariah entered it. He could see Katliana struggling against the vise-like grip Dariah had on her left wrist before he violently pulled her into the taxi to sit between him and Zadikiele. The taxi driver loaded several bags into the trunk. It appeared as though some of the luggage held camping equipment. He overheard Zadikiele order the cab driver to take them to the train station. Jakiele figured the trio would head by train into the Carpathian Mountains and camp out by the lake Synevir while they figured out how best to track down the vampires.

Jakiele headed back to his hotel room and packed up his gear. After leaving his hotel room, he headed to St. Michael's church to wait for his Romanian helicopter pilots. It was not long before they arrived to take him to his destination. It would take an hour or more by helicopter, which would give him time to scout the lake and surrounding forest before Zadikiele arrived. He was using the time he had before he got to the lake to rack his brain and create a plan to rescue Katliana. The only thing he could think of was to try and wait for an opportunity to arise while keeping an eye on Zadikiele and Dariah.

Meanwhile, Mulakai had traveled back to the angelic realm and went to kneel in front of the Archangel mirror. He spoke his required exaltations to the God he served and requested an audience with Gabriel. Gabriel must have been waiting for him as he stepped through the mirror into the heavenly mansion followed by Michael. Mulakai raised his bowed head, and he could see the nervous apprehension on Gabriel's face and the explosive anger on Michael's. Gabriel must have already explained what was going on, and Michael was not pleased it had taken so long for Gabriel to bring him up to speed on recent events.

Mulakai stood back up and greeted them both in warrior fashion before he launched into his explanations about why he had come back and where Jakiele was headed. Michael looked deeply into Mulakai's eyes before he said very quietly, "Mulakai. You are a very loyal friend to Jakiele, which I deeply appreciate." Michael turned his head and glared hotly at Gabriel before he added, "Honesty and integrity seem to be in short supply these days." Michael turned his head back and addressed Mulakai, "It would save a great deal of time if I could simply read your mind and see what you have seen. Would you allow me the honor?"

Mulakai nodded his head quickly in acceptance. Michael took a few steps closer to Mulakai, placed his forehead on Mulakai's, and promptly scanned Mulakai's memories for the information he sought. Then, Michael turned and walked away. He was in deep thought. When he turned back around, his eyes were as cold as blue ice. His voice nearly shook with his internal rage when he turned his laser-focused glare on Gabriel and softly spoke, "I always want to make sure I have all the facts before I make any decisions. If I understand this situation correctly, a vampire has been created somehow, and a human woman in Jakiele's home had miraculously become aware of its existence through the work she does. This woman came to Jakiele for protection because her mother was in his employ and thought they would be safe with him. Jakiele came to the angelic realm to relay this information to me. However, instead of informing me immediately, I was kept in the dark until it became apparent I was needed to save the mirror because demons found out about it and wanted to bring it to the fallen angels! Do my conclusions about sum it up?"

Gabriel's face turned a deep red with embarrassment as he angrily retorted, "Had you not allowed Jakiele to have humans in his home in the first place, you would not have had to be summoned back, Michael! I could have managed everything myself. He was supposed to observe and report on the activities of the humans, not interfere! You know this! I fully intend to bring him up on misconduct charges before the high council when this is over! I gave him 72 hours to try and save the girl, which is more than I should have!"

Michael's voice grew even softer, which was always a dangerous sign. "What you did was put the life of a highly respected and trusted angel in jeopardy because of your arrogance in deciding what I should know and what I should not! I will keep your disobedience in mind. However, you will follow my orders from here on out in the future! Gather up our angel warriors. We will be leaving for Earth in exactly one hour. Have our ship ready to leave. Unfortunately, we cannot all go through the mirror and make it to Jakiele in time to help. I have something I have to do first. Mulakai, go with Gabriel and see it done!"

Gabriel sputtered in utter disbelief, "You would have us take one of our angelic craft to Earth? The humans will see us!" Michael's laugh was hard and bitter when he replied, "They have been seeing us for eons, Gabriel. However, since where we are going is so remote, I think the chances of anyone seeing us are small. Furthermore, if vampires and demons should somehow decide to cooperate, wouldn't it be better if they did see us coming? Think about it. Now, do as I have commanded!"

Michael watched as Gabriel called the angels to him in the great hall and began giving orders before he turned and faced Mulakai to ask him discreetly, "Has Jakiele become romantically involved with this woman? I must know the truth of this, Mulakai." Mulakai looked down at his feet for a moment because he did not want to betray Jakiele's confidence. Nevertheless, Mulakai knew he had to answer Michael honestly. "I do not believe he has, Michael, but I fear he might. I think he has fallen in love with her, and she has with him.

However, Jakiele would never betray us. He feels he must save her, and he will do so whether he gives up his own life in the process or not. He gave me his word of honor. He would not give the demons the mirror, and I believe him."

Michael thought on this for several minutes before he replied, "We are running out of time. Go and aid Gabriel. I must visit the high council of the Dominions and seek their guidance. Meet me at the ship. God speed, Mulakai." Michael went back through the Archangel mirror and disappeared. Mulakai hoped Michael was trying to do whatever was necessary to help them save Jakiele. Unfortunately, trusted friends were hard to come by, even in the angelic realm.

Michael went back to the Archangel realm and went down on his knees in front of the Archangel mirror, transporting him to the Dominion's realm to seek an audience with them. The mirror was only used in extreme cases of importance, and often, an audience would not be granted. Michael got down on his knees and spoke his exaltations to the mirror, and the mirror began to sing. Michael was granted entrance which was a good sign. He was instantly transported to the highest angelic realm he was allowed access to.

The Heavenly entities were mere mists of white smoke and did not like to appear in solid form. Michael got down on his knees and bowed his head, waiting to be acknowledged. Many voices emanated from the swirling vortexes until they came together as a single voice and said only one word, "Michael." Michael stood up and quietly explained the situation as best he could and asked for their aid. The entities listened quietly and respectfully until he mentioned "vampire" and "demon" in the same sentence. The mists swirled all around him in excited agitation until they once again became one. Finally, a high Dominion named Muriel decided to take solid form and appear before Michael.

The other Dominions were swirling incessantly until Muriel held up his hand for silence. "Wait here, Michael. We may be able to help." Then, in one single swoosh, the Dominions disappeared.

Michael had not realized he had been holding his breath in anticipatory fear of retaliation from the Dominions until he let the air out of his lungs in one long gust of air. Michael walked around the room slowly, taking in the details his limited view of the Dominion realm could reveal.

Since these angelic beings were connected to Earthly reality, the mansion's walls were lined with shelf after shelf of scrolls detailing Earth's past and how they had helped guide humanity through all sorts of worldly conflict to harmony. It was not long before Muriel came back through the portal with an angelic mirror that looked exactly like the one in Jakiele's closet. Michael was so shocked and astounded that it took him a moment to speak. Finally, he screwed up his courage enough to ask Muriel, "You want me to give the demons a mirror?" Muriel smirked at Michael and looked at him very gravely before he answered, "Of course. This is what they want, isn't it?"

Michael was confused and did not understand how giving the demons an angelic mirror would solve the dilemma, so he quickly queried, "Yes. However, how is giving them what they want going to help?" Muriel brought the mirror closer to Michael and put it in his hands before he said enigmatically, "Giving them what they desire is the only thing that will bring this matter to a conclusion in a satisfactory manner. So have faith, and all will be as it should."

Muriel once again turned himself into a misty vapor and waited for Michael to transport back to the Archangel realm. Once he got back to the lower heavenly mansion, Michael took the mirror with him up the three flights of stairs which led him to the rooftop. From there, he boarded the special angelic spacecraft to join with the other angel warriors who had already boarded.

Once inside the craft, Michael walked to the front, looked at the angels Gabriel had managed to summon, and addressed them all as one, "We are embarking on a dangerous mission. This mission may cost you your lives. Anyone who does not wish to come may leave now without consequence from Gabriel or me. Demons and vampires may be conspiring against us, and more human lives will be lost if we do not intervene and the life of one of our own, Jakiele." Gabriel was staring at the mirror in Michael's hand and was the first to speak, "You do not seriously intend to give the demons one of our special mirrors, do you, Michael?"

Michael looked down from the small, raised dais he was standing on and leveled a quelling look in Gabriel's direction before he responded, "Silence, Gabriel! The Dominions decided to give them this mirror, and we will do as instructed!" Michael looked out over the many faces of the worried assembly and demanded to know, "What say, you angels? Are you with me or not?"

Although the assembled group of thirty or more angels looked anxious, one of them stepped forward and announced, "We are always with you, Michael. If this is the Dominion's decision, so be it!" Then, one by one, the other angels stood at attention before him, and as one, the angels knelt to their knees, swords in hand, and bowed their heads in respect. Mulakai and Gabriel followed suit. Their devotion and loyalty humbled Michael. Finally, he nodded his head and ordered the pilot to begin their long journey.

It had taken close to two hours for Katliana, Zadikiele, and Dariah to arrive at Synevir Lake. Once they had been dropped off at the nearest town, they had been forced to hike the rest of the way. Dariah had set out at once to survey the surrounding area around the lake to ensure no one else was around while Zadikiele set up camp. Unfortunately, they had only brought one large tent and three sleeping bags with them, along with other essential items. Zadikiele had tied up Katliana to the nearest tree so he could keep a close eye on her while he set about making a small fire to keep them warm. He could feel the antagonism she directed toward him whenever she dared look directly at him. The daggers of resentment emanating from her eyes amused him to no end.

Dariah had tried to engage her in pleasant conversation on occasions, but such efforts resulted in her cussing profusely in her native language, and it annoyed his usually calm facade. He much preferred to keep her tied up with her mouth taped shut so she would be easier to manage. Zadikiele admired her fighting spirit, and the thought had crossed his mind to use her as he had Rochelle, but he did not want to jeopardize his ability to attain the coveted mirror for the fallen angels. So Zadikiele waited patiently until Dariah got back from scouting the area to contact Remiel and tell him what was happening. The only problem was that he would have to leave his human body vulnerable to descend to the Underworld. He did not trust Dariah to watch over him one bit.

It had not taken very long for Dariah to return with news. He could not sense any other beings in the area, and they remained undetected by any rogue vampires. However, Zadikiele gave Dariah the impression that he was not convinced and ordered Dariah to watch Katliana so he could scout the area himself to be sure. What he wanted to do was have a few minutes alone without Dariah's watchful eyes on him so he could feel free to contact the fallen without worrying about whether Dariah was going to look after his human body.

After looking around for the most protected area he could find, Zadikiele found a large tree with a hollowed-out trunk he could easily crawl into and lay down. He covered the entrance to the tree with the surrounding foliage so his body could remain hidden. After laying his body down and closing his eyes, he transported to the Underworld to consult with Remiel. The fallen angels had already convened into the large cavern and were awaiting his arrival to update them on what was happening.

Zadikiele bowed to the large gathering upon entering the cavern, went down to his knees, and lowered his head to await instructions. Remiel was the first to separate himself from the other fallen and walked toward Zadikiele. He placed his right hand on Zadikiele's head and ordered him to rise. Remiel was anxious to hear what Zadikiele had to report by saying, "What is happening, my son? Have you found a way to get the mirror?" Zadikiele had risen slowly to his feet and was apprehensive about revealing he had not been able to get what the fallen coveted.

Zadikiele cautiously replied, "Not yet, Father. I have discovered where the vampire lair is. Dariah and I managed to capture a woman we intend to trade for the mirror. I intend to use her as bait to lure the angels to us. To do so, I will seek out the vampires and demand they assist us, or we will reveal them to the humans and the angels. Either way, they will be destroyed." Zadikiele paused for a moment before he asked the group at large, "How is it these vampires were created in the first place? My understanding is that only a Nephilim who has shared their blood with a human could create one. Weren't all of the Nephilim destroyed in the great flood?"

Uzza rushed forward and glared at Zadikiele before he shouted at him, "It does not matter how one was created! We know that one was made, and you managed to let him escape to warn the angels of their existence! You also allowed my son to get killed to save your skin! Your incompetence knows no bounds! I do not trust your arrogant assumptions. You have no idea whether the vampires will help you or not. More than likely, they will kill you and the others on sight to keep their identities secret. I will be sending reinforcements to you to better your chances of getting what we want." Uzza took a deep breath and went to stand directly in front of Zadikiele before he added quietly, "Succeed in getting what we want, or you and Dariah can most definitely count on answering to me. Begone from my sight, Zadikiele, and do not return to us without the mirror!"

Zadikiele turned to walk away, but Remiel grabbed his arm and led him a few feet away from the other fallen angels for a private conversation before he softly hissed, "Listen to me, Zadikiele, Jakiele was once my closest friend before I betrayed him. He knows you are my son, and if you fail, there will be no life for you on Earth or in the Underworld. Uzza's unrelenting lust for power has worked the others up into a greedy frenzy. With Latkia's death on your hands, there will be no mercy. Do you understand what I am saying?" Zadikiele angrily replied, "There has never been life for me, Father! Eternity without the ability to ever be rejoined with my wife and children has been punishment enough!" Zadikiele forcefully shrugged off

Remiel's restraining hand on his arm and stormed out of the cavern to return to the tree hiding his body.

Zadikiele returned to camp, completely unaware Jakiele had been watching him from a distance with an extended range scope. Jakiele had found a large tree with bushy branches he could sit in and be comfortable. The location afforded him a clear view of the campsite. Since the tree was downwind, his scent would remain undetected. Jakiele wanted desperately to rush in and snatch Katliana from the demon's grasp, but he could not do so without endangering Katliana's life. All he could do for now was wait and watch to see what the demons would do next, follow them, and hope he could somehow snatch her away from the demon's clutches quietly if an opportunity should present itself.

Jakiele felt like at least two hours had passed as he watched the campsite. Dariah had prepared a meal for them to eat, but Katliana was stubborn and refused to cooperate, so Dariah was forced to pinch her nose and shove food and water down her throat. She was coughing, squirming, and trying to resist. Dariah made her continue until he was satisfied she had been given enough sustenance to keep her alive. Dariah was quick to tape her mouth when he was done to keep her quiet. Zadikiele was sitting next to the fire and had watched the whole scenario with amusement. However, his demeanor soon changed when at least fifty other demons appeared stealthily from all sides of the encampment and surrounded them.

Zadikiele surged to his feet instantly with a sword drawn in his hand. Dariah leaped up from his crouched position next to Katliana and drew his sword as well. Jakiele could see Katliana's eyes were wide with fear. One of the demons stepped forward to bow before Zadikiele and dropped down on his knees. The other demons soon followed suit. Zadikiele cautiously sheathed his sword and went to stand in front of the first demon who had fallen to his knees and put his left hand on the demon's forehead. It was revealed to him that Uzza had sent these demons to help him.

Jakiele did not know what was happening, but he felt his stomach drop to his knees. The situation was getting more deadly by the second. It was now more critical than ever for Jakiele to remain unseen. He could handle himself in a fight, but taking on more than fifty demons were pushing the limits of his abilities. There was no way he could protect Katliana while fighting them off simultaneously. From what he could see, the demons had come to the campsite armed to the teeth. Some had swords, others had long sharp spears, while others had to throw stars and knives. He did not see any guns, but he was sure they brought them just in case.

Before long, the large assembly started marching toward the tall peaks of the Gorgany mountains. Zadikiele was in the lead, with Dariah following close behind. Katliana's hands were tied, and she was being led along behind Dariah by a long rope he held tightly in his hands. After the group started marching through the forest, Jakiele followed a reasonable distance behind them, relying on his acute sense of smell to detect any traces of sulfur that could alert him to which way the demons had traveled. It took several hours of hiking before the demons reached the base of the tallest peak. The demons were looking around, trying to decide what direction to head next, when Zadikiele noticed a small rocky pathway intersecting the two tallest mountains.

The rocky pathway almost looked like steps and extended forever. Finally, with no way to see what lay beyond, they had no choice but to follow the path to see where it led next. Unfortunately, the pathway was dark and narrow, and the group had to march single file. Nevertheless, they managed to squeeze through until they reached a small clearing enveloped in a misty fog, making it hard to see where they should go. The demons had all managed to come out of the narrow crevice into the small clearing when a large net came out of nowhere and trapped them all underneath. It was made from some sort of material impervious to being torn or sliced apart by steel no matter how hard the demons tried to escape.

Suddenly, they were surrounded by vampires dressed in ancient armor, with shields, swords, and helmets. One of the vampires came forward and examined the group of captured demons and demanded to know, "Who are you? What are you doing here? Speak, or I will give the command to slaughter you where you stand!" Zadikiele had managed to shove some of the demons surrounding him out of his way so he could address the leader of this group, "I would speak to your superior. There are angels on the way here who have become aware of your existence, and they wish to destroy you! I have come here to help you!"

The vampire who had spoken earlier harshly laughed before he said, "I doubt it, demon. Yes, we know who and what you are. We smelled you the moment you entered our Kingdom. We have been tracking you since the moment you arrived in Cluj Napoca. Do you think of us as fools?" Zadikiele answered him smoothly, "I would never mistake you as a great fool, but my opinion does not negate the fact the angels are still coming, and you will need our assistance. We have something they want." Zadikiele grabbed Katliana by the arm and jerked her forward to face the vampire.

The vampire looked Katliana over thoroughly with a lustful look in his eyes, making Katliana's skin crawl. Zadikiele observed the look, but the vampire quickly concealed his lascivious thoughts. The vampire snapped his fingers and ordered the net to be released. The other vampires quickly disarmed the demons and tied their hands with the same material the net was made from. Then, the vampires led them out of the clearing up a series of steps that would lead the entourage directly into the mountain. A long tunnel guarded closely by posted sentries led down into a series of caves. Zadikiele thought the intersecting caves leading off the main cavern would be dark, musty, cobweb-ridden holes. Instead, the entire network had been converted into luxuriously appointed apartments or the vampires. All were surprised by the opulent surroundings they found themselves in when they were led into the main cavern.

The main room had walls hung with ancient tapestries, decorated like a Turkish palace. A large gold-encrusted throne in the center of the room lined with red velvet sat on top of a large round dais. The dais was surrounded by a circular table with several chairs outside of it. All around the room were computers with vampires sitting in front of them. They were monitoring the security of their various businesses and the surrounding mountains. Lake Synevir was visible on one of the monitors. The vampires had watched every move Zadikiele and the others had made. Finally, the lead vampire who had spoken to Zadikiele led him and the others to the center of the room to stand directly in front of the large dais.

The lead vampire ordered one of the others to get their prince, Mantioch, to let him know they had uninvited guests. The lesser vampire left to do his master's bidding and soon re-entered the room with the prince. Mantioch certainly had a commanding presence, Katliana thought silently to herself. He was very tall and muscular, but not bulky. He could have been Jakiele's twin, with one exception. This creature had black eyes instead of blue, and his facial features were shallower. He wore an oversized flowing black trench coat, black pants, and a crisp white shirt. His feet were covered in thigh-high black shiny boots. His age seemed indeterminate, but he looked like he could be in his late thirties. He looked the group of demons over with casual disdain and took a seat on his throne with great flourish. Once his disinterested gaze landed on Katliana, he gave an appreciative smirk before once again taking on an insouciant demeanor.

Mantioch waved his hand at Zadikiele, and the vampire leader who had been holding onto Zadikiele's bonds shoved him forward and forced Zadikiele to his knees. The vampire unsheathed his sword with his right hand and held it up against Zadikiele's throat. He viciously grabbed Zadikiele's hair and forced his head back with his left hand. The vampire holding him shrieked, "Speak now and tell our prince what you have told me! Now!" The vampire jerked

Zadikiele's hair as hard as he could and held the sword even tighter to Zadikiele's neck.

Zadikiele had to tread carefully, or the game would be over before it ever began. "I would not have come here, my Lord, if I could have avoided it, but one of your own attacked a human girl and killed her in the United States. I became aware of its existence through one of the members of my coven. I tried to cover up the mess, but an angel became aware of the vampire because of this woman!"

Zadikiele pointed an accusatory finger at Katliana before he continued with, "Because of her, the angels will be on their way soon to kill you all! So, we have come to help you." Zadikiele waved both of his arms expansively to indicate the demon horde he had brought with him.

Mantioch listened to the entire dissertation without appearing the least bit interested in anything Zadikiele said until he suddenly jumped up from his chair and crossed the room to stand in front of Zadikiele with supernatural speed. Mantioch grasped Zadikiele's chin in his right hand and bent down to get his face right next to Zadikiele's before he very softly whispered, "You must think me an idiot, demon. One of my disciples would have never bitten a human woman and killed her. No unauthorized vampires have been made in over a thousand years! You would have never offered your assistance unless you had something to gain. I suggest you start telling me the truth, or I will end your miserable existence right here and now!"

Zadikiele's throat worked overtime to gulp in much-needed air before he dared speak again, "If you would allow me, prince, I will prove to you what I have said. I will reveal everything to you if you would but grant me a chance to show you what I have brought with me as proof." Mantioch roughly jerked Zadikiele's head out of his grasp and once again took a seat on his throne before he said, "We shall see demon. Release him!" The vampire who had been holding Zadikiele hostage pulled Zadikiele into a standing position while cutting his bonds with a specially made knife. The knife cut through the silver netting like it was cutting through soft butter. The vampire who released him shoved Zadikiele forward to stand before the prince. However, he made sure to stand right behind Zadikiele with the knife held closely to Zadikiele's back.

Zadikiele raised both of his arms to show he had no other intention but to slowly reach into his coat pocket with his right hand to retrieve the pictures of the dead Asian girl he had been smart enough to bring with him. Zadikiele held them up over his head cautiously so he would not get stabbed. The vampire with the knife to his back grasped the pictures and handed them to another vampire standing nearby, who handed them to the prince. A shocked look quickly ran across the prince's face as he looked at picture after picture in utter amazement before he muttered, "This is not possible. These pictures must be some elaborate hoax or demon trick! I will know the truth of this!"

Mantioch motioned for the Captain of the Guard to come forward and ordered, "I want to know right now if any of our members have traveled recently to the United States. I do not care whether it was authorized for business or not. No one is to leave until I have the answers I seek. Do it now!" The captain snapped his fingers to his fellow guards, and they set about finding out who the vampire was who killed the dead Asian girl if indeed there was one. Mantioch turned his unsettling gaze upon Zadikiele once more and said, "I know there is more to this story than you are telling me. What is it you want, demon!"

Zadikiele now knew he had the prince's attention, but he had to convince Mantioch it was in his best interest to help the demons. He very cautiously stood back a few steps from the prince. He appeared to look down at his boots as though he was deep in thought before he answered, "Before I tell you anything else, would you please do me the honor of revealing to me how you came to be? All my Nephilim brethren were killed in the great flood. Only a Nephilim could have created you. How is any of this even possible?" Zadikiele looked up and had turned in a circle with his hands outspread, indicating he wanted to know how this vampire coven had been formed.

Mantioch stared thoughtfully at Zadikiele as though contemplating answering Zadikiele's presumptuous query. Mantioch gracefully stood up and started pacing back and forth across the large dais before he decided whether he would answer Zadikiele's questions. Mantioch let out a ragged sigh before he replied, "My father was once a famous Nephilim. He obeyed all of God's laws, and he worked hard to provide for my mother and me. He never harmed anyone. He knew about the fantastic boat Noah was making, and he knew something terrible was about to happen. All the other humans and Nephilim made fun of Noah, but my father did not. When the deadly rains started, my father insisted I partake of his blood. I did not want to. Nevertheless, he forced me to do it. I was delirious and sick for three days and could barely move.

When I opened my eyes on the fourth day, the Earth had already been consumed by deep water. As I looked around, I could not see anyone or anything except the topside of Noah's Ark. Strong ropes had tied me to the top of the boat, so I would not be knocked overboard into the storming seas. Somehow, my father ensured I would survive, even though he could have saved himself or my mother instead. He decided my life was more important, even though I woke up a monster. My thirst for blood was unquenchable, and if I did not somehow figure out how to get blood within a month, I would die.

After two more days, my strength, vision, and hearing became more enhanced. It was as though I could hear every heartbeat on the boat while I was slowly being driven crazy with thirst. My time limit was upon me when I had finally managed to loosen the rain-drenched ropes holding me.

The boat was rocking wildly in the storm, and it took every ounce of strength I had to hold on to the end of the rope and secure it to an open-air vent. Finally, I squeezed my body through the vent and lowered myself onto the top floor of the boat with the other end of the rope. Fortunately, no one was on the top floor, so I explored the lower decks. Noah came unexpectedly up the stairs and found me.

My body was shaking all over from being soaked from head to toe from the chilling rain, and I am sure I scared the living daylights out of Noah with my red eyes. He would have run from me and grabbed a weapon, but I was quick to restrain him by putting my forearm around his throat and holding his body close to mine. Noah was a drunkard, but he was not stupid, so I made a deal with him. He would not reveal my identity to anyone, and I would not harm his family or any other human if I could avoid it. Noah was informed that if he did not agree to help me, I would kill him and everyone else on the ark because my thirst was out of control.

Noah led me secretly to the cells below decks where the animals were being kept and locked me in with them so I would not be tempted to take blood from his family. I found out I could mesmerize the animals with my eyes to avoid fear while I drank their blood. The animals gave me the sustenance I needed to survive until the storm was over. I never took any of their lives. Once land was spotted, I bid Noah goodbye and have existed in these mountain ranges ever since. Noah's family was never made aware of my presence. The vampires you see before you have all been created by me, and all are male. We have no use for females other than to see to our needs, and we have never converted any. The only way we can have children is if I decide to convert one, and even then, they must be close to being an adult to preserve our secrecy. Does this answer all of your questions?"

Zadikiele was stunned by what the prince revealed but was quick to latch on to the information he needed to try and sway the prince to his cause when he finally spoke, "The vampire created in the United States was young, and he was a college student at Boston University if such evidence is of any use to you. I was able to track him down and read his memories, and through the images in his mind, we were able to find you. An angel named Jakiele found out where I lived and took the boy from me. We barely escaped with our lives and came here. I am sure Jakiele is somewhere lurking nearby about ready to call in an attack on your fortress since he surely read the boy's memories as well." Zadikiele let the facts sink in before he continued with, "What if I told you there was a way you could be with your father again? Would you be willing to do what it would take to see him and keep your identity a secret a while longer?" The prince became visibly angry, stepped off the dais, and advanced quickly upon Zadikiele.

Mantioch leaned close to Zadikiele and said very quietly, "I do not know what game you are playing, demon, but I know there is no way to be rejoined with my father! The angel you are so worried about following you has already been detained and is in one of my holding cells. As I told you earlier, we have been aware of every move either of you made. We could see his camouflaged armor with our enhanced vision since he could not hide his body heat, and we captured him with little resistance!"

Zadikiele's eyes narrowed with suspicion. If Jakiele had been captured, it was because he wanted to be caught, but he did not bother to correct the arrogant prince's assumption. Instead, he replied smoothly, "Oh, but there is a way, great one." Zadikiele once again pointed a finger in Katliana's direction and said, "She is the one the angel wants, and he will do anything to get her. Jakiele has possession of a mirror which acts as a transportation device used to get from one dimension to another. The fallen, whom I represent, want to use the mirror to transport themselves back to Earth. If we succeed in using her as leverage to get the mirror, you would be able to be rejoined with your father."

Mantioch drew back from Zadikiele in mortified rage. He shouted back at Zadikiele, "My father wanted nothing to do with the fallen angels and all of their twisted, sick plans. I would dearly love to see my father again, but not at the expense of humanity. If I had wanted to kill humans, I could have done so centuries ago! I have no wish to become a part of schemes to gain control of the Earth. The fallen angels had their chance, and they blew it with their never-ending lust for power!" The Captain of the Guard returned to the room and brought a young, frightened, and confused man with him.

The captain shoved the boy at the prince's feet and forced him to get down on his knees.

The captain nodded to the prince and pointed to the boy. The boy had been converted as a favor to one of his trusted council members who had wanted a child of his own, and the prince was now regretting the decision to allow it. The council member named Zebadiah had been with Mantioch since the beginning and was a close friend. Zebadiah was across the room at one of the computer monitors when he noticed his son was kneeling before the prince. He knew his son was in deep trouble if he was brought before the prince in such a manner. So, Zebadiah rushed over to his son's side and waited to hear what offense his son was being accused of.

Mantioch angrily walked up to the boy, pulled him up by the collar of his shirt, and sank his long teeth into the boy's neck to taste the blood rushing through the frightened boy's veins. The blood would reveal every thought the boy ever had. Mantioch saw everything the boy had done in the United States after studying abroad. The blood memories revealed the boy taking advantage of young Andy, who had been passed out from alcohol and could not defend himself. The result was clear why Andy attacked Sue Kwon and killed her. Mantioch threw Zebadiah's son to the ground and placed his foot on the young boy's neck to hold him immobile.

Mantioch withdrew his sword from its sheath while studying Zebadiah very closely. It was their most sacred law not to turn anyone without permission and never harm or be the cause of harm to humans. The boy had been taught thoroughly how to conduct himself and had chosen not to do so. Mantioch would never take one of the vampire's lives without cause, so he handed the sword over to Zebadiah to do what needed to be done. Zebadiah had tears of blood running down his cheeks in sorrow, but he had no choice. He drove the silver sword through his son's heart and cut off his head. Zebadiah handed the sword back to the prince and was soon surrounded by the prince's other high council members, who tried to comfort him and lead him quietly from the room.

Mantioch once again turned his attention back to Zadikiele and firmly stated, "As you can see, we are quite capable of overseeing our affairs. Go back the way you came, and no harm will befall you. Leave now." Mantioch was going to turn away, but Zadikiele's taunting voice stopped him in his tracks. "You might not want our assistance, prince, but know this, if the angels from Heaven decide to come here and destroy you, they will not be led by minor angels. You can bet Michael or Gabriel will be leading them. If they both come here, you and your entire operation will be decimated in a matter of minutes, no matter how many vampires you may have made. They are lethal alone, but when they are together, they are unstoppable, and they will not care about all your self-sacrificing sanctimonious laws! So, you need our help!"

Mantioch's glare at Zadikiele was shrewdly calculating as he turned slowly around and was silent for a moment before he reached a decision. "I have no interest in helping you. I will protect my interests first and foremost. I will be waiting and watching for any avenging angels who may decide to make an appearance, and I will let you know if I need you to help me. In the meantime, you may remain as my guests. Seize them!"

In seconds, the demons were surrounded and bound by the vampires, including Zadikiele. One of the vampires went to Katliana, but the prince stopped him and declared, "Not her. I wish to have her remain at my side. Take the others to the holding cells. Bring the angel Jakiele to me. I wish to converse with him." The vampires did as they were bid and led the demons down a series of steps many levels deep within the mountain until they reached the bottom level. The prison cells where they were going to be held were all carved deeply into the rock and were sealed with heavy steel doors. Small openings at eye level in the doors let in the dank air. Zadikiele and Dariah were put into one cell, and the demons who had joined them were forced into a larger one. Jakiele had been placed in a cell as well, and he smiled as he watched the demons being led into their respective rooms.

The vampires carried down the weapons they had confiscated from the demons and dumped them into a bin near a metal smelter found on the opposite wall where the demons were being held. The guards never knew that Dariah had secretly taken one of the vampires' special knives that could cut through steel. Mantioch and Jakiele had already had a long talk about how Katliana had been kidnapped after Jakiele had decided to allow himself to be captured. It was the only plan Jakiele could think of to ensure Katliana's safety. So far, the prince had kept his word about not helping the demons. Jakiele only hoped the prince would continue to do so.

# CHAPTER 13

Jakiele could feel the demon's evil eyes upon him as he was led out of his cell and up the long staircase to the great room where Mantioch awaited his arrival. As he entered the main cave, his gaze fell upon Katliana, engaged in an earnest discussion next to the prince. Finally, the vampire who led him up the stairs announced his presence to the prince by graciously proclaiming, "The angel, Jakiele, is here as you requested, my Lord."

Mantioch turned his head in Jakiele's direction and snapped his fingers for one of his servants to bring another chair over to the large dais for Jakiele to sit on. Then, without a second glance in Jakiele's direction, Mantioch resumed the earlier conversation he had been having with Katliana while deliberately ignoring Jakiele's presence. Katliana wanted to jump out of her seat and go to Jakiele, but Mantioch forestalled her attempt by placing his hand on her arm to stop her. For some reason, it annoyed the hell out of Jakiele the way the prince assumed a proprietary air around Katliana by laying a restraining hand on her arm. Mantioch seemed utterly oblivious to Jakiele's disapproval of his disrespectful, possessive manner towards Katliana.

Katliana was very much aware Jakiele was growing more annoyed by the second and was very conscious of the prince's plain attempts at rankling Jakiele's calm facade to get a rise out of him.

Katliana worriedly kept looking back and forth between the two men. She desperately wanted to diffuse the rapidly growing tension between the two of them by reiterating what she and the prince had been conversing about. She sweetly said, "Jakiele, you would not believe all of the fascinating histories I have been able to learn from the prince! He has so many fascinating stories about the beginning of the world! Although I disagree with his declaration that the only reason he does not convert any women is he fears they would be too emotional and unstable to want to live for eternity with him!"

Jakiele was careful to hide the sarcasm wanting to drip from his lips when he rejoined, "I am sure he has his reasons, Katliana, whether he has told you the whole truth or not. Perhaps he simply does not want to be tied to one woman for all time?" A tiny smirk had managed to form on his lips when Jakiele made the last comment, although a twinkle showed in his eyes as he gave the prince a private wink to let him know he was joking with him. Mantioch had initially stiffened at Jakiele's casual remarks, but when he realized Jakiele was just teasing him, he relaxed once again into his usual indolent pose.

Katliana turned to look at the prince once more before kindly adding in a gentle tone, "Perhaps you will one day find the right woman, Mantioch. You are certainly sweet and handsome enough, but it is your keen intelligence and sharp wit that ladies of quality would appreciate the most about you in my estimation. Women have changed over the centuries, and we no longer keep our opinions to ourselves, making it easier for you to know what we think. Maybe you might want to consider getting out in the world a bit more and finding out for yourself?"

Mantioch raised a sardonic eyebrow in her direction and looked at Jakiele before he groaned aloud and added, "A woman who speaks her mind and lets you know what she thinks? Dear Lord, God help us all!" The prince let out a chuckle, but then he stood up and started pacing the length of the dais. He turned away from them both, placed his hands behind his back, and closed his eyes.

Mantioch was deep in reflective thought for a few minutes before he turned around to look very intently at Jakiele and waved his hand in Katliana's direction, "She is an extraordinary woman angel. I hope you appreciate the gift you have been given. I am almost tempted to keep her here with me if she would but allow it. However, I have no wish to pluck such a delicate flower, especially since she has some misguided desire to want to be with you!" Mantioch walked back over to Katliana and traced his index finger delicately down her cheek, which caused Katliana to blush a deep red and lower her eyes before he whirled around and faced Jakiele again.

Mantioch grew visibly angry once again when he swirled back around and addressed Jakiele once more, "I saw the way the demons were treating her like a dog and abusing her in the forest! I would never treat a woman so! You had better start doing a better job of protecting her, angel, or you will most definitely answer to me! She will always have a place here with me if she wishes it. I have held up my end of our bargain, and I expect you to keep your word to me that none of my clan will be harmed if I allow you to leave here. You gave me your word of honor none would be harmed if we stayed out of this battle between the angels and the demons. Does your word still stand?"

Jakiele rose from his chair and stood nose to nose with Mantioch before he vehemently voiced his thoughts, "When I give my word Mantioch, I mean it! I cannot promise Michael will heed my words, but I will do all I can to plead for leniency on your behalf. You have stated that you have never harmed humans, yet how are there so many vampires here? They were humans once. How can you possibly expect me to explain the hypocrisy of that to Michael?" Mantioch turned around once more and resumed his incessant pacing before he deigned to answer Jakiele.

"Although I do not feel as though I owe you an explanation, I will oblige you this one time and explain how this whole operation came to be. When I turned into a vampire, I only fed off animals. I made errors in the beginning and accidentally created monsters in the process. Wolves were turning into werewolves, dogs into Chupacabra, etcetera. I tried to track these creatures down and destroy them, but myths and legends about them persisted anyway in ancient folklore. When I tried my hand at taking the blood of humans, I found out how to lure them into a trance-like state and only take enough blood to survive and then erase their memories.

However, as you can see from the vampires I have with me here, it took a while for me to learn how to master the technique of hypnotizing humans. I also had to keep the vampires I converted from making the same mistakes I did. It took centuries to learn how to control our thirst. No new vampires have been created in a millennium, except Zebadiah's son. He, unfortunately, caused the death of the young Asian woman. He has been dealt with and no longer exists in this world. We only exclusively use the blood banks we have purchased to meet our needs. Enterprises we own help keep our existence funded yet keep our lifestyle secret. Our blood banks generously award large sums of money to those who donate. The large amount we offer helps our local community thrive.

Mantioch finished his story and stood waiting quietly for the condemning words he was sure would be uttered from Jakiele's mouth. Nevertheless, the angel surprised him by revealing to him humbly, "Throughout my long centuries on Earth, I have wondered how God could love such contentious, selfish, and narcissistic beings as humans who seem hell-bent on destroying the beautiful planet they have been blessed with and each other. I had almost given up on finding anything redeeming about them until Katliana came into my life and gave me a reason to keep believing. Hearing your tale has given me hope that others in this world also care about watching over God's beloved creation. You have conducted yourself with integrity and righteousness, and I am honored to meet you, Mantioch."

Jakiele held out his right hand for a handshake in a gesture of friendship. Mantioch was stunned, but he grasped Jakiele's hand, and the two became conservative allies. Mantioch beamed a broad smile and ostentatiously announced, "Well, since all has been settled, how about some food? I am sure you both must be famished. Just because I savor the nectar of life does not mean I do not also indulge in the savory luxuries existence still has to offer! Please follow me if you will." Mantioch graciously led Jakiele and Katliana to his private suite, which was more like a small apartment complete with every modern amenity available.

Mantioch's large living room had deep brown leather sofas that rested on thickly piled, maroon-colored carpeting. The rock walls had all been linked with ancient tapestries, which were still in excellent condition. Katliana could not see a speck of dust anywhere. The large rock fireplace in the center of the room had a cheerfully blazing fire, which kept the room at a comfortable temperature. A big-screen television graced one corner of the room and had to be at least five feet long. The trio went through the living room into the dining room, which housed a long antique table. The hand-crafted table looked like it had once belonged to the renaissance era. A sizeable sparkling chandelier hung above the table and looked like it had been made from pure crystals. Several male servants were bustling about, cleaning and setting the table for the evening meal.

The servants did not openly acknowledge the prince had guests in any way, and they kept right on doing what they were commanded to do without so much as a second thought. The servants were extraordinarily proficient and quiet. As Jakiele and Katliana were being shown around the prince's home, Katliana noticed they did not go anywhere near the kitchen where delicious aromas were wafting forth and mentioned it to the prince, "Are we not going to see your kitchen, Prince? Whoever is cooking in there seems to be making something simply divine!" Mantioch laughed heartily and whispered secretly into Katliana's ear, "I am not allowed in the kitchen, my dear, unless I want to lose my manly parts. Johan is my chef, and he originally hailed from France. If I want to continue to enjoy his delicious masterpieces, I must play by his rules and not enter his domain! You will see for yourself very soon why I deign to keep him around."

Katliana giggled at the prince's playfulness. Nevertheless, she was curious how the prince could eat human food, so she asked, "Excuse me, Mantioch, but I was always under the impression that vampires could only consume blood?" Mantioch quickly cleared up the misconception by replying, "No, my dear, vampires need human blood to drink only because our cells die so quickly without it. We get our strength and speed from the cells in our body working at an accelerated rate, and the blood of others keep us strong, but we still need food for nourishment as well."

Jakiele had initially wanted to slam his sword deep into the prince's throat for flirting so outrageously with Katliana. But now he realized the old-world charm and flamboyant mannerisms were just part of the prince's personality, and it did not bother him anymore. So, the tour continued, and the prince proudly showed them to his favorite room, which housed the priceless artifacts and weapons he had collected over his long tenure on Earth.

Jakiele went over to a sword that had to be hundreds of years old and admired the delicate details. Mantioch walked up next to Jakiele and let him know the sword belonged to Alexander the Great. Jakiele was more than impressed with the prince's vast collection of fine art and even some long-lost ancient scrolls belonging to the lost city of Atlantis. Katliana walked from one article of the lost artworks of the past to the next in complete fascination and commented, "I could get lost in here forever, Prince. These treasures are so beautiful. You have excellent taste!"

Mantioch gallantly bowed to her and modestly replied, "You are most kind, Katliana. I should take your advice, venture forth into the world, and find a woman to share it with who would appreciate my love of history as much as you do. In the meantime, I would like to show you another of my favorite pastimes. If you would both follow me?" Mantioch finished his tour with a door that led into the heart of the mountain. He led them to an immense sunken pool filled with frothy aromatic bubbles inside the room. A soft white bathrobe was draped casually over a chair, left by one of the servants next to the edge of the pool. A king-sized bed dominated the rest of the space. It was surrounded by white gauzy curtains casually tied back with golden braided ropes.

In the center of the bed lay a beautiful white lacy gown with a deep red velvet sash. Katliana raised a curious brow in the prince's direction to figure out precisely what he had in mind. Mantioch laughed at her evident confusion and informed her, "I had one of my servants find you some clothing I thought might be suitable for you to use. We do have female visitors from time to time. You will find everything you might need in the dresser next to the bed and shoes in the closet. If you excuse us, I will show Jakiele to his room so we may all get bathed and dressed for dinner."

Mantioch gave Katliana another courtly bow and opened the door for Jakiele to precede him back to the hallway. Katliana had not realized how dirty she felt until she began to undress. She looked in the bedside dresser and found an unused toothbrush, hairbrush, and toothpaste. She found the bathroom on the other end of the room and gratefully began her ablutions. Katliana felt immensely better after brushing her teeth and running the hairbrush through her hair. Upon further examining the dresser contents, she found shampoo, conditioner, and a razor to shave her legs and underarms with.

Katliana brought her bathing items over to the pool and immersed herself into the tub one delicious inch at a time. She lay her long hair back and got it wet enough to wash and rinse it and was going to let the conditioner stay in her hair while she set about shaving her long slender legs. She was starting to feel like herself once more. She did not know Jakiele had slipped back into the room and was watching her slowly shave her legs one at a time. Katliana dipped her head once more in the water to rinse the conditioner from her hair. The hair stood up on the back of her neck as she sensed she was being watched. She looked at the door leading into the room and realized Jakiele had been watching her sensual movements.

Katliana turned a deep red with embarrassment, and her hand flew to her chest as she sank into the bubbles as far as she could.

She did not want him to see any more of her naked body than she had already unwittingly exposed. Katliana was mortified she had not noticed him standing there and demanded to know, "How long have you been standing there, Jake? Don't you knock?" Jakiele walked silently over to the pool and stared deeply into her eyes without ever saying a word.

He was only dressed in a pair of tightly molded men's underwear as he knelt right next to her and grabbed the shampoo. "Sorry to disturb you, but I did knock. I needed shampoo. I will leave you to get ready." Jakiele got up and turned to leave but abruptly turned back around and softly said, "I am so sorry you got dragged into all of this. I feel so badly for you about your friend Kyle. Once I get you back to safety, I promise you that I will not bother you again. You have no idea how much it killed me to see you harmed. I am so sorry I was not able to protect you. Please forgive me, Katliana."

His heartfelt words warmed Katliana's heart and gave her hope that there had to be a way they could have a future together, so she replied, "None of this is your fault, Jake. There is nothing to forgive. Circumstances brought us together, and I know you have done everything in your power to try and save my life. Could you please turn around and hand me the robe?" Jakiele grabbed the robe from the chair and held it out to her while he turned his body around in the other direction to afford her some much-needed privacy. They had less than an hour to prepare for dinner, according to Mantioch, so as soon as Katliana grabbed the robe from his hand, he started once again to leave the room.

Katliana had secured the robe belt around her body when she noticed Jakiele was trying to leave. She halted him by saying, "Jake, please wait. I want to talk to you for a moment if you do not mind." Jakiele paused for a moment and slowly turned back around to stare into her worried green eyes. Katliana knew he would not come to her, so she walked up to stand right in front of him instead. She looked up into his eyes and very seductively said, "We may not have a tomorrow, Jake. We do not know how any of this is going to turn out. I only know I have fallen in love with you, and I want to know at least once what it is like to be loved by you."

Jakiele felt his gut wrench. He wanted to be with her more than anything, but he could not risk the chance she could somehow become pregnant, so he softly said, "I cannot break my vows, Katliana. If you got pregnant, the angels would kill us all. I want to be with you so badly it hurts, but we cannot take the risk. Do you understand what I am saying?" Katliana felt tears well up in her eyes and her heart sink. An idea suddenly crossed her mind, so she whispered into Jakiele's left ear, "Don't you think modern men have ways to avoid such catastrophes? Do you understand what I am saying?"

Understanding what Katliana meant suddenly dawned on Jakiele. Jakiele smiled and went over to the dresser, found what he was looking for, and placed it on the top of the bedside drawer. He laid his body down on the bed and motioned for her to join him. Katliana shyly lowered her robe and climbed into bed next to him. Jakiele would not let their only opportunity to make love go to waste. He shed his underpants and pulled her on top of him so she would not be frightened if she saw his engorged male organ. He pulled her head down to him. The heat exploded between them and quickly became a firestorm of unleashed passion.

Neither could control the raging inferno of lust pounding through their veins as they sealed their lips together and explored each other's mouths with their tongues. Katliana matched his rhythm and was a quick study of what pleased him. He held the back of her head with his left hand and began gently kneading her breasts with his right one. Her breasts became very sensitized to his delicate touch, and the tips turned into rock-hard pebbles. Before long, Jakiele rolled her over onto her back and continued his delicate ministrations with his fingers on her breasts until he replaced them with his mouth. Katliana was lost in a haze of pure ecstasy and closed her eyes to enjoy the exciting new sensations he was creating with his mouth and fingers. A mounting tension caused her body to feel like she was burning from the inside out and consumed every fiber of her being. She began to feel a hot throbbing sensation radiate from her core to her toes.

Jakiele kissed his way down her body and explored every inch of her until he kissed his way back to her feminine core and began to swirl his tongue softly against her womanly nub. Katliana tried to resist and close her thighs to hide from his delicious caresses. Jakiele gently parted her thighs once again and continued what he had started with exquisite tenderness and expertise. Katliana felt her body slowly begin to relax again and felt as though she was climbing toward something she had never experienced before. Jakiele inserted one finger into her tight feminine sheath and started working his magic and taking her body to new heights of pleasure. Katliana began squirming and unconsciously pushing herself onto his finger while Jakiele inserted another as well to ready her untrained body for his. She did not know what her body was striving for until she finally crested the mountain and came apart against his mouth.

Katliana's core was repeatedly convulsing, and she felt like it was hard to breathe. She looked down at Jakiele in complete wonder at what she had experienced. She pulled on Jakiele's head and brought his lips back to her own. In a matter of seconds, Katliana felt her whole body turn to molten lava once again as Jakiele lavished bone-melting kisses on her lips and started caressing her again with his hands. Jakiele broke the kiss to reach over, grabbed the condom off the dresser, and looked deeply into Katliana's eyes before he asked her uncertainly, "Are you sure you want this? I have heard it hurts a virgin the first time, and I do not wish to bring you further pain. However, if we are going to stop, we must do it right now before it is too late. I have fallen deeply in love with you, Katliana. I will respect your decision either way."

Katliana reached both of her hands up, cupped Jakiele's cheeks in her hands, and answered him back softly, "I know what I am doing, Jake. I trust you, and I want you with every fiber of my being. I have fallen in love with you as well too much to stop now." She pulled his lips once again to her own and began kissing him with fierce devotion. Jakiele took his cue and managed to unwrap the package with his fingers and stretch the latex over his massive erection without ever breaking their kiss. His male organ was at the entrance of her tight sheath before he placed his fingers into his mouth to get them wet. He started caressing her nub again with his soft hands and fingers. He felt her body begin to relax, and her thighs began to part widely of their own volition. He wanted to bring her into the vortex of swirling desire once again.

Her eyes had been closed while she was savoring his ministrations, and seductively, she opened her eyes to look deeply into his. His eyes had turned a deep blue as he watched her intensely for any signs of panic. He slowly entered her inch by inch until he reached her maidenhead. Then, with one quick thrust, he pushed through the tiny barrier. Katliana felt like she was being torn apart and seized up in pain while she instinctively tried to close her legs around him. She gasped in pain and turned her head away from him as she tried to hold back tears. Jakiele grasped her chin with his head, turned her face back toward him, and whispered to her, "The worst is over, baby. Relax your muscles and allow your body to adjust to mine."

Jakiele started kissing her again with mind-drugging thoroughness. His fingers continued to work their way around her center with languorous caresses until her body began to respond. She started to writhe anew with anticipation of what was to come. Jakiele slowly began the age-old rhythm of love deep inside her body until she matched his movements with her own. She raised her hips to his to match his rhythm thrust for thrust. She felt like she was climbing the mountain again and was going to come apart against him. His pace grew faster and faster until the climax building within her was upon her before she knew it. He followed soon after reaching his release and rested his forehead against hers while trying to reign in his ragged breaths from the exertion.

Katliana held his head against hers and reveled in the experience they had shared. He had been so tender and loving with her and ever so gentle. Her body was still responding to the aftershocks of the momentous tidal waves of pleasure he had given her. When Jakiele finally got his breathing back under control, he grabbed Katliana, carried her back over to the pool, and washed them both. Neither said a word to the other. Instead, they simply stared deeply into each other's eyes. They knew without saying anything that they had crossed the threshold into another level of their relationship, and there was no going back.

Jakiele gave her another long kiss and left the room to get dressed for dinner. Katliana was quick to follow suit. She did not want to insult the prince by keeping him waiting. The dress left for her was made from the finest silk and fell below her knees. The edges of the dress seemed to be made of antique lace. She quickly donned the red velvet sash and searched for suitable shoes. The red velvet pumps she found in the closet fit her feet perfectly. The dresser by the bed had new sets of unopened panties and lacy bras, so Katliana made effective use of them. She went into the bathroom and fixed her hair before entering the dining room by herself.

Jakiele and the prince were already seated at the table, and both stood up upon her entrance into the dining room. Jakiele had changed into a dark black silk suit and tie with a bright white shirt, while the prince had changed into a similar suit of dark blue. She thought they both looked very handsome indeed. Mantioch studied her for several seconds before coming to stand right in front of her and bowed his head in a courtly gesture. He grasped her hand and placed a kiss on the top before he complimented her, "I see the flower has been plucked, and the rose nectar tasted. I wish you both the best. You look very lovely, my dear. Please have a seat, and I will see to our meal." The prince quickly exited the room to let his staff know they were ready to be served.

Katliana had no idea how the prince knew she and Jakiele had made love, but she was too embarrassed to ask. Jakiele had rounded the other side of the table and grasped her chin in his hand to gently force her eyes to look into his before he asked, "Are you okay? If I hurt you in any way, it was unintentional. Moreover, the prince is right, and you are a feast for the eyes as well as my soul. I only hope you do not have any regrets. Giving yourself to me is a gift I will treasure forever. I love you, Katliana." Katliana reached up to touch the hand holding her face captive and placed it next to her lips to give it a tender kiss before she replied, "I would be lying if I said it did not hurt, and I am a bit sore. You are exceptionally endowed in your nether regions, and there was not much chance of me not being hurt. However, I will tell you it was the most beautiful experience I have ever had in my life, and I am so thankful I could have it with you. Again, I do not have any regrets, and if I had to do it all over again, I would do it again in a heartbeat. I love you too, Jake."

Mantioch cleared his throat loudly to let them know he had re-entered the room not to embarrass them any more than he already had. The trio sat down at the dining room table, and the seven-course meal began with a flourish. The servants made sure their wine glasses were complete with distinctive and flavorful vintages. All empty plates were cleared swiftly. The chef had outdone himself by serving dish after dish of fine French cuisine. Katliana felt stuffed to the gills from the exquisite offerings. She was suddenly exhausted and wanted to sleep, but a loud clanging noise began reverberating through the walls of the cave. It was evident by the screams and the clash of swords ringing against steel that somehow, the demons had managed to escape, and the vampires were doing all they could to keep them away from their prince.

Mantioch and Jakiele jumped up quickly from the table, went to their rooms to get their weapons, and dressed in fighting armor. Katliana was about to follow them out of the cave apartment when both the prince and Jakiele turned around in unison, and Jakiele shouted to her, "No, stay here. Lock the door behind us. Do not come out until one of us comes back for you!" Katliana was about to argue, but by the deadly look on both of their faces, she decided against it and nodded her head in agreement instead. After they had left, she locked the door behind them. The chef came running out of the kitchen and the other servants and looked at her in alarm.

"Mantioch has ordered us to stay here and remain safely locked in. Are there any other exits or entrances I need to be aware of?" Katliana asked them. The vampire servants looked at each other in dismay and fled the room quickly. Katliana was not sure what to make of their odd behavior, so she followed them to a rear exit concealed in the back of the kitchen. This exit must have been carved out in case of a fire or other emergency. She did not know where the exit led to, but the exit could be locked from either side of the heavy wooden door. The servants fled through the exit quickly so that she could bolt the door from her side of the room. She went to the prince's display room, grabbed the ancient sword once belonging to Alexander the Great, and went back to the living room to await word of what was going on. She felt suddenly all alone and terrified for Jakiele.

All she could hear was the clamor of weapons and shouts of men fighting or screaming their last agonizing breaths. She had no way to see what was going on, and it was driving her crazy. However, she had martial arts training, knew how to defend herself if necessary, and she wanted to help if she could. She slowly opened the apartment front door and peered cautiously down the narrow hallway leading back to the main cavern where the commotions seemed to be stemming from. She had barely made it out into the corridor when she felt a steely arm grabbed her around the throat from behind. Katliana felt the cold blade of a boot knife against her vocal cords with her assailant's other hand. She heard the raspy voice of Zadikiele whisper in her right ear, "Hand me the weapon very carefully with your right hand, bitch. I still have a use for you to fulfill. Deny me, and I will kill you where you stand! Do as I say quickly!"

Katliana cautiously handed the ornate sword to Zadikiele with her right hand. He quickly sheathed it beneath his coat with his right hand while he held the knife against her throat with his left. Then, he started nudging her forward into the main cavern entrance. The scene greeting her horrified eyes involuntarily caused a muted scream to well within her throat. Mantioch and Jakiele stood back-to-back with swords in hand, facing a horde of bloodthirsty demons led by Dariah.

The vampires who had not managed to escape were held captive by the demons with their heads pulled back with sharp swords at their throats. Dariah called for the prince's surrender, or further bloodshed would be spilled. Mantioch was about to grudgingly acquiesce to Dariah's commands when shouts from outside the cave made by fleeing vampires caught everyone's attention. As one, all the demons who were in the cavern whirled around in stunned surprise because the entrance to the cave had filled up with angels who were advancing upon them with their swords at the ready.

Michael and Gabriel suddenly appeared from within the multitude of avenging angels and forced their way to the front of the large assembly. The demons gasped in shocked alarm and started to back away from the vampires they had previously held hostage. They looked at each other in shock and confusion as they looked around for a means of escape. The demons knew they outnumbered the angels, but they also knew it would be a long and bloody battle. Zadikiele held his knife even tighter to Katliana's neck as he advanced into the room, which caused Katliana to gasp in fear.

Jakiele and the prince both had their backs to Zadikiele, so they were caught entirely unaware Katliana was being used as a hostage. Upon hearing Katliana's frightened gulp of air, Jakiele spun around and faced Zadikiele with surprise registering across his features, quickly being replaced by a look of pure rage. Zadikiele arrogantly propelled Katliana forward to the side of the large dais Jakiele and the prince were standing on. Zadikiele wanted to ensure he had the two of them clearly in his sites while keeping his back protected from any unwanted attacks.

Zadikiele's raspy voice rang across the room to the crowd of demons as he commanded them, "Stand your ground, all of you, or I will kill you all myself! Take up your arms and destroy them all!" Jakiele urgently shouted to the swarming angels, "Do not harm the vampires! They are not our enemies. These foul demons are.

The vampires agreed to assist me, and I gave my word of honor that they would not be harmed!" The demons were unsure of what to do or what to think when Dariah suddenly lunged toward one of the vampires trying to edge toward the entrance of the cave to escape. Dariah shoved his sword cleanly into the vampire's heart and then withdrew his bloody sword to spin around and cut off the vampire's head. Dariah slowly licked the dripping blood off the blade to taunt the prince. Mantioch inhaled his breath sharply in pain at seeing one of his trusted comrades dispatched so heartlessly.

This brutal action caused the demons to leap into the fray and start attacking the angels as well as the vampires who had not yet managed to escape the large cavern. Jakiele was slowly advancing on Zadikiele with his sword drawn and had a fierce look of concentration that was deeply etched into the lines of his face. Zadikiele stood his ground until, at the last minute, he decided to throw Katliana to the ground. He forcibly held her body to the floor with one booted foot grinding into the small of her back so she could not move. Every time Zadikiele moved to counteract one of Jakiele's mighty thrusts, Zadikiele would grind his foot even deeper into Katliana's back, causing her to scream in pain. Finally, Jakiele stopped moving and waited for Zadikiele to attack while the prince sidled around behind Zadikiele slowly and stealthily.

Mantioch had crept behind Zadikiele as quietly as a slithering snake to plunge his sword deep into Zadikiele's back and slice his weapon through Zadikiele's chest. Zadikiele whirled around in stunned amazement and stood staring at the gaping wound in his chest before he fell to the floor, holding his hands to the wound. Zadikiele stopped breathing within a few quick seconds, and everyone thought he was dead. However, Jakiele was fast as lightning when he scooped Katliana off the floor and carried her to a spot of relative safety off to the side of the large cavern. After that, Jakiele and the prince joined forces again to help ward off the demons who outnumbered the angels three to one in the battle.

It was clear Michael and Gabriel were enjoying themselves immensely as they fought back-to-back against the vengeful demons who wanted nothing more than to spill angel blood and make a name for themselves with a victory. However, they were not watching what Dariah was doing. They should have paid more attention to the way Dariah was silently moving closer and closer to Jakiele. Before anyone even knew what was happening, Dariah threw deadly throwing stars into Jakiele's sword arm, neck, and stomach, which forced Jakiele to lose his grip on his trusted sword.

The room seemed to take on an eerie silence when everyone stopped what they were doing to watch in morbid fascination as Dariah advanced on Jakiele, who had fallen to his knees in pain. Dariah had a long hunting knife stretched across Jakiele's throat in a mere fraction of a second. Dariah grasped the back of Jakiele's hair to force his head back, which also caused the neck wounds to bleed more freely. Michael let out a feral growl and advanced on Dariah's position with lethal intent. Katliana let out a horrified scream and covered her mouth with both hands in sheer terror, knowing Dariah was about to end Jakiele's life.

"Get back all of you, or I will end this angel's miserable life. You know what we came here for! Give me the mirror, or all of you will die! There will be no more death today if you give me what I want! No more games." Michael looked deeply into Jakiele's eyes in muted frustration and turned his head to nod to Gabriel. Michael solemnly said, "So be it, demon. You shall have all you desire." Gabriel went outside the cavern and returned with the mirror the demon wanted so desperately.

Dariah demanded, "Bring the mirror to me and back away all of you!" Gabriel stepped forward and laid the mirror down at Jakiele's feet. Dariah jerked back Jakiele's head with a sharp yank and ordered Jakiele to pick up the mirror and hold it to his chest. Jakiele looked at Michael in confusion, and one would have had to be watching very closely to see the almost imperceptible nod Michael leveled in Jakiele's direction. Then, the angels who had managed to kill many demons started to form a tight circle around Dariah. At the same time, the demons who remained began to edge out of the cavern to make their escape. Within moments, Dariah was left entirely on his own, with his only protection being the mirror Jakiele held tightly to his body. Still, his rapid blood loss was causing him to lose his grip fast.

Michael held up his hand to the angels who were steadily closing in on Dariah and ordered them to stop by commanding authoritatively, "No angels will harm you on my word if you let Jakiele go. Take the mirror and flee, demon!" Dariah did not trust Michael to keep his word, but he had managed to edge closer to the cave entrance. With a mad dash, he grabbed the mirror from Jakiele and fled the cave. Michael held up his hand to restrain the other angels from following and destroying him.

Once Michael and Gabriel were satisfied Dariah was long gone, they gave each other a high-five and smiled in secret at one another. Jakiele was confused at the Archangel's odd behavior, but he was bleeding profusely from his wounds and was about to lose consciousness. Katliana rushed forward and caught his head in her hands before he lost consciousness.

Mantioch was quick to act and gathered Jakiele up into his arms, carried him to his apartment, and headed for his bedroom. Michael gave the signal for the other angels to remain where they were and to stand guard. Michael, Gabriel, and Katliana had followed the prince into the apartment and were genuinely concerned for Jakiele's welfare as he had lost a great deal of blood. However, Michael had been so preoccupied with Dariah he and the others had not noticed Zadikiele slowly make his way out of the main cavern by crawling on the floor and out of the cavern to find his way back painfully to his camp.

# CHAPTER 14

antioch carried Jakiele to the bedroom Jakiele had used previously and gently laid him on the bed before he turned to look at Michael and demanded angrily, "Who are you and why have you come here?" Michael raised a hand to subdue Gabriel, who would have gladly throttled the arrogant prince for speaking to Michael in such a disrespectful tone and gently replied, "I am the Archangel Michael, and this is my second in command, Gabriel. We came to rescue Jakiele from the demons who had taken this woman hostage." He waved a casual hand in Katliana's direction before he continued with, "Jakiele led us to his location through a tracking device he has on somewhere on his body."

Mantioch narrowed his eyes in suspicion before he sarcastically spoke again, "Well, it is good to know Jakiele has such good friends. However, he needs my aid, and if you permit me, I shall see to his wounds." Gabriel started to move forward again to descend on the prince, but Michael waved a restraining hand in his direction. Michael looked the prince directly in the eye and, with a deceptively soft voice, asked, "What exactly are your intentions? His body will regenerate quickly, so how will you be able to help him? You do not intend to share your blood with him, do you, vampire?"

Mantioch stiffened visibly at the hostile question before he testily answered, "You will address me as Prince or Mantioch if you please! Jakiele is my friend and has proven himself to be true to his word, and as such, I will do the same! No, I will not give him my blood, but I do keep human stores of blood locked up in my vault for emergencies. His body may be able to regenerate at a fast pace, but it will not be able to keep up with the blood loss unless I tend to his wounds at once! Now, we can sit and debate this, or I can save his life! Choose quickly!"

Michael nodded his head at once in agreement and led Gabriel quickly out of the room before any more tension could be created between the Archangels and the prince. Michael motioned with his hand in Katliana's direction for her to follow them out. Katliana looked tearfully in the prince's direction before she sweetly bent down to kiss Jakiele on the cheek and followed the Archangels into the living room. The unlikely trio seated themselves on the prince's soft couches and awaited word from the prince on how Jakiele was faring.

Michael and Gabriel had both begun to stare at Katliana with a deep intensity for several long moments until she felt herself turn a bright red with embarrassment at what she was sure was a condemning assessment of her. Michael was the first to speak, "If you did not mind, my dear, I would like to read your memories. I must know all that has happened since I last spoke with Jakiele, as I have only been able to get bits and pieces of the whole story. I am Jakiele's most trusted friend, and I would never do anything to cause him harm. Would you please trust me?"

Katliana was apprehensive. What if Michael was able to see they had made love? Would he strike her down where she sat? Would he kill Jakiele in his sleep? There was no way she would take a chance with Jakiele's life when she replied, "I am sorry, Michael, but my memories are private. So, you will have to speak with Jakiele about anything you wish to know. If you, however, have a question, I will be more than happy to oblige you."

Michael was momentarily taken aback at Katliana's tenacity. Few humans or angels had ever thought to deny his requests.

Nevertheless, he needed information quickly before Gabriel made good on his threat to bring Jakiele up on charges before the high council. Michael decided having Gabriel in the same room with them was not a good idea and contributed to Katliana's apprehensiveness. It became clear that the malevolent way Gabriel was glaring at her caused Katliana's body to quiver in uneasiness.

Michael turned to look at Gabriel and silently nodded for Gabriel to leave him and Katliana alone. Gabriel was disgusted at being summarily dismissed and harrumphed sarcastically, "Well, I guess I should make sure the angels are cleaning up the mess caused here properly! We certainly do not want any more mistakes, now do we?" Gabriel stood up, strode angrily out of the room, and closed the door with a loud bang.

Michael rose from the couch he had been sitting on, knelt in front of Katliana, and gently grasped both of her hands in his. He looked intently into her eyes and explained very softly to her, "Listen to me carefully if you would please, Katliana. I need all the information I can to save Jakiele's life. If you care for him, please let me help him. I beg of you. Is there something you do not wish me to see?" Katliana blushed a deep red and lowered her eyes in embarrassment before she replied in a tentative voice, "Yes, there is. I am afraid you will condemn us to death if you see it. I want you to know I love Jakiele with all my heart. I would give anything to save his life. He certainly risked his own life enough to save mine. If you promise not to use what you see against us, I will help you." Michael already had a good idea of what she was trying not to say, so he gently lifted her chin back up with his right hand, looked into her tear-filled eyes, and said, "If Jakiele made love to you and you both protected yourselves from unwanted pregnancy, what you did is not an automatic death sentence for either of you. If you give me your word Jakiele took the necessary precautions, I will promise you I will not look in on such a private memory."

Katliana openly stared back into Michael's earnest but honest face and quietly nodded to allow Michael to read her memories.

Michael softly whispered to her, "Close your eyes and relax. You will be able to see in your mind all I can see." Katliana did as he instructed and closed her eyes. All the events leading up to seeking Jakiele's aid flashed through her mind in quick succession, even reliving the terrible moments following Kyle's sudden death and the brutal treatment her kidnappers had inflicted upon her. The horrifying memory of meeting the vampire Andy caused her to shudder in horrified remembrance visibly.

After Michael was satisfied with the information he had gleaned from her mind, he lifted his left hand away from her forehead and stood back up. Katliana was relieved Michael had kept his word and had not invaded the sensual memory of making love to Jakiele for the first time. However, she had a few questions of her own to ask Michael, "Where is Mulakai? Why did he not make the journey here with you? I thought he was Jakiele's friend?" Michael smiled enigmatically at her before he answered, "Mulakai has been assigned to England to look after an extraordinary friend of Jakiele's, and we felt it was in the best interest of all concerned that he be dropped off to watch over her and her son. The demons may strike out at them next since she could escape the demon's clutches. Moreover, the woman was privy to much of Zadikiele's operations in the states."

Katliana mulled over the information before she asked her next question, "Do you know if my mother and Caleb are okay? They must be worried sick." Michael hesitated for a moment before he replied, "After Mulakai was able to reach me to fill me in on what was going on, I asked his permission to read his memories. Jakiele had the foresight to share his memories with Mulakai. This information is how I found about the woman Mulakai was sent to protect. Caleb was attacked trying to save you and suffered a major head wound. He is doing well, and he and your mother were taken to one of Jakiele's safe houses in the city to recover. Jakiele made sure they were both safe before he came after you."

Katliana bent her head, covered her face, and began to sob. She felt responsible for this whole mess. If she had never opened the case file, no one would have been hurt, and she would not have been forced to flee Boston to seek Jakiele's protection. Michael bent down once again, freed her tear-soaked hands from her face, and very sternly let her know, "None of this is your fault, Katliana! Demons have been trying to take over the Earth for centuries. It is our job to try and prevent this from happening. One way or the other, they would have eventually tried to come after Jakiele and destroy him. It was only a matter of time before they attacked. Do you understand what I am saying?"

Katliana nodded but continued to let out heart-wrenching cries of distress. Michael stood up and gathered her in his arms. He smoothed back her hair with his hands, uttered soft words of comfort until her body started to relax, and the sobs started to cease. Michael picked her up and tracked her scent back to the room she had previously occupied. He laid her down gently in the bed and covered her with the sheets and blankets until she was securely tucked in. She lay there looking trustingly in his eyes. Michael swept his left hand over her eyes and commanded her to sleep.

The hypnotic voice command Michael used on her brooked no argument from her mortal mind, and she unconsciously gave into the demand without even being aware of it. Michael gave a deep sigh and looked down at her while she slept before quietly leaving the room to go in search of Gabriel. Michael walked into the main cavern and discovered most of the macabre scene had already been thoroughly sanitized. The vampires who had escaped the battle earlier had returned and were uneasily watching the angels thoroughly cauterizing and destroying the remains of both demons and fellow vampires alike.

Michael was the first to notice the blood trail Zadikiele had left behind and followed the bloody path to the cave entrance. Zadikiele had managed to escape, and so had Dariah. Judging from the large blood pools, it had been a slow process for the mortally wounded Zadikiele to make his escape. Michael hoped he did not live long, but he returned to the cavern and ordered the angels to track the trail and report back to him. The angels left quickly to do as they were bid, much to the relief of the vampires, who cautiously went back to performing their duties while trying to avoid making eye contact with either himself or Gabriel.

Mantioch strode back into the large cavern while wiping his hands on a blood-soaked piece of fine linen. Michael walked up to him swiftly and noted the grave expression lining the prince's handsome features. Michael worriedly asked, "Well? Is he going to live?" Mantioch solemnly nodded and replied, "Yes, he will live, but his wounds are severe. He needs rest and nourishment and should not be moved for a few days."

Gabriel had overheard the conversation and angrily walked over to where the prince and Michael were talking and announced, "This cannot be. Impossible! The time limit I gave him is up. He is to stand before the high council and be tried for conduct unbecoming an angel. It has already been arranged!" Michael had had enough of Gabriel's high-handed misuse of authority and was quick to give him a vehement set down, "No one gave you the authority to do any such thing, Gabriel! The only one who can decide what to do with Jakiele is our Heavenly Father and me! If Jakiele needs rest, the council will have to wait. Such will be the end of this conversation! Am I clear?"

Mantioch watched the interaction between the two rival Archangels with a smirk of amusement on his face as he recognized they were competing over who was in charge like two quarrelsome siblings. Gabriel stalked off, muttering under his breath, and continued disposing of any evidence inadvertently left behind from the gruesome battle. Michael once again turned his attention back to the prince and bowed gracefully in front of him before he said, "Thank you for all you have done for us. It is not up to me or the others to judge you or decide your fate before God. Such is God's decision alone. We must leave and continue to track the rest of the demons if possible. My condolences for your many losses in assisting us."

Mantioch continued to wipe his hands as he studied Michael with suspicious eyes and cautiously replied, "I am sorry for your losses as well, Michael. I am sure you lost several good angels today. I also thank you for saving as many of my friends as possible. However, I have no fear of God and whether he knows of my existence or not. God is all-knowing and has been watching me for years, so I live a righteous life and demand all others in my realm do as well. I will make sure Jakiele and Katliana are safe and well before they return to the states."

Mantioch extended his right hand in friendship. Michael quickly seized the opportunity to end the conversation on a positive note and shook the prince's hand. Michael started to walk away and snapped his fingers at Gabriel, which indicated Michael expected Gabriel to follow him out of the cave so they could begin tracking the demon blood trail left by Zadikiele. Gabriel reluctantly followed but not before fixing a hateful glare in the prince's direction. Mantioch insolently gave Gabriel a one-finger salute with a smug smile before turning to walk back to his chambers to check in on Katliana and Jakiele.

The remaining angels Michael had sent out in search of Zadikiele were returning to the cave entrance when Michael and Gabriel came out. They let Michael know the trail had ended at a campsite recently erected next to Lake Synevir. However, the campsite had been recently evacuated, and no traces had been left except for a burned-out campfire. Thus, some of the other demons must have waited around for Zadikiele to return and quickly spirited him away. Michael and Gabriel gave each other concerned glances. Finally, Michael ordered them to return to the heavenly mansion to await word on Jakiele's recovery.

Two days after the wounds had been cleaned and stitched by the prince's personal surgeon, Jakiele made a full recovery without so much as a scar. Mantioch had given Jakiele regular blood transfusions until he was sure Jakiele's body was producing enough blood on his own. Jakiele owed the prince his life, and he was sure to thank him when he finally regained consciousness. However, Mantioch graciously waved off Jakiele's praise and thanks. All he asked in return was if he ever needed a favor, Jakiele would grant it, no questions asked.

Jakiele was hesitant to grant the request, but he reluctantly agreed to the prince's terms since he owed the prince his life. As soon as Katliana had awoken from the forced slumber Michael had induced, she never left Jakiele's bedside, not even to eat. Mantioch had been bringing in her meals so she could stay vigilant at Jakiele's bedside. Jakiele was invigorated, and his body felt renewed as it had not felt in centuries. Finally, he declared to the prince that he was ready to return home, so he decided to get up and get dressed. It was time for them to leave, and Jakiele needed time to ready himself to go before the high council.

Both he and Katliana thanked the prince for all he had done once again, but Katliana made sure to give the lonely prince a giant bear hug and a kiss on the cheek in farewell also. Mantioch was very touched by her gesture and gave her a formal bow and a kiss on the top of one of her hands before he grudgingly released her into Jakiele's care. After that, Mantioch insisted his guards escort them to the train depot and back to the city to make sure they safely made it to Cluj Napoca.

Once Jakiele and Katliana reached the hotel Jakiele had been staying in earlier, he discovered the prince must have already planned for the same room he had previously occupied to be reserved a few more days for them. Jakiele's things were still in the room exactly as he had left them. A chilled bottle of champagne, fine chocolates, and a bowl of ripe delicious fruit with freshly whipped cream lay on one of the bedside tables with a single note which said, "Enjoy, my friends, be well, and God speed your way."

Katliana smiled as she read the note and asked Jakiele, "You do not suppose Mantioch owns this hotel, too, do you?" Jakiele chuckled and said laughingly, "Nothing would surprise me about the prince. But I have no wish to discuss him. I need a shower before I make the necessary travel arrangements. How about you? Would you like to join me?" Katliana blushed a deep crimson. She had never taken a shower with a man before and did not know how to answer him without seeming like a gauche schoolgirl. Jakiele recognized she was still timid and decided to let her decide to join him or not on her own.

Jakiele went into the bathroom, turned on the water in the shower, and set the temperature to a comfortable level. He stepped in and started soaping up his body and slowly washing his hair. Katliana was undecided about what to do, but she finally got up enough courage to go and join him. They made love throughout the day and night. Being able to finally explore each other's bodies and what pleased each other seemed like a treasured gift. Jakiele was a very patient and tender lover and enjoyed showing Katliana how to give and receive pleasure. Jakiele finally got around to making the travel arrangements the following day. He was sure their time together was short, and he intended to make the most of it. The prince had provided them with spare outfits and had packed the necessary means to protect Katliana from pregnancy in the suitcases he had provided for them.

Mantioch was generous and thoughtful to a fault. Jakiele was surprised to find out he respected the prince and was thankful to call him a friend. Katliana and Jakiele ate an excellent late breakfast while they waited for the flight that would take them back home. Jakiele warned her military flights were not very comfortable, but at least any wayward demons watching them would not be able to follow them.

Katliana was apprehensive and unusually pensive on the long flight home as she kept worrying about whether she would ever see Jakiele again. He tried his best to reassure her with warm caresses and kisses, but he was as concerned as she was about Gabriel's vindictive wrath and what future would await him once they arrived back in Washington D.C. Jakiele hired a taxi to take them home. Both were utterly exhausted when they finally got back to Jakiele's house.

Jakiele put in the necessary code to enter the house once they arrived, and the two of them climbed the long staircase to the second floor and entered his bedroom. They quietly undressed and held each other tightly until the following day, when Jakiele knew he had no other choice than to face his fate. He looked into Katliana's sleeping face and kissed her tenderly before dressing in his formal angelic attire. He stoically but apprehensively went into his closet to access the portal that would take him to the angelic realm. He was not surprised to see the mirror was still intact, but he wondered what kind of mirror Michael had given to Dariah. He was sure he would get the answers he sought when he stood before the high council of Dominions.

He went through the portal and went to the great mirror in the center of the angelic realm. He lowered his body to his knees and bowed his head before speaking the required but heartfelt exaltations to the God he served and asked to speak with Michael. Michael appeared before him in the mirror and walked through to join Jakiele in the lower heavenly mansion. Jakiele stood up, and the two warriors embraced each other with their forearms in their typical fashion. Michael was relieved to see Jakiele was well, but the look on his face was gravely serious when he spoke, "You know Gabriel has accused you of gross misconduct before the council, but I will be there to speak on your behalf, and so will Mulakai. The trial will not be easy, Jakiele. Prepare yourself."

Jakiele composed himself the best he could but asked, "Why was Mulakai not present at the battle?" Michael smiled at him and let him know what he had already relayed to Katliana. Jakiele was immensely relieved to know that Mulakai would watch over Rochelle and her boy. It was a massive weight off his conscience, but he was confused about how Michael had even known he had sent her to England or even had knowledge of her existence. Michael simply smiled enigmatically and told him, "I do not tell you everything, Jakiele, but keep in mind there is extraordinarily little I am not aware of regarding angels who are under my guidance. Come, we must leave now."

Michael went back through the mirror and waved a hand for Jakiele to follow him to the Archangel realm. Michael opened the portal to the Dominion realm, where Gabriel and Mulakai awaited them. Jakiele stoically maintained his appearance of calm serenity in readiness to accept whatever fate the Dominions decreed. He resolved that loving Katliana was worth every minute of whatever punishment they decided to mete out.

Gabriel was the first to notice that Michael and Jakiele had stepped through the portal to join himself and Mulakai. Mulakai immediately walked over to greet Jakiele, and the two angels grasped each other's forearms in typical warrior fashion. Gabriel continued to stare smugly at Jakiele, sure in his righteousness of bringing Jakiele up on charges of misconduct. Michael glared hotly at Gabriel for his disrespectful acknowledgment of not only Jakiele's presence but his own as well.

Before long, misty swirls indicated the Dominions were present. It was unusual for them to take any form, but they believed the accused had the right to see their faces if a harsh judgment was handed down. Twelve misty forms took their seats encircling a large stone dais in the center of the room. A large marble podium separated the two circular rows of seats. Muriel's swirling form soon took shape as he stood behind the large podium and began the formal sentencing proceeding.

Michael escorted Jakiele to the center of the large dais before he went back to standing at the outer edge to await instructions from Muriel. Muriel nodded imperceptibly at Michael before turning his perceptive gaze upon Jakiele as though he was studying him intently. Jakiele had his head bowed in respect and then had the good grace slide his body down to his knees to show respect to the Dominions.

The Dominions kept impassive looks on their faces. They were neither angry nor joyous this preceding had been summoned forth by Gabriel. On the contrary, they were knowledgeable beings and would await passing judgment until all the facts were heard. Muriel waved his hand in Gabriel's direction and motioned for him to speak. Gabriel went up onto the dais and addressed the Dominions as a group, "I have requested this audience with you, great ones, as I know you will want to hear the charges I wish to bring against this angel!" Gabriel pointed an accusing finger at Jakiele's bowed head.

"After Michael assigned him to be stationed on Earth, he had the gall to invite humans into his home to become his servants! He became emotionally attached to them and could not properly protect them from the demons who invaded his home and took one of the humans captive! He became so oblivious to his surroundings that he put the mirror Michael had given him in jeopardy of being discovered by the demons! Which, of course, they did. Once they were made aware of the value of the mirror, they thought to trade the mirror for the young girl they had managed to kidnap!"

Gabriel's voice had reached a thunderous pitch as it had slowly risen in anger with each accusatory charge leveled at Jakiele. Finally, he finished his long speech with, "As you know, angels are only allowed to be on Earth to observe and report, not interact with the humans! Not to mention the fact that after he went after the demons to try and save the girl, he openly consorted with the worst sort of monsters and sought their aid, vampires!"

Gabriel fully expected the large assembly of Dominions to be shocked to the core by his last statement, but they merely continued to stare impassively at Gabriel and waited for him to finish his damning assessment of Jakiele. Muriel was the first to speak in a soft tone, "Are these all the charges you wish to level against Jakiele, Gabriel?" Gabriel started to sputter in angry amazement, but he nodded his head. He was indeed finished and had nothing further to add.

Muriel dismissed him with a wave of his hand and motioned for Mulakai to come and stand before them to speak. Mulakai walked slowly to the dais, knelt, bowed his head as Jakiele was doing, and waited to be addressed. Instead, Muriel spoke gently to him and said, "Rise, angel, and speak the truth of what you have seen and heard.

We must know all." Mulakai slowly rose to his feet and placed a reassuring hand on Jakiele's right shoulder in a gesture of support before he reiterated what part he had played in the whole fiasco.

"Yes, it is true Michael permitted Jakiele to have human servants in his home. The housekeeper and chauffer he hired became more like his friends rather than employees. All of them were satisfied with the arrangement, and Jakiele's home was a happy one. His housekeeper has a daughter named Katliana. She came to seek Jakiele's aid after becoming aware of the death of a young Asian girl through her work as a forensic DNA specialist. Jakiele wanted Katliana to turn over the evidence to the proper government authorities, but Katliana adamantly refused.

Jakiele and I soon discovered that the young Asian girl Katliana was investigating had been killed by a rogue vampire. We did all we could to convince Gabriel that we needed to let Michael know what was happening on at least two separate occasions, but Gabriel refused to listen to our requests. It was only after I threatened to seek out Michael myself that Gabriel finally relented and decided to inform Michael, but it was too late. We brought Gabriel back through the portal to view the rogue vampire for himself that Jakiele had managed to capture since our words were not enough to convince him to help us.

The demons installed video cameras into Jakiele's house unbeknownst to him and saw us return through the secret portal. The demons knew Katliana was aware of how the Asian girl died and wanted to use her as leverage to gain access to the mirror. The demons kidnapped Katliana, but Jakiele did all he could to help save her, and she has since been returned safely to his home. Fortunately, he did not bring the mirror with him in his search for Katliana and saved her through his ingenuity and cleverness. It is not his fault any of this has happened, and if he is to be brought up on charges, you may condemn me as well!"

Gabriel gasped in shock at the last words Mulakai had spoken and was about to step forward when Muriel raised a restraining hand to stop him. Mulakai had bent down on one knee beside Jakiele and bowed his head also. Muriel waved his hand to indicate that Mulakai should leave the Dais as it was Michael's turn to come forward next. Muriel waved his hand to let Michael know it was his turn to speak. Michael moved forward to take his place on the dais and calmly stated, "Great ones, it has been a privilege for me to have this angel as my student and to be his teacher. He has ever served Heaven with loyalty and integrity not only to me but to the God he diligently and willingly obeyed. He became emotionally involved with his servants, especially with the young woman Katliana. I believe that he has fallen in love with her.

He also sought out the aid of a lead vampire named Mantioch to save her from the demon clutches. However, he did not cause any of the events that caused her to be kidnapped, and he is not responsible for the death of the young Asian girl. If it is anyone's fault all of this occurred, it is mine. I was the one who trusted Gabriel to inform me if anything unusual was happening with Jakiele. Unfortunately, he chose not to do so until I was forced to take matters into my own hands and summon you for your assistance."

Gabriel stepped back onto the dais without permission and said with an angry retort, "Yes, Michael is the one who willingly gave the demons what they wanted and handed them one of our sacred mirrors! He should be brought up on charges as well! He thanked the vampires for helping us when he should have allowed me to destroy them! They are an abomination and should not be allowed to exist!"

Muriel gracefully went to stand directly in front of Gabriel and quietly hissed, "Think you we have been unaware of Mantioch's existence on Earth angel? We have known about him for centuries after he made his covenant with Noah. Although he made unintentional mistakes at the beginning of his long tenure on Earth, he asked God for the forgiveness of his sins and has lived a righteous life ever since! He also made sure all of you lived! Did he not cease the life of the one who had killed the young girl? You forget yourself, Gabriel! We know everything happening on Earth. Just because we do not always intervene does not mean we are not aware!"

Gabriel convulsively gasped in the air into his tortured lungs, indeed in fear for the first time. This trial was not going the way he had hoped it would. Muriel took a few steps back from Gabriel and addressed him once again, "Your arrogance in assuming what Michael should be informed of and what he should not is what caused this situation to get so out of hand in the first place! Jakiele and Mulakai both sought your assistance, and your blind ambition closed your eyes and heart to the truth! We are the ones who gave the mirror to Michael, you fool! Did you not think we had an ulterior motive for doing so? You had better start following Michael's orders, or it will be you on trial! Am I in any way unclear, Gabriel?"

Gabriel bowed his head in shame and mortification. He had been called out on his behavior harshly in front of the high council and his protégé Mulakai. He walked slowly back off the dais to await the outcome of whatever the high council decided. Michael also turned and walked back off the podium to stand by Gabriel. Michael placed a reassuring hand on Gabriel's left shoulder in support of their long friendship. Gabriel looked up at Michael and whispered the words, "I am sorry, old friend. I made several foolish mistakes. Please forgive me." Michael did not answer him. Instead, he smiled at Gabriel and gave his shoulder a reassuring squeeze.

Muriel stood directly in front of Jakiele and placed his left hand on his forehead. He did not need permission, and he read Jakiele's memories. When he finished, he grasped Jakiele's chin with his hand and forced him to look up. He gave the motion with his hand for Jakiele to leave the dais and go back and stand with Gabriel and Michael. The Dominions, including Muriel, turned into misty swirls of vapor again as they discussed what they would do with Jakiele.

Since they communicated silently with one another, the angels in the room had no idea of the trial's outcome. In moments, Muriel reappeared before Jakiele and addressed the angels, "God created you and the mortals as well. Our God is a kind and loving being. Is it so inconceivable that an angel would also love? However, God does not wish you to mingle with humans and create Nephilim and has decreed that the two species are not allowed to intermingle. Do you love this human Katliana? Would you be willing to do anything to be with her? I must know the truth of this Jakiele!"

Jakiele stood up from his knees and looked directly at Muriel for the first time since the trial began and ardently spoke his deepest desire, "Yes, Great One, I do love her! She has become the very air I breathe and the heart that beats in my chest. I did not mean for any of this to happen, and I would be willing to do whatever you ask of me. Even if doing so means I would never be able to be with her again. Her safety and happiness mean more to me than anything else!" Jakiele's confession stunned the angels. His admission could well mean his death sentence.

The Dominions once again turned into misty vapors of fog and swirled around Jakiele and completely enveloped his body in their presence as they studied him and decided what they were going to do. Once they had reached a decision, Muriel and the others reappeared to encircle Jakiele in a large ring with their hands clasped together and began a sacred chant with their eyes closed and their bodies gently swaying together in unison. Giant sparks of color began to shoot out of Jakiele's body, and a wrenching pain took hold of all areas of his body, forcing him to fall to his knees in agony. Gabriel had to hold Mulakai and Michael back from intervening.

Showers of colored sparks started swirling around Jakiele and moved faster and faster with dizzying speed and light until suddenly, Jakiele went utterly still. The sparks ceased their frenzied dance around his body. Jakiele fell into a deep sleep, and then the Dominions disappeared one by one. Finally, only Muriel was standing over Jakiele's prone body. He lifted Jakiele off the floor and stood him up to face him. Then, with a wave of his hand over Jakiele's face, Jakiele was awake once more.

Muriel addressed all of the angels in the room, "Because of this angel's unwavering loyalty to the God he serves, he has been granted his fondest wish. God commands that he be an angel no more but a mere mortal. He shall have the life he seeks but as a man. Michael, you will take Jakiele back through the portal and retrieve the mirror. You and Gabriel are to seek out the American president and make sure he and the Chinese Ambassador have only memories of friendship and continued cooperation with one another. Plant the memory in their minds that the dead Asian girl simply died of contagion. It was an oversight that the Chinese government was not informed at once. Have them part ways as friends. After all is done, destroy the mirror and any others like it being used. We are finished here."

With a puff of smoke, Muriel was gone. Jakiele was still recovering from the shock of what had happened. He was no longer an angel but a mortal? He felt like he had failed Michael and the others and stood alone with his head bowed in shame. Mortality was a most severe punishment indeed, and as far as he was aware, this form of retribution had never been done before. Michael and the others walked over to the dais and placed their hands upon Jakiele in support. Michael was the first to speak, "I know you are feeling bad about their pronouncement, Jakiele, and you have somehow failed me. However, know I am proud of you and how you have served Heaven. Know I am happy for you. What a glorious gift they have bestowed upon you, my friend! You have been granted an opportunity to have a wonderful life to be lived freely with the one you love without fear. Let me take you to her, and you can tell her the good news!"

Jakiele raised his bowed head and could not help the tears of regret suddenly pouring unbidden from his eyes as he stared back at Michael, knowing the two of them would never again be able to fly together across the vast universe together and share their unique bond. Michael understood what Jakiele must be feeling and added, "We shall ever be friends, Jakiele. I shall check in on you from time to time, and you can always reach me through Mulakai, should you ever need me." Jakiele could not seem to form any words through his stricken throat, so he merely nodded instead. The Archangels led Jakiele back through the portal, while Mulakai stayed behind in the heavenly mansion to await their return to take him to England to begin his first assignment.

After seeing Jakiele safely back to his closet, Michael seized the mirror from its protected resting place, and together, he and Gabriel went back to the lower angelic realm to finish their tasks assigned by the Dominions. Jakiele suddenly felt free for the first time from the weighty responsibilities he was ordered to endure on Earth as an angel. It would take getting used to, but he was looking forward to starting a new life with Katliana at his side.

Jakiele padded softly back to his bed, where Katliana still lay sleeping on her side with her hand underneath her head. He undressed quickly, climbed back in bed, spooned up next to her, and began running his hand up and down her naked thigh. The need to take her as a human male began to throb a steady beat in his groin and grew to almost painful proportions. Katliana rolled over, snuggled into his body, and began running feather-light kisses over his chest and neck. Next, he rolled her on top of him and positioned her thighs to straddle across him as he showed her another position they had not yet tried. Her head was soon thrown back in sheer ecstasy as she quickly adapted and learned how to ride his body with hers. Before long, they were both swept up in a firestorm of passion and desire for one another.

Her first release left her body entirely spent, but soon, Jakiele gave her another and another until he reached his climax. She felt his seed spill deep inside of her, and she reacted with alarm and stared at him with fear and question in her eyes, and she softly whispered, "Oh dear God, what have you done, Jakiele? We did not use protection!" Jakiele looked deeply into her eyes and whispered back, "All is well. The Dominions have decreed that I no longer serve Earth as an angel but as a human. I have a question to ask you, Katliana. Can you love me as a mortal and spend the rest of your life with me? Will you become my wife?"

Katliana was momentarily stunned, speechless before she giddily responded, "Oh yes! I would love nothing more than to spend eternity with you, my love. When can we be married?" Jakiele chuckled softly and kissed her senseless once again before he replied, "Such a thing is up to you. I am sure you and your mother can arrange something amazing. Just tell me when and where to show up and claim you as my own!"

It was Katliana's turn to laugh softly and say back teasingly to him, "I think you have already done so, Jake, but how does a month from now sound? I only want a small wedding here at the house. I do not know many people, so the guest list should be pretty small." Jakiele laughed again with her, rolled her underneath of him, gently pinned her to the bed with his large body, and began nuzzling her sensitive breasts and whispering gently in her ear, "Whatever makes you happy, my lady." Jakiele set himself back to the task at hand and retook her to the heights of passion.

Jakiele and Katliana decided to take a trip to Boston to pay their final respects to Kyle at his tombstone after discussing everything that had taken place and filling each other in on the missing pieces of the bizarre adventure they had shared. Katliana finally felt like she had kept her word to Kyle to find the underlying cause of the mystery of the young girl's death and decided to burn all the evidence in Jakiele's fireplace. She was sad Kyle was gone but was happy he had finally rejoined his family in Heaven. She now felt like she was ready to start her new life with Jakiele.

Jakiele wondered at his good fortune a month later as he stood nervously in front of his fireplace mantle and waited for Katliana to come down the stairs and join him. Anna had done a magnificent job decorating the house with gorgeous pastel flowers and gauzy white fabrics. In addition, she had managed to rearrange the living room into a large seating area to accommodate the guests who had arrived, which included Katliana's aunt and uncle, Mulakai, Michael and Gabriel, and many of Jake's military friends. Jakiele's house was packed to compacity, and all were enjoying the festivities and tasty treats Anna had made for them.

Jakiele was dressed in a black tuxedo with a royal blue cummerbund. His crisp white shirt underneath made his sapphire blue eyes come to life. The music started, and soon, Katliana was being led down the makeshift aisle by Caleb. She was indeed a vision in her frothy white gown, made of the finest silk and lace. She chose not to wear a veil but instead had her hair pinned up in an intricate pattern with fresh flowers laced throughout. Her matching blue sapphire necklace and earrings matched Jakiele's sash perfectly. Soon, the ceremony was over, with everyone wishing them well. The buffet-style meal Anna had arranged in the backyard was soon underway after all the toasts to the bride and groom had been given.

Jakiele and Katliana had only eyes for each other as they danced their first dance together as husband and wife under the makeshift tent erected over the backyard to protect everyone from any prying eyes wishing them or their guest's harm. However, their efforts did not stop Zadikiele, as he had set up in the neighboring trees, to watch the proceedings from a distance through a long lens tripod.

He smugly observed Jakiele and Katliana cutting the first piece of their elegant white cake and sharing a slice. He convinced himself that somehow, the powers above had made Jakiele human. There was no way he could be with Katliana any other way. Then, satisfied he no longer had any need to spy on Jakiele, he jumped down out of the tree and left the area to make his way back to another one of his safe houses. He had a score to settle with Rochelle, and he damn sure was going to make her pay for defying him if it was the last thing he ever did.

Dariah had run away from the prince's cave as fast as he could while carrying the prized mirror back to the campsite he had once inhabited with Katliana and Zadikiele. Unfortunately, the mirror was inordinately heavy and hard to juggle as Dariah valiantly tried to keep it from being damaged in his haste to get it to the fallen angels and accomplish the objective he had been tasked with.

Once at the campsite, Dariah packed up his gear and made for the nearest town to book a passage on the next departing train back to Cluj Napoca. He witnessed the slaying of Zadikiele by the prince, and he was glad for it. He was sick to death of taking orders from Zadikiele when he had the wits and determination to do what was needed and see it done to completion. His father may have been a fallen angel of no regard to the leaders, but he did not intend to be of so low a value to the fallen as his father had been.

Once he made it safely back to the city with his coveted treasure, he checked back into the hotel he and Zadikiele had used earlier. He lay prone on the bed with the mirror down on top of his chest. He closed his eyes and allowed himself to be transported to the Underworld, where he would seek his just rewards from the fallen angels. He walked down the narrow pathway leading him into the main cavern where the fallen were waiting to greet him. Thousands of hands reached up from the molten lava fire pits on either side of the path as lost souls screamed at him to save them from their never-ending torturous agony.

Uzza was the first to come forward with frenzied excitement. He snatched the mirror quickly out of Dariah's tightly clasped hands. Uzza held the mirror in front of him, gazed longingly into it, and declared, "At long last, my brothers! We are finally free. Who dares to come with me?" The other fallen started talking amongst themselves and admiring the mirror Uzza held. The group soon found themselves buzzing with frenzied zeal over what the mirror could do and whether it could lead them back to Earth. Finally, Remiel stepped out from amongst the crowd and went to stand before Uzza.

He held up his hand for silence and cautiously warned, "My brothers, seek caution here, I beg you! We must be certain of where the mirror will lead us first. We must run extensive tests on it and make sure this is not some sort of trap! We do not know where this mirror will take us or whether we can even use it for our purposes!" The other fallen angels would not listen to him. Many gathered in agitated wonder around Uzza and were touching and caressing the delicately framed mirror. Remiel soon realized the fallen had managed to work themselves into a frenzied excitement and were not about to listen to reason or have care for caution.

Remiel started to back away from the rest of the fallen angels as he was sure the mirror had to have been given to Dariah by the Archangels for an excellent reason. He knew there was no way the Archangels would give it up without a fight or without having some plan to trap them. Suddenly, his son, Zadikiele, managed to stumble silently into the cavern entrance. Zadikiele had managed to creep silently up behind Dariah and plunge the knife he held in his hand as deep as he could into the back of Dariah's neck. Dariah crumpled to the floor in shock and disbelief.

Zadikiele could barely stand, but he stood over Dariah's prone body and plunged his sharp blade deep into Dariah's prone body. He wiped the blood-soaked blade clean on his arm before slicing

Dariah's head off with one mighty swipe of the long sharp blade. Zadikiele never said a word but suddenly fell to his knees in agonizing pain from the wound the prince had inflicted upon him. He was barely alive. It had taken every ounce of pure hate to propel him to have enough stamina to complete his objective to stop Dariah from handing over the mirror to the fallen, but he was too late.

Remiel rushed to his son's aid quickly. He removed the long cloak he had been wearing and held it against the profusely bleeding hole in Zadikiele's back. Zadikiele was able to barely whisper to his father, "Do not let them use the mirror. It is a trick. I came back to warn you." Zadikiele could say no more as he lost consciousness in his father's arms. Remiel scooped up Zadikiele's almost lifeless body and rushed out of the main cavern back to his quarters, where he ordered his servants to save Zadikiele's life no matter what, or they would answer to him.

After leaving Zadikiele to their care, Remiel returned to the main cavern and was taken aback by what he saw. The fallen had not noticed Dariah had been killed only a few feet from them because they were all fighting each other to see who would be first to enter the mirror. Uzza and Azza had already gone through, and judging by the number of remaining angels, a good many had followed them through as well.

The mirror began to rise from the grasping, seeking hands of the fallen who had not made it through of its own volition. It hung suspended in the air at least fifty feet above the ground. Frustrated screams and howls of anger could be heard emanating loudly from the mirror. It had positioned itself at an angle where the fallen angels who had been left behind could look up and see the others who had gone into the mirror and that they were trying valiantly to find a way back out. However, the Dominions intended to make sure any who entered would never return.

The fallen angels who had not been able to gain entrance into the mirror stood back and looked up with horror as the hands, nails, and fists of the other angels tried to break the magic surface inside of the mirror and return to the Underworld. The remaining fallen angels left behind slowly turned to Remiel for guidance on what to do next. He was next in the line of succession to rule this dimension of the Underworld and be their leader. One by one, the fallen turned to him, bowed their heads, and fell to their knees in allegiance and respect.

In one substantial black cloud of smoke or fire, Salazar finally decided to make an appearance to see what all the commotion was about. He took one look at the mirror holding the trapped angels. Salazar began to laugh maniacally at the stupidity of the fallen. Then, he turned his malevolent gaze in Remiel's direction. He gave one slight nod of approval and gave Remiel one of the most wicked, evil smiles that Remiel had ever seen, which, to Remiel's mind, meant that he had better not fail as his predecessors had done. Salazar was the one who reported directly to Lucifer on everything that pertained to this lower level of fallen angels.

Remiel vowed to himself he would do whatever he had to for whoever long it took to take vengeance on whoever had wounded his son so gravely. Whoever had done the damage would never be able to hide from him for long on Earth or in the Underworld as he had all the time in the world to let his evil nature come to full force against those who opposed him. He had a clever idea where to start, and he knew he had to be careful, or he too would be the one hanging from the fire pit or worse should he fail.

www.ingramcontent.com/pod-product-compliance
Lightning Source LLC
Chambersburg PA
CBHW021302190726

48288CB00003B/657